Silenced

OTHER BOOKS AND AUDIO BOOKS BY BETSY BRANNON GREEN:

Hearts in Hiding

Never Look Back

Until Proven Guilty

Don't Close Your Eyes

Above Suspicion

Foul Play

Silenced

A NOVEL

BETSY BRANNON GREEN

Covenant

Covenant Communications, Inc.

Cover image by Lawrence Lawry © 2004 Photodisc Green/Getty Images.

Cover design copyrighted 2004 by Covenant Communications, Inc.

Published by Covenant Communications, Inc.
American Fork, Utah

Printed in the United States of America
First Printing: August 2004

11 10 09 08 07 06 05 04 10 9 8 7 6 5 4 3 2 1

ISBN 1-59156-602-9

For my son James,
who takes his responsibility as the big brother very seriously.
I hope all my children will follow in his faithful footsteps.

Acknowledgments

Thanks first to my family for their love, encouragement, and willingness to overlook my shortcomings. Second, to the wonderful, professional people at Covenant, who work so hard to help me transform ideas into books. Third, to my readers across the world, who make it all possible!

CHAPTER 1

On Thursday morning Eugenia Atkins arranged two strips of bacon between the scrambled eggs and put a dollop of real butter on top of a mound of creamy grits. Then she added two buttermilk biscuits to the plate before covering the breakfast with aluminum foil. She slipped out her back door and walked briskly down the sidewalk, pleased to note that her azaleas looked better than the others blooming along Maple Street. As she passed the Riley place, where Kate and Mark Iverson now lived, she raised her free hand to shield her eyes from the rising sun and smiled. It promised to be one of the most beautiful spring days in all her seventy-six years.

When she reached Polly Kirby's house, she knocked on the front door once before letting herself inside. Polly was recovering from hip-replacement surgery, and Eugenia had volunteered to deliver breakfast each morning to her longtime friend and neighbor.

"Polly!" Eugenia called as she climbed the stairs. "It's me, Eugenia."

"Oh, I'm so glad you're here!" Polly cried when Eugenia walked into her bedroom. "I'm starving."

Eugenia eyed the plump woman propped up on a profusion of pillows. "Well, I'm glad I got here before you wasted away to nothing."

Polly giggled. "Oh, Eugenia. You're so funny."

Eugenia pulled the foil off Polly's breakfast and settled the bed tray in front of her friend. "Do you want me to start a load of clothes before I leave?"

Polly shook her head as she took a bite of bacon. "No, my help is coming today, and she'll get me caught up on laundry. But I wonder if you could get the bed a little closer to the window. I can't see a thing from here."

"If you get any closer to that window you'll fall out," Eugenia said. "You'll just have to be content with watching television."

Polly frowned but continued eating. Eugenia was about to say good-bye when they heard the front door open.

"It's just me!" a voice called from downstairs.

"Is that the new Baptist preacher's wife?" Eugenia asked, checking her watch. "Coming to call this early?"

Polly nodded. "She stops by every morning on her way to prayer meeting at the retirement home."

At that moment Cornelia Blackwood appeared in the doorway. Eugenia gave the woman a brief once-over. Cornelia had shoulder-length hair streaked with early gray and a plain face completely devoid of makeup. She perpetually wore a series of baggy jumpers, and all Eugenia could figure was that somewhere along the way someone had said, "This is the way a preacher's wife is supposed to look," and Cornelia took it to heart.

"Good morning!" Cornelia greeted them with enthusiasm, then added, "Praise the Lord!"

"I was just leaving," Eugenia said as Cornelia advanced toward them.

"Then I'm glad I got here when I did." Cornelia grabbed a hand belonging to each woman and addressed the ceiling. "Dear Lord, we just want to thank you for this beautiful day."

Realizing that the woman was praying, Eugenia bowed her head. When Cornelia said "amen," Eugenia added one of her own.

"Looks like somebody needs a hug." Cornelia walked over and gave Polly a firm embrace. Then she looked toward Eugenia—who did *not* need or want a hug.

"I'll get my dish from yesterday on my way out," Eugenia said and hurried into the hall before Cornelia could squash her. "Nice to see you, Cornelia," she called over her shoulder.

Eugenia hurried down the stairs and, after a brief detour through Polly's kitchen for her plate, headed back outside. Instead of returning to her house, Eugenia proceeded around the block—combining Christian charity with invigorating daily exercise. She saw Claudia

Hornbuckle's newspaper lying near the curb, picked it up, then threw it onto her porch. When she walked by the now vacant home of the recently deceased Cora Sue Roper, she paused long enough to pull the For Sale sign from the overgrown front yard. A minute later she ran into Earl Ledbetter Jr., dressed in his policeman outfit.

"Good morning, Earl Jr.," she said.

"Good morning, Miss Eugenia," the boy returned.

"Shouldn't you be in school?"

"Yes'um," Earl Jr. acknowledged. "But today we're supposed to make the letter *C* out of toothpicks, and my mama said I could learn more than that by walking around outside and breathing fresh air." His eyes dropped to the sign in her hand.

"Somebody keeps putting this sign in Miss Cora Sue's yard by mistake," she explained.

The boy studied her for a second, then nodded. "I won't tell anybody you took it."

Eugenia smiled. "Discretion is the sign of a true gentleman." She glanced down at the toy gun he was carrying. "You keeping an eye on Miss Cora Sue's house?"

"Yes, ma'am. My mama said if we don't, hobos might move in."

"Well, I declare, I don't think I've seen a hobo in fifty years, but I guess it's wise to stay on the side of caution. Keep up your watch, and I'll be on my way," Eugenia said as she hurried on. When she reached her yard, she walked around to the back and opened the shed where she kept her gardening tools. After adding the sign to the collection already there, she closed the door firmly and went into the house.

* * *

Mila Edwards stared at the limited wardrobe hanging from the rack in her hotel room and longed for the extensive selection of clothes that was currently in storage in Atlanta. Her father had taught her early in life the importance of making not only a good first impression but a good *every* impression.

Since she figured she'd need all the help she could get to make a good impression on Chief Jamie Monahan of the Albany Police

Department, she settled on the mauve Armani suit, a nice combination of femininity and authority. Her friend Mallory had called it a power suit; she'd said it fairly screamed, "Yes, I'm a woman, and you'd better take me seriously!" Thinking of Mallory made Mila smile, then frown. It had been hard to leave old friends and would likely be even harder to make new ones in Albany, Georgia.

Once she was dressed and ready, she faced the mirror. Her auburn hair was cut in a low-maintenance, layered style and tucked neatly behind her ears. Her dark green eyes were large and fringed with thick lashes. She had inherited straight white teeth from her father and flawless skin from her mother. A healthy diet and strenuous exercise kept her thin. She was more striking than beautiful, which suited her fine. She turned for a side view. If not impeccable, her appearance was at least presentable. Hoping that would be enough, she squared her shoulders and walked outside.

She took a deep breath of magnolia-scented air and marveled at how different Albany was from the gritty, fast-paced streets of downtown Atlanta. The beautiful spring morning improved her mood, and when she saw her candy-apple red Mustang, a smile spread across her face. She and her father had been planning to purchase her first vehicle, but he was killed before they moved past the looking-through-brochures stage.

After he died, she was devastated and alone, but thanks to an insurance policy he'd put in her name, she had a little money. So once the initial, paralyzing grief faded enough to allow her to function—she'd let her daddy buy her a car.

Her father had been leaning toward a reliable Honda with a high safety rating and excellent resale value. But she had bought the brand-new, bright red Mustang. Throughout the purchase process she had agonized over each detail and knew that by the time her car finally arrived at the dealership, all the employees were thoroughly sick of her. But she was very pleased with the final result, and riding in the Mustang made her feel close to her father.

Mila unlocked the driver's door and settled into the soft leather seat. She breathed in the new-car smell and ran her hand lovingly over the steering wheel before heading into downtown Albany. She considered putting down the top but knew that a windblown appearance would not enhance the sensible impression she wanted to make on Chief Monahan, so she settled for an open window.

When she reached the Albany Police Station, she parked her precious car at the curb and studied the entrance with trepidation. A few weeks before, it looked as though her future in law enforcement was over. Then, at the last minute, a job offer came from Chief Monahan. Albany was not a place she wanted to be, but since she had no other options, she had accepted.

Jamie Monahan had been in the army with her father, and she felt sure the chief was doing her a favor. She intended to repay him for his kindness by working hard. But having reached the actual point of no return, her courage failed her.

She didn't want to start over in a new department. She didn't want to face the stares and speculation and unavoidable animosity. After the debacle in Atlanta she wasn't even sure she still wanted to be a police detective. But she needed a chance to redeem herself, and Jamie Monahan was offering that chance. So, with a heavy sigh, she opened the door and got out.

She faltered again when she reached the smokey-glassed entrance. But thinking of her father, she stiffened her spine and pushed into the reception area.

A heavyset officer in uniform had an elbow propped on the large counter/desk combination that dominated the small lobby. He stood up straight when Mila walked in.

"My name is Mila Edwards," she said to the receptionist. "I'm here to see Chief Monahan."

The woman gestured toward the uniformed officer beside her desk as she answered a call.

The officer addressed Mila. "I'm Frankie Cofield. The chief asked me to watch for you."

Mila studied Officer Cofield. His uniform shirt was wrinkled and stretched tightly across a potbelly. An unfortunate halo of fuzzy orange hair—reminiscent of Bozo the Clown—circled his head. She extended her hand. "Pleasure to meet you."

Officer Cofield slowly accepted her hand. "Nice car."

"You really *were* watching for me," she returned, and he smiled.

"I'll take you back to the chief's office."

She nodded. "Lead the way." After a wave to the busy receptionist, Officer Cofield turned and walked through a door to the right. Mila fell into step behind her escort and followed him down the hall.

The everyday police-station noises that greeted her were comforting to Mila as she and Officer Cofield weaved their way through the offices, cubicles, and freestanding desks that made up the bottom floor. She couldn't help but notice that most conversation was suspended as they passed by and that she drew a lot of stares. One tall man, with dark curly hair and bright blue eyes, called out.

"Hey, Frankie! Aren't you going to introduce us?" He gave Mila a flirtatious smile.

Officer Cofield stopped. "Detective Edwards, let me introduce Beau Lambert."

Mila gave the man an icy look. He was very handsome and obviously knew it. His uniform fit his well-defined torso snugly, and Mila guessed that it was custom-made.

"Welcome to the Albany PD." He pulled a small calendar from his pocket. "My schedule's pretty tight, but I think I can work you in next Tuesday."

Mila frowned. "I beg your pardon?"

Beau Lambert gave her another smile. "I make it a point to show all the new girls around town. We'll start with dinner, then hit the high spots of Albany." When she didn't respond he added, "So is it a date?"

The large room was quiet enough to hear a pin drop, and Mila knew the entire day shift was waiting to hear her response. "I make it a point never to date the people I work with. It's unprofessional."

Beau Lambert raised an eyebrow and leaned toward her to whisper, "Well, I'll just have to see if I can make you change your mind."

Mila moved closer and answered, "Don't count on it."

Frankie Cofield stepped between them. "Get back to work, Beau. This way, Detective."

Beau winked at her as he walked back to his office.

"Don't mind Beau," Officer Cofield advised. "He's a good guy, really. Just a little bit of a womanizer."

Mila shook her head. "He must get a lot of rejection if he uses that approach often."

Officer Cofield cut his eyes in her direction. "Nobody turns down Beau. In fact, most times he doesn't even have to ask. The girls just come up and beg him to take them out." Mila was trying to comprehend this when they reached a closed door at the end of the hallway and Officer Cofield stopped. "Well, here we are." He glanced at Mila, then said, "Good luck."

She nodded, and he rapped sharply. "Enter!" a voice from inside called. Officer Cofield opened the door and stepped back, allowing Mila to go in alone.

The office was large and crowded with serviceable furniture arranged in a no-nonsense manner. The desk was piled high with paperwork, files, and computer printouts. Chief Monahan was sitting at the desk. His gray hair was cut military short, and his eyes regarded her steadily over his reading glasses as she approached. He didn't stand or extend a hand toward her, which was a gross breach of Southern etiquette. Alarm bells started sounding in her head as she came to a stop in front of his desk.

Finally the chief spoke. "You're Hal Edwards's little girl."

She nodded. "Yes, sir."

"Made quite a mess out of your career, haven't you?"

She wasn't sure how to answer. "A difference of opinion—"

"Let's get this straight from the start," he interrupted her abruptly. "Opinions have their place—but not in matters involving the chain of command. Orders must be followed. Period." He paused for emphasis, then continued. "Your father saved my life, did you know that?"

She clutched her hands together to keep them from shaking. "No, sir."

"Twice, in fact, during Desert Storm."

She did not want to discuss her father, but since she was at a disadvantage, she forced herself to say, "He was very brave."

Frowning, Chief Monahan agreed. "Your father was one of the best men I've ever known, and he deserves better than what you've done to his name."

Mila felt a blush creep up her neck. Tugging on the edge of her power-suit jacket, she said, "I'd like to explain—"

He raised a hand to cut her off. "I've read the reports and talked to your supervisor in Atlanta. There's nothing you can tell me that will change what I think of you and your recent actions. I don't like glory hogs, and I can't abide insubordination," he told her. "But I pay my debts, so you'll have a job in my department as long as you tow the line. You understand that?"

Several responses ran through Mila's mind, but finally she nodded. "Perfectly."

He glanced at a printout in front of him. "You have a house in Haggerty. I assume you'll be living there?"

Mila's shoulders started to ache with tension. The chief had checked her out very thoroughly. "I inherited a house in Haggerty from my great-aunt, but I'm not going to live there." The chief transferred his hostile stare from the paper on his desk to Mila, and she decided further explanation was necessary. "It was in poor condition the last time I saw it, which was years ago. I'm not much on housekeeping, let alone home repair, so I've put the house up for sale and am planning to rent an apartment here in Albany."

The frown on the chief's face deepened, as if this news only intensified his negative opinion of her. "Make sure personnel has your personal information so you can be contacted when you're off duty."

"Yes, sir."

"Now I'll introduce you to your new partner." The chief picked up his phone, dialed three numbers, and said, "We're ready for you now."

While they waited in uncomfortable silence, the intercom buzzed. "Detective Edwards has a call on line three," a female voice informed the chief.

Mila felt her blush deepen as the chief waved at his telephone. "Make yourself at home," he said with a complete lack of hospitality.

Mila reached across the desk to pick up the receiver. "Edwards," she said.

"Mila? This is Nickel Phelps," the real estate agent handling the sale of Aunt Cora Sue's house announced in her strident voice. "Sorry to bother you at work."

"It's no problem," Mila assured the woman.

"I'm headed out to the property at 312 Hickory Lane and wondered if you'd like to meet me there. We still haven't done a walk-through together."

Mila controlled a sigh. "I know I need to go through the house with you, Nickel, but today isn't good for me. Can I call you tonight and set up a time for this weekend?"

"I suppose," Nickel replied. "But I don't know how you expect me to sell this house for you if we can't even decide on an asking price."

"I take complete responsibility for the delay." Mila glanced at Chief Monahan. "I'll call you later." She had just replaced the receiver when the door to the office opened and Beau Lambert walked in wearing a smug smile.

"Detective Edwards, I'd like to introduce you to Beau Lambert, your new partner."

Mila recognized that her assignment to Beau Lambert was a punishment of sorts and steadfastly refused to give either man any satisfaction. "Officer Lambert and I have already met," she said with a resigned nod.

"It's *Detective* Lambert," the chief corrected her.

"But you can call me Beau," her new partner offered, flashing her a smile.

Mila had to work hard to control a grimace. "Please excuse me, *Detective*. The uniform confused me."

"I like to wear it occasionally," Beau told her. "Helps my rapport with the other guys." He turned to Chief Monahan. "You want me to show her around, sir?"

The chief pushed his glasses up onto the bridge of his nose. "Please. Make sure you take her to personnel and get her tax forms and that kind of stuff filled out." Then he addressed Mila. "Detective Edwards, the only way to get an invitation back into this office is if you do something really good or really bad. I suggest that you stay somewhere in between."

She nodded and moved toward the door, anxious to escape the chief's scrutiny.

"And Beau's a very good policeman. He works hard and *always* follows orders. If you're wise, you'll learn a thing or two from him."

Mila had progressed from humiliated to furious by the time she and her new partner stepped into the hallway outside Chief Monahan's door.

"So, it sounds like your meeting with the chief went well," Beau Lambert said with a teasing grin.

"You think that went well?" she demanded.

He nodded. "Considering what happened at your last assignment, I think it could have gone much worse."

"You know that I was fired from the force in Atlanta?"

"Everybody knows that."

"Great," she said.

Beau laughed. "What I don't know is the particulars."

She gave him a skeptical look. "I'll have to know you for more than fifteen minutes before I tell you all the gory details."

Beau accepted her rebuff good-naturedly. "I guess I can wait for a day or two. And don't worry about the chief. His bark is worse than his bite."

Having come face-to-face with Jamie Monahan's bark, Mila hoped that she'd never experience the bite. "So, are you going to give me a tour of this place or what?"

He raised an eyebrow. "I'll be happy to give you a tour of the department, and my offer to show you around Albany is still open. Since by then I'll have known you for several hours, you could tell me what you did to get fired."

Officer Cofield walked past them as he made this comment. "Give it a rest, Beau," he said in an unnecessary attempt to help her.

"So, you won't date me *or* confide in me?" Beau asked.

Mila shook her head. "Nope."

"Don't feel too bad," Frankie Cofield consoled Beau. "Maybe you'll have better luck with your next partner."

"This is just the opening round," Beau told his fellow officer with a confident grin. "And I've barely begun to fight!"

Officer Cofield shook his Bozo hair as he walked away. "Before you fire the second round, take her to personnel so she'll get paid."

"Not the most interesting area," Beau said as he took Mila by the arm and steered her down another hallway. "But probably one of the most important."

It took almost two hours for her to be thoroughly processed by the Personnel Department. Beau stayed nearby throughout the whole ordeal, and she felt obliged to thank him as they left the administrative area.

"No problem," he told her with a bright smile. "It gave me a chance to charm the new insurance clerk into having me over for dinner."

She frowned. "I can't say I'm glad that I assisted you in your determination to date every woman you see," she said, and he laughed as he began the tour. In addition to the important areas like rest rooms and vending machines, he pointed out each woman he'd been involved with romantically. "Didn't anyone ever tell you that it's not polite to kiss and tell?" she asked finally.

He laughed. "Do I detect a hint of jealousy?"

She gave him an incredulous look. "You certainly do not."

This made him laugh harder. "Well, I never cared that much about being polite." After the tour he offered to take her to a deli across the street for lunch. "Not a date," he hastened to assure her. "We can go dutch."

She shook her head. "No thanks."

With a shrug, he led the way through a door labeled *Investigative Division*. He pushed it open and said, "Here we are." He waited until she had stepped in beside him, then pointed to the left. "The gang task force is over there in the corner. Up front is family protection. The SRO unit is in the back and forensics is downstairs. The detective section is this way." He waved for her to follow him down a row of small offices along the right wall. "The commander's office is the big one on the end, but he's just had back surgery, so for the next few weeks we report directly to the chief."

"Great," Mila muttered. Things just seemed to keep getting worse.

"The other two day-shift detectives, Foley and Bufford, are out on a call," Beau said, explaining the empty offices. "I'll introduce you to them later, but you won't have much contact with them. And here's your new home away from home."

Mila stepped into the small office and had to admit that it did look homey. The walls were a creamy yellow, and the smell of fresh paint still clung to the air. The wooden desk was old and scarred but had been polished until it shone. The swivel chair and computer system were fairly new. There were a couple of framed prints of endangered species on the wall, and a small lamp on the corner of the desk cast a soft light across the room.

"This is very nice." She had expected her work space to be filled with rejected furniture that no one else wanted.

At that moment a petite African American woman rushed in. "Oh!" she said in dismay when she saw Mila. "I meant to get my things out before you arrived." The woman picked up a silver frame from the desk and a nameplate that said *Detective James.* "It was a gift from the guys," she explained. "A little premature as it turned out."

"Detective Edwards, meet Dorcas James," Beau said with a wink at the small woman. "Dorcas, our new arrival."

Dorcas nodded, still clutching her possessions to her chest.

Beau continued, "Dorcas has been with the department for almost ten years. She got her master's degree in December, and everyone assumed the chief would promote her to detective when Potter retired."

Now Mila understood. This woman had fixed up the office for herself, and Mila had slipped in and stolen both her office and her new job. "I'm sorry," she told Dorcas. "I didn't know."

The little woman shrugged. "I'll get another chance."

"Do you want me to help you pack up your other things?" Mila offered, but Dorcas shook her head.

"No, I'll leave them."

Mila couldn't tell if Dorcas was being hospitable or if she thought Mila wouldn't be staying for long. "Okay, thanks."

"No problem."

"Dorcas has been assigned as special liaison to the Investigative Division, so you'll be seeing a lot of her," Beau explained further. "The chief wants her to get as much experience as she can for the future."

For when he fires me, Mila thought to herself. "So, what are we working on right now?" she said out loud.

He pointed to a neat stack of files on her new desk. "The chief kind of reshuffled all the cases, and those are the ones assigned to us.

After you review them, we can talk."

The phone on the desk began to ring, and Dorcas answered it. "James," she said into the receiver. She listened for a second, then extended it toward Mila. "For you."

She took the phone, hoping they would give her some privacy, but neither made a move to leave. With a sigh, Mila turned her attention to the call.

"Mila?" Nickel Phelps's voice came through the phone line. "I went by your great-aunt's house and someone has taken the For Sale sign out of the yard again. You are absolutely going to have to find out who is responsible."

Mila massaged the bridge of her nose where a headache was starting. "I'll check into it as soon as I can."

"Those signs cost money! If this keeps up, I'll have to charge you extra!"

"Yes, I understand," Mila replied, then covered the phone and addressed Beau. "What time will we be through today?"

"I leave at five o'clock sharp," he said. "Unless something big's going on."

Mila removed her hand and spoke to Nickel Phelps. "I can meet you in Haggerty at five thirty tonight," she suggested. "And if you have anything else to tell me, maybe you could leave a message on my cell phone," she added, hoping the real estate agent would realize that calling her repeatedly at work was a bad idea.

"Trouble?" Beau asked after she ended the call.

"Not really." Mila tucked a lock of hair behind her ear. "Some kids just keep taking the For Sale sign out of the yard at my great-aunt's house in Haggerty, and it's bothering my real estate agent."

"I know the chief of police in Haggerty. You want me to call him?" Beau offered. "Maybe he can stake out your house and catch the sign thief."

"No thanks," she replied in a tone she hoped was sufficiently dismissive. "I'll handle it."

"I like your suit," Dorcas said, studying Mila. "Armani?"

Mila nodded.

"It's a brave fashion statement. Most redheads are afraid to wear pink."

Mila didn't really consider herself a redhead and wouldn't wear pink regardless of her hair color. "It's mauve," Mila corrected, beginning to weary of Dorcas. "Now if you'll excuse me, I think I'll get to work." She opened the cover of the top file and began to leaf through it.

Dorcas watched for a few minutes, but Mila steadfastly ignored her. Finally the other woman stood and left the small room. After she had gone Beau said, "I'm just next door. Holler if you need me."

In spite of his overbearing determination to flirt, Beau had been helpful, so she said, "Thanks." She waited until they left her alone, then settled into the comfortable chair in the office she'd stolen from Dorcas and began reviewing the files in earnest.

The first contained a complaint from a citizen accusing a meter maid of consistently ticketing cars before their time ran out. The second involved the disappearance of a German shepherd. Underneath the missing-dog report was a note from Beau which said, *Did you kill someone? Come on, you can tell me.*

Mila smiled grimly, realizing that the chief had assigned her to cases so low profile that she'd never draw attention from the media or the citizens of Albany. And Beau was not going to give up on his quest to learn the details of her past.

When Beau came by to check on her later, she closed the file on a rash of streetlight vandalism and said, "I guess we'll get all the calls about cats stuck up in trees too."

Beau shook his head. "Actually, uniforms will be sent to get the cat down. We'll just be called in later to figure out why the cat was in the tree in the first place."

"So the chief's not going to let me touch anything important?"

"Not at first," Beau acknowledged. "But if you handle this stuff well and without complaining, who knows?"

"I guess I don't have much choice."

After Beau left she skimmed files and mentally planned her trip to Haggerty. She didn't want to walk through her great-aunt's house, and she certainly didn't want to spend time with the ultra-perky Nickel Phelps. Mila had just wondered to herself how much worse things could get when Beau stuck his head through the open doorway into her office.

"The chief has assigned us to an internal committee. First meeting starts in ten minutes."

"What kind of committee?"

"Morale."

With a sigh, Mila stood and joined him at the doorway.

CHAPTER 2

Eugenia was mixing up a batch of tea cakes when her doorbell rang. Only company came to the front door, and she was momentarily stunned since she wasn't expecting anyone. She washed the flour from her hands, walked quickly down the hall and through the living room, and pulled open the door. Cornelia Blackwood stood on her front stoop, a Bible clutched to her thin chest.

"You nearly scared me to death, Cornelia!" Eugenia told the woman irritably. "Why didn't you come to the back door like everyone else?"

"Because I'm here on official business for the Lord, and I know you wouldn't expect Him to come through the back door!"

Eugenia controlled the urge to roll her eyes. "Would you and the Lord like to come back to the kitchen and watch me make tea cakes?"

Cornelia stepped inside and walked to the living room. "I'd like your undivided attention for a few minutes, Miss Eugenia. So if you don't mind, I think we should talk in here."

Eugenia moved a stack of magazines off the couch and pointed for Cornelia to sit in the clean spot. Then she said, "Okay. What's so important that it's got to be discussed in the living room?"

"I was reading in *Guidepost* the other day, and did you know that more than 60 percent of the people in the United States of America don't attend church regularly? *Sixty percent,*" Cornelia enunciated.

"That's bad," Eugenia agreed.

"So I thought to myself," Cornelia continued as if Eugenia hadn't spoken, "we've got to do something to turn the tide. And then the idea came to me that we need to have a Faith Fair!"

"A Faith Fair?" Eugenia repeated doubtfully.

Cornelia clasped her hands together and nodded with enthusiasm. "It can be an annual event. The first one will have to be simple, but we can expand it every year."

"When do you want to have it?"

"Well, my cousin, Gilbert McWayne, wrote the book *A Prayer a Day Keeps the Devil Away,*" Cornelia confided on a seemingly unrelated subject. "I rarely mention it since I don't like to brag. But it just happens that Cousin Gilbert will be visiting us at the end of the month, and I thought we could plan our Faith Fair for that weekend. I'm sure Gilbert would be willing to be our keynote speaker."

Eugenia shook her head. "That sounds like about as much fun as a toothache."

"Oh, I know we'll have to do *more,*" Cornelia assured her. "We can invite all the churches in the area to set up booths explaining about their beliefs or giving away Bibles or whatever!" Cornelia enthused. "We can arrange with a caterer to prepare plate lunches for a reasonable price and print up a bunch of T-shirts. We can have some contests and get the merchants to donate prizes. Then the high school band can play, and I'm sure our children's choir will be glad to perform some hymns."

Eugenia had to admit that Cornelia was on the right track. If the children in the community were involved, their parents would have to come. "That might work," she conceded.

"Then we can end the evening with a huge prayer for our town and our state and the nation!" Cornelia cried. "After the amen we can have fireworks!"

Eugenia gave the kitchen a longing look. "It sounds real good, Cornelia. I'll be there."

Cornelia laughed. "But Miss Eugenia, in order to get the community's cooperation, I'll need you to be on my planning committee."

Eugenia's heart sank. "Me?"

"You've got more influence than anyone in Haggerty, including the mayor," Cornelia said. "If I tell folks you're behind the Faith Fair, then my success is assured."

"You mean the Lord's success," Eugenia said dryly.

Cornelia waved the Bible. "Of course." Then she moved on. "We'll have the first planning meeting at the Baptist Family Life Center at one o'clock on Wednesday afternoon."

Eugenia nodded, more in an effort to get rid of the woman than in agreement. "Okay."

Cornelia stood and trapped her hostess in a vigorous hug. "Thank you so much." She released Eugenia and took a sheet of paper from her huge purse. "Now, if you'll just give me your shirt size I'll order your T-shirt. All the committee members will get one free," Cornelia clarified. "We'll vote on the slogan Wednesday. I've had several suggestions like Give Faith a Chance and Faith Fever. If you have any more ideas, bring them with you to the meeting."

Eugenia controlled a shudder. "I certainly will."

Once she'd shown Cornelia out the front door, she went back to her tea cakes and tried to forget about Cornelia Blackwood and the Faith Fair.

* * *

Mila stifled a yawn and surreptitiously checked her watch. The morale committee meeting had been in progress for almost two hours, and it was now approaching five o'clock. She looked over at Beau. He winked, then sat up straight and addressed the others. "Why don't we table the discussion until next week?" he suggested.

Mila sighed with relief as the people seated around the room nodded in agreement.

"You owe me one," Beau whispered to her as they left the conference room.

"You wanted to get out of there as much as I did, so that doesn't count," she replied.

Beau pulled a set of keys from his pocket. "Well, I've got a hot date, so I guess this is good-bye. For today, at least."

She looked pointedly at the keys. "Aren't you going back to your office?"

"And risk getting roped into doing something that will make me late for my date? No way."

Beau tossed his keys into the air and headed for the front entrance.

Mila watched him leave, then hurried to her office and collected her purse. No one even spoke to her, much less asked her to do anything, so a few minutes later she was in her Mustang, headed for Haggerty.

* * *

When Mila passed the city limits sign, she felt a familiarity that was not altogether pleasant. Even the good memories of her childhood were painful now that her father was gone. She drove around the square and was surprised to find that in the years of her absence nothing had substantially changed. If life was slower paced in Albany than it had been in Atlanta, time stood completely still in Haggerty.

She turned onto Hickory Lane and passed the old homes she remembered from her youth. Several were nicely restored, others falling into dereliction. However, on the corner of Hickory and Chestnut was a sight that startled a little gasp from her. The two old homes that had stood between Aunt Cora Sue's house and the corner for years had been torn down, and a replica of Tara from *Gone With the Wind* had been built in their place. Even utilizing two lots, the mansion had barely a fringe of lawn around it and looked completely out of place in the staid old neighborhood.

Mila was still shaking her head in wonder as she parked in front of her great-aunt's house and forced herself to look at it. The flat roof gave the house the squat look of a shoe box and had been a source of leaks for as long as Mila could remember.

With a sigh she settled back against the seat, planning to wait there in the car until Nickel Phelps arrived. Then she saw a movement in the corner of the yard. Thinking she may have found her sign thief, Mila got out of the car and quietly approached the swaying hydrangea blossoms. When she pulled the branches of the bush aside, she exposed a boy about six years old. There were several badges pinned to his T-shirt, and he had a holster, with an assortment of toy guns attached, strapped around the waist of his blue jeans. His white-blond hair stuck out at odd angles as a result of a few badly placed cowlicks, and his fair skin was generously freckled. Thick spectacles magnified his blue eyes as he looked at her with neither fear nor surprise.

"I'm sorry, ma'am, but I'm afraid I'm going to have to put you under arrest." He extended a pair of plastic handcuffs.

Mila raised an eyebrow. "What is the charge, Officer?"

"Trespassing," he told her solemnly. "This is Miss Cora Sue's yard."

"And why are you here?"

"Watching for hobos," he responded, then shook the handcuffs. "And trespassers."

"What's your name, Officer?"

"Earl Lamar Ledbetter Jr.," the boy responded promptly. "My daddy's name is Earl too, so folks call me Earl Jr."

Mila leaned down so they were eye to eye. "And where do you live, Earl Jr.?"

He pointed behind him to the huge house. "Miss Cora Sue told me I could come over here whenever I pleased." His expression saddened. "Before."

"You and Miss Cora Sue were friends?" she asked.

The boy nodded, staring at his feet.

"I think I'd better introduce myself," Mila said. "I'm Detective Edwards of the Albany Police Department." She showed him her badge. "I just moved from Atlanta, and this is now *my* house."

Earl Jr. took the badge and examined it intently. "Wow." He returned the badge to Mila.

"I'm trying to sell this house, but someone keeps taking the For Sale sign out of the yard. Do you know anything about that?" Mila saw a guilty look cross his face, but he shook his head.

"I didn't do it."

Before she could question him further, a voice called to them from the road. Mila looked over to see Eugenia Atkins approaching them. Miss Eugenia hadn't aged a bit and seemed to be wearing the same blue coveralls she'd had on the last time Mila had seen her ten years earlier.

"Good evening!" the older woman greeted Mila and Earl Jr. simultaneously. Then she held up a plate. "I brought some tea cakes."

Mila stared at the cookies. "I haven't had a tea cake since . . ." She let her voice trail off as the memories came rushing back—Aunt Cora

Sue, standing in the warm, friendly kitchen, humming as she rolled out tea cakes.

"I used Cora Sue's recipe," Miss Eugenia said softly.

"May I have one?" Earl Jr. asked.

Miss Eugenia lowered the plate. "Of course you may. You still protecting Miss Cora Sue's house from hobos, Earl Jr.?"

"Yes, ma'am," the boy acknowledged around a mouthful of cookie. "I thought I'd caught me a trespasser, but Detective Edwards says this is her house now."

"Miss Cora Sue was Mila's great-aunt," Miss Eugenia explained to the boy. "Have a cookie, Mila."

Mila hadn't eaten since breakfast, so she took a cookie with a mumbled thank-you.

Miss Eugenia led them to the porch, and they all claimed a step and sat down. "I caught a glimpse of you at the funeral services for Cora Sue but didn't get a chance to speak. And you didn't stay for the after-funeral meal."

"I had to get back to Atlanta," Mila told her briefly. "Some problems at work."

"It's just as well," Miss Eugenia assured her. "The new Baptist preacher's wife insisted on handling the luncheon, and she's not much of a cook."

"I noticed that there was a new preacher," Mila said, trying to act interested. "What happened to Brother Paul?"

"He developed a phobia about germs and refused to visit the sick," Miss Eugenia informed her.

Mila raised an eyebrow. "A phobia."

"Yes, nowadays people get them all the time. If you don't believe me, just watch the *Maury Povich Show*. In Brother Paul's case, his first symptom was a reluctance to shake hands with people. He said it was germy," Miss Eugenia detailed the preacher's plight. "Then he started washing his hands—and I don't mean just before he ate. He washed them so much the skin was peeling off, and then nobody *wanted* to shake hands with him. He even carried around little moistened towelettes so he could wash when he was away from a sink! But when he refused to visit people in the hospital, the deacons knew they had to handle the situation. I mean, how can you have a preacher who won't go near sick folks?"

"So they fired him?" Mila asked.

"Oh, no, nothing so scandalous. They just offered him early retirement so he'd have the time he needs to free his environment of germs." She grinned at Mila. "He took them right up on it." Miss Eugenia sighed. "This new preacher is from Galveston. He comes highly recommended and has more degrees than a thermometer. But when you get old you become resistant to change, and most of Haggerty is anything but young!"

Mila nodded in agreement. "That was true ten years ago."

Miss Eugenia cackled. "It's even more true now. I heard you had taken a job in Albany," she added, testing the waters. "But you're going to sell Cora Sue's house instead of living here?"

"An efficient apartment in Albany will fit my needs much better than an old house in Haggerty," Mila said. "You understand."

"No, I don't understand that at all." Miss Eugenia ran the last two words together so it sounded like "a-tall." "You used to love visiting here, and I would have thought you'd be anxious to be back in Haggerty."

Mila sighed. "I find it easier just to forget the past completely."

Miss Eugenia nodded sagely. "You miss your father."

"Of course," Mila acknowledged.

"His death was a tragedy."

"And completely senseless," Mila added.

Miss Eugenia frowned. "He was killed on an army helicopter, wasn't he?"

"During a routine practice drill." Mila couldn't keep the bitterness from her voice. "For a long time I was furious with him and the army and the Lord. I'm past that now, but I don't dwell on it."

"And what about your mother? I heard she remarried."

"Yes." Mila looked away. "They live in Florida."

"Do you see her often?" Miss Eugenia prompted.

"No. She and her new husband travel a lot."

Miss Eugenia narrowed her eyes at Mila. "You didn't like it that she remarried."

Mila was stung by this remark. "I don't mind that she remarried. I just wish she'd waited a respectable length of time."

Miss Eugenia considered this for a few seconds. "People deal with grief in different ways. Maybe your mother had to separate herself from everything that reminded her of your father in order to survive."

"Even me?" Mila was horrified by the raw emotion in her voice.

Miss Eugenia reached over and patted her hand. "And now you've lost Cora Sue too. Which is all the more reason for you to come to Haggerty! People here know you and love you."

"Well, it looks like you've started the party without me!" Nickel Phelps called from the sidewalk.

Mila had never been so glad to see anyone.

"Are these homemade tea cakes?" Nickel pointed at the plate.

"Help yourself," Miss Eugenia offered.

Nickel selected a cookie, took a bite, then proceeded up the stairs and unlocked the door to Cora Sue's old house.

Mila followed, steeling herself against the memories she knew would assault her inside. Once she was standing in the living room, she expelled the breath she'd been holding. The house was very different from the way she remembered it. The rooms were empty with only blinds on the windows. The smell of biscuits and cookies baking was gone. It was as if every sign of Aunt Cora Sue had been erased.

Miss Eugenia spoke from the doorway. "Cora Sue donated all the furnishings to the Boys and Girls Ranch. Not that she had much."

"Nothing is left?" Mila forced herself to ask.

Miss Eugenia shook her head. "She said she didn't figure you'd want any of it."

As nausea washed over her, she felt Earl Jr. pulling on her arm. "Miss Cora Sue gave me her picture of Lassie."

Mila looked down at the boy and tears pricked her eyes. "I love that picture," she said in a choked voice.

"You can have it if you want it," he offered kindly.

Mila forced back the tears. "Thanks, but Aunt Cora Sue wanted you to have it."

"She did give you the house," he pointed out. "And it's bigger."

Mila had to smile as Nickel began a quick tour of the house. Once they were back on the front porch, Mila walked to the edge and took a deep breath. Nickel opened a folder with *First Real Estate* printed across the front and removed a sheet of paper.

"I suggest an asking price of $65,000," she proposed. "We'll probably have to settle for $58,000, but it never hurts to start high. Once all the fees are deducted you should clear at least $50,000."

Money had never been a serious issue for Mila. She earned a decent salary and kept her spending within reason. But several weeks of leave without pay had depleted her savings, and she needed the proceeds of the sale quickly.

"Let's just ask $55,000 from the start to save time," she told Nickel, and the agent made a notation in her notebook. "In fact, I won't refuse any reasonable offer."

Nickel seemed pleased, but Miss Eugenia was frowning.

"Since you're not going to make much off the sale anyway, you might want to consider renting it out," Miss Eugenia said. "That way you could keep your options open—in case you decided that you do want to live here after all."

"I'm not going to decide that," Mila told Miss Eugenia firmly. "I'm not even going to stay in the Albany area permanently. It was nice to see you again," she directed toward Miss Eugenia. "And to meet you Earl Jr.," she said to the boy, then turned to Nickel. "Keep me posted." With a wave she hurried to the Mustang and soon was on the highway headed back to her quiet, anonymous room at the Marriott Courtyard in Albany.

She changed into sweats and made use of the hotel's exercise equipment, then showered and fell into bed, too exhausted for a trip down memory lane.

CHAPTER 3

When Eugenia took Polly Kirby her breakfast on Friday morning, she tried to time her visit so that Cornelia would have already come, hugged, and gone. But she had barely pulled the foil off Polly's plate when they heard Cornelia downstairs. The preacher's wife rushed into the room like a storm on the Red Sea and collapsed on the edge of Polly's bed.

"I've had the most wonderful idea for the Faith Fair," she told them. "We could have bumper stickers printed to match our T-shirts. Don't you think they'll be just darling? And very cheap advertising!"

Eugenia looked behind Cornelia and saw Polly mouth, "Tacky."

"Most people don't put bumper stickers on their cars anymore, Cornelia," Eugenia tried.

"Surely they'll make an exception for the Lord!" Cornelia cried.

Eugenia shook her head. "I think you'd be wiser to go with refrigerator magnets or pot holders—something useful that doesn't gum-up your bumper."

"Oh, Miss Eugenia! I love the idea of pot holders," Cornelia gushed. "You're just a genius!"

Cornelia looked ready to hug, so Eugenia moved toward the door. "I'll leave you two ladies to your visit."

"Don't you want to stay and pray with us?" Cornelia inquired.

Eugenia shook her head. "Maybe next time." She saw the look of disapproval on Cornelia's face, but hurried from the room anyway.

* * *

The desk clerk at the Marriott forgot Mila's wake-up call, so her Friday morning got off to a bad start. She didn't have time to consider her wardrobe and pulled on a gauzy floral print skirt, a yellow blouse, and her favorite pair of Cole Haan shoes. Since she hadn't eaten dinner the night before, she knew she had to get some calories in her system to avoid an embarrassing collapse at the Albany Police Department, so she stopped by Hardee's for a biscuit.

When she walked into the lobby at the station, she nodded to the receptionist, then hurried past, using her shoulder to push open the door to the Investigative Division. She came to an abrupt stop when she found Chief Jamie Monahan standing in the doorway to Beau's office.

She decided to give optimism a try. "Good morning."

"You're late," the chief replied with a pointed look at the Hardee's bag in her hand.

Abandoning optimism, but refusing to grovel, she said, "New to the area, traffic and all that."

The chief raised both eyebrows. "I'm sure it must be a real challenge to drive in Albany after dealing with Atlanta traffic."

Mila felt a blush climbing up her neck as the chief nodded at Beau, then walked down the hall and out of the Investigative Division.

"Morning, Beau," she called as she walked into her office.

"Good morning yourself," he replied. "As soon as you get through with breakfast they need you in properties."

"What for?" she asked around a mouthful of biscuit.

"So they can issue you a revolver."

"The chief's going to trust me with a gun?" she asked, walking back to Beau's office. Today, she noticed, he was dressed in a nice suit and tie.

"And keys to our unmarked car too," he told her with a smile.

"Wow. You'd better point me in the direction of properties before he changes his mind."

"Through the door at the end of the hall and to your left. You can't miss it."

Mila found the properties area and filled out the appropriate paperwork. When they handed her the gun and keys, she felt official.

She returned to her cozy little office and barely had time to sit down before Beau burst into the room.

"We've got a call," he informed her.

"Let me guess," she said as she stood. "A cat in a tree?"

He smiled. "No, neighbors complaining about a wailing sound in the apartment next door. Could be a baby crying, could be a ghost."

Mila gave him a dubious look. "I don't know which one to hope for."

They walked out to their unmarked car, and Beau offered to let her drive. She appreciated the show of confidence but declined. "You'd better drive until I learn my way around."

He looked across the top of the sedan. "I thought you were from this area originally."

"My mother was raised in Haggerty, and I spent a lot of time there as a child, but that's been a while," she finished lamely.

"Okay. I'll drive today, but you'd better look over the map on the front seat. I like to split things fifty-fifty."

Mila raised an eyebrow as she settled into the passenger seat. "You do?"

"Well, at least where driving is concerned. I can't work on my social calendar if I have to keep my hands on the wheel." He tapped on the cell phone in his shirtfront pocket.

Shaking her head, Mila picked up the map and started studying. A few minutes later she glanced up and saw that they were driving through a residential area on the fringes of downtown.

"These old houses were built right after the turn of the century," Beau informed her. "It's too close to downtown to attract the yuppies interested in restoration, so most of them have been divided into apartments for the genteel poor."

"The genteel poor?" she repeated.

He nodded, completely serious. "I think this is it." He glanced down at the copy of the complaint to verify the address. "Yep, here we are."

It was a two-story house on the end of Wylam Street, quiet and secluded. There were four mailboxes in front labeled 1412-A through 1412-D, but no names identified the occupants. "Who made the complaint?" Mila asked.

"A college kid in B," Beau replied.

"Then I guess we'll start there."

They walked up onto the wide porch and turned right. There was no doorbell so Beau knocked repeatedly on the screen. Finally a young man opened the door and stuck his head out.

"Are you Spencer Cain?" Beau asked and the boy nodded. "We've come about the complaint you filed."

Spencer stepped out on the porch and lowered his voice. "Hey, like, I never call the police or anything, and I don't want to get anybody in trouble. But that wailing is keeping me awake at night. I can't sleep or study, and I got midterms coming up."

"Which apartment is the noise coming from?" Mila asked.

Spencer pointed behind him. "D. I'm telling you it's creepy—makes my skin crawl." He seemed embarrassed by this comment. "But I guess it could just be a cat."

Mila cut her eyes to Beau, who smiled before asking, "Do you know who lives in apartment D?"

The boy shrugged. "Some older lady."

Mila pulled a tiny notepad from her skirt pocket, preparing to take notes. "How old?"

"Oh, at least thirty," the boy replied. Mila and Beau exchanged another glance as Spencer continued. "You won't tell her I called, will you?"

"We'll try to keep you out of it," Mila promised.

"I just can't keep listening to that racket," Spencer reiterated.

"We understand. When was the last time you saw this . . . elderly woman?" Mila asked.

Spencer considered the question. "A week or so ago, but that isn't unusual. She stays to herself. Which is fine with us, because she is kind of spooky."

Mila looked up. "Spooky?"

"Well, I mean she doesn't come out much," the boy elaborated. "And usually only at night. My roommate swears she's a vampire."

Mila put her notebook away. "We'll check it out," she said, then motioned for Beau to follow her around to the back.

They circled the house, trudging through tall grass until they reached the backyard. The rear porch was smaller than its front counterpart but was divided in much the same way, with both apartments getting half.

They climbed the stairs, and Mila knocked on the door several times, but got no answer.

"You think that Spencer kid was making the whole thing up?" Beau asked.

Mila regarded him with surprise. "Why would he?"

"Maybe he's on drugs," Beau suggested. "Having hallucinations or something."

"Kids on drugs rarely call the cops," Mila pointed out as she pounded on the door again. Then from the other side they heard a low, mournful sob. Their eyes met in mutual astonishment, then the sobbing expanded into a full-fledged howl.

"That's not a ghost or a cat!" Beau said.

Mila frowned. "No, it's a baby." She knocked harder on the door, but still got no response.

"I'll try to force the lock," Beau said.

"Give me just a second," she requested, then addressed the door. "We're detectives with the Albany Police Department. We've been sent here to help you. Please open the door, or we'll have to break it." Mila paused for a few seconds. "You aren't in trouble and we won't hurt you."

The door remained closed so Mila stepped back in defeat. Beau took a position near the door and prepared to force it open. Then they heard the sound of the dead bolt being turned. Beau retracted his shoulder, and they watched the doorknob begin a slow, hesitant revolution. Mila moved in front of Beau as the door inched open far enough to reveal a little girl about four years old with huge brown eyes and long brown hair. Mila knelt down so that she wouldn't be more intimidating than necessary.

"Hi," she said softly. "What's your name?"

"I'm not supposed to speak to strangers," the little girl whispered, tears filling her eyes.

"We're not strangers, we're the police," Mila said. "We'll show you our badges." She removed hers, and Beau did the same. The little girl whimpered when she saw Beau, so Mila motioned for him to stay back. "My name is Mila."

The little girl struggled with the decision for a few seconds, then finally said, "I'm Lily."

"What a beautiful name." Mila moved closer.

"My mommy told me never to open the door while she's gone," Lily confided.

"Your mother would want you to obey the police." Mila looked through the small gap into the apartment. "Where is your mom? We need to speak to her."

Lily's lip began to tremble. "She said she was going for a walk and she'd be back soon, but she's been gone a very long time."

"How long?" Mila asked.

"Three nights."

After a quick glance back at Beau, Mila said to Lily, "One of your neighbors heard you crying. That's how we found you."

Lily shook her head. "I didn't cry. I wanted to," she admitted. "But my mommy said I had to be a big girl and take care of Ben."

"Ben?" Mila repeated stupidly, her heart pounding.

"My baby brother. I can't get him out of his crib. He's too heavy," Lily explained. "All the juice boxes and cookies are gone. I've been making him peanut butter crackers, but he doesn't want them. He just throws them on the floor."

"Why don't you let me come inside so I can get Ben out of his crib," Mila suggested.

"What about him?" Lily pointed at Beau, keeping her eyes averted.

"Maybe he could go and get both of you Happy Meals to eat. How does that sound?"

"Ben doesn't like pickles on his hamburger," Lily said after brief consideration.

Mila spoke over her shoulder to Beau. "Two hamburger Happy Meals, one without pickles." She turned back to Lily. "What kind of drink?"

"Sprite," Lily replied, then opened the door enough for Mila to step inside.

"Hurry," Mila said to Beau before moving into the apartment.

"You expect me to leave you here?" he demanded.

"Just long enough for you to get the food," Mila confirmed. "Lily is afraid of you now, but when you come back with Happy Meals—you'll be her hero."

Beau was frowning, but he moved to the steps. "I should call this into the station."

"Can't you wait until after you bring the food?" Mila suggested. "That will give the kids time to get used to me." Without waiting for an answer she closed the door.

The apartment was cramped and the furnishings below thrift-store standards, but it was neat and clean. Lily led the way across the small living room into the only bedroom. Mila followed in her wake. The bedroom was dominated by a double bed in the center. To the right was a tall chest of drawers and to the left was a crib. Inside the crib stood a toddler, holding onto the rail. On the floor in front of the crib was a semicircle of smashed peanut butter crackers. When the baby saw Mila, he burst into a fresh bout of tears.

"It's okay, Ben," Lily comforted as she hurried over to the baby bed. For the first time Mila noticed that Lily's left leg dragged behind, giving her an unbalanced, twisting gait. Lily hoisted herself up over the rail and plopped into the crib beside her brother. "Ben, this is Mila." The baby cried louder. "Mommy won't mind that we let her in."

"Mommy!" the little boy wailed pitifully, and Mila's chest started to ache.

Lily explained that Happy Meals were on the way, and this cheered Ben somewhat.

"How old is he?" Mila asked, rubbing a spot just above her heart.

"He's two now. He had his birthday last week," Lily replied. "And he needs his diaper changed. Bad."

Mila controlled the urge to shudder. That explained the foul odor in the room. "Will you show me what to do?"

Lily giggled. "You don't know how to change diapers?"

Mila smiled back. "Nope."

Lily pointed at a bag of diapers in the corner. "Get one of those and then make him lie down. He doesn't like it so you'll have to keep telling him."

Indeed Ben resisted the entire process, and by the time Mila was finished she wasn't sure she had the fresh diaper secured well enough to remain in place. Lily must have had similar concerns because she said, "Maybe his pants will hold it up."

Lily climbed out of the bed and the baby started to whimper.

"Will he let me pick him up?" Mila asked.

"I think so." She looked up at the baby. "Ben, Mila is going to get you out of the bed and let you run around. Okay?"

Ben didn't respond, but he didn't start crying, so Mila lifted him out of the crib and put him gingerly on the floor. The baby was happy to be free of his prison. He ran into the living room, around the small kitchen, and then back to the bedroom. His stocky legs and the sagging diaper made this a humorous sight. Lily started chasing the little boy, and soon they were both running and laughing.

While the children played, Mila looked around. "What is your mother's name?" Mila asked Lily.

"Her name is Theresa," the little girl replied. "Theresa Womack."

"And where is your daddy?"

Lily's expression saddened. "He's gone on a long trip. Mommy says he'll be home as soon as he can."

With a grim nod, Mila used her cell phone to call the three local hospitals, but Theresa Womack was not a patient at any of them. Then she checked the funeral homes and county morgue with the same result. These possibilities eliminated, she continued her visual search of the room.

The walls were a utilitarian off-white, but Theresa had made an effort to cheer things up with pictures cut from magazines and mounted on construction paper. There was also a large picture of Jesus taped over the couch and a framed photograph of the family on top of the television. Children's books and Disney videos were scattered around. Mila's frown deepened. The children seemed healthy and well adjusted. The home environment seemed comfortable and safe. So why would a religious, responsible woman just walk off and leave her children?

Lily ran in from the kitchen, Ben on her heels. "Can we watch *Land Before Time*?" Lily asked, retrieving a video from the array on the floor.

"Sure," Mila agreed. "Do you need me to help you?"

Lily shook her head. "I can do it."

Ben sat on the floor in front of the small television and stuck two fingers in his mouth, then waited with patient anticipation while his sister operated the VCR. Mila moved over to the small bookshelf. On the top shelf was a battered set of Childcraft children's encyclopedias. There were several parenting books, a volume that promised it could help you teach your child to read in thirty days, a dictionary, and a home-repair book.

The inconsistencies were gnawing at her. Then Mila saw three small blue books stacked on top of each other, and her heart skipped a beat. She touched the hardback copies of the Book of Mormon.

"We use those at scripture time every night," Lily informed her. "We all have one with our name in it."

Mila opened the top book and confirmed this. Benjamin Robert Womack was written on the inside flap.

"Ben can't read, but he looks at the pictures. I *can* read if my mommy helps me."

Mila put the book back in the stack with the others, then her eyes drifted past the scriptures to a small collection of Relief Society manuals and other Church publications. Mila walked into the bedroom and used a pen to open the top dresser drawer, where she found a neat stack of temple garments. Closing the drawer, Mila considered the situation. She didn't know what had happened, but she was filled with a firm conviction that Theresa Womack did not abandon her children.

There was a brief warning knock on the door, then Beau walked in. Lily gave him a suspicious look, but then her eyes moved to the McDonald's sacks in his hand and remained there.

"She's hungry!" Mila whispered, and Beau nodded.

"I got us one too," Beau said, holding up the bags. "Kind of a party."

"Sounds fun," Mila said as she took the Happy Meals from him. "Will you get reimbursed for this, or do you want me to split it with you?"

"It was only a few bucks," he said dismissively.

"If you aren't going to turn it in, I'm going to pay my share," she insisted. "Otherwise you'll tell people you took me out to dinner."

He laughed. "I hadn't thought of that, but it's a good idea."

"Aren't we going to eat?" Lily asked, and Mila stopped scowling at Beau long enough to distribute the food around the small kitchen table.

"Can Ben drink through a straw?" Mila asked Lily as she pulled the little boy onto her lap to assist him with his meal.

"Yes, but he spills a lot," was the response. This proved to be true. By the end of the meal, both Ben and Mila were damp with Sprite. Lily and Ben returned to their video, while Mila and Beau cleaned up the kitchen.

"I presume you've looked around?" he whispered, and she nodded. "Find anything?"

She shook her head and glanced over at the children to make sure they weren't listening. "The mother's name is Theresa Womack. I found no drug paraphernalia or other signs of illegal activity. They seem like a nice little family. The father's missing in action, but that's not unusual. And this may sound crazy, but I don't think the mother abandoned her children."

He glanced up. "It sure looks that way to me."

"I mean, she did leave them and didn't come back," Mila clarified. "But I think something prevented her from returning."

"What makes you think she didn't just get sick of her boring life and split?"

"Theresa is a Mormon," she told him softly. "A good one."

"How do you know?"

Mila waved at the bookshelf. "Some of the books they have and . . ." It was going to be difficult to explain the significance of temple garments in Theresa's drawer, but she knew she had to try. "Because Theresa wears Mormon underwear." He raised an eyebrow, and she elaborated, "I'm a Mormon too, so I know."

"You're a Mormon?" he seemed more interested in this than her information about Theresa Womack. "You ever met Donny and Marie?"

She gave him an impatient look. "There are over eleven million Mormons, Beau. I haven't met most of them, including Donny and Marie Osmond."

He shrugged. "Too bad."

"Anyway, I think we should consider this a kidnapping." She cut her eyes to the children, but they were completely absorbed in the video. "Or possibly even a murder."

"In that case, I'm calling the chief right now. I bet he'll love your theory," he added with a smile. "A murder or kidnapping instead of a simple case of abandonment."

She refused to allow him to goad her into a reply. Instead she sat down on the floor by the children while he made his phone call. "So, are you enjoying this movie?"

"We've seen it a bunch of times," Lily responded. "Ben likes it though." She studied her brother, then frowned. "Maybe he needs his diaper changed again." She pointed to Ben's sagging britches. "And we haven't had a bath in a long time."

Mila considered this. Once Beau reported the presence of the children, child services would send a representative, and diapering and bathing would be their jurisdiction. "We'll let him finish the video, then I'll change his diaper. We'll decide about a bath later."

Beau walked up behind her as Lily turned her attention back to the television. "Did you get in touch with the chief?"

He nodded. "Yeah."

Mila hated to ask, but forced herself. "What did he think about my theory?"

"He loved it," Beau said sarcastically. "He's sending a team to dust the apartment for fingerprints and do a general search."

A few minutes later they heard sirens in the distance, and Mila hurried to reassure the children. "Some other policemen are coming to look around your house, but they are all nice," she promised. Then she turned to Beau and whispered, "We need to get the children out of here during the search. It will scare them, and they've had enough trauma for one day."

"Remember that park we passed down the street?" Beau asked, and she nodded. "We could take the kids there."

"Sounds good. Let me change Ben while you explain things to the search team." Mila picked up the baby and carried him back to the bedroom. She tried diapering again with worse results. When she finished, Lily laughed.

"You're terrible at putting on diapers," the little girl pronounced.

"I, on the other hand, am an expert," Beau said from the doorway. He stepped inside and gently displaced Mila from her position in front of the baby. With a few deft movements, he had the diaper secured perfectly.

"Where did you learn to do that?" Mila asked, awed.

He winked. "I've got three younger sisters and had to help my mom with diaper duty when they were babies."

They led the children outside and walked them quickly past two patrol cars.

"Do you like going for walks?" Mila asked conversationally to pull their attention from the flashing lights.

Lily nodded. "Mommy took us for walks at night, but it's better in the day."

Mila was still digesting this information when they arrived at the playground.

Lily pointed at the slide. "Ben loves to slide, but you have to watch him, or he'll eat the sand at the bottom." Having delivered her warning, the little girl ran with her lopsided gait to the swings.

Mila let Ben go down the slide a few times, careful to keep him out of the sand. Then they joined Lily at the swings, where she was allowing Beau to push her.

After a little over an hour, Beau watched the two patrol cars drive away from the Womack apartment, headed back toward the station. He pointed them out to Mila. "Looks like the coast is clear." So they collected the children for the walk back home.

"Do you and Ben take naps?" Mila asked Lily.

"Sometimes, but it's too late."

"Too late?"

"If Ben takes a nap now, he won't go to bed at night."

Mila acknowledged her mistake with a weary nod.

"So, tell us what you and Ben have been doing for the last couple of days," Beau suggested.

"We wanted to watch TV, but Ben couldn't see it from the crib," Lily reported while the baby continued to suck his fingers in apparent agreement. "Then I tried to read Ben some books, but I kept forgetting the words. I sang him songs and made him crackers."

Mila smiled at the little girl. "You did a very good job. Your mom will be so proud."

"Is my mommy coming home now?" Lily asked.

"Mommy," Ben whimpered around his slobbery fingers.

Beau and Mila exchanged a look. He shook his head slightly, and Mila nodded. "We're not sure when your mom will be able to come home."

Lily turned her wide, blue eyes to Mila. "Will you take care of us until she gets here?"

Mila swallowed the lump in her throat. “Sure.” She said it casually, but once spoken, the word felt like an oath.

CHAPTER 4

Eugenia was grating coconut for some homemade ambrosia when George Ann Simmons pounded on her back door. "Come on in," Eugenia called, although the invitation wasn't necessary. George Ann was already halfway through the utility room.

"Did you know that Cecil Perkins is missing?" George Ann demanded without preamble.

Eugenia frowned. "Missing? You mean like kidnapped?"

"Nobody seems to know what happened to him," George Ann replied, picking up one of the orange slices that Eugenia had painstakingly peeled and popping it into her mouth. "I made curry chicken last night for supper, and you know how everyone loves my recipe. I had a little left over and thought I'd take it to Cecil and Margaret. When I dropped it by, I asked about Cecil, and Margaret said she hadn't seen him in over a week."

Eugenia was mildly alarmed by this announcement. "A week! And she doesn't know where he is?"

"Says she doesn't care," George Ann confided. "Says it's been peaceful and quiet since he's been gone, and she wouldn't mind if he never came back."

Now Eugenia was scandalized. "Well, what a thing for a wife to say!"

"You might feel that way too if you'd had to live with a man who had a drinking problem," George Ann said.

"Cecil Perkins has a drinking problem?"

"Eugenia! Everybody knows that!"

"Well, I certainly didn't. I just thought he was moody."

George Ann shook her head in despair at Eugenia's naiveté. "Cecil Perkins will come to a bad end. Mark my words."

Eugenia began peeling more orange slices to replace the ones George Ann had eaten. "I saw Mila Edwards yesterday."

"Did you convince her not to sell Cora Sue's house?" George Ann asked.

Eugenia shook her head. "No, I'm hoping that her childhood memories will stop her."

George Ann lifted her chin, which accentuated her long neck, and Eugenia had to turn away. "Well, you'd think that family pride and duty would be enough to stop her."

"Family pride and duty are out of style, and Mila's had a hard time. Daphne remarried soon after her husband's death . . ."

George Ann's eyes widened. "I know. It was positively disgraceful."

Eugenia ignored this and continued. "I just wanted to warn you to be nice if you run into Mila."

"That's an unnecessary piece of advice if I ever heard one," George Ann said crossly. "I'm nice to everyone."

Eugenia restrained a chuckle. "Oh, yes, I've seen how you've accepted the Ledbetters with open arms."

"Oh, well," George Ann said, her chin lifting another notch. "That's completely different. The Ledbetters are pure white trash. Building that monstrosity they call a house—an affront to decent, hardworking people everywhere. And they let that little boy dress up in the most atrocious outfits and skulk around in bushes instead of attending school like normal children." George Ann sniffed. "He probably can't even read!"

"Of course he can," Eugenia responded mildly. "As the child services folks discovered when you called them to report the Ledbetters as neglectful."

George Ann pursed her lips. "You can't prove that I was the one who called," she said. "But goodness knows someone needed to! Those people are irresponsible."

"Not according to child services. They got high marks for home environment."

"They're heathens!" George Ann had warmed to her topic. "They never go to church."

"The Bible says we're not to judge others."

George Ann crossed her arms. "Not everyone caters to the strays and misfits the way you do, Eugenia."

"I'm not encouraging you to befriend Cleo Ledbetter. She's got enough problems without you hanging around her," Eugenia assured George Ann. "I just want you to make Mila Edwards feel welcome in Haggerty if you get the chance."

"I'll be sweet as sugar if I see little Mila," George Ann promised.

"Little Mila is a grown woman now, a police detective with a lot of emotional baggage. If you see her, don't mention her father or her mother. Just concentrate on the happy days she spent here with Cora Sue."

"Yes, ma'am!" George Ann used enough inflection to let Eugenia know she didn't appreciate this advice either. "Well, I guess I'll be going."

Eugenia stood and took a step toward the back door. "Don't rush off."

"There's a Christian Women Supporting Foreign Missionaries meeting tonight," George Ann said as they stepped out onto the back porch. "I guess I'll see you there."

Eugenia shook her head. "I'm helping Kate plant tomato seedlings tonight."

George Ann's eyes narrowed. "It seems like lately you're always doing something else when there's a meeting."

Eugenia dismissed this with a wave of her hand. "I was at the Literary Guild meeting yesterday and the Haggerty Genealogical Society meeting on Wednesday."

"Yes, but when there's a *church* meeting, you're too busy to attend."

"Don't be ridiculous, George Ann," Eugenia said as the other woman started down the steps. "I'll be at Cornelia Blackwood's Faith Fair meeting on Wednesday afternoon and if that isn't church—I don't know what is!"

This seemed to please George Ann. "Well, good."

"You should bake one of your famous key lime pies in case Mila comes back," Eugenia suggested. "I took her tea cakes yesterday, and she seemed to really enjoy them."

A smile curved the corners of George Ann's thin lips. "I might just do that. If she enjoyed your tea cakes, she'll absolutely love one of my pies."

George Ann started across the backyard, then spotted a For Sale sign propped against the gardening shed. "I figured you were the one who was stealing those signs from Cora Sue's yard," she told Eugenia. "You'd better not let Nickel Phelps find out. She'll tear you limb from limb."

Eugenia laughed. "I'd like to see her try."

* * *

When Mila and Beau stepped into the Womacks' apartment, they saw that Chief Monahan and Dorcas James had arrived during their absence. The would-be detective had stationed herself right beside the chief, looking fresh, crisp, and professional in spite of the late afternoon heat. Mila was very aware of her own bedraggled appearance as she approached them.

"Chief, Dorcas," she greeted. "What brings you here?"

Instead of answering the question, the chief waved at the Womack family picture that was now in Dorcas James's capable hands. "Beau, after we get copies of this made, you can start a canvas of the neighborhood. Maybe somebody saw something. Dorcas will work with the Community Relations Department to get pictures to the local television stations. I'll warn child services that we have some customers for them."

As the chief turned to leave, Mila asked, "What about me, sir?"

Chief Monahan's forehead wrinkled with confusion. "What about you?"

"What should I do?" Mila clarified.

"Whatever Detective Lambert tells you to, and try to stay out of trouble." With that, the chief pulled out a cell phone and moved onto the porch to make his call in relative privacy.

"This situation has the potential to turn nasty in a hurry," Dorcas explained to Mila as if she were a dimwit. "If the community feels that the police department mishandled things . . ." She let her voice trail off, the result obvious.

"Have you found out anything about Theresa Womack?" Beau asked.

"According to the Department of Motor Vehicles, she's from Roanoke, Virginia," Dorcas replied. "We're running a check on her now."

The chief came back in, running his hands through his hair in frustration. "Child services is swamped. A caseworker has been assigned, but it will be tomorrow before she can process these kids. We'll take them to a detention center downtown for the night."

"A detention center?" Mila repeated, holding Ben a little closer and reaching down to stroke Lily's silky hair. "You're going to put these two babies in a detention center?"

The chief had the decency to look a little uncomfortable.

"If you're worried about community relations, I'd say that's a good way to get everyone mad at you," Mila continued.

"It's our only option," Dorcas spoke in the chief's defense.

"There's got to be another one," Beau said, aligning himself with Mila, who sent him a grateful smile.

"What if I just stay here with them?" Mila suggested, and the chief frowned.

"That's highly irregular."

"But not unheard of," Beau stepped in again.

Mila lowered her voice. "There's always the chance that their mother will come back on her own. And even if she doesn't, the children will feel safer here."

"They'll actually *be* safe in the detention center surrounded by law enforcement personnel," the chief replied.

Beau took Ben from Mila's arms, then reached a hand out to Lily. "I think we'll wait out on the porch."

The chief waited until Beau and the children were gone, then spoke to Mila again. "You're the one who thinks their mother was killed or kidnapped. That means the children might be at risk too. We need to have them somewhere secure."

"No one has tried to hurt them in the two days since their mother left," Mila pointed out. "And if I'm here, they'll be under police protection."

Beau poked his head in the door and pointed at his watch. "Can we hurry things up? I've got a date tonight."

"Imagine that," Mila murmured.

"It's with a real beauty, and I set it up weeks ago, so I don't dare cancel. But afterwards, I'll come and spend the night here. If both of us provide protection, the kids should be fine."

For the first time the chief looked like he was starting to waver, and Mila's gratitude toward Beau was tempered only by her irritation toward the chief. Why was it that when Beau said something he accepted it so easily?

"Sounds perfect," Mila said with conviction.

"I'll have to get approval from child services," Chief Monahan hedged.

"Give them my cell number if they have any questions." Mila figured that acting like the decision was made was her best bet. Then she walked out onto the porch and spoke to Lily. "I'm going to spend the night here with you and Ben. Can you stay here with Officer Lambert while I run to my hotel and pack a bag?" The little girl nodded, and Mila turned to Beau. "I'll be back as soon as I can."

Mila took their unmarked car and drove to the Marriott. It only took a few minutes to pack an overnight bag, and then she stopped by a grocery store and bought some essentials. Just as she parked in front of the Womacks' apartment, she got a call from the child services caseworker. The woman introduced herself as Wilma Hightower and said that she had been in court all day and still had two emergencies to handle before she could even check to see what was on her desk.

"Chief Monahan says you want to stay at the apartment with the children tonight." Ms. Hightower sounded less than sure about the arrangement. "I presume you have child care training."

Mila thought about the diapering lesson that Lily had given her earlier. "Of course," she replied with confidence.

"Very well," Ms. Hightower agreed with obvious reluctance. "But let me give you my number in case there is an emergency. And I'll come by as soon as I can tomorrow to meet them and start the paperwork."

Mila entered Ms. Hightower's number into her cell phone, then disconnected. Inside the apartment Mila found the children sitting beside Beau on the couch. He was in the middle of *Fox in Socks,* so she took the groceries into the kitchen and put them away while he finished.

When he reached the end he stood. "I've got to go or I'll be late."

"For your hot date," Mila added cynically.

He shot her a smile. "Exactly. Will you folks be okay while I'm gone?"

"We'll be fine," Mila assured him as they walked toward the door.

"See you sooner or later, depending on how well my date goes."

Mila shook her head and closed the door, then locked it. When she turned around, the Womack children were still on the couch, watching her. Their eyes were filled with a confidence that terrified her. She rubbed her hands together. "Okay, Lily, what is our first course of action?"

"Huh?" Lily responded.

"What should we do now?"

"Ben needs a bath. Me too."

"Okay," Mila responded courageously. "You'll show me how, right?"

Lily giggled. "You don't know how to do anything!" She led the way into the bathroom. "First," she instructed, "you turn on the cold water. Then you turn on the hot, but just a little until it's warm. And Mommy always checks it with her elbow before she puts Ben inside." Lily stuck her small elbow into the bathtub to demonstrate.

Mila followed her example and tested the water. "Nice and warm," she pronounced. "So now do we put Ben into the tub?"

Lily giggled again. "You have to take his clothes off first!"

Removing his clothes proved to be almost as difficult as putting them on, but finally Mila had the little boy stripped and into the tub. Lily pointed out the shampoo that didn't sting the eyes, and Mila lathered up Ben's curly hair. Slippery, he was even more difficult to control. For what seemed like hours, he swam and flopped and slithered around in the few inches of water that Mila considered safe. Finally Mila insisted that he get out, and the baby screamed at the top of his lungs.

"Why is he crying?" Mila asked Lily.

"He likes to take a bath."

"But the water's cold."

Lily shrugged. "He always cries when he has to get out."

Mila was reassured by the fact that this was his normal reaction to the end of bath time. She wrapped the unhappy baby in a towel, then held him on her lap while she drained the tub and repeated the warm water testing procedure. "Okay, now it's your turn," she said to Lily.

Lily clutched her clean pajamas to her little chest. "I can't take off my clothes while you're in here."

Mila looked at the baby on her lap. "Ben did."

"That's because he's little," Lily explained.

"Oh." Mila nodded. "I guess I can go into the bedroom and put Ben's diaper on while you take your bath. But I'm going to leave the door partly open so I can hear if you start to drown."

Lily laughed. "I can't drown in that little bit of water!"

Mila hefted Ben and started toward the bedroom. "You don't know how bad my luck has been lately," she muttered under her breath.

Mila read the instructions on the bag of diapers twice, then tried to apply the principles to the squirming two-year-old. When Ben escaped, she examined her workmanship. Only one side was sagging, and Mila felt triumphant.

"I think I did a little better that time," she told Lily when the little girl came out of the bathroom.

"Maybe a little," Lily said with a skeptical look at her brother. "Now we have to put on his pajamas."

This involved a tiny contraption made out of stretchy material and four thousand snaps. Lily giggled each time Mila connected the wrong snaps and was nearly hysterical by the time Ben was dressed.

"There ought to be a regulatory agency for these things!" Mila cried when she finished. "That was criminally difficult."

"My mommy never has trouble," Lily told Mila.

"Mommy," Ben whimpered and stuck his fingers back into his mouth.

Lily hugged her little brother, then asked, "Is it time for dinner yet?"

Mila checked the clock and was surprised to see that it was almost seven o'clock. "Sure. I bought some Froot Loops. How does that sound?"

Lily's mouth opened to form a perfect circle. "Wow. Mommy never lets us have sugar cereal. It gives you cavities."

"Well, we'll just have to brush your teeth afterwards," Mila said as she led them to the kitchen. After dinner Lily reminded her about the need to brush their teeth. "Does Ben have enough teeth to brush?" Mila asked.

"He only has a few, but they still get dirty," Lily pointed out. "And you have to be careful 'cause he tries to eat the toothpaste."

Mila nodded grimly. If the last few hours had taught her anything, she was sure that brushing a two-year-old's teeth would not be the easy proposition it sounded.

Once the children were fed and their teeth brushed, Mila asked Lily what she should do next.

"We get in bed, and then you have to help us read the scriptures." Lily climbed up on the bookshelf and removed the little stack of blue books, then led the way into the bedroom.

Lily showed Mila where the clean sheets were, and Mila replaced the dirty ones in Ben's crib. Then Mila lifted Ben into the crib and watched as Lily hoisted herself up and over the railing. "Do you sleep in the crib with Ben?"

"Usually I sleep with Mommy, but Ben will be scared if I leave him by himself," Lily said wisely.

"That's very kind of you." Mila helped Lily read a few verses of scripture while Ben looked at the pictures.

"Now you read us the bedtime stories," Lily said.

"Which book do you want me to read?"

Lily pointed to the stack on the chest of drawers. "You have to read them all over and over until we fall asleep."

Mila pulled a kitchen chair up to the side of the crib and started to read. After thirty minutes Mila was fighting sleep. Finally she said, "Ben looks sleepy. Maybe we could stop?"

Lily nodded. "Okay, but we haven't said our prayers."

"Ben can say a prayer?" Mila was surprised. The baby had barely mumbled a few words of gibberish since they'd found him that afternoon.

Lily laughed. "No, my mommy always says it for him."

Mila didn't want Lily or Ben to start thinking about their absent mother, so she suggested, "Maybe you could say one prayer for both of you tonight."

"Okay. But we have to kneel down," Lily insisted.

Mila frowned. "If you get out of bed, Ben won't be sleepy anymore."

Lily shrugged. "He'll get sleepy again if you keep reading books."

With a weary sigh Mila helped the children down to kneel by the edge of the crib. Once they were all in position, Lily began. First she listed everything she was thankful for, which included their grim little apartment, their clothes, and the pudding that they'd had for dessert the previous Sunday. Once her list of blessings was out of the way, Lily asked the Lord to help her get big and strong enough to have her leg fixed so she could walk right. Then she blessed her mother and father, which made a lump arise in Mila's throat. Finally she asked the Lord to bless Mila so that she could learn how to take care of them until their mother came back.

Mila was blinking back tears as she put the children into the crib and started rereading the books. Ben fell asleep after three and a half, so Mila stacked the books back on the nightstand. She tucked the covers under Lily's chin, then asked, "What's wrong with your leg?"

"I have a curvature," the little girl pronounced carefully, "in my back. I'm going to have a bunch of operations when I get bigger."

Mila nodded, then pointed at the sleeping baby. "Will he wake up during the night?"

"Maybe," Lily replied. "But don't worry. If he does I'll sing him some songs."

Mila was deeply touched. "You are a very good sister."

Lily smiled. "That's what my mommy always says."

Mila stayed in the bedroom until Lily fell asleep, then went into the living room to wait for Beau. It was almost one o'clock in the morning before he knocked on the door, and Mila had fallen asleep on the couch.

"I wasn't kidding about that being a date I couldn't afford to miss," he whispered when she let him in.

"You *were* kidding about spending the night with us. It's morning," she pointed out.

He laughed as he walked into the kitchen and looked through the grocery bags still on the tiny counter. He pulled out a bag of Oreos. "Mind if I have a few?"

"Help yourself," she invited.

He popped two cookies into his mouth. "Want some?"

Mila shook her head. "No, that Happy Meal had my week's limit of fat grams."

His eyes scanned her thin frame. "You could use a few fat grams."

"Obesity runs in my family, so I'm kind of fat-phobic."

"Fat-phobic?"

"Afraid of gaining weight," she clarified. "So I exercise and watch what I eat."

He nodded as he crammed two more cookies into his mouth. "Kids okay?"

"They're fine. Any new developments on our case?" Mila asked.

Beau swallowed a mouthful of cookie. "Yeah. Theresa Womack was missing before she disappeared."

Mila was astounded both by this news and the fact that it had been shared with Beau and kept from her. Even considering Chief Monahan's animosity, it was an unforgivable violation in police procedure. "What do you mean by *missing*?"

"Theresa Womack and her husband own a house in Roanoke, Virginia. According to the police chief in Roanoke, in the middle of February Theresa took her kids and left. She didn't notify the babysitter or tell her neighbors or hire a real estate agent. Finally neighbors complained about the grass getting too long, and a couple of uniforms were sent to check it out. From what they could tell, she packed up a few necessities and just drove away."

"What about the husband?"

"Gone too. He was accused of stealing from his company and got fired from his job. He reacted violently and caused some property damage. He skipped town before he could be arrested. They found a postcard in the apartment that the chief thinks was from him. It was addressed to a post office box that Theresa had rented."

"What was on the postcard?"

"Just a phone number," he said.

"I guess you tried the number?"

"Belongs to a disposable cell phone that was used only once and disposed of immediately afterwards."

"Last Tuesday?" Mila guessed, and Beau nodded. "What was the postmark on the card?"

"London."

Now this was a surprise. "The husband was in London?"

"Must have been for a while. He probably decided it was safe enough now to come back. Our best guess is that he set up the meeting during the phone call. They met, Theresa got in his car, and they drove away."

"Leaving their children to starve? No way." Mila watched Beau eat for a few minutes, then asked, "Why did Theresa come to Albany in the first place?"

"No idea why she came to Albany. Dorcas is trying to track the car. We assume she drove it down here, but it's possible that she sold it somewhere along the way and came to Albany on the bus or something."

"Why wouldn't she just go on to London and join her husband immediately?"

"Our working theory is that Larsen Womack split after he was fired, and then the wife left separately, maybe for an unrelated reason."

Mila was furious and had to work hard to keep her emotions in check. "You and the chief and Dorcas have developed a working theory without me?"

Beau looked uncomfortable. "We tossed around a few ideas."

"And what was the unrelated reason you came up with that made Theresa leave her home in Roanoke and move into a dumpy apartment in Albany right after her husband disappeared?"

"We don't have one."

Mila gained some satisfaction from this admission, but as her anger ebbed, the hurt increased. The chief was taking advantage of her concern for the children to exclude her from the investigation. "Who fired the husband?"

"A pharmaceutical company called Ryathon."

"What did Larsen Womack steal?"

"We don't know. The chief's got Dorcas on it." Beau closed up the bag of cookies and put them on the tiny counter in the kitchen. "Since everything seems fine here, I think I'll go home and crash for a few hours."

She nodded. "Sleep quick. The kids will probably be up soon, and I'll need your help."

She heard him groaning as he walked toward the door. "Do you think we'll get overtime for working on Saturday?" he asked.

"I doubt it, since we volunteered for this extra duty."

"One of us did, anyway."

She knew he was trying to coax her into a better mood, but she couldn't force herself to cooperate. Finally he waved and stepped out into the night. She watched as he climbed into the unmarked car, then she locked the door behind him.

CHAPTER 5

The Womack children slept in until five o'clock the next morning, giving Mila almost four hours of sleep. She convinced them to watch a video for an hour and dozed on the couch, but she still felt like a zombie as she made breakfast. After their meal, she dressed Ben under Lily's watchful eye. Once the children were settled in front of the television watching a video about singing vegetables, Mila took a shower.

When she rejoined them in the living room she considered calling Beau, but took pity on the other detective and decided to wait. As Mila settled on the couch, the video ended, and Lily turned off the television. "Mommy doesn't like us to watch too many videos."

Mila glanced at the clock. It wasn't quite eight. "So, what will we do next?"

"You could read us some books," Lily proposed.

The thought of the books she had read several times the night before crossed her mind with dread. "The bedtime stories?" she asked.

Lily laughed. "No, these." She picked a stack from the bookshelf, and they settled on the couch to read.

"Don't you get sick of hearing these same books?" Mila asked after they had been through all of their daytime selection twice.

Lily considered this, then shook her head. "No."

"Is there anything else we could do?" Mila asked.

"We could play house. I'll be the mom, and Ben will be the dog, and you'll be the baby."

Mila nodded vaguely, grateful for the reading reprieve. Then the phone rang. It was Wilma Hightower, the child services caseworker.

Mila told the children to play without her for a few minutes, then took the phone into the little kitchen so she could converse without being overheard.

"How are things with your little charges?" Ms. Hightower asked.

"Considering everything, I'd say they're great," Mila told her. "We've been reading the same books over and over, and now we're going to play house."

Wilma chuckled. "Sounds very entertaining and therapeutic. What have you told them about their mother?"

Mila looked across at Lily, who smiled back with a serene, trusting expression. "Not much. I'm sorry, but I just didn't know what to say."

She heard Wilma sigh. "That's okay. I'm used to dishing out bad news."

Her tone sent a chill up Mila's spine. "Have they found her body?"

"No, but after this much time we have to accept the very real possibility that she's not ever coming home." There was a brief pause, then Wilma said, "I've got a couple of appointments this morning, but I'll be there as soon as I can."

* * *

The ambrosia turned out even better than Eugenia had hoped, and on Saturday morning she took some over to the Iversons next door. "Why are you dressed for work?" she asked Mark when she saw him sitting at the kitchen table.

"I'm going into the office for a couple of hours today," he replied.

"Where are the kids?" Eugenia asked, taking two bowls from the cupboard and two spoons from a drawer.

"Watching television," Kate answered. "What's that?"

"It's ambrosia," Eugenia explained as she dished them both up a generous helping. "The recipe calls for a little brandy, but since you're teetotalers, I used vanilla instead."

Mark stared at the concoction suspiciously. "We really appreciate that."

"Try it," his wife Kate encouraged him after eating a spoonful. "It's delicious, and a little vanilla won't hurt you."

Mark stirred the fruit mixture. "I know it won't hurt me," he said, but instead of putting any into his mouth, he stood. "I think I'll save mine for tonight since I really need to get on in to work."

Eugenia gave him a knowing look, but moved toward the back door herself. "And I'd better get Polly her breakfast before she starves. Kiss my babies for me!"

"I will," Kate promised.

Eugenia crossed the Iversons' lawn and let herself into Polly Kirby's house. Upstairs she found Polly watching *Seven Brides for Seven Brothers* on the classic movie channel. Polly held up a hand to keep Eugenia from speaking until a commercial started. Then she was all smiles.

"Good morning, Eugenia." Her eyes zeroed in on the foil-wrapped plate and Tupperware container in her friend's hand. "What's for breakfast this morning?"

"The usual eggs and bacon, but I brought you some homemade ambrosia for dessert," Eugenia said. "Minus the brandy so Kate and Mark would eat it."

"I think I'll have dessert first," Polly said as she took a bite. "Delicious—although I'll admit that I've always taken wicked pleasure in eating *real* ambrosia. I mean, how else can you enjoy brandy and stay respectable?"

"Speaking of brandy," Eugenia said, moving a little closer to the bed. "Did you know that Cecil Perkins had a drinking problem?"

Polly nodded. "Why, of course. Everybody knows that."

Eugenia was still shaking her head when she let herself out Polly's back door.

* * *

After her conversation with Wilma Hightower, Mila received instructions from Lily on her role as baby of their pretend family. Her major duty seemed to be to cry—a lot. Ben scrambled around on all fours in a realistic imitation of a good-natured dog, while Lily cooked, cleaned, and disciplined Mila as necessary.

Mila's throat was getting sore from the constant wailing by the time Beau arrived at noon. He was carrying McDonald's sacks, and the children greeted him with enthusiasm. "It's not fair that I spend hours reading, bathing, diapering, and pretending to be a baby to win their affection, and all you have to do is show up with hamburgers," Mila complained as she settled the children around the table and distributed their lunch.

"Sounds like someone got up on the wrong side of the bed," Beau murmured. Even after only a few hours of sleep he looked disgustingly fresh and well rested.

"*Someone* got up too early from any side of the bed," Mila corrected, then she stared at her hamburger. "I guess fast-food two days in a row won't kill them." She took a bite. "Or me."

Once they were finished eating, Mila told Beau it was his turn to watch the children while she made some phone calls. She suggested that he assume her role as baby in the make-believe family, but he convinced the children to reread books instead of playing house. Giving him a look over her shoulder to let him know that he'd gotten off easy, she went into the bedroom and closed the door.

After several calls to long-distance information, she finally reached the bishop of the Roanoke Second Ward. Mila identified herself, then told him about Theresa's disappearance and the children's plight.

"I'm so sorry to hear that," he said, obviously shaken. "Do you expect to find Theresa soon?"

Mila paused, then said, "We don't. If she deserted the children, there's the chance that she will change her mind and come home voluntarily. But if she was kidnapped or even murdered, she may never return."

"I hope that nothing terrible has happened to Theresa, but I'm sure that she would never desert her children." The bishop sounded positive.

Mila was pleased by his response. "I don't think so either, based on what we've been able to learn from her apartment and the children. Unfortunately that might mean that Theresa is dead."

"If that turns out to be the case and funeral arrangements become necessary, I'll be glad to handle them, since she didn't have any family."

"She didn't have *any* family?" Mila repeated in surprise. Dorcas and Beau and the chief probably knew that, but hadn't gotten around to sharing it with her yet.

"None that I knew of," the bishop was continuing. "She and Larsen were both orphans. In fact, that's how they met—at an orphan support group."

Mila immediately realized the implications of this for Lily and Ben. If neither parent could be located, the children really were alone in the world and at the mercy of a flawed and overburdened social services system. "So the children have no one?"

"Well, Larsen lived with a foster family for most of his teenage years. He was never actually adopted, but he spoke of them fondly, and they visited occasionally."

Mila sighed with relief. "Can you contact them and let them know the situation?"

"They are on a mission right now. Somewhere in South America, I think," the bishop informed her. "I'll call Salt Lake and find out for sure."

"If they're on a mission they won't be much help."

"I'm pretty sure the foster parents have a son," the bishop added thoughtfully. "I want to say that he's a professional surfer, so it might be hard to locate him, but I can try."

"Please do," Mila requested, although she didn't see how the man could be of any help even if the bishop did locate him. "I understand that Larsen was fired by Ryathon Pharmaceuticals. Is there anything you can tell me about that?"

There was a brief pause. "I've heard some rumors, but I don't feel comfortable repeating them," the bishop said finally. "What I can tell you is that Larsen Womack had a current temple recommend and seemed honest and trustworthy."

Mila thanked the bishop and gave him her number in case he thought of anything else that he wanted to tell her. When she walked back into the living room, Beau glanced at her, then his eyes fell to the cell phone in her hand. "Checking in with your boyfriend?"

"No." She took the book from Beau's hands and gave it to Lily. "Could you show Ben the pictures for a few minutes while I talk to Beau?" The little girl nodded, and Mila pointed into the kitchen.

Beau followed her. "I was talking to the Womacks' bishop," she whispered. Seeing the blank look on Beau's face, Mila generalized her terminology. "Their minister."

Beau nodded in comprehension. "What did he say?"

"He agrees with me that this is not a case of willful abandonment, and he said that, in his opinion, Larsen Womack was an honest man."

Beau shrugged. "Ministers always give folks the benefit of the doubt."

"He also said that Larsen and Theresa were both orphans. Did you know that?"

Beau shook his head. "I've told you everything I know."

She paused long enough to let him know she doubted this. "Anyway, if that's true, then the children have no relatives to accept custody. Larsen did live with a foster family for several years. The parents are on a mission for the Mormon Church, but there's a foster brother."

"I'll get Dorcas to check it out," Beau promised.

"You said we could play hide-and-seek," Lily called from the living room.

"And I always keep my promises!" Beau assured her. "I'll be it first." He covered his eyes and started to count. Mila rolled her eyes as the children rushed to hide.

Wilma arrived right as they finished dinner. Mila offered the child services caseworker some of their frozen lasagna, but she declined. Once they were all settled in the living room, Wilma chatted with the kids for a while.

"Mila tells me that you like books," Wilma said finally, and Lily nodded. "I brought one of my favorite books to read to you."

Lily snuggled a little closer to Mila, then nodded. The book was about a rabbit that found a rainbow and then lost it. The basic concept was that the rainbow and its beauty still existed in the rabbit's memory and could still bring him happiness. But the words seemed empty to Mila, and she felt herself tense up as Wilma delivered the bad news. Ben had dozed off in Beau's lap while the rabbit was searching for his rainbow, but Lily was listening closely.

"So just like the rainbow in our story, your mother has gone away, but you will always remember her and love her, and in that sense she'll always be with you."

Mila watched Lily's expression go from confused to horrible comprehension. "Isn't my mommy coming back? Ever?"

Wilma spoke with practiced care. "I'm sure your mother didn't want to leave you, but she did, and now arrangements will be made for someone else to take care of you."

Tears spilled over onto Lily's pale cheeks. "I want Mila to take care of me and Ben until Mommy comes back."

"You'll stay here until Monday," Wilma said evasively as she stood. "Now you sit here and let Officer Lambert read a book to you while I talk to . . . Mila." Wilma made a little face when she said the name, and Mila realized that she disapproved of the familiarity that had developed between her and the children.

She followed Wilma to the door, and they stepped outside. "So, what happens now?"

"From what we have been able to determine there are no relatives; therefore, the children will be placed in foster care until their parents are found or declared legally dead. Unfortunately, the foster care system is bursting at the gills. I've managed to find a place for each of them, but they'll have to be separated."

"Oh, no!" Mila objected. "They can't be separated."

"I know it sounds cruel, but it's probably for the best," Wilma told her. "If both parents are dead, the children will be in long-term foster care and might eventually be candidates for adoption. The boy will be easy to place, the girl more difficult because of her handicap."

Mila swallowed a lump in her throat. "She has curvature of the spine. She said it can be surgically corrected."

Wilma nodded. "It can be, but she will require several expensive surgeries, and most people don't want to take on a child with problems."

Finally the full impact of what Wilma was saying dawned on Mila. "So they'll be separated permanently? Ben will be adopted, while Lily spends her life in foster care?"

Wilma pulled her keys from her purse. "Almost certainly." When Wilma looked up, Mila saw compassion in her eyes. "I hate to separate them too. But I can't allow the little boy's future to be restricted by his sister's limitations."

"If the family who adopts Ben would just meet Lily . . ." Mila began, but Wilma cut her off with a wave of her hand.

"Most couples want to start out with one baby—not two children. And certainly not one who will spend the better part of a year in the hospital."

"Ben depends on Lily."

"The adoptive parents will want the baby to depend on them," Wilma pointed out gently.

"But their mother could turn up at any minute! Their father too!" Mila pleaded.

"If Mr. Womack turns up, he will be facing felony charges and will probably spend the majority of his life in jail. Mrs. Womack may face charges as well and will almost surely lose custody of her children if she reappears."

Mila felt ill. The children would be raised apart, without the gospel. Everything Theresa had worked for was going up in smoke. "There has to be another way."

Wilma flashed her a smile and started toward the street. "Short of you becoming a foster parent, I can't think of one. Bring them to the police station on Monday morning. I'm going to have them meet with a child psychologist."

When Mila returned to the living room, she found Beau reading to Lily. Ben was still sleeping, cradled in the crook of the policeman's arm. She lifted the baby and moved him into the crib, then sat next to Lily and listened to Beau read until the little girl nodded off. Lily roused for a few seconds while Mila tucked her into bed. Her little arms went around Mila's neck, and she whispered, "Is my mom really gone, or did I dream it?"

"She's lost," Mila told her honestly. "But remember, Lily, your mother loved you very much. She'll come back if she can."

A tiny smile touched Lily's mouth as she curled into the covers and went back to sleep.

"They're going to separate the children," Mila told Beau when she walked back into the living room. "They think Ben can be adopted, but they'll put Lily in permanent foster care."

He nodded. "I figured they would, since the little girl is crippled."

"She's not crippled!" Mila was horrified. "She has a curvature of the spine that can be fixed. And she's smart and kind and she's taken care of Ben all by herself for days."

"Hey!" Beau interrupted, staring at the moisture on her cheeks. "One of the first rules of police work is you have to check your emotions at the door."

Mila wiped her face and took a deep breath. "Yeah, well I never was very good at following the rules."

"So I've heard," Beau told her with a smile. "Maybe this would be a good time for you to tell me why you lost your job in Atlanta."

She knew he was trying to distract her, and it worked. "Do you expect me to believe that the details of my termination are a complete secret?" she demanded.

"Not completely. We heard that you disobeyed a direct order and that nobody would hire you except the chief because he was in debt to your daddy."

Humiliation washed over Mila in steady, sickening waves. "I had my reasons for disobeying an order."

"I'm sure you did," Beau replied. "And they were . . ."

She gave him a shaky smile. "None of your business."

"You're just making me more curious by withholding information," he warned. "If necessary I'll date someone in Atlanta's Internal Affairs Division so I can get the scoop."

"Even you wouldn't go that far. I've seen the women in internal affairs," she attempted a joke.

"That's the girl. Fight back," he said, pleased. "And actually I was relieved to find out that the chief hired you because your daddy saved his life. Up until this morning the rumor was that the chief hired you for romantic reasons."

Mila stared at him. "You thought there was a romance between me and the chief?" she asked, incredulous.

He laughed. "I have to admit I was ready to give you and him Academy Awards for your impressions of hate."

She scowled. "Now you know we weren't acting."

"I'd much rather work with a rogue detective than the boss's girlfriend," Beau assured her. "And the chief will learn to love you. Just give him time."

She lifted an eyebrow. "Rogue?"

"If the lovely Italian leather shoe fits," he pointed at her feet, "wear it."

"What do you know about lovely Italian leather?" she asked.

He lifted his foot. "Gucci," he said with reverence. "From one clotheshorse to another."

She had to laugh, then he said he'd better go. "Don't want to be late."

"Let me guess, you've got a hot date."

He winked. "See you tomorrow."

After Beau left, Mila walked around the apartment, straightening things up. As she stacked the bedtime books and folded little clothes, her heart started to ache. Maybe it was the fact that she'd lost her own father and knew how shattering it could be. Maybe it was because she'd grown up without siblings and almost envied Ben the love of a sister. Or maybe it was her connection through the gospel with Theresa Womack. But whatever the reason, Mila knew that she couldn't let this happen. Her father hadn't taught her to be a victim, so she knew she couldn't just sit by helplessly. *Use your resources,* her father had always said. But how?

For several crazy minutes she considered putting the children in her car and driving off for places unknown. But it didn't take long for her to realize that making herself a fugitive would not help the children in any meaningful way. She considered a few, slightly better options—like impersonating a relative and forging a will for Larsen and Theresa Womack that left the children in her care—before deciding to take the issue to the Lord.

Mila felt much better after her prayer, although she still didn't know what course to take. She showered and drank a low-fat protein shake. Then she sat on the couch and studied the situation out in her mind again. Finally she smiled when she remembered Wilma Hightower's parting remark. Child services was probably the only place in Atlanta where she still had contacts and even friends. It might take all night long, but, with the Lord's help, by Monday morning Mila intended to have things worked out to her satisfaction. She picked up the phone and dialed her friend Mallory's home number.

* * *

On Sunday morning the children slept in until six thirty. After breakfast Mila dressed them with increased proficiency, then helped them brush their teeth. She suggested that she might be able to find something for them to watch on television, but Lily shook her head. "We can't watch TV," she said. "It's Sunday, and we have to have church."

Mila had considered taking the children to one of the wards in Albany, but decided that was beyond her capabilities. "We can't go to church today," Mila began, wondering how she was going to explain that to the children without losing their confidence.

"We never *go* to church anymore," Lily said. "I mean, we have our own church here."

Mila was nonplussed. Theresa Womack didn't take her children to church? They read the scriptures and said their prayers, but they didn't go to church? It was another strange inconsistency. "How do you have church at home?"

"We sing songs, and then Mommy tells us stories and reads to us out of the scriptures."

Mila smiled. "You'll show me how. Right?"

Lily giggled. "I always show you everything!"

Throughout their home Primary, Mila couldn't help but think about Theresa Womack and the kind of woman she had been. Her children were healthy and well behaved. Lily was responsible and very routine oriented. But they rarely left the house, at least not in daylight, and had church at home. Theresa was hiding for some reason, and Mila felt sure if she could figure that out, she would have the key to Theresa's disappearance.

They finished their Primary meeting at eight, and without videos or toys to entertain the children, Mila was afraid that she was in for a very long day. But Lily requested some paper and pencils and helped Ben draw pictures. When they got bored with that, Mila let them help her make milkshakes. Then they made a Lego town until lunchtime.

Beau arrived in time to eat a sandwich with them. While eating, he examined the Womacks' television. "No cable?"

Mila shook her head. "Just rabbit ears, but the reception is pretty good. Why?"

"Because the Braves are playing this afternoon."

Lily looked up from her sandwich. "You aren't supposed to watch ball games on Sunday. It's not righteous."

Beau's eyes moved from the little girl to Mila. "Well, maybe I won't be spending the afternoon here after all."

The kids talked Beau into reading to them for a little while when they were finished with lunch. Then he left to watch the ball game, and Mila and the children played Simon Says and Mother, May I.

Mila fed them Hamburger Helper for dinner, and then they settled on the couch to read. After the children were asleep, Mila dialed Mallory's number. "So?" she asked her friend.

"I've called in every favor anyone ever owed me," Mallory replied. "You'll be in my debt until the day you die."

"I don't mind that," Mila said with a smile, "as long as you got the desired results." Mila listened while Mallory itemized the arrangements. When her friend finished she said, "You're right. I'll always be in your debt."

"I'll figure out some way for you to repay me," Mallory predicted.

They talked for a while, and when Mila turned off her cell phone, she had a satisfied smile on her face.

CHAPTER 6

On Monday morning Eugenia served Polly breakfast, then she settled comfortably in a chair by the bed and asked if they'd found Cecil Perkins. Miss Polly paused between bites of scrambled egg to shake her head. "I called Margaret yesterday, and she said she thought he might be in Mobile."

Eugenia frowned. "Why would he be there?"

Polly shrugged. "Margaret said Cecil always was fond of Mobile."

"Did she call the police or anything?"

"I think so," Polly replied. "Not that it was necessary. Half the town has called them about Cecil by now."

While Polly finished eating, Eugenia stood and straightened the room. She felt Polly's eyes on her several times and finally asked, "Have I grown another head or something?"

"What do you mean?" Polly responded.

"Well, you're staring at me like I'm from another planet!"

"I am not!" Polly objected to this accusation. "I was just . . . looking."

"Why?"

"To see if it's true that you've been gaining weight."

"Me?" Eugenia put a hand to an ample hip. "What makes you think I've gained weight?"

"Well, George Ann brought me a piece of homemade cherry pie last night, and while she was here she mentioned that she thought you had gained a few pounds. So I was trying to decide for myself, that's all."

"And what was your conclusion?" Eugenia asked in a menacing tone.

Polly knew what side her bread was buttered on and replied cautiously, "I think you look just fine."

Eugenia was not mollified. "I may have gained a pound or two over the holidays," she acknowledged. "But what business is it of George Ann's, I'd like to know? And if she wants to make it her business, why doesn't she just ask me instead of discussing it with half the town?"

Polly held up her fork in alarm. "My gracious, Eugenia. I'm hardly half the town! And if you want to find out why George Ann is making your weight her business, why don't you ask her?"

Eugenia nodded grimly. "I believe I will."

* * *

Mila woke up on Monday morning with butterflies in her stomach but tried to ignore them. She took a shower and when she returned to the bedroom, she found Lily holding Ben in the crib. The little boy was almost as big as Lily, so the sight would have been comical if it hadn't been so sad. Mila increased her resolve to protect them and solidify their relationship.

"I told Ben about Mommy being lost," Lily said, her big eyes bright with unshed tears. "But I don't think he believes me."

"Mommy?" Ben repeated and looked around the room. "Mommy!"

"He misses her," Lily explained.

Mila lifted them out of the crib one at a time, then sat beside them on the big bed. She handed Ben his favorite book and said, "I know you both miss your mother. I lost my father several years ago, and I still miss him."

"Your daddy got lost, just like our mommy?" Lily asked.

"Sort of," Mila hedged.

"Were you sad?"

"I cried until I thought I would die," Mila admitted. "But I didn't. And you won't die either, because you've got to take care of Ben."

Lily nodded. "I know."

Mila smiled and held out her hands for Ben. "Let's read this book, then we'll go eat some cereal. After that we'll have to get you dressed because we have a busy day."

Mila fed, bathed, and dressed the children, then let them watch PBS until Beau arrived to take them all to the station.

"How are they?" Beau asked her once they were on their way.

"Pretty good," she replied.

"And how are you?" he pressed.

She smiled. "I've got a plan. How I am depends on how well it works."

"Uh-oh," Beau said with dread. "Are you going to give me any details?"

"No," she replied. "If you don't know my plan, you can't be blamed if it goes wrong."

Beau shook his head. "Working with you is scary but never boring."

This time Mila laughed. "I'll take that as a compliment."

When they arrived at the station, Wilma was there with a child psychologist. "We're going to talk to the children for a little while," she told Mila. "I'll bring them back here when we're finished."

Mila nodded, then gave both children a hug before they left with the child services caseworker.

"The chief is holding a meeting in the conference room," Beau told her. "He wants us there, pronto."

She followed him to the conference room where the chief was sitting at the head of the table. Dorcas was right beside him, looking perfect as always. Mila was introduced to the liaison from the mayor's office and a representative from internal affairs. Then the chief waved impatiently toward a couple of empty seats.

"The Womack case might be bigger than we thought." He glanced at Mila, who stayed put; she could tell that he wasn't pleased to have her involved in anything big. "Our investigation of the husband, Larsen Womack, has led us to the unhappy conclusion that Theresa Womack was probably kidnapped and possibly murdered by her husband."

Beau grimaced. "Mila has a problem with any theory that casts Larsen Womack in the role of a criminal," he said, and she cringed as the chief's eyes swung toward her.

"Why?" he asked.

Before Mila could answer, Beau continued, "Because the Womacks wear special underwear."

The chief's eyes were boring holes through her, and Mila was afraid she was going to spontaneously combust. "Special underwear?"

Mila tried to ignore the chief's obvious dislike for her personally and concentrate on the matter at hand. "That is only part of why I'm convinced that the Womacks were good Mormons. I talked to their minister, and he said he believes Larsen was honest."

"Do you have any concrete evidence?"

"No."

The chief frowned. "Then sit down."

Mila remained standing and heard Beau sigh behind her.

"I'd like to speak to you for a few minutes before this meeting continues," she told the chief. "Privately."

Color suffused Chief Monahan's heavy cheeks, and she wondered if he'd heard the romance rumors. "Whatever you've got to say to me can be shared with the entire group," he growled.

She squared her shoulders, then nodded. "Very well. I plan to become a foster parent for the Womack children."

There were a few seconds of silence, then the chief burst out in a humorless laugh. "Thanks for the comic relief, Detective. Now if you'll sit down we'll get busy."

Mila held her ground. "No, really. I started the application process to be a foster parent about a year ago in Atlanta and even though I never completed it, I got far enough for emergency approval."

"Why would you apply to be a foster parent?" the chief demanded. "Do you make a habit of collecting stray children?"

She refused to let him get to her. "No, sir. I didn't have any particular children in mind at the time. I just thought it was something I might want to do."

"Then why didn't you complete the process?"

She looked him straight in the eye. "Because I got involved in a fight for my career and decided that should take priority."

The chief made a dismissive gesture with his hand. "It's very nice of you to offer, and I'm sure everyone is very impressed by your Christian charity," he said. "But it is out of the question." He turned to Beau. "Why don't you bring everyone up to speed on the case."

"Actually, it's a done deal," Mila persisted, and the chief turned hostile eyes back to her. "The state director of child services has arranged it. As of eight o'clock this morning I was approved as a foster parent in Dougherty County, pending the housing inspection, of course."

"Housing inspection!" the chief sputtered. "You think they'll approve that hotel room you're staying in?"

Mila shook her head. "No, sir. I plan to move to my great-aunt's house in Haggerty for as long as I have the children."

"I won't have it!" the chief thundered. "And if you'll stop thinking of yourself for just one minute you'll realize that you can't be a single foster parent for children who have just lost their mother and do your job here at the same time."

"I agree." She could tell by the look on his face that she'd caught him off guard. "That's why I'd like to apply for a leave of absence."

Chief Monahan's expression was now wavering between angry and incredulous. "You haven't even worked here for a full week, and you're requesting a leave of absence?"

She nodded. "Yes, sir."

"And who will do your job while you're babysitting?"

"Dorcas," Mila said without hesitation.

The chief's eyes narrowed. "You realize you're putting your career on the line."

Mila took a deep breath. "Yes."

The chief shook his head in disgust, then looked away. "It's your life. You can finish trashing it if you want to."

Mila moved to sit down, but the chief's voice stopped her. "During your 'leave of absence' you won't be assigned to the Womack case. Is that understood?"

Mila glanced at Beau. "Yes, sir."

"Then we'll dismiss you before continuing this *official* meeting."

She nodded and turned toward the door. With her hand on the doorknob, she addressed the chief. "However, as Lily's and Ben's foster parent, I expect to be informed about any and everything that might affect their health, safety, or happiness." Then she opened the door and stepped into the hallway.

Mila leaned against the wall and took several deep breaths. Once she had control of herself, she went to her office and sat down, waiting for the children to finish their meeting with the psychologist. Wilma and the children found her there thirty minutes later. Mila smiled when she saw Lily and Ben.

"Well," the caseworker said. "I guess congratulations are in order, Miss Foster Parent. Although I'll admit it was quite a surprise to find out that you had friends in such high places."

"Hey," Mila said with a smile. "It was your idea."

Wilma shook her head. "Girl, you are crazy. I'd lecture you about all the responsibility and liability and accountability that you've taken on, but something tells me you won't listen."

"I've made up my mind," Mila agreed.

"Well, I requested a home inspection so we can get the kids situated. They'll call you on your cell phone to set up the appointment."

"Thanks, Wilma. I guess I'd better tell my real estate agent to take my house off the market."

Wilma walked them to the parking lot, and after the children were strapped into the backseat of the Mustang, she spoke to Mila through the driver's window. "You call me if you need something," she told Mila. "Anything."

Mila smiled. "Thanks. In fact, I already have a favor to ask."

Wilma rolled her eyes. "Me and my big mouth."

"I need the furniture and things from the Womacks' apartment. The children's toys and clothes and beds—everything. But I'm afraid the chief will refuse the request if it comes from me."

"Because the case of their mother's disappearance hasn't been solved?" Wilma guessed.

"No, because he hates me."

Wilma considered this. "Oh, I see."

"I could buy new furniture, but the kids will be happier if I can surround them with familiar things." *Besides, using the Womacks' furniture would preserve more of my shrinking funds,* Mila added silently. Now that she had taken an unpaid leave of absence, she was going to have to be very careful with money.

Wilma frowned. "I'll ask, but don't get your hopes up."

Mila laughed. "You look like a woman used to getting her way."

Wilma's eyes narrowed. "How'd you get to know me so well in such a short period of time?"

* * *

Mila and the kids stopped by the hotel, where she packed up her belongings then checked out before heading toward Haggerty. On the way, she called Nickel and broke the bad news.

"But I had two interested buyers!" Nickel cried. "It's been a complete waste of my time."

"I will sell it eventually, and I promise to let you handle it," Mila cajoled. "But right now I need a house."

As soon as she disconnected the call with Nickel, her phone rang again. It was Beau. "You could have prepared me for that little ambush," he said.

"I wasn't sure where you stood on the issue," she replied. "And I didn't want to put you in an awkward situation."

"Oh, yeah, I was real comfortable standing there without a clue while you threw your career in the toilet."

"I'm sorry," she said honestly. "But I have to do this."

There was a brief silence, then Beau said, "There's going to be a big meeting tomorrow morning, and you should probably be there to protect your interests."

"You're not supposed to tell me anything about the case, Beau," Mila reminded him.

"Some people understand what it means to be partners," was his reply.

She cleared her throat, then asked, "What time?"

"Nine. The pharmaceutical company Larsen Womack worked for is sending a representative, and from what I understand, several people have applied to take temporary custody of the children."

Mila knew this news should fill her with relief, but it didn't. "Larsen's foster parents?"

"Yeah, I think they're trying to get discharged from their mission work early. But in the meantime, the Womacks' preacher in Virginia and even the CEO of the pharmaceutical company offered to take the kids. None of them have a better claim than you do though," Beau said as if reading her mind. "Your only real threat comes from Larsen Womack's foster brother. A guy named Quincy Barrington Drummond the Fifth."

"You're kidding."

"Nope," Beau assured her. "I can't decide what ticks me off more, the name itself or the fact that five different sets of parents saddled their own kid with it."

Mila laughed, and it helped her to relax a little. "The bishop in Roanoke said he was a beach bum."

"I don't know about that, but according to the chief, he's self-employed, unmarried, and lists his parents' home as his permanent residence."

Mila sighed. "He doesn't sound like too much of a threat."

"You can decide for yourself. He'll be at the meeting tomorrow morning. And speaking of the meeting . . ."

"What?" Mila asked.

"Don't you think it would be a good idea if I knew all the details of what happened in Atlanta before then—just in case it comes up?"

"It won't come up," she said, then turned off the phone and saw Lily watching her.

"Where are we going?" the little girl wanted to know.

Mila smiled and said, "We're going home."

CHAPTER 7

Eugenia Atkins was on her way to take Florence Higginbotham to pay her water bill when she saw Mila Edwards pull her fancy little red car to a stop in front of Cora Sue's house. She was pleased to see Mila and amazed to see the two children who emerged from the car along with Cora Sue's grandniece.

"Who's that?" Florence asked with mild curiosity.

"That's Daphne Roper's girl, Mila," Eugenia replied, hoping there wasn't a line at the waterworks so she could be done with Florence quickly and get back to Hickory Lane to check on things.

* * *

Mila extricated the children from the backseat of the Mustang and stood them on the sidewalk in front of Aunt Cora Sue's house. Ben stuck his fingers in his mouth while Lily eyed the shoe-box-shaped structure.

"This was my great-aunt's house," Mila told them. "When she died she gave it to me."

The house was a little uninviting, and Mila decided to let them play outside first in hopes that they would bond with the new location quickly. She led the way into the backyard, and while the children explored, she made phone calls, arranging to have the utilities turned back on.

As she finished, she heard a voice calling from the side of the house. "Hellooo!"

"We're in back!" Mila answered, and soon Eugenia came round the camellia bush wearing a wide-brimmed straw hat to shade her face from the sun.

"Well, who do we have here?" the older woman asked, studying the children.

"Miss Eugenia, I'd like to introduce you to Lily and Ben," Mila said, swatting at a mosquito making a feast of her left forearm. "I'm going to be their temporary foster parent."

"It's nice to meet you," Miss Eugenia said to the children, then turned back to Mila. "And what brings the three of you to Haggerty today?"

Mila waved at the house. "It looks like I'm going to live here for a couple of weeks."

Miss Eugenia clapped her hands with joy. "It was Cora Sue's dearest wish. I declare, if I'd known you were coming, I would have aired out the place. It's dusty and musty and—" Miss Eugenia looked toward old house. "Maybe worse."

Before Mila could respond, they heard another voice. "Is anybody home?"

"It's that nosy George Ann Simmons," Miss Eugenia whispered. "Coming to find out what's going on over here!"

Mila was wondering if Miss Eugenia had a higher purpose for her own visit as Miss George Ann appeared. "Good morning! I brought you one of my key lime pies!"

"Hello, Miss George Ann." Mila lifted the damp hair off her neck, silently lamenting the heat and humidity that played havoc with her attempts to be impeccable. "That was very nice of you to make us a pie," she added, taking the plate Miss George Ann extended.

"Mila and these children are going to live in Cora Sue's house," Miss Eugenia informed her old friend. "Isn't that wonderful?"

Lily overheard this remark and asked Mila, "We're going to live here?"

Mila decided to approach the subject carefully. "Would you like to?"

"I guess," Lily replied, then pointed at the huge house next door. "Why can't we live there?"

Mila laughed. "Because it's not our house."

"Whose house is it?" Lily wanted to know.

"Oh, dear me," Miss George Ann said, her voice dripping with disdain. "It belongs to an undesirable named Cleo Ledbetter." She turned to Mila. "Cleo is short for Cleopatra—heaven help us."

"Well, whatever her name is, she has a very nice house," Mila said diplomatically.

"Nice!" Miss George Ann exclaimed. "It's a disgrace. I'm sure she bribed every official in Dougherty County in order to build it on that lot."

"Cleo won the Florida state lottery last year," Miss Eugenia explained for Mila's benefit. "Ninety million dollars."

"Doesn't that beat all?" Miss George Ann demanded. "Decent people have to go through life pinching pennies, and trash like Cleo Ledbetter win ninety million dollars."

"Goodness knows you've never pinched a penny in your life," Miss Eugenia retorted. "And Cleo's not trashy."

"Her family lives in an assortment of trailers south of town," Miss George Ann fired back, her long neck stretched in an unbecoming manner. "And you know what they say. You can take the trash out of the trailer, but you'll never . . ."

"Nobody but you would say anything of the kind," Miss Eugenia interrupted.

"And the whole neighborhood looks like a junkyard," Miss George Ann continued.

"It *is* a junkyard," Miss Eugenia provided. "The Ledbetters run a used car parts business."

Miss George Ann sniffed. "And Cleo's married to a man who works for the county sewer."

"Water treatment plant," Miss Eugenia corrected.

"Whatever." Miss George Ann waved a dismissive hand.

Miss Eugenia addressed Mila. "I say you've got to respect a man who still gets up and goes to work every day after his wife wins ninety million dollars."

Miss George Ann didn't seem impressed by this. "You'll do well to stay away from Cleo Ledbetter," she told Mila. "All the sensible folks in town do," she continued with a look at Miss Eugenia, who apparently didn't fall into the sensible category.

"Well, it was nice of you to stop by and give us all this *sensible* advice, George Ann," Miss Eugenia said. "But we're kind of busy here, so why don't you go home and count your daddy's money while I show Mila around." Miss Eugenia turned her back on the other woman and walked toward the house.

"Well, I never . . ." Miss George Ann replied.

Mila wasn't sure what to do. Finally she decided to ride the fence. "Thanks for the pie."

Miss George Ann nodded stiffly, then stomped out of the backyard.

"Don't mind George Ann," Miss Eugenia said when Mila joined her by the house. "She's always crabby." Miss Eugenia opened the door, led the way inside, and looked around the dreary living room. "How soon are you planning to move in?"

"Immediately," Mila responded.

"Dear me. I'll hurry home and call the ladies in my Sunday School class and ask them to get over here and start cleaning."

Mila smiled. "Thanks, but I've hired a professional cleaning service. They should be here any minute."

Miss Eugenia raised her eyebrows. "Oh, well, that was very *sensible* of you."

Mila had to laugh. "I thought I'd let the kids play in the backyard until the cleaners get here. Then we'll go back to Albany and pack up their things."

Miss Eugenia frowned. "I guess I'll head on home. Do you remember where I live?"

Mila smiled. "Of course. Your azaleas are always spectacular."

"Come see me once you get settled in," Miss Eugenia invited. "And if you need me for anything, just holler."

* * *

The cleaning crew arrived, and Mila showed them what to do, then took the children back outside to play. Mila heard a rustling noise behind her and turned to see Earl Ledbetter Jr. decked out in full police regalia, standing behind an overgrown oleander bush. "Hey, Earl Jr.," Mila said.

The little boy approached them, a walkie-talkie clutched in his hand. "Ma'am, I warned you before about trespassing. I let you off last time, but unless you have some proof that Miss Cora Sue gave you this house, I'm afraid I'm going to have to arrest you."

Mila looked down at the Womack children. "The kids too?"

He nodded solemnly. "Afraid so."

Mila pointed at the equipment hanging from his belt. "But you only have one set of handcuffs."

This didn't faze him. "I'll have to call for backup." He depressed a button on the walkie-talkie and then explained the situation.

After a few seconds a voice replied, "Release the prisoners, Earl Jr., then come on home for lunch."

The boy looked up, an embarrassed blush creeping across his cheeks. "Looks like it's your lucky day, ma'am. I've been instructed by my superior to let you go."

Mila put her hands on her hips and faced Earl Jr. "We're going to have to come to some kind of arrangement. I'm moving into this house, and I can't have you always trying to arrest me."

Before the boy could respond, a woman wearing a neon pink wind suit and high-heeled house slippers fringed with black fur emerged from the back hedge. "Earl Jr.!" she cried. "Didn't your daddy tell you to come home for lunch?" The woman stopped short when she saw Mila. Jet-black hair, expertly styled, swung becomingly around her pretty face.

Mila extended her hand. "I'm Mila Edwards. You must be Cleo."

"I must be," Cleo agreed, blowing her bubble gum with her colorful lips. She squeezed Mila's hand briefly. "I thought Earl Jr. had made you up."

"I'm real enough," Mila told her, then introduced the Womack children. "We're going to be moving in, for a couple of weeks anyway."

"It'll be nice to have neighbors again," Cleo said, polishing the nails on her right hand against the wind suit jacket. Cleo was definitely over the top fashionwise, but somehow it seemed to work for her. "We've missed Miss Cora Sue." She put her hand on Earl Jr.'s shoulder and pointed him toward the hedges. "If my son here becomes a nuisance, just send him home."

"Is he really a policeman?" Lily asked, and Cleo laughed.

"No, he's just in a law enforcement stage. A couple of weeks ago he thought he was an alien abandoned by his mother ship on this backward planet. Before that he was a cowboy and wouldn't eat anything unless it was cooked on a campfire. As stages go, the law enforcement one isn't so bad." Cleo took a couple of steps toward the hedge, then turned. "I thought you were trying to sell this place."

"I was," Mila acknowledged.

Cleo watched her closely, obviously sensing that there was more to the story. "I considered buying it myself," she told Mila. "If I bulldozed this house I could have a decent yard, but I figured that might push the folks of Haggerty to murder me in my sleep."

Mila smiled. "Surely they wouldn't go that far."

Cleo shrugged, indicating that she wasn't at all sure. Then she motioned toward the children. "So, what's their story?"

While the kids played, Mila explained about Theresa Womack. By the time she was through, Cleo was dabbing her eyes with a Kleenex. "These poor little darlings!" she exclaimed.

"It's a sad situation," Mila agreed. "Ben asks for his mother sometimes, but he doesn't really understand. Lily grasps more, but . . ."

Cleo shook her head. "No, children can't understand forever. Which is a blessing, really. Somewhere in her little mind, she's sure she'll see her mama again, and that keeps her from grieving too much."

"That's what I think too," Mila said.

Cleo glanced back at the house. "When are you moving in?"

"Soon. And I hope it passes the child services housing inspection." Her cell phone started to ring. "Could you excuse me for a minute?" Mila asked as she checked the number of the incoming call. "This is the caseworker from child services."

"Take your time. I'll watch the kids," Cleo offered.

Mila stepped around to the side of the house and spoke briefly to Wilma. When Mila returned, Cleo asked about the inspection. "The inspection is set up for Wednesday," Mila told her.

"Before then you'll need to get some furniture," Cleo pointed out.

"I've asked permission for the furniture from their apartment to be brought here," Mila told her. "I think it will make the children feel more at home."

Cleo nodded in agreement. "I'm sure that's true. I grew up poor so I know most of the child services folks. Who's your inspector?"

"Leonard Pusser," Mila provided.

"Old Sour Pusser," Cleo said with a frown.

Mila knew the nickname couldn't be considered a positive sign. "What's wrong with Mr. Pusser?"

"He's mean and picky and—" Cleo searched for the right words. "It's very bad luck that Miss Cora Sue's house isn't in great shape."

Mila smiled. "A friend of mine works for the state director of child services in Atlanta, and she's helping me get everything arranged. So I'm not really worried about passing the inspection."

Mila's friend in high places didn't impress Cleo. "Well, you should be worried. Sour Pusser hasn't got any friends, and he doesn't do favors. He'll go straight by the book, and based on what I've seen of your great-aunt's house, you've got a snowball's chance in a fiery furnace of getting that place approved."

Mila's heart sunk. "I need to look settled and responsible by Wednesday or child services will assign the Womack children to different foster homes. I don't have time to find and rent another house." *Nor the money,* Mila added silently.

Cleo pursed her very pink lips. "There are some good things about this house."

"Like what?" Mila asked.

"You own it outright, for one thing."

Mila smiled. "I *guess* that could be considered a good thing."

"But Sour Pusser will flunk you for a loose screw. You've got to find somebody who can do a detailed safety check."

"How will I find someone on such short notice?"

A smile lighted Cleo's face. "I could ask the contractor who built my house to send some guys over. He made a fortune off of me, so I don't think he'd say no."

Mila felt gratitude welling up inside her and was afraid for a minute that she was going to cry. "I would really appreciate that."

"I'll get Earl Sr. to cut your grass tonight."

"I'd hate to trouble him. I was planning to hire a lawn service."

Cleo laughed. "For this tiny little yard? That's silly. It will only take a few more circles on the riding lawnmower."

"Well, thank you," Mila said, then asked, "and if Mr. Pusser still won't pass the house?"

Cleo frowned. "We'll cross that bridge if we get to it."

Lily ran up, dragging Ben behind her. "He needs his diaper changed."

Cleo put a finger under her nose. "In a hurry."

Mila lifted the baby and carried him into the house where the cleaning crew had just finished. She wrote them a check, then changed Ben's diaper. When she walked back outside, Cleo asked, "When will you know about getting the kids' stuff from their apartment?"

Mila shrugged. "I talked to the child services caseworker, and she said she made the request but hasn't heard back from Chief Monahan. I left him a message myself, but he hasn't returned my call." She didn't add that this was no surprise.

Cleo considered this for a few seconds, then started punching numbers on her cell phone. "I made contributions to a lot of political campaigns when I was trying to get this house built," Cleo told Mila, confirming Miss George Ann's suspicions about bribery. "I'll talk to a few members of the Albany City Council and see if we can encourage the police chief a little."

While Cleo was talking, Mila went inside to retrieve a quilt and some lunch. Mila called the children as she came out, then spread the quilt on the grass. Earl Jr. radioed his headquarters to request a fifteen-minute break, and permission was granted. Mila handed out juice boxes, then put aerosol cheese on saltine crackers. Ben fell asleep during the picnic, and Mila laid him out on the quilt while Lily and Earl Jr. went to check the front yard for hobos.

Cleo had finished her political arm-twisting so Mila left Ben under her watchful care while she followed the older children. Halfway through their inspection, a large truck with several ladders attached to the top and Wilhite's Contracting painted on the sides came to a stop at the curb.

Mr. Monroe Wilhite himself had come to do the inspection and walked with Mila through the house. When they returned to the front door, she asked, "How does it look?"

"Some of the wiring and plumbing should be replaced, but I don't think it will affect your inspection," Monroe replied. "There are some minor things like loose floorboards, exposed wires, and some old fuses that can be handled easily. The only big thing we'll need to do is get rid of that old floor furnace. That metal grate in the floor gets hot during the winter and is a safety hazard."

"If we take out the furnace what will we do for heat?"

"I recommend that you put in a heat pump."

"What will that involve?"

"We'll have to install a duct system and the unit itself. This is a small house so it's not as bad as it sounds."

"How much will it cost?"

He gave her a number.

Mila considered this. The amount required to fix the furnace would effectively empty her savings account. "Living in this house is a temporary thing," she told Monroe. "As soon as the Womack children are settled I'll move to an apartment in Albany, so I don't want to put a lot of money into the house."

"The improvements I'm talking about will make the house sell faster when you put it back on the market," he assured her. "And without them there's no way you'll pass the child services home inspection."

Finally she nodded. "Can all that be accomplished by Wednesday?"

Monroe smiled. "No way."

Mila's heart sank.

"The small stuff can be done by Wednesday. We'll cover the metal grate, and if you show the child services inspector the work order for the new heat pump, that should satisfy him. I'll have a crew over here this afternoon."

Mila felt greatly relieved. "I can't thank you enough."

Monroe smiled. "I'd do most anything for Cleo Ledbetter." With that remark he walked out to his truck. Mila stared after him, surprised by his response. Miss George Ann had given her the impression that Cleo was the local pariah. All she could figure was that Monroe really *had* made a fortune off of Cleo and that was how she had won his loyalty.

CHAPTER 8

Eugenia had seen George Ann twice during the day, once at Cora Sue Roper's old house and later at a meeting of the garden club, but on neither occasion found an opportunity to confront the woman in regard to the rumors about her weight gain. She was returning home, enjoying the sunset, when she noticed that Mark's car was in the driveway. She promptly made a turn up toward the Iversons' back door.

"Hellooo!" she called as she walked through the laundry room and into the kitchen. The family was gathered around the table, eating dinner.

"Hey, Miss Eugenia," Kate greeted. "Would you like to join us?"

"Don't mind if I do." Eugenia got a plate and the necessary utensils out of the cupboards, as familiar with Kate's kitchen as she was with her own. Once she was settled at the table, she said, "There's a new girl in town named Mila Edwards. Well, actually she used to live here as a child, but she's moving back, at least temporarily."

"I guess you've been helping her get settled," Kate said with a covert look at her husband.

"I saw that look," Eugenia scolded as she dished more Jell-O onto Emily's plate. "And I did check on her. I'm sure she'll need some help, especially since she's foster parenting two precious little children." She turned and addressed Emily and Charles. "Not any more precious and sweet than you are, though!"

"I've got a busy day planned tomorrow, but maybe I can go by and see her on Wednesday," Kate said.

"That would be nice," Eugenia replied, then turned to Mark. "Did you know that Cecil Perkins was missing?"

Mark nodded, his expression carefully neutral. "I heard that."

"Well, since you're an FBI agent, shouldn't you be looking for him?"

Mark put down his fork and raised his eyebrow. "Not unless I'm told to."

"Besides, Cecil Perkins has been found," Kate contributed.

Eugenia frowned. "How did you know? And why didn't anyone tell me?"

Kate shrugged. "Miss Eva Nell came by this afternoon collecting for the March of Dimes, and she told me."

"So, where is he?" Eugenia demanded. "Cecil, I mean."

"In jail somewhere in Florida," Kate responded.

"In jail!" Eugenia was aghast. "In Florida!"

Kate nodded. "Apparently he drove down there and found a bar, then stayed drunk for several days until they finally put him in jail. They had to wait for him to sober up so he could tell them where he lived."

"Well, I declare," Eugenia said. "When is he coming home?"

Kate stood and got the milk from the refrigerator, then refilled Emily's cup. "According to Miss Eva Nell, not anytime soon. She says Miss Margaret won't pay his bail and won't go get him."

Eugenia put her own fork down at this announcement. "You don't mean it."

"That's what she said," Kate confirmed. "But I can't really blame Miss Margaret. Living with a drunk must be pure misery."

"*You* knew Cecil has a drinking problem?" Eugenia asked in amazement. Then her eyes narrowed in Mark's direction. "Did you tell her?"

Mark held up his hands in surrender, and Kate laughed. "Mark doesn't tell me *anything,* you know that. And nobody had to tell me about Mr. Perkins. It was obvious."

Shaking her head, Eugenia stood. "Well, thanks for dinner, but I'd better head home." She took her dishes to the sink and rinsed them thoroughly, then returned to the table long enough to kiss Emily and Charles. She was headed for the back door when she paused. "Do you think I've gained weight?" she asked them.

"I wouldn't answer that under threat of death by torture," Mark replied.

Kate laughed again. "Why do you ask?"

"Because Polly told me that George Ann thinks I have," Eugenia divulged grudgingly.

Kate nodded. "She told me that too."

Eugenia's lips parted in shock for a few seconds, then she pressed them together in a grim smile. "Well, that does it. I'm going to have a talk with Miss George Ann Simmons."

* * *

It was getting dark by the time Mila and the children arrived back at the Womacks' apartment. She fed them a quick supper, then gave them baths. She was halfway through the bedtime book-reading routine when her cell phone rang. She checked the number and swallowed hard.

"This might be important," she told Lily. "Can you show Ben the pictures in his scriptures until I get back?"

Lily agreed, and Mila stepped into the bedroom before pushing the talk button. She could feel Chief Monahan's hostility through the phone lines. "A crew from the Evidence Department will pick up the children's personal effects tomorrow morning and transfer them to your home in Haggerty. Beau is on his way over with cartons you can use for packing."

Mila sighed with relief. "I appreciate that very much, but you don't have to waste manpower. I'll be glad to arrange for a moving company . . ."

The chief cut her off. "I don't want civilians pawing around in potential evidence. It's bad enough that we're disturbing that apartment at all."

Mila's gratitude evaporated. "It's important for the children to have their things, and if any of the stuff ever becomes evidence, you'll know where it is."

"Next time maybe you could use regular channels instead of going behind my back," the chief suggested, his tone barely civil.

"You ignored requests from me and Wilma Hightower. I was left with no other choice," Mila said, taking responsibility for Cleo's actions.

"This isn't Atlanta, where important friends can bail you out of trouble. Here it's following the rules and the chain of command that matter."

"I thought what matters is the Womack children," Mila responded, then hung up. She was still trembling an hour later when she tucked Lily and Ben into the crib.

Mila spent most of Monday night packing and woke up on Tuesday morning with gritty eyes and aching muscles. The confidence she'd been garnishing about her ability to parent the Womack children suffered a setback when Ben dumped his bowl of instant oatmeal all over his head during breakfast. This required an unscheduled bath and a clean outfit for the errant toddler.

As a result, Mila didn't have much time to invest in her own appearance. In her haste she put on a Fendi skirt with a Hugo Boss jacket and didn't realize it until she was already on the way to the police station. With a shrug she decided that she might not be impeccable, but at least her mixed designers matched her mixed emotions.

During the drive to Albany, Mila called Wilma Hightower and told her that the chief had agreed to let them use the Womacks' furniture.

"Glad to hear that," Wilma said. "And I heard that there's a big meeting about the case this morning."

"I'm on my way there now," Mila confirmed.

"I'll keep my fingers crossed for you," Wilma promised.

As soon as Mila ended that call, her phone rang again. "Did you steal something in Atlanta? Is that why they fired you?" Beau asked.

"Good morning to you too, Beau."

"Someday I'll catch you off guard, and you'll spill your guts."

"Dream on."

He sighed. "So, what are you going to do with the kids during the meeting?"

"I'm bringing them with me. I want the chief to have to look into their little faces when he makes decisions about their future."

"Oh, great," Beau replied. "It sounds like this meeting is going to be as much fun as the last one."

"I'm not going to antagonize the chief," she assured him. "If he'll be reasonable, everything will be fine."

"I just have one request."

"Which is?"

"Promise me you'll be on your best behavior."

"Why start now?" Mila asked.

"Have you forgotten that your competition's going to be there?"

"My competition?"

"Quincy Barrington Drummond the Fifth."

Mila glanced at the children in the backseat. "I'd never let someone named Quincy beat me at anything."

Beau laughed. "Famous last words."

* * *

When Mila and the children arrived at the Albany Police Station, she led them directly toward Beau's office. Mila glanced into the neighboring cubicle that had briefly been assigned to her; she saw that Dorcas had already put the pictures of her kids back on the desk.

Beau met her at the door to his office. He greeted Lily and Ben, then asked, "You ready to go?"

She nodded. "As ready as I'll ever be."

"This way." He inclined his head. "The chief is having a little premeeting with staff before the visitors arrive. We might as well let him see that you're here now."

"Oh, boy," Mila replied grimly.

Beau led her to the small conference room. The chief and Dorcas James were already there and looked up with a nearly identical mixture of surprise and displeasure when Mila walked in with the Womack children.

"*Miss* Edwards," the chief emphasized the lack of *detective* associated with her name. "What brings you here this morning?"

"Child services notified me that there was going to be a meeting today," she replied, which was the truth if not the whole truth. "Since I have temporary custody of the children, I'm entitled to attend."

The chief looked at Mila and Beau, but didn't contradict her. "You can stay, but the children can't. It's not appropriate." He pushed his intercom and ordered his secretary to the conference room. When she arrived he said, "Erma, take the children and entertain them for the next hour or so."

The woman looked startled for half a second, then coaxed Ben and Lily out of the room with the promise of M&Ms.

"Now sit down, both of you," the chief said to Mila and Beau with ill-concealed impatience. "We've got several items of business to go over before the others get here." Chief Monahan referred to an agenda in front of him, then turned hostile eyes to Mila. "I presume that the children are adjusting?"

Mila gave him a grim smile. "Yes, sir. Thanks for asking."

The chief was prevented from a reply when Beau had a small coughing fit. Mila pounded on his back, and when he got himself under control, she noticed that his eyes were watering. "Are you okay?" she asked him.

"No, you're killing me," he whispered under his breath.

Chief Monahan gave Beau a long look, then said, "Larsen Womack's foster brother will be at the meeting, and he's also applied for temporary custody."

"Any chance he'll get awarded?" Beau asked.

The chief shook his head. "Slim to none."

Mila didn't realize how tense she'd been until she felt her shoulders sag with relief.

"However, he could cause trouble for us," the chief continued. "Bad press, that kind of thing. So we'll do what we can to keep him happy."

Mila nodded along with everyone else. She didn't have a problem with the foster brother being happy, as long as he left the children with her.

Dorcas leaned forward and said, "I find it a little convenient that he lives in California and just happened to be attending a surfing convention in Tampa when Theresa Womack disappeared in Albany."

The chief nodded. "That is quite a coincidence."

Mila looked blankly between the two of them. "Are you saying that the foster brother is a suspect in Theresa's disappearance?"

"Not officially," the chief clarified.

Mila couldn't let it go. "Does this man have a criminal record, something to make you suspicious of him?"

"No," the chief admitted. "But we're looking at all angles."

"Good," Mila replied. "Because that one is terrible."

Beau was into another coughing fit when a knock sounded on the door. "Our guests have arrived," the chief said with a hard look at Mila. "Beau, get yourself under control and let them in."

CHAPTER 9

Mila watched as Beau ushered the new arrivals inside and introductions were made. First was Lionel DeFore from Ryathon Pharmaceuticals. He was wearing an expensive suit and a cheerful smile that seemed rather out of place to Mila, considering the circumstances. Then she turned her eyes to study Larsen Womack's foster brother, who was something of a surprise.

She had expected Quin Drummond to be younger, with shaggy hair, wearing cut-off jeans and flip-flops. But he was in his thirties and wore neatly pressed khaki pants and an oxford shirt. His brown hair was trimmed short, and the only indication that he earned his living by surfing was the peeling skin on his sunburned nose. He gave the group a collective smile as introductions were made. He looked cute and shy and harmless. Mila sighed with relief as the chief asked Beau to bring everyone up to speed on the case.

The detective moved to the front of the room. "Theresa Womack left her apartment last Tuesday morning. She told her children that she would return shortly, but she never did. On Friday a neighbor called in a complaint about noise in the apartment next door. Detective Edwards and I answered the call and found Lily, age four, and Ben, age two, alone. Pictures of Mrs. Womack have been circulated throughout the immediate vicinity and downtown Albany in general. While some people claim to have seen her, none remember if it was on one of the days in question.

"Through the subsequent investigation, we learned that Mrs. Womack and her husband, Larsen, own a home in Roanoke, Virginia. Mortgage payments are up to date thanks to automatic deductions made from the modest balance in their joint checking account, but all utilities were canceled and the house is deserted. Larsen Womack hasn't been seen since February, when he was fired by Ryathon Pharmaceuticals. Theresa and the children left Roanoke the next day and came to Albany for an undetermined reason."

Beau paused for a deep breath, then continued. "The neighbors here rarely saw Theresa and claim never to have seen the children. The owner of a local used bookstore says that Theresa Womack was a regular customer. She also claims that Theresa told her Larsen was abusive and might send someone looking for her. For this reason the store owner was reluctant to discuss Mrs. Womack, even with police officers."

Mila started to object, but Quin Drummond beat her to it. "That is ridiculous," he said, taking the words literally from her mouth. "Larsen was not abusive."

"I'm just presenting what we've gathered so far, Mr. Drummond," Beau explained. "And whether the accusation is true or not, that is what the bookstore owner said. I talked to her myself."

"There has to be some mistake," Quin Drummond insisted.

"There may be," the chief conceded diplomatically. "We're not drawing conclusions here, we're just reviewing the data." He turned to Beau. "Go on."

"We aren't sure that Theresa's presence here and her subsequent disappearance have anything to do with the events that happened in Roanoke, but we can't ignore the possibility. So Ryathon sent Mr. DeFore." Beau nodded at the man in the expensive suit. "I'll turn the floor over to you, Mr. DeFore."

Mr. DeFore smiled again. "Thank you, Detective Lambert. I've been instructed to help in any way I can. What do you need to know?"

"First tell us what Mr. Womack did for Ryathon," the chief suggested.

"Well." Mr. DeFore's frown looked as artificial as his smile. "I don't know exactly how to say this . . ."

"Just say it," Chief Monahan requested.

"Larsen Womack isn't a brilliant scientist. He's more of a plodder." Mr. DeFore glanced up to see if his audience comprehended his veiled meaning. "Which is almost as valuable to a drug company as a genius," he was quick to assure them. "Getting drugs approved is a very tedious business. It's hard to find quality scientists who are willing to do the drudge work."

"Larsen Womack is that kind of scientist?" Dorcas clarified. "Only smart enough to do the boring stuff that doesn't get any glory?"

"Exactly." Mr. DeFore seemed pleased by the woman's grasp of the situation. "Larsen was dependable and steady and the last person I would have expected to go off the deep end."

"What do you mean by that?" Mila asked.

"Larsen had always been one of the first employees to arrive every morning, but around Christmas he started arriving late."

"How late?" Mila demanded.

"Sometimes it was noon before he showed up."

That was certainly late by anyone's definition, so Mila didn't comment.

"We don't have a strict dress code at Ryathon, but we do expect our employees to be neat and clean," Mr. DeFore continued.

"And Larsen Womack wasn't complying with this?" the chief guessed.

Mr. DeFore's expression became one of distaste. "I had several complaints about his general appearance, and it was even reported that he smelled of alcohol."

"Did you personally witness any of this?" Mila asked skeptically.

"I noticed that he often came to work in wrinkled clothing and was rarely clean shaven, but I never smelled alcohol."

"He was fired for sloppy appearance and tardiness?" Mila inquired with obvious disbelief.

"Oh, no," Mr. DeFore replied. "Larsen was fired for stealing."

"No way!" Quin Drummond said at the same time Mila said, "I don't believe it." She had to smile. At last she had an ally.

Beau took up the questioning. "What is he *accused* of stealing?"

"While in the process of submitting new drugs to the FDA, Larsen had brief access to sensitive documents relating to a synthetic blood thickener that we hope to have on the market by the end of the year. You may have heard our advance advertising about the drug called Ryanex?"

No one claimed to have any knowledge of this, so Mr. DeFore continued. "It has been in the research stages for almost five years."

The chief frowned. "And why was the information Larsen Womack had access to so sensitive?"

"Because it contained enough technical data to allow someone to steal our research and market a similar product, cutting into our sales."

"So Mr. Womack was fired for stealing the research on your new synthetic drug?" Beau clarified.

"Actually, no. He was fired for stealing $88,000 from the department's submission account. We didn't discover that the express mail envelope containing all the FDA papers was missing until *after* Larsen left the building."

"Why was this information in an envelope?" Beau asked.

"Because he was supposed to submit it to the FDA, but it never arrived. Larsen Womack stole it instead."

"If Mr. Womack was a minor employee, why did he have access to company money?" Dorcas asked, and Mila had to admit it was a good question.

"There are many costs involved in getting drugs approved," Mr. DeFore explained patiently. "Sometimes additional tests are requested, new packaging, labeling, mail costs—"

Chief Monahan held up a hand. "We get the idea. So Mr. Womack could write checks on this company account to pay for expenses relating to the submission of new drugs for approval from the FDA?"

Mr. DeFore nodded.

"Eighty-eight thousand dollars is a lot of postage," Mila said.

Mr. DeFore acknowledged this with an inclination of his head. "The account was also used as a temporary holding area for other money, while waiting for a permanent transfer."

Now Mila understood. "A slush fund."

Mr. DeFore's smile faded slightly. "Yes. I guess you could call it that."

"Wherever the money came from," the chief said, "you're saying that Larsen Womack stole it."

Mr. DeFore's smile returned in full phony force. "Yes, he wrote a check for the entire balance. That's why we had to terminate his employment."

"He stole $88,000, then showed back up at Ryathon so you could fire him?" Mila asked. "Doesn't that seem a little strange to anyone besides me?"

Quin Drummond's eyes met hers across the table. They were gray, like thunderclouds. "It seems *very* strange to me," he said.

The chief ignored them both. "Strange or not, Larsen Womack came to Ryathon on February 17, at which time he was told that he was being let go?"

"Correct," Mr. DeFore said.

"Did you handle it personally?" the chief continued.

"Yes," Mr. DeFore replied.

"Did you ask him about the money?" Dorcas wanted to know.

"Of course," Mr. DeFore confirmed. "He just laughed. When it became clear that he wouldn't answer my questions, I told him I had no choice but to call the police. That's when he started knocking over tables. He even managed to set the lab on fire. By the time the police arrived and the fire was under control, we realized that Larsen was gone, along with the information for the FDA."

Beau leaned forward. "I presume the police went to his house?"

"Yes. His wife claimed to have no knowledge of the stolen money or Larsen's whereabouts. She was understandably upset when she learned what had happened."

"I'm sure," Mila muttered.

Mr. DeFore sat down, and Beau reclaimed the floor. "The Roanoke police determined that when Larsen Womack left Ryathon the day of the fire, he took the envelope containing the sensitive information with him. When Theresa disappeared, they concluded that she had joined him in hiding."

"But we know that wasn't true," Mila pointed out.

"Correct," Beau agreed. "But we believe that before they went their separate ways, Larsen gave the missing envelope to his wife."

"Then what?" Mila asked.

"Larsen may have told his wife to hide here until the police in Roanoke quit searching for him. We don't know why he chose Albany, but her lease on the apartment was signed on February 20, so we know she didn't stop anywhere else first," Beau explained. "We found a postcard in the apartment postmarked in London, so we assume that Larsen left the country for a time. Or, if Larsen Womack *was* an abusive father, Theresa may have taken the opportunity presented by his legal problems to run. In which case Larsen may not have known where she was until recently."

Chief Monahan cleared his throat. "Whether he knew where she was all along or just located her, we believe that he sent the postcard and arranged for her to bring him the envelope on Tuesday of last week."

Beau addressed his next remarks directly to Quin Drummond. "Theresa's daughter, Lily, claims her mother was wearing a Sunday dress and tennis shoes. The comfortable shoes indicate that she was planning to walk a significant distance from the apartment. And what would you wear if you were going to see your husband for the first time in several weeks? How about a nice Sunday dress?"

Mila wished she had thought to ask Lily about Theresa's apparel. Then she realized that Beau must have been the one who did and glared at him, but he wouldn't meet her eyes.

"The fact that Theresa set the meeting up *away* from the apartment and their children leads us to believe that she didn't completely trust him," Beau said, "which supports the abuse theory."

The chief nodded. "That makes sense."

"That's crazy," Quin disagreed. "Larsen didn't even spank his children. I'll never believe he was abusive."

"Another possibility is that they met away from the apartment to protect the children in case Larsen was being followed," Beau proposed.

"By who?" Mila demanded. "The Roanoke police?"

"When you make deals with criminals, things can turn ugly," Beau pointed out. "If Larsen was going to sell the information, he might have taken this precaution to protect his family from the prospective buyers."

Mila preferred this theory to the abusive father scenario but still couldn't picture Larsen Womack in the role of a thief.

"Larsen was not a criminal," Quin insisted. "There's got to be another explanation."

"When was the last time you saw your former foster brother?" the chief asked, his voice surprisingly gentle.

"I haven't seen Larsen in a while, but I spoke to him regularly on the phone," Quin said. "And even if Larsen did completely lose his mind, Theresa wouldn't have stayed around and let him hurt the children. And she wouldn't have agreed to live a life of crime, surviving on stolen money and hiding from the police either."

Chief Monahan gave Beau a quick look, then said, "A lot of otherwise intelligent women stay in abusive situations, hoping that their spouse will change. But in either case, we have reason to believe that Larsen was not planning to reunite with his family after he got the envelope from Theresa."

"Why wouldn't he?" Mila asked with a frown.

"Because he was having an affair with a coworker," Beau said.

Quin Drummond laughed out loud. "Larsen was so shy it took him almost a year to get up the courage to ask Theresa out on a date. There's no way he had a girlfriend on the side."

Mila nodded in agreement. "I talked to the Womacks' bishop in Roanoke. He said Larsen Womack had a current temple recommend." She turned to Chief Monahan. "That means that Larsen Womack had a recent interview with his bishop and would have had to answer questions about his personal life." Explaining temple worthiness was almost as difficult as explaining the significance of garments, and finally she floundered into silence.

"Are you saying that Mormons don't lie?" the chief asked menacingly.

Mila was taken aback. "Of course not. Mormons are human just like everyone else. But lying in a temple interview would be a serious thing."

Chief Monahan gave Mila a satisfied look. "So is adultery, even to Baptists."

There was a brief silence, then Beau said, "This *other* woman may have encouraged Larsen to steal the money and the information on the new drug. The postcard from London suggests that they may have intended to live out of the country once they retrieved the information and sold it."

Dorcas asked Mr. DeFore, "Do you have a name for the woman Larsen Womack was allegedly involved with?"

The Ryathon executive shook his head. "No."

"But she was an employee?"

Mr. DeFore blushed. "According to rumor, yes."

"Somebody at Ryathon knows who she is," the chief said to Dorcas. "Make some calls and once you have a name, check her out through Roanoke PD."

Dorcas nodded as she made notes in her daily planner.

Quin leaned forward. "I don't buy any of this, but if Theresa had the envelope and she met Larsen with it last Tuesday, why didn't she come back to the apartment and her kids?"

"Maybe Larsen couldn't risk her telling anyone about him, so he killed her," the chief suggested.

Quin shook his head. "That is *beyond* ridiculous."

"He would have to be a monster to kill his own wife and leave his children unattended and defenseless," Mila added.

"Maybe Larsen's girlfriend handled the envelope exchange," Beau suggested in an obvious attempt to help Mila's cause. "She might have killed Theresa so she could have Larsen without strings attached."

This theory was only marginally better than Larsen murdering his own wife, so Mila couldn't generate any enthusiasm.

"Or, if Larsen Womack was planning to sell the information to a third party, they would have a significant monetary interest in that envelope," Beau proposed. "They might have killed Larsen and Theresa to get it."

"Any evidence of the new product on the market?" the chief asked Mr. DeFore.

"None that I'm aware of," the man from Ryathon Pharmaceuticals replied matter-of-factly. "But it would take several weeks to produce the drug, even with our research. Not to mention the time it would take to go through the FDA approval process."

"We don't even know for sure that Theresa and Larsen are dead," Mila pointed out.

"And until we have a body we can't eliminate the possibility that Theresa ran off with her husband or just ran off period, abandoning her children in the process," Beau said.

Mila resisted the urge to rub her temple where a headache was forming. "What if Larsen was set up?"

"Framed you mean?" Dorcas asked, and Mila thought she saw sympathy in the other woman's eyes. That just made her head hurt worse.

Mila licked her lips before proceeding. "Maybe he ran away from Ryathon to keep from getting arrested for something he didn't do. He told Theresa to take the kids and hide in a separate location for their safety. He might have figured out a way to use the envelope to prove his innocence and contacted Theresa. She met him last Tuesday, but somebody was watching and either killed or kidnapped them both."

Quin looked pleased for the first time since the meeting began. "I prefer that theory."

Chief Monahan shook his head. "Well, I don't. It's just useless speculation," he pronounced as if his theories were built on firm and overwhelming evidence. "Until you can show me something concrete to change my mind, I'm going with the Roanoke Police Department's position that Larsen Womack is a fugitive from justice and our best suspect." He turned to Dorcas. "Is there any chance that we can interest the FBI in the case?"

"I'll call the resident agent here in Albany and see what I can do," Dorcas offered.

Mila felt drained, like she had a few years ago after a long bout with the flu. "So where does the investigation go from here?"

"Not your concern, Miss Edwards," the chief replied with obvious satisfaction.

There was a knock on the door, then a woman pushed it open without waiting for an invitation. She waved to Dorcas, who hurried into the hallway. Everyone waited quietly during the short discussion. When Dorcas returned she looked pale, and the chief asked what the interruption was all about.

"I'm afraid I have what may be bad news," she said slowly.

"Just what we need," Beau grumbled.

"The guys from evidence who are packing up the things from the Womacks' apartment for transfer to Detective Edwards's house in Haggerty found signs of a search."

The chief frowned. "Of course they did. Our guys searched the place meticulously last Friday."

Dorcas shook her head. "No, sir. They found evidence of another search, one that took place after fingerprint filament was used."

There was an ominous silence, then Beau said, "Sounds like maybe Theresa didn't turn over the envelope after all."

* * *

While the others discussed this new development, Mila mentally reviewed the contents of her Prada handbag and regretfully determined that she didn't have any headache medication. Resisting again the urge to rub her temple, she tried to concentrate on the conversation around her.

Quin Drummond was posing a question. "If she didn't give the envelope to Larsen or whoever she met, where is it?"

Mila smiled. If her head weren't hurting so badly, that would have been exactly what she asked.

"Maybe it was still in the apartment on Friday, and our guys missed it." Beau didn't look happy as he suggested this.

"I hope it was, so whoever was still looking found it," Quin said, and dread started forming in Mila's stomach. "Otherwise they might search again."

Dorcas frowned. "There's no way to know for sure. Until that envelope is located, the Womack children might be in danger."

The chief considered this for a few seconds. "In a way, that might be an advantage. If we know what Larsen or whoever wants, and where they'll look to get it, we can be prepared."

Mila's gaze locked on Chief Monahan. "You can't use the children like bait!"

"Of course I'm not going to use the children as bait," the chief snapped. "I'm just saying that until an arrest is made, we'll have to be particularly vigilant."

Mila was not convinced. "If I find out that you are using the children to *attract* a criminal, I'll stop you—even if I have to go to the press."

Chief Monahan's eyes narrow ominously. "If you do, not only will you be fired, but I'll make sure you never see those kids again."

"Okay everyone!" Beau broke in. "We won't advertise the children's location or try to attract the criminals in any way. But if whoever it is doesn't have what they want, chances are they'll try to search the Womacks' things again or possibly even talk to Lily. Since the things from the apartment and the Womack children will all be at your house in Haggerty, that gives you a lot of responsibility," he told Mila.

Quin addressed the chief. "I have a possible solution. If you'll let me take the children back to California with me, they would be far away from this situation."

"I'll have to fight you on that one," the chief said without the hostility that had been evident when he spoke to Mila. "You can't guarantee their safety, even in California. And until my case is solved, I can't let evidence and potential witnesses leave my jurisdiction. Child services has already appointed Detective Edwards as their temporary foster parent, which means that the Albany Police Department will be providing twenty-four-hour protection."

Mila almost laughed out loud. The chief elevated her quickly back to the rank of detective when it suited his purposes.

Quin said, "I won't fight you on the custody issue or insist on taking the children to California. But I would like to help protect the children until things are settled." His expression was still benign, but his tone was firm. "And if I have reason to believe that the children aren't safe, *I'll* go to the press, and I don't think you'd be able to prevent me from seeing them again."

The chief didn't look happy, but he nodded.

Then Quin turned to Mila. "I have a pop-up camper. Would you mind if I set up camp in your backyard for a while?"

Mila opened her mouth to object, but before she could speak, Chief Monahan said, "That's perfect! You and Detective Edwards can work out the details after our meeting."

"And while I'm sure that Detective Edwards is very capable, I think we need a better plan to protect the children," Quin said.

Chief Monahan looked irritated, but gave him a conciliatory smile. "I'll arrange for cooperation from the Haggerty Police Department, and you'll be in the backyard. I think the children will be perfectly safe. Now, let's end this meeting and get back to work."

Mr. DeFore smiled at the assembly. "Ryathon is very anxious to retrieve the stolen information," he reminded them. "I've been authorized to make a sizable contribution of funds to make that happen quickly. All we ask in return is that the envelope be given to us as soon as it is found."

Even Chief Monahan looked displeased by this remark. "Are you offering us a reward to get us to do our job?"

"Of course not!" Mr. DeFore backpedaled smoothly. "We just want to help with the costs of the investigation."

"The city of Albany pays for police investigations," the chief responded coldly, and Mila was glad to have the pharmaceutical company on the chief's bad list. "Beau, you call Winston Jones in Haggerty. And Dorcas, you'll contact the FBI."

"Yes, sir!" they chorused.

"Then this meeting is adjourned until further developments."

Mila left the conference room quickly and found Quin Drummond waiting for her in the hallway. "I need directions to your house," he explained.

"Of course," she said and pulled a blank piece of paper from her purse and started to write.

When she handed him the list of directions he said, "I'm anxious to see the children." He looked around, and she knew he wanted her to arrange a quick meeting at the police station.

Instead she gave him a cool, professional smile. "You'll be seeing a lot of them during the next few days if you have your camper in my backyard. We'll meet you in Haggerty."

He paused for a second, then nodded in acceptance and walked toward the front of the building. Mila followed him as far as the lobby and watched through the smoked glass as he got into what looked like a candy-apple-red 1967 Mustang with a pop-up camper attached.

She watched in stunned silence as he pulled away from the curb and headed toward Haggerty. The only thing cooler than a new Mustang was an old one.

"Detective Edwards?" the receptionist pulled Mila out of her daze.

"Yes?"

"I've called Erma and asked her to take the Womack children to Detective Lambert's office."

Mila nodded. "Thank you." She turned and walked through the door to the Investigative Division, still in shock. The phone on Beau's desk was ringing, and she answered it automatically. "Edwards."

"May I speak to Uncle Beau, please?" a high-pitched female voice said tentatively.

"Uncle Beau?" Mila repeated. "You mean Detective Lambert?"

"Yes."

Mila looked around. "I'm sorry, but he's busy. Can I take a message?"

"I just wanted to remind him about our date tonight."

Mila got a sick feeling in the pit of her stomach. "Your date?"

There was a giggle. "Tell him he'd better not be late." Then the call was disconnected.

Mila was still holding the receiver when Beau walked in. "What's the matter?" he asked. "You're as pale as a ghost."

Mila hung up his phone. "That was your date for tonight," she forced herself to say. "Making sure that you weren't late."

His face turned red. "Oh."

"Why does she call you Uncle Beau, and why does she sound like she's a minor?" Mila demanded.

He frowned, then closed the door. "Because I am her uncle, and she is a minor."

Mila was completely confused. "Then why are you *dating* her?"

Beau laughed. "I'm actually babysitting her while my sister goes to night school, but if the guys got wind of that they'd rag me, so I just say it's a date."

Mila stared at him in astonishment. "So all these dates you couldn't be late for were really babysitting appointments?"

He put a finger to his lips. "Shhh! Sometimes I go on real dates!" he said, defending his masculine charm. "But other times I babysit."

She shook her head. "Why didn't you just tell me the truth?"

"I would have," he replied. "Eventually."

Before she could respond, the door flew open and Lily rushed in, followed closely by Ben and a harried-looking Erma. "Mila?" Lily said, pulling on her arm. "Are you sick?"

Mila forced herself to smile as she lifted Ben into her arms. "No, I'm fine," she assured the little girl. "Say good-bye to Miss Erma and Beau."

"Good-bye," Lily spoke for both children.

"Thanks," Mila told the secretary. "We'll talk more later," she promised Beau over her shoulder, then led Lily out into the hall.

CHAPTER 10

During the drive to Haggerty, Mila called the moving and storage company in Atlanta and confirmed that her clothes would be delivered that day. She was getting desperate for more wardrobe options. As she turned onto Hickory Lane, she saw Quin Drummond's classic Mustang parked in front of her great-aunt Cora Sue's house. She pulled in behind him and unloaded the children.

Lily and Ben were thrilled to see Quin, and Mila fought back a bit of jealousy. They gave him a tour of the backyard and rode with him while he pulled his camper into place. Then they watched as he set up his temporary home.

Mila watched too, surreptitiously from the kitchen window, until a rental truck containing three police officers and the Womacks' furniture arrived. Quin offered to entertain the kids while she supervised the unloading process. Mila accepted gratefully, then went into the house, where she had to make hasty decisions about room arrangements. Throughout this process the doorbell rang, as the ladies of Haggerty did their Christian duty by welcoming Mila with casseroles. She tried to act properly appreciative and stacked them in the refrigerator.

Once the evidence guys left, she went out to check on the kids. Both were asleep in the camper, so she went back inside and spent the next few hours arranging Theresa Womack's things in Aunt Cora Sue's little house. She called the moving company again, and they assured her that their truck had left Atlanta early that morning and would deliver her belongings before sunset.

When the kids woke up from their naps, they came to find Mila, and she was disproportionately glad to see them. While Lily was telling her every detail of the pop-up camper's interior, Beau Lambert walked in. He greeted the children, then let them take him on a tour of the house.

"Interesting," he said when he returned to the living room, where Mila was putting books on the shelf. "It's got that unimposing, just-above-a-cardboard-box-under-the-interstate feeling."

"Thanks," she said. "That's what I was going for."

He laughed briefly, then his expression became more serious. "You've got your revolver, don't you?"

Mila glanced at her purse on the top of the bookshelf. "Yes, why do you ask?"

"I wasn't sure just how far you or the chief was taking this leave of absence stuff, and I think you should be armed."

"Do you really think someone will search through this stuff again?"

Beau shrugged. "Never hurts to be prepared. Where's surfer boy?"

"He's set up his little portable house out back," Mila responded absently. "If the chief would consider *all* reasonable possibilities, we could solve this case much more quickly. He's so stubborn and afraid that I might actually be right about something."

"You're being too hard on him," Beau chided. "He has let you take this pretend leave of absence and didn't block your attempt to become a temporary foster parent."

Mila bristled. "He couldn't have stopped me."

Beau raised his eyebrows. "You're not the only one with powerful friends, Mila. The chief has to take every aspect of the case into consideration, and I think he's given you some leeway."

"So you believe that a normal, religious man like Larsen Womack went as crazy as the chief claims?"

"What I think is that you are too emotionally involved in this case," he said, and she looked away. "Is that what happened in Atlanta? You got involved with a suspect or something?"

"Of course not," Mila said irritably, but his guess hit a little too close to home. "And quit trying to change the subject. We've got to figure out how to prove Larsen Womack's innocence to the chief."

He studied her for a few seconds, then said, "As far as Mr. Womack and his innocence is concerned, in my experience, where there's smoke—there's fire."

Mila sighed. "I don't know why I expect anyone to believe that Larsen Womack did not kill his wife," she said wearily. "But I'll admit that I'm a little nervous. What if someone does try to search the house or harm the kids? What if I can't protect them?"

"You'll be fine. You've got me for support whenever you need it and the beach bum guarding your back. And here's the second line of defense right now." Beau pointed to a Haggerty police car as it pulled to a stop at the curb.

A large man with a deep tan and receding hairline, wearing a khaki uniform climbed out from the driver's seat and walked up to the porch. Beau introduced him as Haggerty police chief Winston Jones.

Mila extended her hand. "It's nice to meet you."

"Likewise." Winston Jones cleared his throat. "I'll have a patrol car drive by every hour during the day and more often during the night."

Mila smiled at him. "Thanks."

"I have a limited staff," Chief Jones warned her. "But I'll do what I can."

"I appreciate that very much."

"Well, now that I've put you in such good hands, I guess I'll head back to Albany," Beau said. "I've got big plans for tonight."

Mila gave him a bland look. "I'll just bet you do."

Beau waved and hurried down the sidewalk toward the unmarked car. As he drove away, Mila saw Miss Eugenia walking up the sidewalk.

"Well, I'm glad to see that our local law enforcement is giving you a nice welcome, Mila," the old woman said, her eyes narrowing. "I'm surprised, but glad."

Chief Jones smiled. "You know me, always friendly."

Miss Eugenia frowned. "I can't say that I know that at all." She turned to Mila. "So are you moved in?"

Mila nodded. "Pretty much."

"Well, don't worry about dinner," Miss Eugenia said. "I'm bringing a chicken casserole."

"Oh, you don't have to do that. People have been bringing in food all afternoon."

"None of it will be as good as my chicken casserole," Miss Eugenia assured her, then she glanced at the house. "Heard that Monroe Wilhite was fixing the place up for your inspection. Mind if I look around?"

"Help yourself." Mila waved toward the door.

Once Miss Eugenia was inside, Winston whispered, "Bringing in food is Haggerty's way of politely sticking their nose in your business."

Mila nodded. "I spent enough time here as a child to understand how it is."

"You spent time here as a kid?" Winston seemed shocked by this revelation. "I can't believe I'd be able to forget someone who looks like you." His regret over this comment was immediate and obvious as he blushed to the roots of his receding hairline.

Mila carefully controlled a smile. "Thank you for the compliment. I'm Daphne Roper's daughter, Miss Cora Sue's grandniece."

Winston frowned. "It seems like I do remember Daphne having a little girl. I guess somewhere along the way you grew up."

"It happens to the best of us."

Winston laughed, then called to Miss Eugenia. "If you've snooped around enough, I'll drop you off at home on my way back to the station."

The elderly lady stepped out onto the porch. "I'm perfectly capable of getting home by myself."

"But there's no point in that since I'm here." Winston took Miss Eugenia by the elbow and led her down the steps.

"I'll be back in a little while with your dinner," she called to Mila.

After all the company left, Lily helped Mila organize the videos while Ben played with his Legos. Finally, just as Mila had given up all hope, the truck with her clothes and her bed arrived, and she was afraid she would cry with joy. The driver apologized profusely, claiming that he had been lost for the last several hours.

"Took a wrong turn and didn't realize it until I was miles out of the way," he told her as he stacked boxes on his dolly.

She forgot her irritation in her excitement to have her clothes back. She had him bring the boxes into Cora Sue's old room and stack them neatly in a corner. Once her bed was set up, she gave the driver a modest tip and closed the door behind him with a relieved sigh. The first box contained her summer suits. She picked up one of her favorites and was pressing it fondly against her cheek when Quin Drummond spoke from the doorway.

"Lily let me in," he said. "I hope you don't mind."

She put the suit back into the box and tried to hide her embarrassment. "Of course not. You're welcome here anytime."

"Thanks."

She opened two more large boxes; one contained shoes, and the other, her casual clothes.

"Is that more of Larsen and Theresa's stuff?" Quin asked.

She shook her head. "No, this is mine. It was delivered from Atlanta just a few minutes ago."

"Oh, well I guess you'll feel more comfortable here with your knickknacks around."

She laughed. "I don't have any knickknacks. Well, not a lot of them. I've always rented furnished apartments, so the only piece of furniture I actually own is my bed. These boxes contain my *clothes.*" She couldn't keep the reverence from her voice as she said the word.

"Wow," Quin stepped in and examined the boxes. "You have a lot of clothes."

"It's a weakness, I'll admit it," she said sheepishly.

"There's nothing wrong with looking nice." His eyes flickered over her face and hair. Then they heard a knock on the front door.

"Hello!" Miss Eugenia called as she let herself in. "Anybody hungry?"

Mila and Quin walked into the kitchen where Miss Eugenia was unloading a box of food. She had not only chicken casserole, but also a green salad, cornbread, and an apple cake for dessert. Mila introduced Quin, and Miss Eugenia promptly invited him to dinner. He looked to Mila for permission, and she nodded.

"Goodness knows Miss Eugenia has brought enough to feed an army."

The children were called in and washed up, then they settled at the table. After the blessing, Miss Eugenia bustled around the kitchen, filling glasses, wiping counters, and rinsing dishes. Mila fed Ben, while Quin encouraged Lily to eat. He finally resulted to bribery, but both children ate a hearty meal.

"You two make a good team," Miss Eugenia observed as she cleared the children's dishes away.

Mila wasn't sure how to respond, and Quin looked equally at a loss for words. So she just smiled at him. "Since Lily and Ben ate well, I think we should reward them with a video."

"Can I pick?" Lily asked, already running to the little cupboard.

Mila agreed conditionally. "Yes, but choose something Ben likes."

Once the children were settled in front of the television, Mila fixed a plate of salad. She noticed that Quin had helped himself to healthy portions of everything, but there was still a lot of food left over. "Won't you eat with us too?" she invited Miss Eugenia, who was just finishing a sinkful of dishes.

The older woman smiled. "Oh, well I might have just a bite." She dried her hands, then pointed at Mila's plate. "You don't like chicken casserole?"

Mila shook her head. "I'm sure it's delicious, but I'm watching my weight."

"Humph," Miss Eugenia said scornfully. "You don't have any weight to watch. You're as skinny as a rail."

"Not naturally, though," Mila explained. "I have to work at it."

Quin refrained from comment, but Mila saw him smiling as he took a big bite of cornbread.

Miss Eugenia waved her fork around the kitchen. "You've got it looking pretty good in here."

"Thanks," Mila replied.

"And you won't have to worry about cooking meals for a while. The ladies of Haggerty will see to that."

"We've already got enough food to last for weeks," Mila acknowledged.

"And that's mostly from the Methodists. Once the Baptists find out that you've moved in, they'll be knocking down your door, with Cornelia Blackwood, the new preacher's wife, leading the way." Miss Eugenia leaned forward and whispered, "Watch out for Cornelia. She bursts into spontaneous prayer without warning. So if she grabs your hand, bow your head."

"I'll remember that."

"And she's a hugger," Miss Eugenia continued.

"A hugger?" Mila repeated.

"She read a book about hugging improving your health or something equally ridiculous. So she hugs—a lot."

Mila smiled. "When Mrs. Blackwood visits I'll be prepared to pray and be hugged."

Miss Eugenia squinted, her attention focused on the living room. "What is that cross-stitch on the wall?" she asked.

Mila glanced over her shoulder at the Families Are Forever cross-stitch. "My mother made it. It's kind of a Church slogan."

Miss Eugenia paled. "Did you join the Mormon Church?"

"I've been a member of the Mormon Church all my life," Mila replied. "My father was a member, and my mother joined shortly after they married."

Miss Eugenia put a hand to her chest. "Cora Sue never breathed a word."

"Mother didn't want anyone to know," Mila explained. "I guess she wanted to spare Aunt Cora Sue's feelings."

"Daphne is a Mormon?" Miss Eugenia clarified doubtfully.

"Sort of," Mila replied. "She did get baptized, but after she remarried she sent me this box full of what she termed 'your church stuff.' She said that Terry went to the Church of Christ, and she planned to attend there with him." Mila turned away from the cross-stitch and poked at her salad. "Apparently her feelings for the gospel were like her feelings for my father—temporary."

"Well, I declare," Miss Eugenia said, and Mila couldn't tell if it was their membership in the Church or her mother's defection that warranted the exclamation.

"Quin's a member of the Mormon Church too," Mila told her, hoping to deflect some of Miss Eugenia's attention from herself.

"You don't mean it."

Quin smiled. "It's true."

"Mormons are not so different from members of other Christian religions," Mila told their stunned guest. "We believe in the Savior and the Bible and a lot of the same things Protestants believe."

Miss Eugenia nodded finally. "I know that. My neighbors Mark and Kate Iverson are members of the Mormon Church, so I've learned quite a bit about your religion over the past few years. And there's another young couple in town who are Mormons, but he's in the state senate, and they live in Atlanta while congress is in session."

Mila was surprised by this information. She didn't remember ever hearing of members of the Church in Haggerty.

"It's a funny thing," Miss Eugenia picked up her train of thought. "When I was girl, it was just Baptists and Methodists around here. You'd meet an occasional Presbyterian or Episcopalian, but I never even saw a Catholic until after I was married. But now we've got our own Mormons and Catholics right here in Haggerty."

"Times change," Mila acknowledged. "And it's a credit to the town that people of different religions can get along well together."

Miss Eugenia nodded. "That's the truth. There are some fine folks in this town. In fact, Cornelia is planning an interdenominational Faith Fair for the end of the month," she mused. "Kate said she'd attend the first meeting tomorrow afternoon as the Mormon representative. Maybe you'd like to come too?"

Mila was so thankful to have a good excuse. "I'm sure it will be very nice, but I can't leave the children."

"I'm warning you that Cornelia Blackwood is serious about this Faith Fair, and if you don't come to her, she'll come to you."

"A pushy type?" Mila guessed.

"That's putting it mildly. Since I'm a Methodist she doesn't affect me as much as the Baptists, but she's really causing a stir in town."

"What does she do?" Quin asked.

"It's not just one big thing—it's a whole series of little things. She's young and sees us as a lot of old folks who need to change their ways."

Mila nodded in comprehension. "And the town doesn't appreciate that."

"For instance, she's worried that people don't go to church enough, so she's having this fair, complete with T-shirts and visors. She even tried to do bumper stickers, but we convinced her that would be tacky and a waste of money."

"Getting people to go to church more often is a good thing," Quin defended the preacher's wife.

"Oh, yes. No one disagrees with her purpose—it's her methods that get her in trouble. If someone chooses not to be a part of her Faith Fair, it looks like they don't believe in going to church."

Mila smiled. "Maybe if you let me borrow your Faith Fair T-shirt it might impress Mr. Pusser from child services."

Miss Eugenia raised an eyebrow. "Even if I had my T-shirt, it wouldn't do you any good. It would swallow you whole."

There was a knock on the door, and Mila went to answer it. Cleo Ledbetter was standing on the porch with Earl Jr. by her side. "We're eating dinner," Mila told them as she opened the door. "Would you like some?"

"We've already eaten," Cleo returned. "Earl Jr., you sit there by the kids." Cleo walked on into the kitchen. "Hey, Miss Eugenia," she greeted the older woman. "And who have we here?" she asked, giving Quin a speculative glance.

"Quin Drummond," he introduced himself and held out a hand.

Cleo accepted his hand and held it longer than necessary. "And what brings you to our little neighborhood, Quin?"

"He's Lily and Ben's . . . uncle," Mila explained. "He's staying in my backyard for a few days to visit."

Cleo walked over and peeked out the kitchen window. "Well, you'd better move that thing before Sour Pusser gets here in the morning. He's not crazy about homes on wheels."

"I'll move it before the inspection," Quin promised.

Cleo took the seat beside him. "Well, Quin Drummond, you are about as cute as can be. Are you married?"

"Cleo!" Mila and Miss Eugenia said simultaneously.

"What?" the other woman asked. "I'm just checking him out for Mila here."

Mila felt a blush surge across her cheeks, and Quin smiled.

"No, I'm not married."

"Any prospects?"

"No. Most girls lose interest when they find out what I do for a living."

"Which is?" Cleo probed.

"I surf."

Cleo furrowed her delicate little eyebrows. "On the Internet?"

"In the ocean," Quin clarified.

"Is that a bona fide profession?" Miss Eugenia wanted to know.

He shrugged. "I guess anything a person does to support himself could be considered a profession."

Miss Eugenia didn't seem to have an argument for this, so she said, "Well, I'll be."

"Did you need something, Cleo, or are you and Earl Jr. just visiting?" Mila asked.

"Visiting mostly," Cleo replied. "Earl Sr. is watching a baseball game, and I thought you might be nervous the night before your big inspection, so I brought some cards. A few good games of gin rummy will take your mind off Old Sour Pusser."

"Why don't we play bridge instead?" Miss Eugenia suggested. "It's a much more intelligent game."

"I don't know how to play either one," Mila confessed. "My father didn't allow face cards in our house."

Cleo and Miss Eugenia looked down at the deck with uniform sorrow. "Why?" Miss Eugenia asked.

"It's a religious thing."

"Mormons don't believe in face cards?" Miss Eugenia was appalled. "Kate and Mark never breathed a word!"

"It's not a commandment," Mila explained. "It's kind of like caffeinated drinks—something that's left to the individual conscience."

"Every time I think I know all the Mormon rules I find another one," Miss Eugenia grumbled, and they all laughed.

Then Mila felt Lily tugging at her sleeve. "You can borrow these if you want."

Mila looked down at the Little Mermaid cards clutched in Lily's small hand. "Thank you, Lily," she said, then she turned to her companions. "Go fish, anyone?"

"I'll deal," Miss Eugenia said, taking the cards from Mila. "And don't you dare mention this to anyone. If my bridge club members find out I've been playing a baby game with cartoon cards, I'll be a laughing stock."

Miss Eugenia insisted that they keep score. While they played, she asked Mila if there had been any progress in finding Theresa Womack.

"No," Mila was sorry to report.

"Got any King Tritans?" Miss Eugenia asked Quin, and he shook his head.

"Go fish."

"I've had some experience with the FBI," Miss Eugenia told them as she added the card she had drawn to her hand. "Mark Iverson, my Mormon neighbor, is an agent. Maybe if you tell me the details I can be of some help."

"And I've got plenty of experience with crime!" Cleo said with a cheerful smile. "Maybe I can help too."

Mila didn't actually believe either one of them could help solve the mystery of Theresa's disappearance, but she gave them the details that were a matter of public record. When she finished, Miss Eugenia was frowning. "So, the two of you are completely certain that Larsen Womack was not a criminal?"

"Completely," Mila and Quin confirmed in unison.

"Then if the chief isn't looking for another suspect, I guess you'll have to do it yourselves."

"If it all started in Virginia, the only sensible thing to do is to go there," Cleo contributed. "You got any Flotsam and Jetsams?" she directed toward Mila.

"No," Mila replied.

"If you were in Roanoke, you could interview neighbors and coworkers yourselves instead of having to take other people's word for what they said," Cleo pointed out.

"Going to Virginia is an idea," Mila admitted. "But I can't leave the kids."

"I'll take care of the kids," Miss Eugenia offered.

"I'll help," Cleo added.

"And the chief would be furious if he found out I was conducting a separate investigation," Mila murmured.

Miss Eugenia waved her cards. "You don't care about that."

Mila smiled. "That's almost true."

"But it might be dangerous to show up in Roanoke asking questions about Larsen and Theresa," Quin said. "After all, they are both *missing*."

"Then you can go with her for protection," Miss Eugenia suggested.

Mila was embarrassed. "Oh, I couldn't ask Quin to do that."

"Actually I think it's a good idea," he said thoughtfully. "We could fly up and back the same day and no one would even realize we were gone."

"I'll think about it," was all Mila would agree to.

After Miss Eugenia and the Ledbetters left, Mila and the kids walked Quin out to his camper. He offered to give Mila a tour, and since she couldn't decline without being rude, she accepted. The camper was small, but every inch of space had been put to good use, providing him with all the modern conveniences.

"You have everything," she remarked as her eyes scanned across the microwave, electric can opener, and dishwasher.

"Where do you sleep, Uncle Quin?" Lily wanted to know.

He pointed to the sitting area at the front of the camper. "The couches combine into a queen-size bed. Supposedly the kitchen table can be turned over and made into another bed, although I've never tried that."

"Can we stay out here with Uncle Quin?" Lily asked. "And sleep on his table bed?"

"Not tonight," Mila said firmly. "Maybe another time."

Lily frowned, but didn't complain. "Can we watch his teeny-tiny television for a few minutes?" She pointed toward the compact entertainment system embedded in one wall.

"You might need a magnifying glass." Mila took a step forward and examined the six-inch screen.

Quin walked over and turned on the television, then popped in a Disney video. "Kids have good eyes. They'll be fine."

Lily and Ben sat down and offered to make room for Mila, but sitting on Quin's couch/bed didn't seem appropriate, so she shook her head and sat on one of the benches that surrounded his kitchen table. Quin sat across from her, necessarily quite close in the cramped quarters, which Mila found oddly unnerving.

"So, have you thought any more about going to Roanoke?" he asked.

Mila pulled at the collar of her blouse, suddenly warm. "I'd like to talk to the people up there personally, but I can't leave the children," she told him. "I trust Miss Eugenia, but she's old, and I only met Cleo a couple of days ago."

He nodded. "I understand. It wouldn't be wise to take any chances as long as there's a possibility that the kids are in danger." He moved the salt and pepper shakers around for a few seconds, then said, "Maybe I'll go on by myself."

Mila was pleased and impressed by the suggestion. "That would be very helpful."

He grinned. "I'll do it then. Tomorrow I'll make plane reservations, and then we can compile a list of everyone I need to talk to while I'm there."

Mila chewed her lip. "You won't get as much cooperation as I would, but if that's the best we can do . . ."

"What? You don't think they'll be terrified into spilling their guts when I tell them what I do for a living?" Quin teased, and she had to laugh.

"I doubt if I could terrify them into spilling their guts either, but they'd have to take me more seriously since I'm a police officer," she said, then stood and called to the kids. "Time for bed."

"Can Uncle Quin read us our bedtime stories?" Lily wanted to know as Mila collected them from the couch.

Mila was trying to decide how to respond when Quin answered for her. "Thanks for inviting me, Lily, but I'd better save that for another night."

Mila was relieved. Having him inside the house while they went through their bedtime routine would have been awkward for her. He was very considerate, and she felt a surprising and unexpected tenderness toward him. With Ben on one hip and Lily holding her other hand, she turned to him. "Good night."

"Good night." He held the door open as they climbed out of the camper, then waved as they slipped through the back door into the house.

Mila bathed the kids quickly and snapped Ben into his sleeper in record time. They climbed onto the double bed and read the Book of Mormon, then Mila read the bedtime books in order without having to be prompted. She supervised the saying of prayers, speaking for Ben, but when she tried to lift him into his crib, he started to cry.

"I think he wants me to lie down by him again," Lily said.

"If you don't mind, that probably would make him happy," Mila said and gave her a boost into the crib. Then she put Ben beside his sister, and this time he didn't whimper.

Mila checked on them every few minutes and finally found them asleep, arms around each other. She couldn't bring herself to separate them, so she spread the blanket over them both and tiptoed back to the living room. She curled up on her unattractive couch and stared at the cross-stitch her mother had made, proclaiming the eternal nature of the family. It was impossible to explain, but living in a ramshackle house, her career in ruins, and a virtual stranger camping in the backyard, she felt more at peace than she had in a long time.

CHAPTER 11

On Wednesday morning Mark Iverson had to lean down to adjust his tie in the mirror that topped his wife's dresser. It was an authentic reproduction of a dresser used a hundred years before, when people were shorter. He gave the knot of his tie another tug, then reached for his FBI credentials and the stake calendar, tucking them in his shirt pocket before pulling on his suit coat. Being bishop of the Albany Second Ward and the resident agent for the FBI in Albany sometimes seemed like a conflict of interest. At other times, he had to look around to make sure which role he was in at the moment.

He walked into the kitchen and was greeted by a heartwarming sight. His wife, Kate, was making pancakes while his two-year-old son, Charles, watched. His daughter, Emily, who would be four in October, was sitting at the table.

"I'm drawing you a picture to put on your wall at work," she told Mark when she saw him.

"I think there might still be one blank spot on my wall," he said, thinking of the hundreds of drawings that Emily had already given him. He walked up behind his wife and put his arms around her waist then drew her close. "Good morning," he said, nuzzling her hair.

She relaxed against him. "Good morning, yourself. Would you like some pancakes?"

He reluctantly released her and picked up his son, who was standing too close to the stove for his comfort. "I think I'll just have cereal. How about you, Charles?" he asked as he held the little boy high above his head.

"Pancakes!" Charles squealed.

Mark settled him into the high chair and complimented Emily's artwork, while Kate put a plate of pancakes on the table. He got a bowl of cereal, then watched with tenderness as Kate fed Charles, pretending that the fork was an airplane to encourage him to eat.

"Miss Eugenia came over a little while ago on her way to take Miss Polly breakfast," Kate told him in between pancake landings. "She says that girl who used to live here—Mila Edwards?" She paused, and Mark nodded to indicate that he remembered the name. "Well, it turns out she's a member of the Church. She has been her whole life, but no one in Haggerty knew."

Mark felt his stomach tighten. He'd gotten a call about Mila Edwards and her foster children the day before. He didn't know she was LDS, but he did know that her situation was a potentially dangerous one. "Um," was all he could say.

"Miss Eugenia says her foster children are almost the exact same ages as Emily and Charles," Kate continued. "So after I make bread this morning, I thought the kids and I would go over and meet them."

"Why don't you wait until Sunday and meet her at church?" he suggested.

Kate laughed. "We live in Haggerty, remember? If I wait until Sunday, I'll be the last person in town to meet her."

"I know you mean well, but this is a busy time," Mark tried. "She's in the process of moving into her great-aunt's house and child services is doing a home inspection and . . ."

"How do you know so much about them?" Kate interrupted him.

He shrugged, trying to act casual. "I hear things."

Kate considered this for a few seconds, then shook her head. "We won't stay long, but I don't want to wait until Sunday. There are so few members of the Church in this area, and we should stick together."

"I'm sure Miss Eugenia and her buddies will smother Sister Edwards with kindness without your help," Mark insisted, making another attempt to discourage his wife.

"Which is precisely the point. *I'm* a Haggerty lady just like Miss Eugenia and her smothery buddies."

He couldn't tell her anything confidential, so he had to skirt the issue. "What I know about Mila Edwards I learned officially, so I can't give you the details. But being around them could be dangerous."

Kate frowned. "That's even more reason why I should offer my support and friendship."

Mark shook his head. "I'm sorry, but I can't allow you to take the children into a hazardous situation."

"You can't allow it?" Kate repeated, as if she couldn't believe she'd heard him correctly.

Mark took a deep breath, then said, "I'm going to have to insist that you stay away from Mila Edwards until her situation is resolved."

The silence that followed his words was deafening.

"Are you forbidding me to visit her?" Kate asked finally.

"Don't look at it that way." He watched the emotions play across his wife's beautiful and expressive face. First confusion, followed by hurt, eventually turning to anger.

"You *are* forbidding me!"

"I wish I could explain, but I can't. Please just trust me on this."

Kate walked over to the sink and started filling it with warm water. "Since I've promised to obey, I guess I don't have much choice."

"We'll talk about it more when I get home." Mark joined her by the sink and leaned down to give her a kiss, but she pulled away. He watched her wash dishes for a few seconds, but when she didn't acknowledge him, he turned and said good-bye to his children, then left for work.

* * *

When it was time to dress for her home inspection, Mila was thrilled to have her entire wardrobe at her disposal. She chose a pair of linen pants and a white cotton shirt. The ensemble fit the no-nonsense impression that she wanted to convey to Mr. Pusser. Once she was dressed and ready, she woke up the kids. While fixing their breakfast, she peeked out the kitchen window. As promised, Quin had decamped for the inspection. She found him sitting on the front porch steps, reading the newspaper.

"Good morning," she greeted from behind him.

He turned around and smiled. "Good morning."

"Would you like to join us for breakfast?"

"Thanks, but I fixed a bowl of oatmeal before I packed up."

"Sorry to put you to that extra trouble."

"No problem," he assured her. "When will the child services guy be here?"

"I'm supposed to meet him at the police station at nine."

"What were you planning to do with the kids?"

"Cleo invited them to wait at her house."

"When you're ready to go, I'll take them over and stay there until you're finished," he offered. Once again he saw a need and filled it without being asked.

"Thank you," she said softly.

"And we can exchange cell numbers so you can keep tabs on us."

She had just been about to suggest that and was glad he spoke first. She gave him her cell number and accepted a piece of paper with his written on it. Seeing his handwriting for the first time, a cramped little scrawl, gave her a warm feeling. Determined to stay focused on the inspection, she folded the paper and put it in her pants pocket. Then she turned the children over to Quin and drove into Albany to collect Mr. Leonard Pusser.

Mila had mentally pictured Mr. Pusser as a small, wiry man with mean eyes. In reality Mr. Pusser was a tall, thickly built man with mean eyes. He was waiting impatiently in the reception area of the police station when she arrived, ten minutes early. Mila introduced herself, and he suggested that they go so he could "get this over with."

Clinching her teeth to keep from making a comment she knew she'd regret, Mila led the way outside. When Mr. Pusser saw her Mustang, he shook his head. "Not a very practical family car."

Mila looked at him in surprise. "I'm not allowed to have a Mustang?"

"Well, there's no written law, but some vehicles are more family friendly," Mr. Pusser said, making a note on his clipboard, and Mila knew she was off to a bad start. "Was the car seat installed by a professional?"

Mila shook her head. "I put it in myself."

This didn't seem to bother Mr. Pusser as much as the Mustang. "Just take it by the Health Department and get it safety checked, then mail a copy of their certification to my office."

Mila nodded.

"I'll follow you," he said, climbing into a sensible, family-friendly minivan.

Mila led the way to Haggerty and tried to resist staring at Mr. Pusser in her rearview mirror. She prayed for the Lord's help and then found a country station and sang along to buoy up her spirits.

When she parked in front of Aunt Cora Sue's house, she immediately sensed a difference. She couldn't pinpoint the source of change until they reached the porch. A couple of rattan chairs had been put on the porch, giving the house a friendly, we're-here-to-stay kind of look. She saw Mr. Pusser glancing around as she unlocked the door.

She pushed into the living room and had to suppress a gasp of surprise. The room was still neat, as she had left it. But strategically placed in various locations around the room were nice touches that made the room more inviting. There was a little vase with fresh flowers on the bookshelf. An expensive wooden chess set covered most of the scars on the surface of the coffee table. Several educational videos were scattered in plain sight. A lovely crocheted afghan was draped across the back of the couch, and a set of Norman Rockwell prints were arranged on the living room walls.

"Nice," Mr. Pusser said as he looked around. "I love Norman Rockwell, and I believe that a good game of chess will stretch a child's mind farther than a week of school." He picked up one of the videos. "I don't believe children should watch much television, but this is one of the few video series I endorse."

Mila was too shocked to form a response, so she just smiled. They continued through the transformed house. Magnetic alphabet letters arranged artfully into short words on the refrigerator. More flowers, a small portable stereo playing classical music, and Theresa's parenting book open to the chapter on nutritional meals were on the little table by the bed.

In the children's room the small touches became huge ones. Brightly colored *Star Trek* posters hung on the walls. A solar system comforter covered the bed, and the crib was full of pillows made in the shape of planets.

Mr. Pusser picked up a lamp shaped like the sun. "Very educational," he remarked. "I'm a *Star Trek* fan myself. Just be sure to remove the pillows from the crib before you put the baby to sleep."

Mila nodded, still dumbfounded.

"Where are the children now?" he asked.

"Next door," she managed. "With Cleo Ledbetter and their father's foster brother."

Mr. Pusser made a notation. "The children can only be left with approved sitters. Mrs. Ledbetter is approved, but the foster brother will have to be processed."

She flinched. "I'm sorry, I didn't know."

"It's not a problem," he assured her, pulling a sheet of paper from the back of his clipboard. "Make a list of anyone who will keep the children on a regular basis along with their contact information, then mail it to me with the car seat inspection report," Mr. Pusser said as they stepped back onto the front porch

"Okay."

"I see that you've had the metal grate for the old floor furnace covered. I presume you're planning to put in central heat and air?"

"Yes, sir. Monroe Wilhite is handling the work for me and said to tell you he'd get you the paperwork when it's completed."

Mr. Pusser nodded as he made more notations. They walked out into the backyard, and he checked it for poison ivy and other poisonous plants. Fortunately, Mr. Pusser didn't have a problem with dandelions. Just as he tore off the top of the form, Quin and the Womack children walked through the hedges that separated Aunt Cora Sue's yard from Cleo's. Ben was up on Quin's shoulders, looking happier than Mila had ever seen him. Lily was skipping along lopsidedly beside them, and Mila's heart skipped a beat.

Mila made brief introductions. "Quin, this is Mr. Pusser. Mr. Pusser, Quin Drummond."

"You the foster uncle?" Mr. Pusser asked, and Quin nodded.

"Does that camper parked in front belong to you?"

Quin lifted Ben off his shoulders and turned the little boy loose in the front yard. "Yes."

Mr. Pusser frowned and looked back at Mila. "What is the relationship between the two of you?"

Mila was startled. "We don't have one. Quin is just visiting the kids for a few days before he heads back to California."

The child services inspector seemed dubious. "If the two of you are cohabitating that will affect your suitability as a foster parent."

Mila was too embarrassed to respond.

"I'm not staying in the house," Quin explained. "I'm going to set up my camper."

"Not on this premises, you're not," Mr. Pusser said firmly. "That's cohabitating."

"Okay, I won't park it here," Quin agreed.

Mr. Pusser examined him through narrowed eyes. "You'd better not. I'll be checking back from time to time." He handed the top copy of the inspection form to Mila.

She stared at it for a second, then looked up. "I passed?"

The inspector acknowledged this with a brusque nod. "Contingent on my receipt of the items I requested."

"I'll take care of that immediately," Mila promised.

With one last, long look at Quin, Mr. Pusser walked down the sidewalk and got into his van. They watched him drive away, then Cleo slipped through the hedges.

"I didn't want him to see me," she whispered. "Earl Jr. was in his space stage the last time Old Sour Pusser inspected our house, and I was afraid he'd remember where he saw those things last."

"Thanks for loaning us all that stuff," Mila told the other woman with a grateful smile. "And I told him you were watching the kids. He said you were approved."

Cleo seemed pleased. "You never know the mood Old Sour Pusser will be in, but he ought to think I'm approved. He knows me better than I know myself." She glanced over at her son. "And you can keep the space stuff. Earl Jr. never repeats a stage."

"Mr. Pusser inspects your house often enough to remember your decor?" Mila asked in surprise.

"Every couple of months," Cleo confirmed.

"Why?"

Cleo shrugged. "Lots of reasons. Mostly because I'm not popular here in Haggerty. The neighbors call and complain to child services."

Mila was shocked. "The people of Haggerty seem so nice and that sounds just . . . petty."

"Nothing I can't handle," Cleo replied. "So, I was right about Old Sour Pusser's objection to the camper?"

Mila nodded. "You were right." She watched Lily run around in unbalanced circles while Ben picked dandelions.

"Where are you going to park your home on wheels?" Cleo asked Quin, stepping a little closer to the man than absolutely necessary.

"I don't know," he replied.

"You can set it up in my backyard—what there is of it," Cleo proposed. "That will keep you close to the kids."

Mila regretted that Quin would have to move, but had to admit that transferring to the Ledbetters' yard was the simplest solution. So she didn't object as Quin accepted Cleo's offer. They walked over to Cleo's backyard and watched Quin back his camper into the corner. Then he started setting up his campsite again. Miss George Ann came up during this process and made no attempt to hide her horror.

"I knew it was just a matter of time before you tried to set up a trailer park here!" Miss George Ann cried. "There are regulations about such things inside the city limits!" She turned to address Mila. "Before you know it, she'll have rusty junk cars lining the street!"

Mila intervened quickly. "Quin is *my* guest—not Cleo's. And he's just camping here for a few days. We have permission from the police," she added.

Miss George Ann lifted her head higher into the air. "Can I speak to you privately, Mila?"

Mila followed the older woman to the side of the house near a cluster of honeysuckle bushes.

"Goodness gracious, Mila," Miss George Ann said, her long neck stretched to the limit. "What is going on?"

Mila moved closer. "Cleo is letting Lily and Ben's uncle set his camper up in her yard because the child services inspector won't allow him to stay in my yard."

"Dear me!" Miss George Ann replied with a sniff. "You're fraternizing with that Ledbetter riffraff?"

Mila's eyes narrowed. "Cleo has been very helpful. Now if you'll excuse me." She started to walk away.

"Mark my words, developing a friendship with Cleo Ledbetter will bring you grief!" Miss George Ann predicted. "And if you're intending to live here you need to get these dandelions treated." The older woman frowned at the flower-dotted yard. "They'll spread onto all the lawns in the neighborhood if you don't."

Mila nodded and kept walking.

When she returned to the backyard, she learned that Cleo had invited them for lunch. "We have to celebrate the fact that you passed inspection," Cleo said. "I think you charmed Old Sour Pusser."

"No." Mila felt a blush creep up her cheeks. "It was all the little extras you scattered around the house that convinced him I was a fit foster parent."

Cleo laughed. "I guess that did help a little. I know Old Sour Pusser like the back of my hand. So how about lunch?"

Mila looked over at Quin, and he shrugged. Then she saw the baby jam a fistful of dandelions into his mouth. Mila ran over and picked up Ben.

"He eats everything," Lily said as Mila frantically tried to get the weeds out of Ben's mouth. "One time he even ate a bug, and my mommy cried." The mention of her mother seemed to take all the play out of Lily. She stopped running and watched the dandelion removal process.

When Mila was reasonably sure she had saved Ben from dandelion poisoning—if there was such a thing—she picked up the little boy and said to Cleo, "I guess the kids do need to eat something besides dandelions."

Cleo looked back over her shoulder. "What? Are y'all some kind of health-food junkies?"

Mila smiled at the baby in her arms. "No."

The Ledbetters' house was even more impressive on the inside. Cleo and Earl Jr. gave them a full tour. Mila had been to Graceland once and noticed that Cleo and Elvis had similar tastes. The house was ostentatious and gaudy and way too big, but still managed to feel fun and homey. There was a gorgeous spiral staircase that Cleo told them was only for show.

"It's pretty, but way too much trouble," she explained, then showed them the elevator tucked discreetly underneath. "I'll save the playroom until after lunch," Cleo whispered to Mila as she seated everyone around a gorgeous round wooden table in the kitchen that looked like something out of *Southern Living*.

Once they were eating homemade vegetable soup and grilled cheese sandwiches, Mila said, "This is good. Did you make it?"

Cleo hooted with laughter. "Me? I can't even operate a can opener. No, Earl Sr. comes home at lunchtime and cooks for us."

Mila tried not to think about Earl Sr.'s profession and whether or not he had washed his hands before preparing lunch as she encouraged Ben to eat his sandwich.

"If you cut it up in little pieces he can feed himself," Lily told her. Mila complied, and soon the little boy was eating happily.

Cleo watched Mila pick at her own sandwich and finally said, "Earl Sr. is the cook of our family, but I could probably throw together a salad if I tried real hard. And there's plenty of dandelions in the backyard."

Mila was embarrassed. "This is fine," Mila replied, taking a big bite of the sandwich for emphasis. It had been a while since she had eaten real cheese and for a few seconds she couldn't concentrate on anything but the delicious taste. "Ben's the only member of the family that eats dandelions." At the mention of the word *family* she got a lump in her throat and had a hard time swallowing.

Quin seemed to notice her discomfort and distracted Cleo by asking questions about the house until everyone was finished eating. Cleo led them from the kitchen into a huge room full of toys.

"This looks like a Fisher Price warehouse," Quin said as Lily hobbled toward a playhouse and Ben climbed up a miniature slide.

Mila laughed in agreement. "Disneyworld can't be better than this."

Cleo watched Earl Jr. as he called to Lily from a two-story plastic fort. "Earl Jr. doesn't enjoy it as much as I thought he would. I guess playing by yourself isn't much fun."

"No plans for more children?" Mila asked, then regretted the personal question as Cleo's face clouded with pain.

"Are you kidding?" Cleo demanded. "Child services could take Earl Jr. away from me any day."

Quin frowned at this remark. "Surely not."

Cleo shrugged, but didn't say she was teasing. "Anyway, my doctor says it would be dangerous to try again."

"I'm sorry," Mila said.

Cleo expression became wistful. "It's funny how life works out. I have a sister who's never been married, still lives with my mother, and is pregnant with her third child. It seems like the Lord would have wanted to send those babies to me instead."

"I have a lot of questions to ask somebody when I get to the other side too," Mila agreed. "Like why my daddy had to die when I was so young." She took a deep breath, then moved away from that subject. "I'm sorry about your sister."

Cleo accepted Mila's remark with a nod. "I don't see much of my family anymore. I don't want anyone setting a bad example for Earl Jr., and that pretty much sums up my family—bad examples."

"I'm glad you won that money so you could move away from them."

Cleo smiled. "Me too."

"I guess you miss them though," Quin said quietly.

Cleo shrugged and the feathers that circled her neckline undulated along with her shoulders. "I do miss them sometimes, but me and Earl never really fit in there any better than we do here." She waved her hand to encompass Haggerty.

Mila frowned. "Why?"

"Well, for one thing we got married and stayed that way—rare in our neck of the woods. And we had actual jobs and didn't enjoy running from the police. It's funny, now we live around people we have more in common with, and they think we're trashy!"

Mila winced. "Once they get to know you, they'll see that they were wrong."

Cleo shrugged again, but didn't comment.

They let the children play for a while, then Mila said it was time to go home for a nap. Ben objected loudly, and to calm him Mila had to promise that they would come back the next day.

"Come every day," Cleo offered. "It'll give Earl Jr. something to look forward to."

They walked into the ornate entry room and past the huge staircase, and when they reached the front door, Mila and Quin thanked their hostess again. "Lunch was delicious," he said.

"Thanks for having us," Mila added.

"Anytime," Cleo said graciously.

"Why don't you let me reciprocate by having you all over tonight?" Quin offered.

"You're inviting us to your little campsite?" Mila clarified, and Quin nodded.

Cleo looked between the two of them, then said, "I'd love to, but Earl Sr. wants to go out for Chinese tonight." She addressed Mila. "Of course, that's no reason why you can't accept. Ben and Lily need to spend as much time with their uncle as they can before he leaves."

Mila nodded. "That's fine with me. What time?"

Quin glanced at his watch, then said, "Seven o'clock."

"We'll be there." Then Mila took the Womack children to her great-aunt Cora Sue's house and put them down for much-needed naps.

* * *

Mila spent the afternoon entertaining ladies from Miss Eugenia's Sunday School class and accepting casseroles. By the time she went to get ready for dinner at Quin's, she had a refrigerator nearly bursting with foil-covered dishes.

She changed clothes three times before finally settling on a pair of Cavalli jeans and a lacy Versace peasant blouse. The children were excited so they left a few minutes early and walked through the hedges to Quin's campsite.

Mila had expected him to serve hot dogs or even have a pizza delivered. But when they settled around the collapsible picnic table, she saw that he had grilled a chicken, tossed a salad, and even baked a cake.

"This looks wonderful," she complimented him, and he smiled.

Lily dominated the dinner conversation, speaking both for herself and for Ben. When they were finished eating, Quin let them roast marshmallows over the ash that had once been charcoal in the barbecue grill. He instructed them on the process, and Mila looked around. The camp was austere but pleasant.

While the children warmed marshmallows, she said, "You're so calm. You never seem stressed about anything."

He considered this, then shook his head. "I try not to let things bother me."

She laughed. "I wish I could learn that technique. Everything bothers me."

"Like what?" he looked genuinely curious.

"I worry that I'll get fat or that I'm overdressed or underdressed. I'm never satisfied."

"That's funny," he said. "I'm almost always satisfied."

She shook her head. "Total opposites." She watched Ben stuff a marshmallow into his mouth, then said, "Tell me about surfing, all your trophies and everything."

"I don't compete much anymore. Mostly I go to competitions to promote my boards and stay on top of changes in the sport. I also do some endorsements and some consulting work."

"And you enjoy it?"

"I make enough money, I'm my own boss, and I get to travel all around the world. What's not to like?"

"Don't you ever wish for more structure?" she asked.

He thought for a minute, then shook his head. "Not really."

"You never dream about a wife and family living in a cottage with a picket fence?"

He laughed. "Sometimes I dream about a wife and family, but I picture them on a beach in Maui, carrying custom-made surfboards. And I can't imagine being fenced in—even by a picket."

Mila smiled. "And I can't imagine living without a fence of some kind. It seems like you'd always be off balance." She studied him for a minute. "I sort of envy you, though. All that freedom and loving what you do for a living. I'd hoped to enjoy police work that much, but so far it's just a job."

A fine, misty rain started falling, and Mila called to the children. "We'd better get inside," she told Quin. "Thanks for dinner."

"You're welcome," he replied, then it started to rain in earnest, and the children screamed in unison. "You grab Ben, and I'll take Lily," he suggested.

Mila nodded and grabbed the baby, then they headed through the hedges and up onto the back porch of Aunt Cora Sue's old house.

Mila unlocked the door, and they rushed into the small kitchen, dripping all over the floor.

"That was so fun!" Lily shrieked. "Can we play in the rain some more?"

"Not tonight," Mila told her. "We've got to get these wet clothes off of you before you catch a cold." Mila walked into the bathroom, and Quin followed, still holding Lily. "Wrap her in that towel until I can get Ben bathed," she instructed, and he did.

Mila ran some warm water, then wrestled Ben out of his clothes. She put him into the tub and rinsed him thoroughly, then wrapped him in another towel and handed him to Quin. "His things are in there." She pointed to the children's room. "I'll help Lily."

When Mila got into the bedroom a few minutes later, Ben was wearing his diaper backwards, and Quin was staring at the footed sleeper in utter confusion. The fact that he knew less about child care than she did made her like him even better. She took over and soon had Ben ready for bed. She let Quin read stories until the children fell asleep. Then they tiptoed out of the bedroom.

Mila picked up Ben's towel and rubbed it on her wet hair as she listened to the rain pounding on the roof. "Will you be okay in your little camper during this storm?" she asked.

"If it gets too bad I'll climb into the Mustang," he said.

"If it gets too bad you can sleep on the couch."

He grinned. "I'd hate to see what Mr. Pusser would have to say about that."

"Cohabitating," Mila predicted with a smile.

"Good night." Quin opened the door and stepped into the driving rain. She watched until he disappeared through the hedges, then she closed the door.

After changing into pajamas, Mila turned on the television to check the weather. She had just settled onto the couch when there was a knock on the door. The rain seemed to isolate her from the rest of the world, and she felt very alone. There was another knock, and she realized she was going to have to answer it soon or the children would wake up. So she got her revolver from her purse and walked to the door.

"Who's there?" she asked, hoping her voice didn't betray her anxiety.

"Mark Iverson," came the reply. "FBI."

She unlocked the door and pulled it open.

"You shouldn't just take someone's word that they are with the FBI," Mark scolded mildly as he stepped into her living room.

She held up her gun. "I was prepared in case of trouble. Besides, Miss Eugenia told me about you."

He nodded. "She's always at least a step ahead of me. I guess she also told you that I'm the bishop of the Albany Second Ward," he said.

Mila smiled. "She told me you were a member of the Church, but I don't think she mentioned that you were the bishop. What should I call you? Bishop or Agent or Bishop Agent?" she teased.

"Mark will be fine," he told her with a smile. "And it's actually in my capacity as bishop that I'm here, not for the FBI. I'll request your records on Sunday. But I've talked to Chief Monahan and until things are secure here, I hesitate to assign home and visiting teachers. If you need anything in the meantime, feel free to call me." He extended a card listing his home, work, and cell numbers.

"Thanks." Mila studied the card carefully. "But it's starting to look like my stay here will be brief, so you might want to wait about requesting my records."

Mark frowned. "I won't make a request until you let me know one way or another. In the meantime I've written directions to the chapel on the back of my card. Our meetings start at nine."

Mila turned over the card. "Thanks." After a brief pause she said, "If you've talked to the chief, you've gotten a very one-sided perspective. The chief is convinced that Larsen Womack is a criminal and that he poses a danger to his children."

"You don't share his opinion?"

"He was an active member of his ward in Roanoke, so I'm having a hard time picturing him as an extortionist and murderer."

"From the Mormon perspective Larsen Womack isn't a likely criminal," Mark concurred.

Mila laughed with relief. "Maybe you can talk some sense into the chief!"

Mark shrugged. "I doubt it. And unfortunately being a bishop has taught me that membership in the Church doesn't guarantee virtue or honesty."

Mila was terribly disappointed. "So you agree with Chief Monahan?"

"I don't agree with anyone. I'm not even officially involved."

"The FBI isn't going to look into Theresa Womack's disappearance?"

"Chief Monahan requested assistance, but I can't do anything about it unless my superiors decide to reopen that case."

Mila frowned. "Reopen?"

Mark looked like he regretted this admission. "You know that Ryathon is pushing for fast approval of a new synthetic drug?"

Mila nodded.

"Just before Larsen Womack disappeared, the FBI office in Roanoke received an anonymous tip that the new drug was unsafe and that documents sent to the FDA had been falsified."

Mila was thrilled. "You think the tip came from Larsen?"

"Maybe," Mark acknowledged the possibility. "I spoke with the agent in Roanoke who handled the case, and he said that after Larsen disappeared they investigated thoroughly and couldn't find any evidence of wrongdoing."

"But by then Ryathon would have had time to cover their tracks."

Mark spread his hands. "But without Larsen Womack or his research, there's no case."

"I have this unpopular theory that Larsen is running for his life, and a plot to suppress evidence of a dangerous new drug would really give me some leverage."

Mark shook his head. "Sorry. The drug seems safe." He took a step toward the door. "But if you come across evidence that suggests otherwise, let me know. Right now I'd better get home. And speaking of home," he began, and a frown settled over his handsome features. "My wife wants to come visit you, welcome you to Haggerty and all that, but I've asked her not to. Because of my line of work, my children are at risk enough. I hope you understand."

Mila nodded. "I do."

"Good, because Kate certainly doesn't," he muttered.

"In fact, I'd like to ask all the ladies in town to stop bringing food. I have enough casseroles now to last until Christmas, and there's no point in the ladies putting themselves in the line of fire—just in case."

"I think that's wise. And please call if you need me as your temporary bishop or . . . anything." After a quick wave, Mark Iverson walked out into the rain.

CHAPTER 12

On Thursday morning when Mark awakened, Kate was already up. He knew she had tossed and turned all night because he hadn't been able to sleep either. With a sigh he walked into the bathroom, postponing the moment he'd have to go downstairs and face the cold shoulder again.

There was a loaf of wheat bread on the counter when he walked into the kitchen. It was wrapped in clear plastic, and *Mila Edwards* was written across the top. He felt Kate staring at him and raised his gaze to meet hers. There were purple smudges of exhaustion under her eyes, and he felt a pang of guilt.

"Miss Eugenia is going to take that over to Sister Edwards, since I'm not allowed," Kate said as she turned toward the table where the children were eating cereal.

Mark fixed himself a bowl, then joined them. "Mama's letting us have Froot Loops," Emily told him. "And it's not even my birthday."

Mark glanced at his wife, but she kept her gaze averted. "Well, it must be some kind of special occasion. Maybe it's Christmas."

Emily giggled. "There's no tree or stockings!"

Mark tugged one of her pigtails. "Then I guess your mother has her own reasons for letting you have a breakfast treat."

"Do you have a reason, Mama?" Emily called to Kate.

"Just hurry and eat before I change my mind," Kate replied.

Mark finished his cereal, then rejoined his wife by the sink. "Why don't you see if Miss Eugenia is available to babysit tonight?" he suggested. "We could go out to dinner."

Kate pulled the plug from the drain and reached for a dish towel. "It probably wouldn't be a good idea to leave our children here with only an elderly woman for protection. You never know when a murderer might happen by."

"Kate," Mark began, but she cut him off.

"You're going to be late for work." She walked to the high chair and extricated little Charles. "Let's go up and make your beds," she told the children.

Mark watched them leave the room, then let himself out the back door and drove to Albany.

* * *

Beau called during breakfast on Thursday morning. Mila held the phone in the crook of her neck while spooning instant oatmeal into Ben's mouth. She'd learned her lesson about trusting the baby with the whole bowl.

"I thought you'd forgotten about us," Mila said.

"I tried," he admitted. "I'll never be able to get you out of my mind until you tell me about Atlanta," he teased.

"Of all the approaches you've used so far, that one is the most tempting," Mila told him.

Beau laughed, then said, "I talked to Wilma, and she said you passed your inspection. I guess you're happy about that."

"I'd be happier if you could find our missing person so my little charges could go back home," Mila answered, careful to phrase her response so that the children wouldn't understand.

There was a brief pause. "Mila, you know that's unlikely to happen."

She sighed. "Even if the worst is confirmed, at least they would be able to move on with their lives. It's the uncertainty that drives me crazy." She knew she was putting him in an awkward situation by asking questions, but couldn't help herself. "Have you made any progress on the case?"

"None," he reported. "In fact, the case is so cold that the chief is moving it to the back burner until we hear something from the FBI."

"Do you think they'll help?"

"He just asked them to reopen their investigation at Ryathon. He thinks Larsen stole the formula for that new drug and was planning to sell it on the black market. Theresa's death was incidental to that. I guess he's hoping if the FBI solves the mystery of Larsen's disappearance, Theresa's will be solved in the process."

"What do you think, Beau?"

"I think that's all we've got."

There was a knock on the front door, so Mila ended her conversation with Beau and lifted Ben, still smeared with oatmeal, from the high chair and went to answer it. She looked out the living room window and saw Miss Eugenia standing on the porch.

"Kate Iverson sent you this bread," Miss Eugenia said when Mila opened the door. "Mark won't let her welcome you in person, and she's as mad at him as I've ever seen her."

"Come in," Mila invited, and the older woman accepted promptly. "Mark came by last night and explained his reluctance to have his wife and children over here until we're sure it's safe. In fact, would you ask the ladies from town not to bring in any more casseroles. We have enough to last us months and . . ."

"You think someone might get shot trying to deliver food?"

"It's possible. And a steady stream of strangers coming to the door makes it difficult for me to watch for someone who means the children harm."

Miss Eugenia nodded. "I'll take care of it." She looked at Ben. "He needs a bath."

Mila laughed. "It's just oatmeal. How did the Faith Fair planning meeting go yesterday?"

Miss Eugenia followed her into the kitchen and watched as Mila scrubbed Ben's face. "It wasn't as productive as Cornelia had hoped. Halfway through making the assignments for the fair, George Ann volunteered to be president of the newly formed Faith Fair Committee. Cornelia said we didn't need a president, mostly because she didn't want to yield any authority—especially not to George Ann. So after thirty minutes of very unuplifting arguing, we dispersed."

"That's the end of the fair then?"

"Oh, no! Cornelia won't give up that easily. We're meeting again on Sunday afternoon, and all the controversy will likely draw a big crowd."

When Miss Eugenia was on the porch saying her good-byes, a Taurus station wagon pulled up and parked at the curb in front of Aunt Cora Sue's house.

"Well, speak of the devil," Miss Eugenia murmured. "If it isn't Cornelia Blackwood herself."

Mila turned and studied the woman who climbed out of the station wagon. She had a large Bible clutched in one hand and a small casserole dish in the other. She approached the house with long, purposeful strides.

The preacher's wife pulled Miss Eugenia into a firm hug. "I'm pleased that we're calling at the same time."

"Actually I was just leaving," Miss Eugenia said, disengaging herself. "Mila, may I present Mrs. Cornelia Blackwood. Cornelia, this is Cora Sue Roper's grandniece, Mila Edwards."

"It's such a pleasure to meet you." Cornelia tilted her head for a second. "You look like you could use a hug."

Mila braced herself as the other woman enfolded her in a pair of strong arms. Mila glanced over Cornelia's head and saw Miss Eugenia roll her eyes. "Let her go before you strangle her," Miss Eugenia said, and Cornelia laughed.

"Oh, you're such a card." She turned her attention back to Mila. "I've brought you a nice casserole for supper," she said. "My husband is the preacher at the Haggerty Baptist Church, and I'd like to invite you to services on Sunday."

"Thank you," Mila responded, "for the casserole and the invitation."

"Mila's a Mormon," Miss Eugenia informed the preacher's wife with obvious delight, and Cornelia's face lost all its color.

"Oh, my," she whispered, actually taking a step backward.

"It's okay, Cornelia. Mormonism isn't catching."

Cornelia laughed again, but this time it was forced. "Of course not. Well, regardless of your religious orientation, we want to welcome you to town. It's a lovely place to raise children."

"Mila's a police detective, and the children she's tending are in danger. It's awfully brave of you to visit, knowing you might get shot."

Cornelia grasped both women by the hand. "Dear Lord!" she cried, her eyes open and looking heavenward. "Please protect this house from the devil! Amen!" The prayer ended, and Cornelia spoke to Mila. "I'd better be getting home. I'll leave you in the Lord's hands."

"Thanks again!" Mila called after her.

"Don't rush off!" Miss Eugenia added, a mischievous smile on her face. "Mila looks to me like she needs another hug!" But the preacher's wife was gone. "Ahh," Miss Eugenia said with a satisfied smile. "It's rare for me to get the upper hand with Cornelia Blackwood. I couldn't let the opportunity pass."

Miss Eugenia took the casserole from Mila's hands and moved back into the house. "Let me see if this is what I think it is . . ." She pulled off the foil cover and made a face. "That's what I thought. Her specialty—beanie weenies."

When they got into the kitchen they found Cleo going through Mila's refrigerator.

"Have you already spent all your millions and now have to scavenge for food?" Miss Eugenia asked.

Cleo laughed. "No, I've still got a few dollars left, and actually I'm sorting casseroles for Mila."

"Sorting them how?" Miss Eugenia wanted to know, coming closer to watch over Cleo's shoulder.

"I'm dividing them between things Mila can actually use and things I can take home for the stray dogs."

Miss Eugenia gave Cleo a look of grudging respect. "Now that's time well spent." She handed her the beanie weenies. "Add this to the dog pile."

After Cleo and Miss Eugenia left, Mila let Lily choose a coloring book and settled Ben in front of a stack of Legos before taking out the card Mark Iverson had given her the night before. She moved into the bedroom so the children couldn't overhear her conversation, then dialed the Iversons' home number. A few seconds later a woman's voice answered. "Hello?"

"Is this Kate Iverson?"

"Yes," Kate confirmed.

"I'm Mila Edwards, and I wanted to call to thank you for the bread you sent over with Miss Eugenia."

"Oh, you're welcome. I'm sorry I didn't deliver it myself," Kate sounded embarrassed.

"Actually, that's something else I have to thank you for," Mila said, weighing her words carefully.

"You want to thank me for not delivering the bread personally?"

"Yes. I'm a detective for the Albany Police Department, and the children in my care may be in danger. Both their father and mother have disappeared under questionable circumstances, and we're afraid that they might be targets as well. Well-meaning Haggerty ladies coming by to meet me and dropping off casseroles makes my job harder and increases the risk for the children. I've asked Miss Eugenia to discourage people from bringing in food, but you figured it out for yourself. I guess having an FBI agent for a husband helps you to understand situations like this."

There was a brief silence, then Kate said, "Yes, I had an advantage over the other ladies in town. I look forward to meeting you on Sunday, and if there's anything I can do before then, without making matters worse for you, please let me know."

"Thank you. We'll see you on Sunday." Mila hung up the phone, pleased with herself.

Quin knocked on the back door a few minutes later. Mila put in one of Cleo's educational videos while she and Quin discussed his upcoming trip to Roanoke. "Did you make a plane reservation?"

He nodded. "I leave tomorrow morning and come back late tomorrow night."

Mila made a notation on the paper in front of her. "It will probably be better to go to the Womacks' neighborhood in the early evening, when people are home from work, so why don't I set you up an appointment at Ryathon first?"

"Fine with me," Quin replied.

"I'll arrange with Mr. DeFore to take you on a tour of the facility, show you the area where Larsen worked, introduce you to his coworkers, that kind of thing. Then you'll want to interview people without Mr. DeFore, or they'll be intimidated."

"What if Mr. DeFore won't leave?"

"You'll have to insist."

When the video was over, Lily asked Mila to invite Earl Jr. over so they could play. Mila called the Ledbetters, but Cleo said Earl Jr. was at school.

"I have to send him every once in a while to avoid extra visits from child services," she explained. "But he'll be home at three o'clock, so bring the kids on over then. He'll be tickled to have company."

Mila agreed, then hung up and told the children that their playtime would have to be postponed. They took the news bravely but seemed sad, so Quin suggested that they take a walk.

"We could go up to the town square and show the kids around."

"It makes me a little nervous having them so far from the house."

Quin frowned. "Has something happened that makes you think they're being watched?"

"No," she admitted.

"Please, Mila!" Lily begged. "Let us go for a walk."

"I guess a short one will be okay," Mila gave in, then she leaned forward and whispered to Quin, "I'll take my gun just in case."

They walked up Hickory Lane and turned on Maple, which led them directly into the heart of Haggerty. As they circled around, Mila pointed out things she remembered and changes that had been made. "That library building is new," she told them. "The city hall and police station look just the same." When they passed a shoe store, she paused to look inside. "Edith's Shoe Emporium," she said reverently. "Miss Edith has wonderful taste in footwear."

Quin laughed. "Do you want to go in and look around?"

"Maybe another time when I'm alone," she said, giving the window display one last, longing glance.

They made their way slowly back toward home. When they turned onto Hickory Lane, Lily pointed a finger. "Whose car is that?"

Mila frowned as she stared at the late-model sedan parked in front of her house. It didn't exactly look familiar, but something about it made the hair on the back of her neck stand up. Then she glanced up onto the porch of Aunt Cora Sue's house and saw two people sitting in Cleo's rattan chairs. One was a thin man. The other was a plump woman with tightly permed blond hair and a tie-dyed, one-size-fits-all pants set that proclaimed a decided lack of taste.

"Just what I need," Mila muttered under her breath.

"Who is that?" Quin asked.

Mila reached down and picked up Ben, then increased her pace. "My mother and her husband."

"Hey, sweetie!" Daphne Roper Edwards Fisk called to her daughter over the porch railing. "I was so thrilled when I found out you were staying here! Aunt Cora Sue must be smiling from ear to ear."

Mila nodded a greeting to Terry and introduced Quin and the Womack children. "What brings you here?" she asked while enduring a quick embrace from her mother.

"Terry has business in Macon, so we were going to spend the night in Albany and invite you out to dinner. But when we got to the hotel, they said you'd checked out, so I called Jamie Monahan. Then he told me all about these poor little angels and all that you were doing to protect them!" Tears filled Daphne's large green eyes. "I convinced Terry to drop me off here and go on to Macon. He can come by and get me in a few days, and in the meantime you'll have an extra pair of helping hands."

Mila sifted through all the information her mother had just given her, and then said, "You're staying *here*? For a few *days*?"

Daphne nodded. "To help you."

"There are only two bedrooms," Mila said.

"I don't mind sleeping on the couch, or we can double up," Daphne replied. She smiled down at the children. "Now let's get you little darlings inside. Terry, would you mind riding into Albany and picking up pizza for lunch?"

"We've got a refrigerator full of casseroles," Mila said irritably.

Daphne addressed Lily and Ben. "We can either have casseroles or pizza for lunch. Who wants pizza?"

Both children raised their hands. So did Quin Drummond. "Sorry," he told Mila. "But I never have really liked my food all mixed up in a casserole."

"I don't care," she said finally, although she did. Why did her mother have to come in and take over immediately? They had been getting along fine.

Daphne sent her husband off for pizza, then followed Mila into the small house. "Oh, everything looks so nice," Daphne praised as she looked around. Her eyes settled on the cross-stitch. "You've even put up my little picture." She turned warm eyes to her daughter, and Mila knew she had read more into it than the action deserved.

"I had to make things look homey so I could pass the child services inspection," she said. They sat in the living room, and Daphne alternated between asking Quin questions and singing songs with Lily and Ben. Both children loved her instantly, much to Mila's disgust.

Terry returned with the pizzas, and they all ate their fill. Then Quin helped Mila put the children down for their naps. When they returned to the living room, Terry was gone. "He had to be in Macon at five o'clock," Daphne explained. She turned to Quin. "So your parents are on a mission?" she asked, just as if she were still an active member of the Church.

"Yes, they're in Argentina."

"Did you serve a mission?"

"I went to Kansas," Quin replied, and although Mila was annoyed by her mother's presence, she was pleased to have this piece of information.

"No surfing there," Daphne said with a smile.

"I guess the Lord didn't want to tempt me," he acknowledged.

"Quin surfs for a *living,*" Mila felt obligated to tell her mother.

"Oh! Have you won a lot of contests?"

"A few," he admitted.

"Tell us about them."

Mila settled back, expectantly. Maybe having her nosy mother around wasn't going to be so bad after all.

At three o'clock they took the children over to the Ledbetters and introduced Daphne to Cleo and Earl Jr. The Ledbetters were predictably taken with Daphne, and Mila felt her resentment grow.

When it was time to go home, Daphne walked ahead with the children, leaving Mila and Quin following in her wake. Mila invited Quin to share a tater-tot casserole for dinner, but he shook his head. "I think I'll just make a sandwich in the camper." He cut his eyes over at her. "That will give you and your mother a chance to visit."

Mila frowned. "You just don't want her to interrogate you anymore."

He laughed. "I didn't mind that. But the two of you don't seem very comfortable together."

"My mother and I were never close."

"A daddy's girl, huh?"

She nodded. "I guess, and I haven't been around her much since she remarried—six months after my father died."

"Ah," Quin said with an understanding nod. "And that seemed like a betrayal to you and your father."

Something about the way he said it made her reaction sound childish. "Yes, that's pretty much how I felt."

"But it's been several years now and you're older. So you can put that behind you."

Mila shrugged. "Now I feel like she's trying to force herself into my life."

"Maybe she thinks that's the only way she can get in," he suggested.

"Well, I'll humor her, but you'd better come over for dessert, just in case we're sitting there staring at each other with nothing to say."

"It's a deal. I'll even bring the dessert."

She couldn't help but smile. "Come about seven."

Mila transferred her clothes from the extra bedroom to the one she would have to share with the Womack children while her mother was in residence. Then she went into the kitchen to help her mother with dinner. While they heated up the casserole, Daphne talked. She told Mila all about Terry's business and how successful it was. "He doesn't travel a lot, but when he does, he insists that I come with him."

As opposed to *her* father, who always traveled alone. Mila got the point.

"We have the nicest little house right on the water. You're going to have to come down for a nice long visit."

"I'll try, if I ever get a break between cases," Mila semipromised, although she had no desire to see the house. Her parents had always lived in post housing.

Quin arrived before she lost her patience, and she gave him a grateful smile. He had double-chocolate ice cream, which they dished up and ate around the small kitchen table. Ben got most of his on the outside instead of the inside, so Quin took him to the bathroom and put him into the tub.

Mila let Lily bathe herself, but stood outside the door as a precaution. When the children were dressed in their pajamas, they ran into the living room and asked Daphne to read the bedtime books. This was a high honor, and Mila couldn't help but feel a little left out.

As Daphne began reading, the doorbell rang, and Mila opened it to find Beau. "Well, I'm glad you could take time out of your busy schedule to visit us," she said as he walked in. The children barely gave him a look before returning their attention to the book Daphne was reading. Somehow that made Mila feel better.

"I can't spare you much time. I have a date at eight o'clock," he told Mila with a wink. "A real date. She's a gymnast from the University of Georgia," he added as if that would help her understand the urgency.

Mila rolled her eyes, then offered Beau tater-tot casserole and double-chocolate ice cream, both of which he declined. Then she told him about Quin's information-gathering mission to Roanoke the next day.

"That's a good idea," Beau said. "Although I'll deny it if you tell the chief I said so. How come you're not going with him?"

"I didn't want to leave the kids with a babysitter."

Daphne looked up. "That's not a problem now. You can leave them with me."

"I can ask Winston to check on them more often while you're gone," Beau offered.

"And Miss Eugenia and Cleo both said they'd help," Quin reminded her.

"It might be too late to get a seat on your flight," she hedged.

"I'll give the airline a call," Quin offered. He pulled out his cell phone and walked into one of the bedrooms.

"A last-minute ticket is going to cost a fortune," Mila whispered after Quin was gone.

"He'd only be able to get a fraction of the information you would," Beau hissed back. "With that laid-back, California attitude, the folks in Virginia would eat him alive. It's a waste of time unless you go too."

"Part of that devil-may-care, easygoing manner is an act," Mila said, and Beau raised an eyebrow. "He's smarter than he lets on."

"Hmm." Beau gave her a speculative glance as Quin returned.

"I got you on the flight," Quin said. "We leave at eight in the morning."

"Which means you need to be at the airport by seven o'clock," Beau advised. He checked his watch. "Well, I don't want to keep my date waiting. Call me when you get back. I'll be anxious to hear what you find out on your trip."

"Just don't mention it to the chief."

"Are you crazy?" Beau asked as he reached for the front doorknob. "If he gets news that bad, he might shoot the messenger."

"He'll hear about our trip," Mila said, walking with him onto the porch. "I just don't want him to throw up any roadblocks in advance."

Beau nodded. "I understand."

"I'd tell you to have fun on your date, but I'm not sure what that would entail."

He laughed. "Yeah, it would probably be better to tell me to behave myself."

"I'll call you on Saturday morning—early."

He waved good-bye, and she went back inside.

* * *

It was dark by the time Mark Iverson left Albany, and for the first time since his marriage he dreaded going home. He'd tried to call Kate a couple of times during the day, but only got the answering machine. Since explaining about Mila Edwards and the Womack children would be a breach of confidence on several levels, he was probably in for more of the silent treatment.

There wasn't a single light showing through the windows of their house, and as Mark pulled into the driveway, he felt a wave of apprehension. Was Kate mad enough at him to leave? She had promised him for better or worse throughout eternity, so he knew she wouldn't go away permanently, but the possibility that she might have made an unscheduled trip to visit her mother in Utah did cross his mind as he unlocked the front door and stepped into the entryway.

"Kate!" he called, but got no response.

He put his keys on the round inlaid wooden table in the middle of the small room, then took a step toward the kitchen, hoping to find a note. He didn't see her until he walked into the dining room. She was standing behind the table in the dark, wearing a lacy black dress.

"Kate?" he said, but she didn't answer. Instead she struck a match, and in the tiny illumination he could see that the table was set for two with their good china. She lit one candle and then another. Some of the tension left his shoulders.

"Welcome home," she whispered.

He drank in the sight of her for a few seconds, then crossed the room and gathered her gently into his arms. "I've missed you." He meant to kiss her once, but it was several minutes before they pulled apart.

"I'm sorry," she whispered. "I know you were just trying to keep me and the children safe." His head lowered toward hers, but Kate put a finger on his mouth. "If I don't get the chicken out of the oven it's going to be inedible."

"Suddenly I'm not very hungry." He reclaimed her lips briefly, then said, "Where are the kids?"

"They're spending the night with Miss Eugenia," Kate replied.

"I presume this means you've forgiven me?" he ventured.

Instead of answering, she moved back into his arms.

CHAPTER 13

When Mila woke up on Friday morning in Theresa Womack's lumpy bed, she looked over into the crib to see Lily and Ben. Both were still asleep. She tiptoed past the other bedroom where her mother was ensconced comfortably on Mila's bed. Based on the soft snoring coming through the door, Mila determined that her mother was also still asleep. So she walked into the bathroom.

For the flight, Mila dressed in a long denim skirt that wouldn't show wrinkles, a brown button-up blouse, and a soft linen jacket. She styled her hair, applied her makeup, then went into the kitchen. While nibbling a piece of toast, she tried to decide whether or not to wake up the children. Before she came to a decision, her mother appeared in the doorway.

"I meant to get up early and have breakfast made before you left," she said. "But I slept in."

"It's okay," Mila assured her. "I'd probably get sick on the plane if I ate more than this."

"You look beautiful," her mother said with a wistful smile. "Impeccable."

Mila had to smile back, and some of her resentment left. "Thanks." She glanced toward the bedrooms. "Do you think I should tell the kids good-bye? I don't want them to wake up and feel like I've abandoned them too."

"Let them sleep. I'll explain," Daphne promised.

There was a soft knock at the back door, and Mila smiled. "That will be Quin."

She opened the door and let him in. He was wearing jeans and a light brown jacket with leather elbow patches. It was almost as if they had coordinated their wardrobes. Her eyes moved from his dark, spiky hair to his soft gray eyes.

"Want some dry toast?" she offered.

"It's tempting, but I already had a bowl of cereal."

Mila turned to say good-bye to her mother and saw that Daphne had started making breakfast. "I want it to be ready and waiting when those babies wake up."

Mila felt a little surge of tenderness toward her mother and pushed it back quickly. "Well, I guess we should go on."

Quin glanced at his watch. "It's a little early still."

She shrugged. "You never can tell what traffic will be like. Am I driving or are you?"

"Either way is fine with me," he said in his accommodating way.

She smiled. "Then I'll drive. I love my car."

Mila turned back to her mother and went over all the emergency numbers, safety precautions, and contingency plans. Finally Daphne held up a hand. "You're going to Virginia, not the moon. I can handle things for a day."

Then there was a knock on the back door. Mila opened it to admit Cleo and Earl Jr. "Good morning," Mila said. "Not going to school today?" she asked the little boy.

"He's been three days this week," Cleo replied. "And since kindergarten isn't mandatory, that's enough to keep child services off my back."

Mila studied the cat-eye glasses perched on Cleo's nose. The frames were leopard print, to match the leotard Cleo was wearing.

"I didn't know you wore glasses," Mila remarked.

"I don't," Cleo said, reaching up to touch the glasses fondly. "But they were so cute I had the optometrist put clear lenses in them for me." She looked around. "Where's Lily and Ben?"

"Still asleep, but I'm sure they'll be up soon," Mila predicted.

"You have a seat at the table, and I'll fix you some hot chocolate," Daphne told Earl Jr., and the little boy obeyed.

Then Miss Eugenia walked in the back door carrying a grocery bag.

"I didn't expect you to come over this early," Mila told her.

"I've already taken Miss Polly her breakfast, so there's no reason to delay. Besides, today is Winston's day off, and I promised if he'd spend it with us, I'd make him a banana pudding."

Mila was pleased by the thought of the police chief being with the children while she was gone. Miss Eugenia started unloading her grocery sack onto the counter. She had whole milk, eggs, sugar, vanilla, bananas, and Nilla Wafers.

Cleo frowned as she examined the items. "I thought you said you were making banana pudding."

"I am," the older woman acknowledged.

"Then where's the pudding?"

"I declare!" Miss Eugenia shuddered. "You can't make a real banana pudding with the instant Jell-O kind. You have to boil custard."

Cleo frowned. "Why?"

Miss Eugenia put her hands on her hips. "Because it's the right way to do it. Now make yourself useful and put the vanilla wafers in the bottom of this casserole dish."

Cleo shrugged, then concentrated on her task as Winston walked in. "Morning ladies."

The kitchen was too small for so many people, and Mila backed up close to Quin.

"You sit in the living room and listen for those children, Winston," Miss Eugenia told him in a no-nonsense tone. "Daphne is working on breakfast, and I'm making your banana pudding so that it will be ready to eat by lunchtime."

Winston didn't have to be told twice. He retreated to the relative safety of the living room, and Mila wished she had an excuse to join him.

"The banana pudding won't be ready to eat until lunchtime because you have to give the cookies time to get soft," Daphne told Cleo from the stove, where she was frying bacon.

"Even I know that," Cleo responded as she spread cookies in the casserole dish.

Then Miss Eugenia hollered, "What are you doing?" and everyone jumped. Mila was relieved when she realized that Miss Eugenia was pointing at Cleo.

"I'm putting the cookies in the bottom like you said," Cleo responded.

"But you're not making sure they're all face up!"

Cleo glanced at the cookies. "They'll taste the same either way. Besides, who'll know."

"We will!" Miss Eugenia cried. "There's a right way to do things, Cleo!"

Cleo shook her dark head. "People keep telling me that, but I can't say that I agree. My mama used to say that there's more than one way to skin a cat, and I figure that goes for making banana pudding too."

"Well, I declare, we may never get this banana pudding finished if you can't follow the simplest instructions," Miss Eugenia said in despair.

"You'd better get on to Albany, honey," Daphne told Mila.

Quin led the way out of the kitchen, and she followed him with a nervous look back at the ladies.

"Don't worry about them," Winston told her quietly. "I won't let them come to blows. Think of it this way: what criminal in his right mind would take on all of them and me too?"

Mila had to smile. "I do feel better now. We'll be back tonight."

They stepped outside, and Winston locked the door behind them.

* * *

Mila and Quin flew from Albany to Atlanta, then had to change planes for the flight into the airport in Roanoke. When they walked into the terminal in Roanoke, Lionel DeFore was waiting to meet them. Mila had to struggle to hide her surprise.

"Mr. DeFore," she said. "We weren't expecting to see you until ten o'clock at Ryathon."

The man smiled. "I know, but I decided to meet your plane and show you some Virginia hospitality. Now if you'll follow me, my car is this way."

Mila reached out and touched his arm. "While we appreciate the offer, we'd rather have our own transportation while we're here, so we'll rent a car."

"Oh, you're welcome to use my car and my driver all day. He'll take you anywhere you wish to go, and he knows his way around Roanoke, which will save you time."

Mila stepped closer. "I'm sure you realize that as a police detective I have to be very careful not to accept any favors that might be misconstrued as bribery."

Mr. DeFore's face fell. "Oh, dear me, yes, I do see."

"We'll rent a car and then follow you to Ryathon."

The Ryathon executive still looked unhappy, but he nodded. "Very well. We'll be watching for you out front. It's a small airport—we won't be able to miss each other."

While they were standing at the Hertz counter waiting for their rental car to be processed, Quin asked why she had refused Mr. DeFore's offer. "Something tells me it doesn't have anything to do with police ethics."

She nodded. "Mr. DeFore's offer of his car and driver might just be a way of keeping tabs on us while we're in Roanoke."

"Or it might just be a friendly gesture of hospitality, like he said."

She shook her head. "Being a police officer has taught me to expect the worst from people, and they usually don't disappoint me." The man behind the Hertz counter handed Mila a set of keys and had her sign for the car. Then they followed him outside. "And when Mr. DeFore asks about our plans for the day, which he will, we'll be vague."

"So he can't follow us?"

"Or talk to the people we want to interview before we get to them. And he may offer to go with us, or take us out to dinner . . ."

"And if he makes any of these very sinister suggestions, we'll refuse?" Quin guessed, a smile playing at the corners of his very nice mouth.

Mila decided to overlook his teasing tone. "We will definitely refuse," she murmured, dragging her eyes from his lips.

Quin and Mila climbed into the rental car and drove around to the front of the airport where a sleek black car was waiting. Mila pulled in behind it and then followed as the driver moved into the sparse traffic.

"I get the impression that you don't like Mr. DeFore," Quin said as they drove.

"Actually, that's true," Mila admitted.

"What is it about him that bugs you?"

"He's a little too . . . smiley."

Quin raised an eyebrow. "Smiley?"

"He's always smiling—even when it's not appropriate."

"It might just be a nervous habit, like nail biting."

"Whatever it is, the man gives me the creeps. And I fully expect him to try some stall tactics once we get to Ryathon."

"Why would he want to stall us?" Quin asked.

"Maybe *stall* was a poor choice of words. I think he'll try to make us waste our time—thereby keeping us from learning all we can."

"Why?"

"Because I'm convinced that Ryathon Pharmaceuticals is somehow behind Theresa Womack's disappearance."

While Quin considered this, Mila followed Mr. DeFore's car into a parking lot in front of a modern steel and glass complex. "Impressive," Quin said.

"There's a lot of money in drugs, even the legal kind," she responded with a quick smile.

Mr. DeFore stepped from his vehicle and hurried toward them. "Let me take you inside, then I'll give you the grand tour."

"Could we just get an abbreviated tour?" Mila asked with a meaningful glance at Quin. "We're really pressed for time."

Mr. DeFore seemed disappointed, but nodded. "Of course, whatever fits your plans best. Then I've made reservations for lunch."

Mila cut her eyes over at Quin. "We appreciate that very much, but we don't have time for a sit-down lunch on this trip. We'll just grab a sandwich and eat in the car between stops."

Now Mr. DeFore looked crushed. "But Roanoke is such a lovely place, and if you rush through your visit, you'll miss so much!"

"Maybe we can come back another time for fun, but this trip is strictly business," Mila told him. "Now, let's start that tour."

Mr. DeFore took them through the glass doors into a sumptuous lobby. He pointed out the huge oil paintings of the company's founder, his son, and grandson on the lobby wall. "The grandson, Brandon Ryan, is the current CEO."

"Will we be meeting Mr. Ryan today?"

"He's not on the schedule, but I'll check and see if he's available."

They went through the administrative area quickly, took a cursory glance at the marketing and public relations area, then spent almost an hour in the production shed—which was the size of three football fields.

"So is this where all of Ryathon's drugs are made?" Mila asked.

"Oh, no!" Mr. DeFore said with a little laugh. "We can only handle the production of experimental drugs here. We have two manufacturing plants in Nevada and three in Mexico." Mr. DeFore excused himself to confer with the receptionist. When he returned, he said that Mr. Ryan was available to see them now, so they would interrupt their tour at this point.

"Before we leave, I'd like to see the lab where Larsen worked," Mila said. "And we want to talk to some of his coworkers."

Mr. DeFore nodded. "Of course, but we'd better catch Mr. Ryan while he has a break in his schedule."

If the parts of Ryathon Pharmaceuticals they had seen up to this point spoke of wealth, the executive suite fairly screamed it. Crystal chandeliers cast a tasteful glow on dark wood-paneled walls. The furnishings were understated and tasteful and, Mila guessed, probably priceless antiques. She knew such trappings were intended to intimidate, and she tried to resist, but she couldn't.

Mila had expected Brandon Ryan to be the stereotypical business tycoon, but in reality he was a slight, colorless man. His pale blond hair was a little too long and had a tendency to fall in a clump onto his forehead. In spite of the warm spring weather, he was wearing a sweater, and his watery-green eyes and pasty complexion indicated that he was in less-than-excellent health.

He met them at the door of his huge office as his secretary, a modern-day Attila the Hun, ushered them in. Mr. DeFore made introductions, then Brandon Ryan motioned to a grouping of leather couches and chairs that managed to almost look cozy.

"Please have a seat. Detective Edwards, I understand you're here to learn what you can about Larsen Womack."

Mila nodded. "Yes, sir, and we appreciate you allowing us access to your facility."

Brandon Ryan waved a hand. "Please, call me Brandon."

Mila had no intention of doing so and made a mental note not to address him by any name for the rest of her visit. "What can you tell us about Mr. Womack?"

The CEO crossed his legs and leaned forward, a look of what seemed like genuine sadness on his face. "I didn't know him well, of course. I have over two thousand employees at this facility alone."

"We understand."

"But on the few occasions that I was around him he seemed like a nice guy, and his department always got high ratings during evaluations."

"Did you personally witness any of his erratic behavior right before he was fired?"

Mr. Ryan shook his head. "No. He did make an appointment to see me a week or so before, but he didn't show up."

"That is typical of his behavior during those last few weeks of his employment," Mr. DeFore contributed.

Mila resisted the urge to give their voluntary guide an irritated look and continued her questioning of Mr. Ryan. "And you don't know what he wanted to talk about?"

Mr. Ryan seemed surprised by this question. "Well, I just assumed he wanted me to help him keep his job."

"You think he planned to confess and then lost his courage?"

"That's what I assumed."

"We understand that you have a new drug coming out soon." Mila kept her tone aggressive.

"Yes," Mr. Ryan confirmed. "We are very proud of it."

"I guess it will make you a lot of money."

Mr. DeFore looked scandalized, but Mr. Ryan smiled. "Yes, of course we stand to make a great deal of money off the new drug, but we have millions of dollars invested in it, so we won't show a profit for a year or so. That's why the FDA keeps competitors from copying new drugs for a time."

"To give the developing company time to recover their costs," Mila guessed.

"Yes."

"Has there been any controversy over this new drug?"

"Very little," Mr. Ryan replied. "It has few side effects, and the benefits far outweigh the drawbacks."

Conscious of the minutes that were passing quickly, Mila stood. "Well, thank you for your time."

"Let me give you my card." Mr. Ryan pulled an embossed business card from his shirt pocket. "Please feel free to call me on my private line if you think of any more questions."

"That was nice of him," Quin whispered to Mila as they walked into the hall.

"A little too nice. He's hiding something," she hissed back, and Quin laughed softly.

"You don't trust anyone!"

"And I predict that after participating in this investigation you'll have learned to think just like me." Mr. DeFore was holding an elevator for them, so they hurried to catch up. As they rode down to the laboratory where Larsen Womack had worked, Mila thought about her prediction and felt a stab of regret. Quin was so open and trusting. She hated to think about him becoming as cynical as she was.

CHAPTER 14

The laboratory was just what Mila expected—modern and immaculate. Mr. DeFore led them through it, then took them to the submission division where Larsen had worked.

"I'd like to see his office," Mila requested. "I'm trying to get a feel for him, so it would be helpful."

"This whole wing was remodeled after the fire," Mr. DeFore reported sadly. "And there was so much smoke and water damage, everything had to be discarded."

"So nothing that Larsen Womack used is still here?"

Mr. DeFore shook his head. "Not so much as a stapler. It was all insured," he explained. "It didn't make sense to sift through the soggy mess trying to recover bits and pieces that were still functional."

Mila had to admit that the excuse was reasonable, but something about Larsen Womack being completely obliterated made her uneasy. "Can we speak to his coworkers now?"

"You're welcome to speak to anyone," Mr. DeFore told her. "We sent out a company memo instructing everyone to cooperate completely."

Mila gave Quin an "I-told-you-so" look.

"Let me step into the lab and see if they can stop what they're doing now."

Once Mr. DeFore was gone, Mila said, "They sent around a company memo."

Quin smiled. "Why is that bad?"

"If I got a memo from my boss telling me that a police detective was coming to investigate an employee, telling me to cooperate completely, between the lines I would read, Be careful what you say."

"But then, you have a very suspicious nature," he reminded her.

She nodded. "It's part of my job."

Mr. DeFore returned and cheerfully ushered them into the lab. He introduced them to the staff, which consisted of a man named Pierce Maxwell—who had replaced Larsen—a secretary, and two lab assistants. "Is there someplace where we can talk to them *privately*?"

Mr. DeFore pointed to his left. "You may conduct your interviews in this empty office." Then he turned to the secretary. "And Mrs. Harmon will call me when you're ready to complete the tour."

As Mr. DeFore left the lab, Quin leaned forward and said softly, "At least he didn't try to sit in on your interviews."

The office is probably bugged, she wrote on her notepad and held it up for him to see.

"Thanks for the warning," he whispered. She nodded, then turned the page in her notebook, trying not to think about his mouth in such close proximity to her ear. She could hear him laughing quietly as she asked Pierce Maxwell to join them in the temporary interview room.

"Thank you for giving us a few minutes of your time, Mr. Maxwell," Mila began once they were all settled. "Or is it Dr. Maxwell?"

"I do have a PhD, but I don't use my title. Please call me Pierce."

Mila made a notation, then said, "Ryathon seems like a wonderful place to work."

Pierce nodded. "It's fantastic. I still feel like pinching myself to be sure I'm really here."

Mila raised an eyebrow. "You haven't been employed long?"

"Only about a month," he replied.

"So you didn't even know Larsen Womack."

He shook his head. "No."

"Based on his work, what can you tell me about him?"

Pierce Maxwell looked surprised by this question. "I haven't seen any of his work. I guess it was all destroyed in the fire."

Mila tapped her pen against the little notepad. "You're telling me that Larsen Womack worked here for five years and every piece of paper, computer disk, or application that he wrote to the FDA was destroyed?"

"Yes," Pierce confirmed. "You could probably get copies of the applications he filed with the FDA from them, but I haven't seen anything."

"Well, then maybe you could just tell us generally how things work here," Mila suggested, her lips pursed.

For the next few minutes, Pierce Maxwell explained the research and submission process at Ryathon.

"So you test the products before you submit them to the FDA?" Mila asked.

"Oh, no!" Pierce seemed to think this was very funny. "All the testing is either done on site where the drugs are manufactured, or a company is hired to handle the testing. Mostly what I handle is paperwork."

Mila remembered Mr. DeFore's comments about Larsen being a plodding, unimaginative scientist, perfect for the boring job of submitting new products to the FDA for approval.

"If you don't do any testing here, then why do you need this expensive lab, and why do you need two research assistants?" Quin asked, and Mila sent him a look of respect. It was a good question.

"Occasionally the FDA will request additional tests, and if they aren't too extensive, we do them here. But Womack did a lot of *unrequired* testing. It was like a hobby for him."

"And Ryathon didn't mind?"

"No, from what I understand, the CEO liked Womack and considered his lab sort of a pet project. Apparently he felt that the continuous testing reduced the number of mistakes making it to the market."

Mila felt Quin's eyes on her, but resisted the urge to glance at him.

"What kind of mistakes?" Quin asked, and Mila felt like a proud parent. He was learning fast.

"Minor stuff, too much of this or too little of that. Sometimes there are problems in production." Pierce looked around. "We're kind of scaling back now. One of the research assistants has taken a job in another department."

"So Mr. Ryan doesn't want you to continue Larsen's practice of testing everything?"

The scientist shrugged. "Guess not."

"Well, thank you for your time," Mila said with a tone of dismissal. "If we think of anything else, we'll call you."

"Would you like me to send in one of the assistants?" he asked as he left, and Mila nodded.

"You were right about Mr. Ryan not being completely honest with us," Quin whispered. "He knew Larsen better than he admitted."

"And the question is, why did he lie?"

Before they could continue their conversation, a pretty young woman walked in and sat in the chair vacated by Pierce Maxwell. "My name is Stacy Logan," she told them.

After providing their names, Mila asked, "How well did you know Larsen Womack?"

The girl giggled. "Not at all. I just graduated from Virginia Tech at Christmas and was hired at the end of March." She waved vaguely toward the lab. "Sandy's new too."

This time Mila did allow herself a quick glance at Quin before she continued her questioning. "So, no one in this department actually worked with Larsen Womack?"

"Only Carol, the secretary."

"Well, thank you for your time, Miss Logan. Would you please ask Carol to come in?" Once the girl was gone, she spoke quietly to Quin. "Maybe they were so cooperative because they knew we couldn't find out anything from people who didn't know Larsen."

Carol Harmon appeared to be in her early forties. Her hair was frosted a soft, streaky blonde to hide the gray, and she was fit and trim, like someone who exercised daily. She would have been attractive except that her face had a pinched, bitter look.

"From what I understand you are the only person left in the department who actually knew Larsen Womack," Mila began.

Carol leaned back in the chair, making herself comfortable. "I guess that's true."

"Why don't you tell us a little bit about yourself."

"Well, I've been with Ryathon for almost eighteen years. I'm divorced, no children."

"Do you enjoy working here?"

"Oh, yes. My major in college was chemistry, and I loved all the lab work and experiments that Larsen used to do."

Mila raised an eyebrow. "Ryathon was fortunate to find a secretary with a chemistry degree."

Carol gave a self-deprecating laugh. "Oh, I didn't graduate. My husband was a medical student, and I had to interrupt my education and take a secretarial job here to get him through school." She looked up and shrugged. "Age-old story. He let me put him through school, then dumped me for another woman. I think about going back and finishing my degree sometimes, but . . ."

That explains the bitterness, Mila thought. "Can you tell us what happened to Larsen Womack?"

The secretary looked uneasy. "I really don't like to talk about that."

"Why?"

Carol glanced out into the lab. "I don't want to be called upon to testify against him if they ever catch him."

Mila closed her notebook. "I'm with the Albany police, and we don't have any actual jurisdiction here. Mr. Ryan is allowing us to question you, but it's not really official."

"So you're saying that whatever I tell you can't be used against Larsen?" she clarified.

"That's what I'm saying."

Carol took a deep breath, then said, "I worked with Larsen for five years. He was the best boss in the world—quiet and a little nerdy, but calm and steady. He never overreacted to a problem, he arrived for work every morning at seven fifteen, he always brought a sack lunch, and he even had particular ties for each day of the week. He was a very routine-oriented person."

"But that changed?"

"About a year ago Ryathon hired a research assistant named Belinda Wallace." The lines around Carol's mouth deepened as she remembered. "Belinda was a flirt, and it amused her that Larsen was shy and happily married. So she made up her mind from the start to corrupt him."

"And was she successful?"

Carol nodded. "It was like a military campaign for Belinda. First she claimed to have car problems and asked Larsen if he could give her a ride to work and back every day."

"And he agreed?"

"Unfortunately," Carol confirmed. "When she saw that Larsen brought his lunch, she started bringing hers too. He ate at his desk, but she talked him into going outside to the picnic tables. And she was always going into his office, distracting him."

"How?"

"She'd say she was wearing a new dress or new shoes and ask him if he liked whatever it was." Carol leaned forward and lowered her voice. "One time I even heard her say she was wearing new underwear."

"Did she show her underclothes to Larsen Womack?"

"Not that I saw, but I couldn't keep an eye on them all the time," Carol said wearily. "Then they started working late." Carol gave them a significant look.

"How late?"

She shrugged. "Belinda told me that they just waited for everyone else to clear out, then they would go to her house and spend the evening together."

"Do you think that was true?"

"Belinda wasn't above lying, but Larsen started looking so guilty that I think there was at least some truth to it. Then one day he came in smelling like alcohol, wearing the same clothes he'd had on the day before. He had a wild, terrified look in his eyes, and when Belinda told me he'd spent the whole night with her, I believed it."

Mila heard Quin sigh, but kept her attention on Carol. "Do you also believe that Larsen Womack stole the money from the company account?"

She nodded. "It might have been Belinda's idea, but Larsen was the only one who could sign the checks."

"Do you know how his wife felt about all of this?"

Carol frowned. "The wife is always the last to know. I'm proof of that."

"Tell us about the day of the fire."

Carol rubbed her hands along her arms as if she felt a chill. "Larsen was late, but then that had become the usual. Belinda wasn't here either. Mr. DeFore came in and told me to call him as soon as they arrived. Larsen finally got here about noon, but Belinda wasn't with him. He said she was taking the day off and he had just come in for a few minutes."

"Did you call Mr. DeFore?"

"I warned Larsen first, but then I called him. I felt I had to."

Mila nodded. "We understand. What happened when Mr. DeFore arrived?"

"They went into Larsen's office, but their voices were so loud that I could hear most of what was said," Carol reported. "Mr. DeFore told Larsen about the shortfall in the submission account and accused him of taking it. Larsen laughed and accused Mr. DeFore of trying to frame him. I heard a crash in the office, and Mr. DeFore came out. He said Larsen was becoming violent and told me to leave the area while he called security to come and take Larsen from the building."

"When did the fire start?"

"I'm not sure. It was total pandemonium for a while. The security guards arrived, and the police were called, and then we noticed the fire. In the process of trying to put it out, I lost sight of Larsen. By the time the police arrived, he was gone."

"Do you think he started the fire on purpose?"

"That's what Mr. DeFore thinks," Carol said. "But even in the confused state Larsen was in, I can't imagine him risking the lives of all the people at Ryathon."

"So how do you think the fire started?"

"I think it was an accident and Larsen just took the opportunity to leave."

"What happened to Belinda Wallace?" Mila asked.

"I don't know. She never came back to work after that, and they finally hired a replacement."

"What about the other research assistant?"

"Her husband got transferred, and they moved to Wyoming."

"Did you ever talk to Theresa Womack after all this happened?"

Carol shook her head. "No, but she e-mailed me occasionally."

Mila sat up straight. "Have you heard from her lately?"

"No, not for a couple of weeks."

"What did she say in her e-mails?"

"Mostly asking if I'd heard from Larsen, and once she asked if I knew anything about an express mail package Larsen had prepared for the FDA."

"What did you tell her?" Mila asked, trying to sound casual.

"I told her all I knew was that Larsen was carrying it around the morning of the fire. I didn't know if he took it with him when he left, or if it was destroyed in the fire."

They thanked Carol Harmon and exchanged cell numbers in case they needed to get in touch with each other. Then Mila asked the secretary to call Mr. DeFore and tell him they were done.

Mr. DeFore was back in minutes and again offered to take them out to lunch, but Mila said they had several other stops to make and their flight left that evening. She thanked him again for his cooperation, then they walked out to their rental car.

"Well, what do you think?" she asked Quin. "You knew Larsen. Is what Carol Harmon said possible?"

He didn't look happy. "She had worked with him for five years," Quin began slowly. "She seemed to know him well, and the changes she described were gradual. I guess it's possible that he let a flirtation go too far."

"With the help of a conniving woman," Mila said with a nod.

"I'm not saying that's what happened," Quin added. "But I guess I have to say it was possible."

"That was interesting that Theresa e-mailed Carol about the package."

"It doesn't make sense. Why would Theresa be asking about that package?"

"That's why it's interesting." Mila pulled out the road map.

Once they were headed toward Bishop Lytle's dental office, Mila said, "Carol didn't like Belinda much."

"Yeah, I noticed that," Quin agreed with a smile.

"She could have been making all that up to cast Belinda in a bad light."

"Why?" Quin asked. "The woman doesn't even work there anymore."

"Maybe we should determine exactly where she is," Mila said and pulled out her cell phone. She called Beau and asked him to run a check on Belinda Wallace. He came up with a Steve and Belinda Wallace and gave her the address. Mila repeated it for Quin, who wrote it down. "Can you check a little more? See if she's still married or divorced, that kind of thing."

"Sure," Beau agreed. "As long as the chief doesn't catch me."

"If he says anything, tell him you're doing it for me. You know how much he loves me."

Beau made a choking sound as Mila said good-bye.

She smiled over at Quin. "We'll add that address to our tour of Roanoke."

The meeting with the bishop didn't take long. He reaffirmed his opinion that Larsen was a good husband and father, although he admitted that his last interview with Larsen had taken place in October of the prior year. After they left Bishop Lytle's dental office, they went through a Burger King drive-through and ate their lunch while searching for Belinda Wallace's house.

The research assistant's neighborhood was a fairly new development where the houses were similar and built very close together. They identified Ms. Wallace's house from some distance because of the tall grass and collection of newspapers on the driveway. They walked up the sidewalk and rang the doorbell, just to be sure. The sound of the bell echoing inside confirmed their suspicions.

"She's gone," Quin said.

"And has been for some time," Mila agreed. She led the way to the house on the right, but no one was home. A Doris Creel, who was more than willing to talk, occupied the house to the left.

"I retired from the phone company a few years back, and after my husband died I decided I didn't want to fool with a big yard and all that. So I bought this garden home," Mrs. Creel said by way of introduction.

"How long have you known Ms. Wallace?" Mila asked.

"She and her husband moved in about a year ago," the woman reported. "But I think they're separated. Belinda never would give me a straight answer on that, but I haven't seen him around for months."

Mila pulled out a picture of Larsen Womack and showed it to Mrs. Creel. "Do you recognize this man?"

The woman nodded. "Oh, yes, that's Belinda's new boyfriend."

"What makes you say that?" Mila asked, displeased.

"Because she told me so," Mrs. Creel replied. "Besides, he was over at her house all the time."

"Do you know how long Ms. Wallace has been gone?"

"She packed up and left on a night sometime before February 20. I already told the police all this."

Mila couldn't make herself refer to Theresa's husband as Belinda's boyfriend when she pointed at the picture. "Was this man with her?"

Mrs. Creel thought for a minute. "You know, I think he was."

"Could you identify him?"

"Heavens no. It was dark, and I only caught a glimpse of him."

"You don't happen to have a picture of Ms. Wallace, do you?" Mila asked on impulse, and the woman smiled.

"As a matter of fact I do." She left the door for a few minutes and returned with a snapshot. "This was taken at our neighborhood cookout last July. There's Belinda." She pointed to a plump woman with mousy brown hair.

"Do you mind if I keep this?" Mila waved the picture. "I'll return it after I make a copy."

"I don't mind," Mrs. Creel said. "Is Belinda in some kind of trouble?" she added with just a touch of malice.

"I don't know," Mila replied honestly. "Thanks for your time."

As they walked back to the car, Quin said, "Her story corroborates Carol Harmon's."

"Doesn't it, though," Mila returned grimly, then she looked down at the snapshot in her hand. "Belinda's not very attractive. It's hard for me to believe that Larsen would sacrifice his family for her."

"Actually, her plainness makes her more believable to me," Quin said with obvious reluctance. "A beautiful woman would have intimidated Larsen completely."

They climbed into the car, and Mila added the picture of Belinda Wallace to her Womack file. Then, using the map, Quin gave her directions to the Womacks' neighborhood.

This was also a new subdivision, but it was in a rural area with large houses and generous lots. The Womacks' house was a two-story colonial, and in spite of the fact that no one had lived there for several months, the grass was neatly cut. As she pulled up to the curb, Mila glanced over at Quin and saw a sad look on his face. The fact that he was personally involved with the Womacks came back to her forcefully.

"This must be hard for you," she said quietly. "Seeing the house empty."

He nodded. "But I have to do whatever I can to help Larsen and Theresa—even if it hurts."

She smiled. "That's the spirit. Now let's go interrogate the Womacks' neighbors."

They talked to ten different neighbors and found out very little except that they were taking turns cutting the Womacks' grass. Mila was impressed by their neighborliness until someone admitted that they were doing it to keep the subdivision as a whole from looking trashy. Mila thought about Cleo and about Miss George Ann's assertions that the Ledbetters were trashy. And yet Earl Sr. had cut the grass at Aunt Cora Sue's house out of simple kindness. Deciding that the definition of trashy was varied between individuals, Mila continued with her questions.

They left the Womacks' neighborhood two hours later and headed for the airport. As they drove, they discussed their findings. "Other than Pierce Maxwell's comment about Larsen's lab being a pet project of Mr. Ryan's and Carol's claim that Theresa e-mailed asking about the express mail package, we don't know much more than we did when we came," Quin said.

"We do have a name for his supposed girlfriend," Mila pointed out. "And a picture."

This caused a concerned look to cloud Quin's features. "It sure does look like Larsen was involved with Belinda Wallace and that they probably ran off together."

"Maybe," Mila replied, frowning at the road in front of her.

He seemed surprised by her response. "What do you think?"

"I think that we learned exactly what Ryathon wanted us to hear. The only member of Larsen's department that is still employed there is Carol Harmon, and, amazingly, she gives us a story that supports the theory Mr. DeFore presented in Albany. Larsen went crazy, stole money, was going to steal their research, ran off with the lab assistant."

"You think Carol was lying?"

"I think that's very likely," Mila confirmed. "If you think about it, Carol's story was full of holes. If Larsen and Belinda ran off together, why did Theresa and her children disappear as well? And why would Theresa e-mail asking about the express mail envelope?"

"So Mr. DeFore or Mr. Ryan told her what to say?"

"Or maybe Carol made up the story herself. She almost has a degree in chemistry and would probably be able to read lab results. She had access to every test run in that department, not to mention Larsen's phone messages and computer."

"You think Carol Harmon stole the information on the new drug and then set up Larsen?"

Mila shrugged. "It's a possibility."

"What would be her reason for saying that Theresa asked about the envelope?"

"All I can think of is that Ryathon wants us to think that envelope was burned in the fire along with every other piece of paper Larsen Womack had written during his five years of employment."

"I thought that was weird too."

Mila frowned at the road. "I can't shake the feeling that someone is leading us around by the nose."

"Ms. Harmon?"

"Or Mr. DeFore or Mr. Ryan or even Larsen himself."

Quin sighed. "So we're no closer to solving the mystery than when we got here this morning."

She couldn't help but smile. "Cases are only solved quickly on television. In real life it usually takes weeks of hard, tedious work."

"Well, I'm glad you're with me on this one, because I have a feeling that you don't give up easily."

She was disproportionately pleased by his remark. "It's true that I always do my best, but this case is special. Even though I've never met Theresa or Larsen, I feel connected to them. And I'm crazy about Lily and Ben. So I guess you can say that I'm emotionally involved too." She changed into the exit lane that would take them to the airport. "And all my instincts tell me that the key to solving this mystery is to find Belinda Wallace."

Once they were settled on the plane, headed to Atlanta, Mila opened her notebook and her file and reviewed all the information they had on the Womacks and Ryathon Pharmaceuticals. It was warm in the plane and quiet, since they only had a few fellow passengers, and at some point the gentle vibration of the jet engines must have lulled her to sleep. Her eyes flew open when the pilot announced their descent into Atlanta, and she realized that she was cuddled against Quin Drummond's shoulder.

She jerked away from him, terribly embarrassed. "I am so sorry," she said, although the words didn't come close to expressing the depth of her mortification.

Quin smiled. "You weren't bothering me a bit," he assured her. "In fact, it was kind of nice."

She felt a blush creep up her neck and into her cheeks. "I don't know what came over me. I rarely sleep on planes and *never* on other people."

"You can't let your guard down—even for a minute?" His tone was kind.

"Something like that," she admitted, turning away from his gaze. "You're a very restful person." She paused, then added, "I guess I feel safe with you."

"I'll take that as a compliment."

She managed a half smile. "You should. I never relax."

"Why not?"

"Because for as long as I can remember, I've been trying to prove myself to someone."

Quin looked genuinely perplexed. "Who?"

"Well, first my father. He had very high expectations. Then in school it was my teachers, and in college my instructors. Once I decided to join the Atlanta PD, I had to prove myself to my entire precinct."

"Most people probably feel intimidated when they start a new job."

"It's worse for women," she assured him. "We have to do twice as well as men to get half the credit."

"Being a woman can't be harder on credibility than being a surfer," he said with a smile. "Nobody takes me seriously, but I've never considered life a competition."

She studied him through narrowed eyes. "I think you like it that way. If no one takes you seriously, it gives you an edge."

He laughed, but was saved from a response by the flight attendant asking them to prepare for landing.

Hartsfield-Jackson International Airport in Atlanta was much busier than its counterpart in Roanoke, and it required every bit of their concentration to make their way to their connecting flight, which was loading by the time they arrived. The flight to Albany only took twenty minutes, and soon they were climbing into Mila's cherished Mustang.

"So, you love your car?" he asked as she pulled up to the tollbooth.

She paid for the parking, rolled up her window, then nodded. "Just thinking about it makes me smile."

"I love mine too. It was my dad's when he was a kid."

"I wondered how you were able to . . ." She almost said "afford," but changed quickly to, "find a classic like that."

He smiled, and she wondered if he could read her mind. "Talking him into selling it to me was the hard part," he said. "And I'm not exactly poverty-stricken, you know."

She thought about the little pop-up that he pulled behind his father's Mustang and the fact that he used his parents' address as his own. "I didn't say you were."

This time he laughed. "But that's what you were thinking."

She couldn't deny it and didn't like the feeling that he was making fun of her, so she was quiet for the rest of the drive. When they arrived in Haggerty, they found Winston Jones sitting on the front porch in one of Cleo's rattan chairs.

"Is everything okay?" Mila asked with a nervous glance at the front door.

Winston stood. "Oh, yes, ma'am. Everything's fine. They've fought about everything from how many eggs you should put in a batch of cornbread to whether you should plant your garden before or after Easter. I could handle all that, but when they started talking about . . ." He blushed. ". . . Female things, I had to get out."

Mila controlled a smile. "I can't thank you enough for spending the day here. I know it was a huge sacrifice."

Winston shrugged. "Not that bad. They fed me good." He waved and walked toward his patrol car. "And Monroe Wilhite had a crew here most of the day. I think he's got your central heat and air system installed."

"That's wonderful," Mila said as she unlocked the front door.

Lily screamed with delight when she saw them. Mila greeted the little girl, then Ben held out his arms to her, and she thought her heart would burst. She lifted the baby and carried him with her as Miss Eugenia herded them into the kitchen.

"I saved you some banana pudding," she told them. "One of my better batches, if I do say so myself."

Daphne gave Mila a quick hug, then took Ben from her and pointed to a piece of paper on the counter. "Monroe left that and said you need to send a copy to that child services inspector."

"I'll do it first thing on Monday," Mila said as her eyes scanned the invoice. "I'm sure he also wants me to pay him."

Miss Eugenia laughed. "I'm sure he does."

"I fixed a pot roast for supper, and there's plenty left," Daphne said, elbowing her way in front of Miss Eugenia. "Would you rather have some of that first?"

Quin gave Daphne a charming smile. "Lunch was a hamburger eaten in the car hours ago, so I would love some of that roast." He turned to Miss Eugenia. "But I'll be sure to save room for pudding."

"I'll bet you've never had a real banana pudding before," Miss Eugenia predicted as Daphne fixed plates for Mila and Quin.

"You're right, but I'm really looking forward to trying some," Quin replied, with a covert wink at Mila.

"There's plenty more if you're still hungry after eating this," Daphne told Quin as she put his plate on the table in front of him. "And you'd better eat more than the vegetables," she told Mila, putting a second plate in front of her daughter.

Mila didn't even pretend to hide it when she rolled her eyes. "I told you, I can't please anyone." She ate a few bites of the tender roast, then asked, "Where's Cleo?"

Miss Eugenia sat between Mila and Quin. "She took Earl Jr. home to spend some time with his daddy, but I expect she'll be back now that you two are home. So, what did you find out in Roanoke?"

Mila put down her fork and sighed. "A lot of nothing. Or at least nothing we can make sense of." She succinctly outlined their moderate discoveries and tentative theories.

"I'll bet the secretary was secretly in love with Larsen, and her jealousy of the research assistant caused her to make up the awful rumors," Daphne hypothesized.

Miss Eugenia shook her head. "More likely the president of the company offered her a big raise if she'd tell it his way."

"Anything is possible," Mila said wearily, the long day starting to catch up with her.

There was a quick knock on the back door, and Cleo walked in, followed closely by Earl Jr., who had a play gun in front of him and was searching corners as they went. Beau Lambert brought up the rear.

"The kid's got good form," he said as he watched Earl Jr. check the room.

"Sit down, Detective Lambert," Daphne commanded with an almost girlish smile. "I'll dish you up some supper."

"As much as I'd like to try some of that roast, I have a dinner date and had better not lose my appetite," Beau told Daphne as he sat beside Mila.

Cleo took the seat next to Beau and asked, "So, how was it?"

Mila repeated her spiel with less enthusiasm this time.

"Nice and pat," Beau said with a frown when she finished.

"A little too pat, if you know what I mean," Mila murmured.

"I know exactly what you mean," Beau acknowledged. "But it's going to take a lot more than suspicions to get the chief to change directions on this case."

Mila stabbed a tender carrot. "Tell me something I don't know."

Having circled the kitchen twice and opened every cupboard door and drawer, Earl Jr. stopped his search, apparently convinced that the area was criminal free. He approached Mila and said, "I'm going to have a birthday on Wednesday, and Mama's letting me have a party. You can come of you want."

Mila smiled into the solemn little eyes. "Why, thank you, Earl Jr. We'll plan to be there."

"I can't believe my baby is going to be six!" Cleo tousled the little boy's hair. "It seems like just yesterday we were bringing him home from the hospital."

Earl Jr. started to squirm under his mother's sentimental attention, so she patted the seat of his pants before sending him off to play with Lily and Ben.

"He seems excited about his birthday," Mila said once the child was gone.

"Up until now we've always just had a family party, but since he started school this year he wants to invite his *friends*." Mila could tell that Cleo was pleased that her son was more popular in town than she was. "And I thought, heck, we'll just invite the whole kindergarten at Haggerty Elementary."

Quin raised an eyebrow. "How many children is that?"

"About one hundred," Cleo said, and gasps were heard around the table. "They probably won't all come!" Cleo told the group.

"I love birthday parties," Daphne said, pulling an extra chair up to the table. "Have you chosen a theme?"

"Earl Jr. is determined to have a police party."

"What in heaven's name is a police party?" Miss Eugenia demanded as she dished up generous helpings of banana pudding.

"It's a new idea," Cleo admitted. "But I figure I can pull off the world's first police birthday party."

Mila laughed. "You can play pin the badge on the police officer."

"And you can serve doughnuts with candles in them!" Daphne contributed.

"Hey!" Beau objected. "That's a cheap shot."

"I like Mila's idea about pin the badge on the cop, and it might be fun to fingerprint the kids."

"We have a bunch of those identi-kits with a little snapshot and fingerprint in case the child ever turns up missing," Beau said with his mouth full of banana pudding. "I could get a couple of volunteers to make one for each kid, and then your party would have a practical purpose."

"Thank you." Cleo agreed to this plan eagerly. "Could you ask the volunteers to wear their uniforms? That will make it seem more authentic."

Beau nodded. "Sure. I'll wear mine too, so there will be lots of uniforms around. And I could drive a squad car into your backyard and show the kids some of the more interesting features."

"Like the siren?" Cleo suggested.

"The neighbors will love that," Miss Eugenia muttered.

"Maybe you could show them how to use handcuffs," Daphne ventured. "Or something quiet like that."

"Heck, I could even teach them the Miranda statement," Beau offered.

"That might be going too far," Mila said with a frown.

"I don't believe there is such a thing as going too far," Cleo assured her with a smile. "For party favors I could fix up little bags with a badge and toy guns . . ."

"Oh, no!" Miss Eugenia objected. "That would *definitely* be going too far. People are very sensitive about promoting violence these days."

Cleo shrugged. "Okay. I'll think of something else."

"It sounds like fun," Beau said as he pushed away from the table. "Thanks for the banana pudding, Miss Eugenia. And what time do you want me and my fellow officer here on Wednesday?" he asked Cleo.

She considered this for a few seconds, then said, "Four thirty."

"Will do," he agreed.

Mila walked Beau to the front door and stepped out on the porch so they could talk in relative privacy. "What will it take to get the chief to reconsider his position about Larsen and Theresa?" she asked.

Beau frowned. "At this point he doesn't really have a position. The FBI has decided that a few anonymous phone calls accusing Ryathon of wrongdoing doesn't justify reopening their investigation. The case of Theresa Womack's disappearance is unsolved, but not a priority. There have been no further attempts to search the Womacks' things or approach the children." Beau held out his hands in a little shrug. "For now you're just taking a leave of absence to babysit until arrangements can be made for the kids."

It was what she expected him to say, but she was still unhappy. "Quin says his parents have received an early release from their mission so they can apply as foster parents for Lily and Ben, at least temporarily. They should be back in the States within a week or so."

"That sounds like the best thing for everyone. The kids will have some stability with people who love them, and you can get back to work."

"Hmm," Mila responded noncommittally. "So we're giving up? On the case, I mean?"

"Unless you can come up with something substantial and change the chief's mind. What's the next step in your unofficial investigation?"

"I need to find out all I can about Belinda Wallace."

"She's the woman Larsen Womack was involved with?"

Mila grimaced. "Supposedly. I'm convinced that finding her will answer most of our questions." She glanced up at him. "That's where you come in."

He smiled. "You want me to look for Ms. Wallace?"

She nodded. "If you can do it without getting in trouble."

"I've already got Dorcas working on it."

Mila was surprised. "She's bound to know you're doing it for me."

"She knows."

"Then why is she doing it?" Mila asked.

"Because she's a nice person and she owes me a favor. I'll let you know as soon as she finishes her search. Now I'd better go." He gave her a quick wink. "Don't want to keep my date waiting."

Mila rolled her eyes. "Tell your niece hello for me."

He scowled, then headed down the steps toward his car. As Mila watched him go, she wondered why Dorcas James was helping her, especially since it meant being on the opposite side of the Womack issue from Chief Monahan. Deciding to wait until her head was clear before trying to analyze the situation, Mila went into the kitchen. Miss Eugenia was clearing the dessert dishes, and Daphne was washing them while Cleo told them about her plans for the official invitation to Earl Jr.'s birthday party. "I thought I'd fix it up like a warrant for their arrest," she said.

"Heaven help us," Miss Eugenia muttered.

Daphne bravely took a stand against the older woman. "I think that sounds cute."

Miss Eugenia put the remnants of her banana pudding in a small bowl and covered it with plastic wrap. "I'll take this to Polly tomorrow. This will cheer her up almost as much as a juicy piece of gossip." She glanced at Mila, who was yawning. "Cleo, collect Earl Jr. and let's head home. Mila is exhausted."

After their guests left, Mila offered to help her mother put the children to bed, but Daphne declined her assistance. "I can handle these precious babies. You go on and get some sleep. I can get these babies ready for bed and slip them into the crib without waking you."

Too tired to argue, Mila gave Lily and Ben a hug, then said good night. Once she was settled in Theresa Womack's bed, she closed her eyes and let her mind drift back to that moment on the plane when she woke up with her cheek pressed firmly against Quin Drummond's shoulder.

CHAPTER 15

On Sunday morning Daphne let Mila sleep in until eight o'clock. By the time she showered, dressed, and walked into the kitchen, the Womack children were scrubbed, fed, and ready for church.

"I don't know how you do it, Mom," Mila said, truly impressed.

Daphne seemed pleased by this remark. "I have experience in this area," she replied modestly.

Then Mila noticed that her mother was wearing a Sunday dress. "Are you going to church with us, Mother?" she asked, trying not to sound hopeful.

"Of course," Daphne responded, putting a turkey breast into the oven to cook while they were gone. "How could you handle the children alone?"

"I don't know," Mila admitted. "But I thought you might be uncomfortable at church."

"Why?"

"Well, you've left the Church," Mila reminded her, and Daphne laughed.

"I haven't *left* anything, honey. I just go to church with Terry because that makes him happy. One day you'll find out that in marriage compromises have to be made. I still pay my tithing, and I'm hoping that soon Terry will overcome his prejudices against the Church and let me attend the ward in Tallahassee."

Mila was dumbfounded. "But if you haven't left the Church, why did you send me the Families Are Forever cross-stitch and all the LDS books?"

Daphne gave her a quizzical smile. "Why, honey, I thought those books would be a comfort to you. They were mostly your father's, and sometimes holding things that belonged to a person makes you feel close to them. And I didn't want you to forget that families *are* forever."

Mila frowned as she tried to adjust to this whole new way of thinking where her mother was concerned. Daphne walked over and patted her shoulder.

"You look just like your father when you frown," she said.

Mila poured milk onto her cereal. There was a noise at the back door, and she glanced up to see Quin sticking his head inside. She hadn't realized until she saw him that ever since she woke up, she'd been anticipating this moment. His dark hair was spiked up in the artfully casual style that so suited him. He was wearing a crisp, white short-sleeved shirt that set off his deep tan. Across his arm was a suit coat, and in his hand was a scripture case.

"Don't you look wonderful this morning!" Daphne exclaimed, saying what Mila felt but would never dare admit.

A little blush stained Quin's cheeks, and if anything he looked even better. "Thanks. Is everybody ready to go?"

"Mila's eating a bowl of cereal," Daphne said, announcing the obvious, and Mila rolled her eyes at Quin. "Why don't you sit and have a bowl too."

"Thanks, but I fixed my own breakfast."

"Now, there's no need for you to do that anymore," Daphne said. "As long as I'm here, I'll be cooking three meals a day, and you might as well share them with us."

Mila ate a few bites of her cereal to avoid a lecture from her mother in front of Quin, then they filed outside. Lily was given permission to ride with Quin to keep him from being lonely, then the small Mustang procession made its way toward Albany.

When they arrived at the chapel, Miss Eugenia met them at the door.

"I thought you were a Methodist!" Mila cried in surprise, and Miss Eugenia seemed to think that was very funny.

"Why I am! I just come to church with Kate so I can help her with the babies." She shifted a stocky toddler higher onto one hip and said, "This is Charles, and that," pointing at a little girl, "is Emily.

Kate plays the organ, and since Mark has to sit on the stand, my presence is essential."

Mila smiled. "I've no doubt about that."

Miss Eugenia greeted the Womack children and Quin, then turned to Daphne. "Mila told me you were a Mormon, and I'll admit that was quite a shock."

Daphne laughed. "Don't hold it against the Mormons," she said.

Miss Eugenia raised an eyebrow. "Maybe you have some sense after all. Now let's get into the chapel before all the good seats at the back are taken."

Mark Iverson left the stand briefly to welcome them, and Miss Eugenia introduced them to ward members until the meeting started. "This is a special friend of mine," she told them when a tiny man came in, leaning heavily on a walker. "Elmer Stoops, meet Mila Edwards, her mother Daphne, her friend Quin, and her foster children, Lily and Ben."

Brother Stoops was so short that he had to look up to see any of them. He regarded the strange group through thick lenses, then smiled, exposing a set of dentures that seemed too big for his mouth. "Always happy to meet friends of Eugenia's." He turned and scooted his walker forward. "Did you finish *Jesus the Christ*?" he asked Miss Eugenia.

"Yes, and I loved it!" she exclaimed. "Now I'm starting *The Articles of Faith*." She turned to Mila and Quin. "Don't you just adore Brother Talmage?"

Mila blinked twice. "You've read *Jesus the Christ* and are now starting on *The Articles of Faith*?" she confirmed.

"Oh, yes. I've read the Book of Mormon four or five times and the Doctrine and Covenants twice. Then Elmer started me on books like *The Miracle of Forgiveness* and *A Marvelous Work and a Wonder.*"

"Eugenia is an insatiable reader," Brother Stoops told them. "She's already finished *Understanding Isaiah* and is well into the works of Brother Talmage."

Mila was impressed, but a member of the bishopric had stepped to the podium to start the meeting so she couldn't ask more questions. She glanced up at the organ and saw Kate Iverson, who gave her a quick nod of greeting before she began playing the opening song.

After sacrament meeting, Daphne and Miss Eugenia took the children down to Primary, while Quin and Mila waited in the chapel for Sunday School to begin. Kate Iverson joined them a few minutes later.

"I've got to go play the piano in Primary, but I did want to meet you," she said a little breathlessly. "I'm Kate, and you must be Mila." Her inquisitive eyes turned to Quin. "And I guess this is your husband."

Mila felt her heart pound as she shook her head. "No, this is a . . ." for lack of a better word she borrowed Miss Eugenia's terminology, "friend. Quin Drummond."

"Oh," Kate seemed surprised, but recovered quickly. "Well, welcome to both of you. How's motherhood?" she asked Mila.

"Much harder than I expected," she responded honestly.

Kate laughed. "Tell me about it. Well, maybe I'll see you later." With a wave Kate walked out of the chapel.

Mila and Quin sat in awkward silence after Kate left. Kate's assumption that they were married was a natural one, she told herself. They were sitting together at church, so of course she would think they were husband and wife. She was sure that the attraction she felt for the surfer couldn't be that obvious.

"Miss Eugenia is well read," Quin remarked, startling her from her disturbing thoughts. "I've been a member of the Church all my life, and I've never read *Jesus the Christ* from beginning to end."

"Me either," Mila agreed. "Miss Eugenia is a remarkable and confusing woman."

"But that banana pudding stuff she made was wonderful."

Mila shook her head in mock disgust. "Isn't that just like a man. Always thinking with his stomach."

Quin's laugh was a soft, bubbling sound that seemed to come from deep within. Mila was still savoring it when Daphne and Miss Eugenia rejoined them.

"What's so funny?" Daphne wanted to know.

"Quin was just saying how good your banana pudding was," Mila told Miss Eugenia, and the other woman smiled as she settled her substantial girth into the open space beside Elmer Stoops.

She gave Quin an approving look and said, "I'm always glad to meet a man with good taste."

After the meetings, Daphne invited Miss Eugenia to come over for Sunday dinner, but she said she always ate with Kate and Mark. "Polly used to cook for us, but now that she's an invalid, Kate and I share the duty."

"And we sure will be glad when Miss Polly gets back on her feet," Kate said, coming up behind them.

They said their good-byes and headed to the parking lot.

"Now I know *you'll* eat with us," Daphne said to Quin as they walked toward the Mustangs.

"Actually, I've already accepted an invitation to eat with the Ledbetters," Quin said. Mila refused to examine the wave of disappointment that washed over her.

"Well, come later on for dessert," Daphne suggested.

Lily was reaching for the passenger door of Quin's car, but Mila called her back. "You ride home with us, Lily. Your Uncle Quin has plans this afternoon." The words came out a little sharper than Mila intended, and she regretted them as she felt Daphne and Quin both staring at her. Thankfully, Lily didn't object, and soon they were headed back toward Haggerty.

The turkey dinner was delicious, but Mila couldn't enjoy it for thinking about Quin next door eating with the Ledbetters.

"Is your meat dry, honey?" Daphne asked as she watched her daughter push food around on her plate.

"No, it's perfect. I'm just not very hungry."

"I wonder what Cleo is serving," Daphne thought aloud with a shrewd look in Mila's direction.

Mila frowned. "Why would I care?"

"That's a very good question," Daphne acknowledged, then she pointed at Lily's empty glass. "Mila, honey, will you pour Lily some more milk?"

After the children were down for their naps, Mila and her mother settled on the couch in the living room. "Aunt Cora Sue would be so pleased if she could see how you've fixed this place up," Daphne said.

"It's not permanent," Mila told her. "I'm just staying here until the Womack children are settled one way or another."

"Hmm," Daphne murmured.

Mila didn't even want to know what that little sound meant, so she ignored it. "How much longer is Terry going to be in Macon?" she asked, not sure what answer she was hoping for. Her mother was a big help with the children, but her presence was stressful, and Mila had enough anxiety in her life.

"Oh, Terry's through with his business in Macon. I told him to go on home, and I'll catch a bus when things are settled here."

Mila was horrified. "You stayed here just to help me?"

"Partly," Daphne admitted. "But mostly I stayed because Terry says the time has come for me to reclaim you."

Mila raised both eyebrows. "Reclaim me from what?"

"Your father's memory," Daphne replied. "I've let him have you long enough."

Mila felt the air leave her lungs. "What do you mean?"

"Your relationship with your father was so strong that there was never much room for anyone else—even me. The two of you were so alike, had so much in common. Sometimes I felt like you both just tolerated me."

Mila wanted to object, but couldn't think of anything to say.

"That's why it's been so refreshing to live with Terry. He's not the man your father was, but we enjoy each other's company. We both like garage sales and playing cards and watching television, things your father abhorred. And he thinks I'm funny and clever and *smart*."

Mila was brought up short by the truth of this comment. When her father was alive, her mother was never included in any type of intellectual conversation, and if Daphne ever tried to offer an opinion, the colonel treated his ditzy wife with a sort of fond contempt.

"You weren't happy with Daddy?" Mila asked, a little knot of dread forming in her stomach.

"I loved your father," Daphne replied carefully. "But I didn't appreciate his frequent assumption that I was stupid, and I hated the military life. All the moving." She couldn't suppress a little shudder. "I would just get settled in a place, find the dry cleaner who used the right amount of starch, the grocery store that gave double coupons, and make a few friends. Then your father would get transferred again. He'd go off to his new assignment and leave me to pack up our home, sever all ties, and arrive at the new post to start all over again."

"It must have been hard on you," Mila realized for the first time.

Daphne shrugged. "It was lonely. I finally decided it would be less heartbreaking if I didn't *make* any new friends at the next place, but officers' wives are the greatest people in the world, and I couldn't help myself. Your father had his work and you had him. If it weren't for all the friends I made . . ." Her voice trailed off.

"Why didn't you tell Daddy you wanted him to quit?"

"Can you imagine the colonel stuck in a regular nine-to-five job?"

Mila couldn't. "No. But you had a right to be happy too."

Daphne sighed. "I would have been *happy* in Haggerty, but that would have required your father to retire from the army and get a boring little job. No trips to Washington, no speeches at patriotic occasions, no political banquets. He would have been miserable. Since it was either him or me, I figured it might as well be me."

"Why didn't you tell me sooner?" Mila forced herself to ask.

"Well, in order to strengthen my relationship with you, I knew I would have had to step between you and your father. I was afraid that would hurt you. Now I think I was wrong. I should have fought for you instead of accepting life on the outskirts."

Mila adored her father but finally had to face the fact that he never really gave up anything for her. Daphne, on the other hand, had dedicated her life to Mila's happiness. She thought about all the volleyball and softball games and debates that she spent watching the door, hoping that her father would find time in his busy schedule to come. Usually he didn't, but on those few occasions that he did—she was walking on air. With shame, she realized that she never gave a thought to her mother, who never missed any of her activities.

"I was so mad when you married Terry."

Daphne seemed genuinely surprised. "Why, honey?"

"I felt abandoned."

Daphne stroked Mila's cheek. "I invited you to come with us to Florida."

"That seemed disloyal to Daddy. Almost like spitting on his grave."

"Which is what you thought I was doing?" Daphne guessed, and Mila's blush was confirmation enough.

"Why *did* you have to marry so soon after he died?"

"Well, like I said, I'd been lonely for a long time. And there was the issue of money."

"Money?" Mila asked in confusion.

"I got a small pension, but there was only the one insurance policy, and I wanted you to have that."

"I thought it was in my name."

Daphne shrugged. "If your father had ever given a thought to his own mortality, I'm sure he would have gotten a policy with you as the sole beneficiary."

Mila felt the world tilt. "So the insurance money should have been yours?"

"It could have been," Daphne agreed. "But you needed it more than I did."

Mila's hands were trembling, so she clutched them together in her lap. All this time she thought her father had provided for her, but really it was her mother. "You had to marry Terry because you were broke?"

Daphne laughed at this. "Certainly not. Since we always lived in post housing we didn't own any property, but we did have some savings and a few stocks and bonds. My plan was to get a job, and I could have lived comfortably. But then I met Terry, and he had a nice little house in Tallahassee and no plans to ever move. So I accepted his proposal."

"You don't love him?" Mila was aghast.

Daphne laughed again. "Of course I do. Terry is a wonderful person, but I don't want you to think I was miserable with your father. There were many good things about my life with him, and most of the unhappiness was my own fault. And I did put my foot down a couple of times."

Mila leaned forward with interest. "When?"

"Once was when you were born," Daphne told her. "Your father wanted to name you after his grandmother."

"I thought he *did* name me after his grandmother."

"Oh, yes, Mila was his grandmother's name, but not her whole name. Her middle name was Henrietta, and I drew the line there."

Mila reached out and covered her mother's hand with her own. "Thank you." Mila was mostly joking, but tears sprang into Daphne's eyes.

"I love you," Daphne whispered fiercely.

"I love you too, Mom."

They sat in companionable silence until Lily and Ben woke up. Then they took turns reading books. Beau called and Winston stopped by for a few minutes, but Quin never did come and get the dessert that Daphne had promised him. Mila resisted as long as she could, but when Daphne was putting the children to bed, she couldn't take it any longer. She walked out the back door, through the hedges, and to the little campsite in the corner of the Ledbetters' yard.

Quin was sitting in a lawn chair under the shadow of his little porch awning, and she didn't see him until she was very close. "Oh," she cried, startled. "Why are you hiding out here in the dark?"

He laughed, and her knees went weak. "I'm not hiding. I just wasn't expecting company."

Mila looked around. "Did I interrupt something?"

"No." He pulled open another chair. "Have a seat."

He didn't seem compelled to make polite conversation, so after a few minutes of silence she said, "Nice night."

"Yes."

She turned and faced him. "You never came for dessert. I guess you were having too much fun with Cleo, who I might remind you is a married woman."

Even in the dim light she could see his eyebrows shoot up. "I'm very well aware of Cleo's marital status," he assured her. "And I did come for dessert, but I saw you and your mother engrossed in conversation and decided to let you talk."

Mila's unreasonable anger disappeared as she remembered the topic of their conversation. "I've taken my mother for granted and idealized my father."

"It's natural to remember only the best things about loved ones who have died," he said softly. "And I think most mothers are taken for granted by their children."

She stood and paced before him. "But don't you see? I not only revered and adored my father, I built my life around him. The career I chose, the clothes I wear, even the foods I eat are an effort to be like him. But if he wasn't perfect, where does that leave me?"

"Nobody is perfect, Mila," he said softly. "And you shouldn't define yourself based on other people's opinions."

She collapsed back into the chair, her nervous energy spent for the moment. "How are you able to accept people at face value?"

"What makes you think I do?"

"Because you never insinuate that I'm not trying hard enough to solve the case or find fault with my efforts to care for Lily and Ben. You don't even seem to notice if I'm impeccable, and you never correct my grammar."

"You're right. Other people's shortcomings don't bother me. Just my own. But I honestly don't find anything to criticize about you. I think you are just about perfect."

She was astounded. "Me? Perfect?"

He nodded.

She shook her head. "I'm far from perfect. For instance, I don't think I'm cut out for motherhood."

He laughed again, and she gave him an irritated look. She hadn't expected censure from him, but she hadn't expected him to make fun of her either. "I'm glad all my problems are providing you with so much amusement."

"I'm not laughing at you or the difficulties of motherhood. I think it's funny that you thought you could slip into the role of single parent of two young children *without* having problems."

She grimaced. "Conceited, I guess."

"No, but maybe a little overconfident. Don't get discouraged, Mila," he encouraged, and a shiver ran down her spine. Her name sounded different somehow when he said it. "Most mothers get to start off with one child at a time and have nine months to prepare. You got a double dose of motherhood suddenly and can't expect to adjust immediately."

"My mother has been a huge help."

He nodded. "Yes, you're lucky that she chose such a good time to visit."

Mila leaned back and took a deep breath of honeysuckle-scented air. "You always make me feel better," she told him. "Maybe you're in the wrong line of work. You could be a counselor or therapist."

He laughed again, then apologized quickly. "I'm sorry!" He forced his face into a stern expression. "I have been told I'm in the wrong line of work before, but nobody ever suggested that I go into psychoanalysis."

"Let's try and avoid the word *psycho,* especially in relation to me," she requested. "Speaking of your career, do you have a lot of trophies?"

"I have a few," he acknowledged. "I use some of the best ones when I do seminars or endorsements. The rest are stored at my parents' house. I told my mom to throw them away, but she won't."

"How are you able to work the Church into your life as a surfer?" She hated herself for asking, but felt that she had to know.

"Being a surfer is no different than any other businessman who is required to travel a lot," he told her. "I make an effort to be back home on weekends, but when I can't, I arrange for a substitute."

"What's your calling?" she asked.

"I'm a Primary teacher."

She smiled. "That's sweet."

"I teach the eleven-turning-twelve-year-olds," he added. "I have eight boys and two girls in my class."

The smile faded from her face, and she put her hand over her heart. "In which case, you deserve a medal."

He laughed. "That's what the bishop said when I accepted the call."

"Do you have any pictures?" she asked.

"Of my primary class?"

"No. I mean, I wouldn't mind seeing a picture of your class, but I meant surfing pictures."

There was a brief silence, then finally he said, "My mother has a lot. I just have a few snapshots. Most of them are kind of old."

"Can I see them?" she asked, intrigued by the reluctance she heard in his voice.

"Well, I don't know," he hedged.

"What's the matter? Are the pictures all of competitions you lost?"

He laughed again, but now the nervous undertone was unmistakable. "No."

"Then why don't you want to show them to me?"

He cleared his throat. "Because I'm only wearing a bathing suit."

She narrowed her eyes at him. "What kind of bathing suit?"

"Just the regular kind."

"Then why would that be embarrassing? Don't all surfers wear bathing suits?"

"Yes, and I wasn't embarrassed at the time. I was on the beach with other people who were also wearing bathing suits. But here," he waved around at the little campsite, "I just think I'd be uncomfortable."

She considered this for a few seconds. "Would it make you feel better if I put on my bathing suit?"

The pause was longer this time. Finally he said, "No, I don't think that would improve the situation at all."

She laughed, extremely pleased by the unexpected direction the conversation had taken. After a few minutes, she said, "I could probably find some pictures of you on the Internet."

"You probably could," he acknowledged. "But I wish you wouldn't."

She was surprised to realize that at that moment she would have promised most anything to please him. "Okay," she told him, a little breathless.

He gave her the sweetest smile and put a warm hand over hers. "Thanks. Maybe someday you can come to one of my competitions, and I could give you surfing lessons."

"Sounds fun," she said in what she hoped was a casual tone.

He leaned toward her, and as his lips hovered over hers a voice spoke from the Ledbetters' patio. "Mama said for me to come out and sit with you awhile," Earl Jr. reported, then he glanced at Mila. "She said you might be lonesome."

Quin grinned down at her, then eased back into his lawn chair. "Pull up a seat," he invited the boy.

"Just take mine," Mila suggested as she stood. "I'd better get home."

Quin rose from his chair and walked her to the hedge. "Good night."

"You too," she whispered. Then she ducked through the bushes and hurried to Aunt Cora Sue's back door.

* * *

Mila let herself in and found that Daphne had the children asleep and had gone to bed herself. Mila slipped into the bedroom she shared with Lily and Ben and removed a stuffed animal from the crib. She stroked the sleep-warmed cheeks, tucked the sheet securely around Lily, then turned to go, but a little voice stopped her.

"We need to get Earl Jr. a birthday present."

Mila leaned down and spoke to the little girl through the bars of the crib. "You're right, we do. Maybe we can make a trip to Wal-Mart tomorrow. What should we get him?"

"He already has a lot of policeman stuff," Lily remarked.

"Yes, any attempt to increase his law enforcement collection would just be a duplication," Mila agreed. Then a thought came to her. "Unless . . ."

"What?" Lily asked, excitement in her voice.

"I have a real police badge from my job in Atlanta. We could give him that." Mila had been trying to think of a way to get rid of the badge, and this seemed like the perfect opportunity.

"I don't think he has *any* real stuff," Lily said, her expression rapt.

"The badge it is, then," Mila said. "I'll ask my mother to wrap it up for us. Now you'd better go on to sleep."

"Can we still go to Wal-Mart tomorrow?" Lily asked. "Even if we don't buy anything for Earl Jr.?"

Mila smiled. "What would we buy?"

"Maybe some toys for Ben," Lily suggested.

"How about some toys for you?"

The little girl giggled. "That too."

Mila ruffled her hair. "I've always wanted to be a mom," she confessed softly.

This sent Lily into a new fit of giggles. "You can't be a mom!" she cried.

Mila was surprised by the child's innocent vehemence. "You mean because I don't have a husband?"

"No!" Lily squealed. "Because moms are *soft*."

Pasting a smile on her face, Mila told Lily good night and headed for the bathroom. But as she prepared for bed, Lily's words haunted her. She didn't know if the hardness Lily was referring to was mental or physical, but either way it made her sad. After checking to be sure all the doors were locked, Mila climbed into bed quietly so she wouldn't wake the children and tried not to think about her lack of softness or Quin and his ready smile. She didn't succeed on either count.

* * *

On Monday, Cleo and Earl Jr. stopped by on their way to school so that he could deliver their birthday invitation personally. The arrest warrant was startlingly realistic, and Cleo laughed when Mila pointed this out.

"I've seen a few of the real things," Cleo admitted. "Didn't they turn out cute?"

"I don't see how anyone would *dare* not attend!" Mila teased, and Cleo laughed.

"That's the general idea."

As Cleo and Earl Jr. were leaving, Quin stepped up on the porch and invited the children to come to his campsite for a while. "I thought you might need a little time to go over your file on Larsen and Theresa," he explained after the children had run out into the yard.

"That was awfully nice of you," Cleo said, giving Mila a sly look.

"I could use an hour or so," Mila replied, trying to ignore Cleo. "Then we were going to make a trip to Wal-Mart to buy toys. I'm sure the kids would like it if you'd come along."

"Sounds fun," Quin accepted the invitation.

"I hate Wal-Mart," Cleo informed them as if she'd been included in the invitation. "And Earl Jr. has to go to school so he can pass out his birthday warrants. But thanks for inviting us!" She gave Mila another shrewd look as she called to her son and led him through the hedges.

Quin watched her go, then said, "I guess I'd better watch them close. Otherwise Ben might start eating dandelions again."

Mila laughed. "Miss George Ann wants me to get rid of them, and Ben is cheaper than a lawn service."

"But imagine what Mr. Pusser would think if he drove by and saw Ben grazing in the backyard."

"You're right," Mila said with a nervous glance at the road. "Keep a close eye on Ben."

Once Quin and the kids were gone, Mila went back into the house. Daphne was happily cleaning the kitchen so Mila went into her bedroom and called the Albany Police Station. When the receptionist answered she asked to speak to Dorcas James.

"James," the other woman answered a few seconds later.

"Dorcas, this is Mila."

There was a short pause, then Dorcas said, "I presume you want the report on Belinda Wallace?"

"Yes."

"There's no record of a divorce between her and her husband, Steven. He worked construction, did some landscaping, and the odd carpentry job. According to their tax return, he did pretty well financially, but he didn't have an employer, per se."

"So there's no way to tell when or if he left the Roanoke area."

"Right. Although I'm pretty sure he's gone. There's been no activity in their checking or savings accounts for almost three months, and both still have small balances. The house is about to be repossessed for nonpayment. I don't think they would let that happen if they had a choice. I ran a check on both social security numbers, and no one has used them to get a job or a loan or anything."

"So they've disappeared off the face of the earth?"

"That's how it looks."

"Just like Larsen and Theresa."

"The similarities are striking," Dorcas admitted.

"Do you think they're dead?"

"I think that is a very likely possibility. If not dead, they must be in deep hiding."

Mila chewed her lip. "Is this enough to convince the chief to take another look at things?"

"I'll run it past him, but don't get your hopes up."

"Thanks for trying."

After she ended her conversation with Dorcas, Mila went to check on her mother. "Need some help?" she asked when she saw that Daphne was making apple pies.

Her mother shook her tightly curled hair. "No, but I'd enjoy some company."

Mila smiled. "Let me get my notes, and I'll work at the kitchen table."

For the next hour Mila organized her notes while her mother worked behind her. Finally she said, "You remind me of Aunt Cora Sue."

Daphne frowned. "Are you calling me old?"

Mila laughed. "No, I'm calling you a good cook."

Her mother's face brightened. "Oh, well I won't argue with that. Although being a good cook has its drawbacks. It makes you fat."

This was a touchy issue with Mila, and she was sure it didn't come up by mistake. Before replying she looked at her mother, cheeks rosy with the effort of rolling out piecrusts, a dusting of flour on her nose, and she felt an aching tenderness spread through her. She wanted to walk over and put her arms around her mother, but it was too soon for that. So instead, she said, "Weight's not important. It's who you are inside that counts."

The rolling pin in Daphne's hand hesitated for a second, then began its steady movement. "Do you really mean that?" Daphne kept her eyes averted, but Mila could hear the tears in her voice.

"I really do," Mila assured her. "Now, won't you let me peel apples or something?"

Daphne smiled. "No, but I'll let you eat an apple. You're too thin."

"It's what's *inside* that counts," Mila teased.

"That's only true until you keel over from malnutrition."

Mila ate an apple and was headed out to get the children when the phone rang. It was Cornelia Blackwood. "Good morning!" the woman greeted. "Did you enjoy my casserole?"

"We didn't eat it last night. We're saving it for a special occasion," Mila said diplomatically, then she smiled thinking of the doggie feast Cleo was planning.

"Oh, well, that's fine then," Cornelia said. "I started the prayer tree this morning and asked everyone to remember you and those little children to the Lord. And I told the ladies to stay away from your house until further notice."

Mila smiled. "I appreciate both very much."

"Oh, and one other thing. I'm organizing a group of concerned citizens to picket the capitol in August against abortion. Can I add your name to the list?"

"I'm not sure what my situation will be in August," Mila hedged. "I'd better not commit to anything yet."

This seemed to satisfy Cornelia, and after a quick phone prayer Mila was able to end the conversation.

* * *

Since the car seat was in Mila's car, she drove her Mustang on the Wal-Mart adventure. Mila allowed the children to pick out two toys each, and Quin insisted on paying for their selections. They left Wal-Mart and drove to the Health Department where they had the car seat installation approved.

"This all seems kind of unnecessary," Quin remarked as a county employee checked all the straps and buckles.

"Mr. Pusser already disapproves of my Mustang," Mila told him. "I decided I'd better get this car seat installation approved before he decides to revoke my passing grade on the home inspection."

Quin nodded after a second's consideration. "I guess anything you can do to keep Mr. Pusser away is a good thing."

They returned to the house on Hickory Lane in time to eat a Cleo-approved casserole for dinner followed by Daphne's apple pie. After dinner, Daphne sent them outside while she straightened up the kitchen. Mila and Quin watched the fireflies while the kids played with their new toys on the porch. When Daphne joined them, she and Mila reminisced about Cora Sue until it was time for the children to go to bed. Daphne took them inside, conveniently leaving Mila and Quin alone.

"Okay, you've heard all about my childhood," Mila said. "Now why don't you tell me about yours."

Quin shrugged. "What's to tell? I was a regular kid."

"When did Larsen join your family?"

"When he was fifteen and I was fourteen."

"Was it an easy adjustment?"

"Yeah, pretty much. We'd had foster kids before, but most of them were younger than me and just staying until they could be placed for adoption. But when Larsen came, we knew it would be for good."

"Why didn't your parents ever officially adopt him?"

"Larsen didn't want to be adopted. He loved my parents, and he was always telling them how glad he was to be a part of our family. But he didn't want to give up his own name. He felt like that would be disloyal to his biological parents," Quin explained. "And it wouldn't have made any difference. He's my brother, adopted or not."

Mila nodded. "When did you start surfing?"

He leaned forward and rested his face in his hands. "A cousin took me surfing for the first time when I was about seven."

"And you loved it from the start?"

"I felt completely at home," he acknowledged. "My cousin talked to my parents about letting me take lessons."

"That was brave of them to agree."

"My parents are practical folks. They knew they couldn't keep me out of the water, so they decided they wanted me to know everything about safe surfing."

"How old were you when you entered your first contest?"

He had to think for a few seconds. "I think I was about twelve."

"And how long did it take you to start winning?"

"I won my first competition," he admitted, and she couldn't control a gasp. "It was just a small, local event."

"You're a surfing prodigy," she pronounced reverently.

He laughed. "Maybe I *was* a prodigy. Now I'm an old man playing a young man's game."

"You're not old!" she defended him.

"I'll be thirty-two next month and if I don't retire soon, I'm going to start getting beat out by twelve-year-olds."

She nodded. "The new crop of prodigies."

"That's why I want to shift my energies to my surfboard business, but if it flops . . ." He let his voice trail off, the consequences obvious.

"You could start surfing in competitions again."

"Once you stop, it's hard to start again. Especially at a level sufficient to earn a living."

"And support a business," she added with a yawn.

He stood and reached out a hand to pull her to her feet. "Well, I've bored you long enough for one night. At least you should be able to fall right asleep."

She looked down at her hand, still held firmly in his. "You didn't bore me, but I am tired."

He gave her hand a final squeeze and let go. "See you in the morning."

"Good night," she said with a wave. Then she watched as he crossed the lawn and pushed his way through the hedges into the Ledbetters' backyard.

CHAPTER 16

On Tuesday morning, Eugenia stopped by George Ann's house on the way home from taking Polly her breakfast. She had seen George Ann at the Faith Fair meeting on Sunday afternoon and wanted to confront her about the rumors she was spreading, but decided to wait until they could talk privately. On Monday she saw George Ann at Wal-Mart and again at the Haggerty Library, but both times the gossip-monger had disappeared as soon as she caught a glimpse of Eugenia.

Having decided to bring the mountain to Mohammed, Eugenia raised her hand and knocked firmly on the door. George Ann looked less than pleased when she saw the identity of her guest. "I should have known it was you," she said, her lips pursed in disapproval. "No one else is rude enough to call so early."

Eugenia pushed her way inside and came quickly to the point of her visit. "Why have you been telling everyone in town that I'm fat?"

George Ann put a hand to her long neck. "I did no such thing!"

"Are you denying that you told people that you thought I'd gained weight?"

"I may have mentioned it to a few people, but certainly not *everyone* in town!" George Ann replied.

"Why?"

"I was concerned because I know you have high cholesterol and are supposed to be on a low-fat diet."

"So why didn't you just ask me?" Eugenia demanded.

"I was planning to," George Ann assured her, taking a step back in the small entryway, "if I got a consensus, but I didn't want to upset you if your weight gain was just my imagination."

"Humph," Eugenia said disdainfully. Then curiosity forced her to ask, "So, what *was* the consensus?"

George Ann shook her head. "My results were inconclusive. Since everyone in town is scared of you, no one would give me a straight answer."

Eugenia pointed a stern finger at her friend. "So you *admit* that you asked everyone in town!"

"Oh, Eugenia," George Ann responded in obvious despair. Then there was a knock on the door.

"Looks like you have more rude friends than just me," Eugenia said with satisfaction.

George Ann gave her a sour look, then pulled open the door. Cornelia Blackwood stood on the small porch. "Good morning!" she cried with Christian zeal. "I'm here soliciting participants for a march against abortion in August. May I put you both on the list?"

George Ann agreed with a stiff, unenthusiastic nod, but Eugenia shook her head. "Sorry, Cornelia, but I can't march for anything. Arthritis, you know."

George Ann frowned. "I didn't know you had arthritis."

Eugenia waved dismissively as she walked past Cornelia and headed down the porch stairs. "Anyone who lives to be our age has arthritis, George Ann," she said over her shoulder. "Ask everybody in town—they'll tell you."

* * *

Once the children were fed and settled in front of the television watching an educational video, Daphne sent Mila into town to pick up a prescription at Haggerty's only drugstore. On the way back home, Mila couldn't resist a brief foray into Edith's Shoe Emporium. While she was examining a pair of sandals, she heard a voice on the next aisle.

"Can you believe the nerve of that woman? Having a birthday party on Wednesday night?"

In the South, Wednesday night was more closely protected than Sunday, and this comment wasn't surprising. Mila slipped off her shoe and tried on the sandal, then another woman said, "That just proves Cleo's heathenish nature."

That got Mila's attention, and her heart started to pound painfully.

"And as if that's bad enough," the second voice continued. "Can she really believe we'd let our children attend a party at that horrible house after she's thumbed her nose at all of us?"

The first woman responded. "Cornelia said anyone was perfectly justified in declining the invitation and attending church as usual."

"If Cornelia's not sending her daughter, I'm certainly not sending mine," the second voice said with cruel precision.

The first voice was laced with satisfaction. "We'll see how proud Miss Cleopatra Ledbetter is when her son doesn't have a single guest at his birthday party."

The voices moved away, and Mila stood holding the sandal, frozen with shock. The depth of their hatred for Cleo alarmed her, but the fact that the women were going to take out their ill will on Earl Jr. broke her heart. Finally Mila forced herself to put down the sandal and walk out the door. By the time she reached the white house surrounded by gorgeous flowers, she was crying.

"I declare!" Miss Eugenia cried when she saw her. "Did something happen to the children?"

Mila had to think for a minute, then shook her head. "No, Ben and Lily are fine. But I was in Edith's Shoe Emporium a few minutes ago and heard some women talking," she blubbered. "No one's coming to Earl Jr.'s birthday party tomorrow night!"

Miss Eugenia frowned. "I thought Cleo said she invited the whole kindergarten at the elementary school."

"She did! But no one's going to let their children come because they hate Cleo."

Understanding dawned suddenly on Miss Eugenia's features. "Well, we'll just see about that," she said grimly. "Come in and get comfortable. I've got some calls to make."

Mila sat on the couch in the cluttered living room, sniffling occasionally while she listened to Miss Eugenia work. The older woman dialed a number, and when the call was answered, she said, "Renita? This is Eugenia, and I've got something important to tell you, so listen closely. Unless you want everyone in this town to know that I saw your husband coming out of that adult bookstore in Albany, your son will be at Earl Jr.'s birthday party tomorrow night. And bring a nice present." Without waiting for a response, Miss Eugenia disconnected and began dialing again.

"Now we'll go to the heart of the problem," she murmured. "Cornelia? Eugenia. I've heard an awful rumor that no one is planning to attend Earl Jr.'s birthday party tomorrow. Do you know anything about that?"

Miss Eugenia held the receiver away from her ear so Mila could hear the response. "Well, the party is on *Wednesday* night," Cornelia said. "Besides, some people don't feel like Cleo Ledbetter is a good influence for young children. And if people think that, there's nothing I can do."

"You could encourage people to go by the party first and then go to church. That way the children won't be at the Ledbetters' long enough to be negatively influenced."

"You are overestimating *my* influence," Cornelia replied. "I can't force folks to attend Earl Jr.'s party."

"Uh-huh. Well, let me put it to you this way, Cornelia," Miss Eugenia said grimly. "If your daughter is not at that party tomorrow night, I won't support your Faith Fair. In fact, I'll go around town telling everyone who'll listen that it's an awful idea and encourage them not to participate either. Then we'll see how much influence *I* have."

Miss Eugenia continued to hold the phone out, but there was only silence on the other end. Finally Cornelia said, "I'll do what I can."

"That's all I'm asking," Miss Eugenia said. "It would be a shame for all those T-shirts to go to waste. Consider the birthday party an opportunity to witness to an unbeliever. The Lord seemed to put a lot of stock in that sort of thing."

Miss Eugenia made several more calls threatening to resign from boards and discontinue financial contributions to various organizations. Then she hung up the phone. "That should take care of it."

Mila smiled at the old woman. "Thank you."

"Believe me, it was my pleasure," Miss Eugenia said, looking very happy with herself.

* * *

After dinner that night, Mila and Quin settled in the lawn chairs under the awning of his camper. While enjoying the cool breeze, she told him about the birthday boycott and the way Miss Eugenia handled it.

"It was nice of a hardened, suspicious police detective like you to take an interest in a little boy's birthday party."

"Miss Eugenia is the one who took care of the problem."

"But she never would have known if you hadn't told her," Quin insisted, reaching over to take her hand in his.

They were quiet for a few minutes, then Mila said, "You're a puzzle to me."

His eyebrows shot up in surprise. "How so?"

"Well, for one thing, you're so low-key. Beau is always after me to tell him what happened in Atlanta that got me fired, but you've never asked. I can't decide if it's because you didn't know that I was fired or if you aren't the curious type."

His fingers held hers more tightly. "I did know, and I'll admit to a certain amount of curiosity. But I knew that when you were ready to tell me, you would."

"I guess I'm as ready as I'll ever be." She pulled her hand from his and walked a few feet away before she began. "My partner and I had been tracking a rapist-murderer for weeks, but we were always a step behind. Finally we caught up with him in an apartment late one night. His latest victim was already dead, but we had him cold."

She clasped her hands together and forced herself to go on. "While my partner was calling for backup, the suspect ran. I shot at him, but he kept going and disappeared at the end of the hallway. My partner followed him, and I picked up the radio and explained the situation to our supervisor. He told me to pursue the suspect."

"But you were scared to follow him?" Quin guessed softly.

She shook her head. "No, it was the children."

"The children?"

"The dead woman had two little boys. They were crying and clinging to my legs, begging me not to leave them. I told my supervisor about them, but he insisted that I follow my partner." She looked up. "How could I leave those kids there with their mother's dead body?"

He shook his head, obviously understanding her plight. "So you disobeyed the order."

She nodded. "I waited until the backup arrived. By then my partner was back. He'd lost the guy."

"You had a hard choice to make," Quin said slowly. "I can't say you made the wrong one."

She turned tortured eyes to his. "If I'd have left the kids they would have been scared, but alive. I chose to stay, and the next night the guy killed again—another woman dead and three more orphaned children. And this time it was on my conscience."

"Did they catch him?"

"Yes, but not before he ruined another family."

Quin was quiet for a few minutes and when he did speak, he was right behind her. "There's no way to know for sure what would have happened to those children if you had left them. In their state of terror they might have fallen out the window or down the stairs or run into traffic."

She shrugged, acknowledging the possibility of this.

He put his hands on her shoulders and turned her to face him. "But the important thing is that it's in the past. You made the decision and, right or wrong, it's over. Now you have to look to the future."

She released a deep breath. "I think I need a hug," she whispered. "And since Cornelia Blackwood isn't here, could you give me one?"

He hesitated for just a second, then his arms went around her and pulled her close. She closed her eyes, feeling completely secure for the first time since her father died.

* * *

On Wednesday morning, Wilma Hightower from child services called and asked Mila to bring Lily and Ben into Albany at ten o'clock. "I've got them appointments with a pediatrician, a dentist, and a grief therapist," the child services caseworker explained. "It's routine, but necessary, and I don't dare put it off any longer."

Mila checked her watch. "The kids have a birthday party tonight. What time do you think we'll be finished?"

"No later than five," Wilma promised.

When Mila told her mother that the children had appointments in Albany, Daphne insisted on baths and fresh clothes. "I feel like I should go with you," Daphne said, chewing her bottom lip. "Most kids get scared at doctors' offices, even if their parents haven't disappeared under mysterious circumstances. But I promised Cleo that I'd help her get the party set up."

"I can handle it," Mila said, hoping she could. While her mother spruced the Womack children up, she walked over to the Ledbetters' backyard, intending to see if Quin had time to accompany them to Albany. But when she stepped through the hedges, she realized that was not a possibility.

Quin's pop-up was gone, and the small backyard was crawling with people. Cleo was supervising the placement of pulsating red lights in the middle of checkered tables and waved to Mila. "What do you think?" she called from across the yard.

"I think it's great," Mila replied, her eyes searching for Quin. "But you're not going to have room for the games."

"We're having them inside."

"You're going to let one hundred five-year-olds run through your new house?"

Cleo nodded with the serenity of a person who could afford major repairs.

"Where's Quin?" Mila was finally forced to ask.

"He went into Albany to pick up the ice sculpture for me," Cleo responded.

Mila was tempted to tell her that she might be going a little overboard, but refrained. "I've got to take the kids in for checkups."

There was a honk from the road, and Cleo turned toward it. "That must be the caterers. See you when you get back."

Left alone in the middle of the party preparation, Mila turned and headed back home.

"How are things going over there?" Daphne asked when she walked into the kitchen.

"Busy," Mila replied, irritated with Cleo for taking up Quin's time when she needed him.

* * *

Mila met Wilma at the child services building, then followed her across town to the pediatrician's office. As Daphne had predicted, both children reacted badly to the strangers, and by the time they reached the therapist's office, Mila felt like she needed counseling herself.

"The pediatrician recommended that Lily see a specialist," Wilma told her as they strapped the children into the Mustang.

Mila nodded. "She probably had one in Roanoke. I'll check into it and arrange for the records to be transferred."

"And he says that Ben's lack of communication skills isn't something to worry about yet. If he's still not talking in six months, we'll look into a speech pathologist."

During the drive back to Haggerty, Mila called Dorcas and asked her to check out an orthopedic specialist in Roanoke who might have had Lily as a patient.

It was almost five o'clock when Mila reached Hickory Lane. Traffic was backed up for several blocks, so she parked in the first available spot, and they walked to Aunt Cora Sue's house. They barely had time to grab their gift and hurry next door. Feeling hot, tired, and even more irritable than before, Mila followed her mother and the Womack children through the hedges.

The Ledbetters' backyard was packed with children and party personnel. Two tables near the house were completely covered with presents, and the guest of honor was standing on the patio with his mother, accepting good wishes. As they waited their turn in line to tell Earl Jr. happy birthday, Mila's eyes searched for Quin.

"He's directing traffic," Daphne said after a few minutes.

"Who?"

Daphne regarded her daughter with wise eyes. "Who were you looking for?"

"No one in particular."

Daphne laughed. "Well, no one in particular is helping people with this horrendous traffic jam that Cleo inadvertently created."

Mila ignored her mother and pretended to be engrossed in the handcuff display that Frankie Cofield was presenting a few yards away.

"I told him he should have worn a clown costume for the occasion," Beau whispered from behind her in an obvious reference to Frankie's resemblance to Bozo.

Mila had to smile. "It was nice of him to donate his time."

"Frankie's a nice guy. He's just in the wrong profession. He should join the circus or the rodeo."

Mila shook her head in mock disgust. "Don't you have something you should be doing?"

"I'm supposed to be helping in the fingerprint room," he said. "I just took a break to see if any of the kiddies had a pretty, divorced mom."

"You are incorrigible," Mila said, and he laughed.

"I try." Beau winked, then melted into the crowd.

After they spoke to Earl Jr., Daphne offered to take the children on through all the rooms, so Mila wandered back outside. She wanted to check out the traffic situation, but saw Miss Eugenia ensconced at a table in the center and joined her instead.

"Taking roll?" Mila asked.

"Indeed I am," Miss Eugenia replied. "And it looks like everyone is present and accounted for."

"Who would dare defy you?" Mila teased.

"No one with any sense." Miss Eugenia looked at the swarm of children. "Sometimes I regret that motherhood passed me by."

"It's a lot harder than it looks," Mila told her. "If I didn't have my mother here to help me I'd have probably thrown myself off a cliff by now."

Miss Eugenia cackled with laughter. "You be sure and tell her how much you appreciate her, you hear?"

Mila nodded.

"The practice is good for Daphne. Someday you'll have children of your own, and she'll be a grandmother."

"Not if Lily is right about me." Mila laughed, but it came off a little artificial. "She says I can't be a mother because I'm not *soft*." She held up her arm and flexed her biceps.

Miss Eugenia didn't laugh, but regarded her seriously before saying, "Softness is more a state of mind than a body condition."

Mila met the older woman's eyes, then blinked back tears as Quin came up behind her and squeezed her shoulders.

"Having fun?" he asked.

She nodded. "It's a great party. How's the traffic?"

"A mess," he admitted, pulling a chair up beside her. "Chief Jones and his deputies have taken over, and I wish them luck." He looked around. "It's hard to believe, but I think every one of the kindergartners actually came!"

Mila smiled, then leaned close to him and whispered, "Miss Eugenia is a force to be reckoned with."

He turned so that their faces were only a few centimeters apart. "I won't ever cross her, that's for sure."

"Earl Jr. is about to cut his cake!" Lily cried as she and Daphne and Ben returned to the table.

Mila pulled away from Quin and avoided her mother's gaze as they all watched the cake-cutting ceremony. A few minutes later Cleo came over, flushed with success.

"Didn't it turn out great?" she asked, her eyes sparkling with excitement. "And you know, these snooty ladies aren't that bad. I might even start going to church every now and then and donate to a couple of local causes." She flashed them all a smile. "I promised myself I wasn't going to buy their friendship, but since they've made the first step . . ."

"It's very wise of you to show your appreciation to the town by cooperating with your neighbors," Miss Eugenia agreed with a quick look at Mila. "You can catch more flies with honey than with vinegar."

"I've never had much trouble attracting flies," Cleo teased. "But I don't mind being sweet every now and then."

As the party started to wind down, Daphne took Lily and Ben home while Mila and Quin helped Cleo clean up. There were two huge tables covered with gifts, and Mila asked Cleo how long she thought it was going to take Earl Jr. to open them all.

"I figure most of tomorrow," she replied with a smile. "I told him he can keep five, and we'll donate the rest to the Goodwill. We don't want Earl Jr. to be spoiled."

Mila was impressed, but before she could comment, the caterer stepped up beside Cleo and cleared his throat. "We're all packed up and ready to go."

"Let me go get my checkbook," Cleo said and hurried into the house.

Left alone, Mila walked over to where Quin and Earl Sr. were helping to load the rental company truck. She stood mesmerized, watching Quin's muscles flexing as he lifted chairs. Then he glanced over and saw her. After a quick wink, he returned to his task. Mila pulled at her shirt, suddenly feeling too warm.

Once the truck was loaded, the driver and his assistant climbed into the cab and drove out of the Ledbetters' backyard. Quin walked over to where Mila stood, wiping sweat from his face onto the sleeve of his T-shirt.

"Why did you help the rental people do the job they were getting paid for?" she asked him with a teasing smile.

He laughed. "I figured the sooner I got rid of that truck, the sooner I could get my campsite set up so I can go to bed. I'm exhausted."

"Cleo's kept you pretty busy today?"

He gave her an incredulous look. "She nearly killed me! I'm just glad that Earl Jr. only has one birthday a year."

"It was nice of you to help."

"I wanted the people of Haggerty to see that Cleo has friends, not just employees."

Mila resisted the urge to throw her arms around his neck.

He pointed toward the road where his Mustang and camper were parked. "You want to give me a hand?"

She knew he didn't really need any help, but was glad for the chance to stay with him, so she nodded. She rode in the passenger seat while he backed the camper into its spot in the Ledbetters' backyard, then she waited by the pop-up while he returned his car to the street. When he returned, it only took a few minutes to re-create his campsite.

"Well, I guess I'll let you get to bed," she said once it was finished.

He grabbed her hand. "Don't go yet. Let's just sit out here and enjoy the breeze." She looked at her hand in his and nodded.

He opened two folding chairs and placed them side by side under the little awning that covered the entrance to his pop-up. After they sat down, he reclaimed her hand and instead of enjoying the breeze, she spent the next few minutes trying to get her heart rate under control.

Finally she asked, "So, have you missed surfing the last few days?"

He seemed to consider this for a few seconds, then nodded. "Yes, I miss it."

"You're probably getting out of practice," she said.

"Probably," he agreed. "But I don't mind."

"You don't?"

He leaned close. "No, because I'd rather be with you." Their eyes locked for a few seconds, then his lips touched hers gently.

* * *

On Thursday morning Mila woke up late, feeling happier than she had in years. She listened for the sounds of her mother and the Womack children, but the house was quiet. She stood, stretched, then went to investigate.

Daphne had a plate of breakfast waiting for her in the microwave, and there was a note saying that she'd taken the children with her to the grocery store. *And don't worry,* her mother had written at the bottom. *Winston Jones is escorting us.* Mila smiled. That did make her feel better.

Once she had eaten enough of her breakfast to keep from upsetting her mother, Mila dressed for the day, then went out in search of Quin. She found him looking under the hood of his Mustang. She had wondered if they would feel awkward together, this first meeting after their kiss the night before, but Quin's smile was the same as always—open and friendly.

"Good morning," he said.

"What are you doing?" she asked, moving up close enough beside him for their arms to touch.

"Changing the oil."

"You do that yourself?"

He gave her a horrified look. "I wouldn't let anyone else touch my car!"

She laughed. "I guess that proves who loves their Mustang more. I don't even wash mine personally."

"I'd be glad to check your oil while I'm at it," he offered.

"Thanks, but I just got it serviced a couple of weeks ago." She stretched her hands above her head. "I can't seem to wake up."

He smiled. "I noticed."

She lowered her arms and looked at the sky. "I wonder what the weather forecast is for today."

"Why?"

"The air is thick, and you see how everything has kind of a yellowish cast?" He nodded. "That sometimes means severe weather." She glanced into the backyard at his campsite. "I'll go inside and see if there are any warnings out, but you might want to batten down your hatches—just in case."

He smiled. "I will. Thanks."

Mila had just turned on the television and was searching for a weather report when the phone rang. It was Dorcas James. She had the name of Lily's specialist in Roanoke and a recommendation for one in Albany. Mila thanked her and, after she hung up the phone, had to admit that in spite of her best efforts not to, she was starting to like Dorcas.

When Daphne and the kids got home, Winston and Quin both helped unload groceries. Then Winston said he needed to get to his real job, and Daphne shooed everyone else into the backyard so she could prepare lunch.

Quin and Mila sat next to each other on the back steps, watching the children play. "Did you find out about the weather?" he asked.

"I missed the weather report, but if there was severe weather they'd interrupt regular programming." She looked up at the sky. "We'll just have to keep an eye on it."

A few minutes later, Miss Eugenia came out the back door. "Mother got rid of you too?" Mila guessed.

Miss Eugenia smiled. "She invited me to lunch but *did* suggest that I wait out here with the two of you. She says she's preparing something special, which has me intrigued."

Mila took in Miss Eugenia's polka-dotted summer dress, knee-high hose rolled down to just below the knee, and a pair of open-toed pumps that had to be thirty years old. "How come you're all dressed up?" she asked.

"I've been to one of Cornelia's Faith Fair planning meetings, and I declare, by Saturday, I might need anxiety medication."

"It's not going well?" Quin asked.

"Oh, I guess it's going fine. It's just that Cornelia can't do anything tastefully. With her—the bigger the better."

"I guess I should be glad that I won't have to deal with her much." She turned to Quin. "Mrs. Blackwood doesn't like Mormons."

Miss Eugenia frowned. "Why, that's not true. She thinks you're wrong in your beliefs and might be a little suspicious of you since Mormons are known for proselytizing, but she likes you fine."

Mila was surprised by Miss Eugenia's defense of the woman. "I thought *you* didn't like her!"

"I don't particularly," Miss Eugenia admitted. "But I've never known anyone who lives her religion more than Cornelia Blackwood. She gets up at the crack of dawn and leads a prayer meeting at the nursing home. Then on her way back home, she goes by and sees homebound members of the congregation. She might not make a good casserole, but if there's ever anyone in town that's sick or bereaved or just new, Cornelia will be one of the first to call with a covered dish."

"I thought she was just trying to save my soul," Mila said.

"That too," Miss Eugenia admitted. "But you've got to give Cornelia credit. She read that article about people not going to church, and she could have been like the rest of us, shaking our heads in despair over the moral decline in America, but instead she decided to have a Faith Fair." Miss Eugenia looked pointedly at Mila. "And she's invited the Mormons."

Mila wasn't impressed. "She had to do that, in order to be interdenominational."

"No, she didn't," Miss Eugenia countered. "There's four churches in Haggerty—all different religions."

Quin stepped into the conversation, and Mila suspected that he wanted to avoid an all-out fight. "I have a question for you, Miss Eugenia."

The older woman narrowed her eyes at Mila, then turned to Quin. "I'll answer it if I can."

"I served my mission in Kansas and spent a lot of time in a very religious area similar to Haggerty. Most people there belonged to a church even if they didn't go every week. I expected them to be interested in what I had to say, but I found that it was harder to teach religious people than it would have been to teach someone who had never heard of Jesus. They were unreceptive and almost hostile toward the LDS missionaries. Why is that?"

"Well, for one thing, once people are saved they don't feel a need to do much else. Or if they are involved with their church and are happy, they don't want to change."

"That explains the disinterest, but not the hostility," Quin agreed. "We believe in Jesus, so why did they call us blasphemers and accuse us of being members of a cult and swear that we are going to the devil?"

Miss Eugenia looked mildly uncomfortable, and Mila felt certain she had heard these accusations directed toward Mormons as well. She leaned forward, anxious to hear what Miss Eugenia would say.

"I can't speak for all Protestants," the older lady began carefully. "But according to my observations it mostly has to do with the definition of *grace*. I was taught that once a person accepts Jesus Christ as their Savior, then they are saved and assured a place in heaven."

"We believe that too," Quin said. "I accept Jesus Christ as my Savior and know that without His atoning sacrifice I would be going straight to the devil when I die."

"Another area of concern for the preachers that I've heard address the subject stems from the Mormon belief that you can improve your situation in heaven by good works here on earth. The general opinion of Protestant ministers seems to be that this doctrine blasphemes the Atonement, makes it seem insufficient."

"But any improvement in our eternal situation is really just a by-product of righteous living," Quin told her earnestly. "We do good works because we love the Savior."

Miss Eugenia nodded. "I know that. But it's confusing for people who don't know much about your church. And these basic areas of confusion are exacerbated by all the anti-Mormon activists who plant seeds of suspicion."

"That's the group that I can't understand," Mila said.

"It's partly to do with money," Quin told them. "Some people make a living by protesting the Church."

"That doesn't seem very Christian," Miss Eugenia remarked.

"I know that I can't imagine picketing a building owned by another church the way some people do when a new temple is built," Mila agreed.

"And sometimes the demonstrators are people who used to be Mormons," Miss Eugenia added.

"I *really* don't understand that," Mila said.

Quin shook his head. "Me either. I think it was Elder Maxwell who said that when some people leave the Church, they can't leave it *alone*."

"Anyway," Miss Eugenia reclaimed the floor, "there are a lot of false rumors about Mormons that get spread around, and that's another good thing about Cornelia's Faith Fair. It gives people an opportunity to explain their beliefs."

"Just getting members of various religions to work together is a good thing," Mila had to admit.

Before anyone could comment further, Daphne opened the door and called them inside, ending the religious discussion.

"This better be good," Miss Eugenia grumbled. "I'm stiff all over from sitting on these steps."

Daphne ignored the complaint and squinted at the sky. "Looks like we're in for stormy weather."

Miss Eugenia stood slowly, massaging her lower back. "Yes, the weatherman said severe thunderstorms."

The secret lunch turned out to be a taco salad, which Miss Eugenia said she had never had. It was a big hit and by the time they retired to the living room, the sky was dark and the clouds were heavy.

"I hope you thought to pack up your camper," Daphne said, glancing out the window.

Quin winked at Mila. "It's packed up tight."

"You'll need to stay in here with us until the bad weather passes," Daphne told him. "Campers and such can be very dangerous in a storm."

"I'd better get home myself," Miss Eugenia said. "Thank you for the taco salad, Daphne. It was good."

"I'm glad you enjoyed it," Daphne replied, obviously pleased.

Quin got to his feet. "The wind is blowing pretty hard. Why don't you let me drive you home?"

"Well, that's a really gentlemanly offer, and I'll be pleased to accept," Miss Eugenia told him with a smile.

After they left, the phone rang, and Mila answered it and listened for a few seconds, then covered the mouthpiece and said, "It's Cleo inviting the kids over to play." Mila glanced out the window. "Do you think the weather's too bad?"

Daphne shook her head. "I can listen to weather reports from there as well as I can from here, and playing with Earl Jr. will distract the children from the storm. I'll walk them over." She addressed Lily and Ben. "Can you kids get your raincoats? We're going to play with Earl Jr."

"We're on our way," Mila told Cleo, then hung up.

"You have to stay here and wait for Quin to come back," Daphne said. "I'll take the kids by myself. That will give you and Quin time to go over your case."

Mila felt like she should argue, but before she could come up with a good response, Daphne had the kids' coats on and they were out the door.

"Keep an eye on the weather and come home if it starts to get bad!" Mila called after them, and Daphne nodded. Mila closed the door, then stood at the front window and watched the wind blow. Quin returned a few minutes later.

"Whew!" he said as he hurried inside. "That wind nearly knocked me down." He closed the door and looked around. "Where is everybody?"

"Cleo called and invited Ben and Lily over to play. Mother thought that might help keep the children from getting scared by the storm so she walked them over. She promised to bring them back before the weather gets too bad." Mila's eyes drifted back to the window.

Quin shifted his weight from one foot to the other, drawing Mila's attention. Suddenly the little house seemed even smaller, and the air around them was heavy and close. She knew Quin felt it too, since he stayed by the door instead of walking into the room.

Mila cleared her throat. "Mother suggested that we could spend the time working on the case."

He took a hesitant step forward. "I guess we could do that."

"I'll get the file." Mila went into her bedroom, and when she returned, he was sitting on the couch. She sat beside him and opened the file. He reached over to pick up a picture, and their hands touched incidentally. Mila jerked, almost as if she'd been shocked.

"The FBI hasn't been able to find Belinda Wallace or her husband," Mila said in a strangled voice. "Either they are using false identities or they're dead. Here's the personal information on them." Mila held out the fax sheet, but her hands were shaking, and it fell to the floor. They both leaned down at the same time and bumped heads.

Quin took the file from her lap and put it on the end table, then he took both of her hands in his. "This is silly."

"What?" she asked, staring at their entwined fingers.

"Sitting here pretending like we don't want to kiss each other."

"I," she began, then faltered. "I, well," she tried again. Then she leaned toward him and whispered, "So what are you waiting for?"

He smiled as their lips met. When they pulled apart, her voice shook as she said, "In spite of the impression I've given you, I really don't kiss just anyone."

"I don't consider myself *just anyone,*" he countered.

"After all, we are good friends," she managed. "I'm comfortable with you. I guess it's not unreasonable that I would want to kiss you."

He laughed and said, "Just admit that you find me attractive."

She pressed her lips together in a semipout. "I don't want to."

This seemed to amuse him even more. "What do you like best? My eyes? My hair? The fact that I surf for a living?"

She reached up and rubbed his spiky hair. "I love your eyes and your surfing ability, but I guess the thing I find the most irresistible is your casual I-just-wet-it-and-run-my-fingers-through-it hairstyle."

Quin laughed. "I do just wet my hair and run my fingers through. It's not a *style,* it's a lazy habit."

She had to laugh too, and before she knew it they were kissing again. Mila lost track of time for a while and when she became aware of her surroundings again, she realized that even though it was early afternoon, the sky was black as night. Then the phone rang. It was Daphne asking them to come over and help her get the kids home.

"They're tired and ready for naps, and I'd like to get them home before the storm starts. But the wind is blowing so hard I don't think they can walk, and I can't carry them both."

"We're on our way," Mila replied. When she looked up, Quin was already at the door.

"We'd better hurry," he said. "The rain won't hold off much longer."

Mila and Quin ran next door, fighting the strong wind. Daphne met them at the door and distributed the children, Lily to Mila and Ben to Quin. As she adjusted Lily's raincoat, Mila glanced into the living room where Cleo and Earl Jr. were sitting stiffly on the couch.

"Why don't you and Earl Jr. come with us?" Mila asked, concerned by the pallor of Cleo's skin.

"Earl Sr. is on his way," Cleo replied faintly. "We'll be fine."

"And we've got our shoes on," Earl Jr. contributed, sticking his feet up for Mila to see.

"So you'll be prepared in case you have to leave the house?" Mila guessed.

Earl Jr. frowned. "No, in case lightening strikes us. Rubber soles," he added for clarification.

"I don't think there's much chance of lightning striking you in the house," Mila told him.

"It's easy to get electrocuted in a thunderstorm, even inside," Cleo said. "You can get shocked if you're on the phone, and I saw on the news one time where a man was taking a shower and got hit by lightening. He was thrown clear out of the bathtub without a stitch of clothes on."

"Now that would be my worst nightmare," Daphne said with a little smile as Mila walked over to stand close beside Cleo.

Mila patted her friend's pale fingers. "You look scared to death."

"I am," Cleo admitted. "When I was a kid I used to get under my bed every time it rained. I've outgrown that, though," she said with a longing gaze at the stairs.

"Well, we're right next door, so call if you need us."

"We will," Cleo promised.

Quin opened the front door just as fat raindrops started falling from the swollen sky. "We'll have to make a run for it," he called over his shoulder to Mila. She nodded, and they plunged into the storm. By the time they stepped into Aunt Cora Sue's house, everyone was soaked to the skin.

They all worked quickly to get the children into dry clothes, then Daphne turned to Mila. "Quin and I will put these babies down for their naps. You get some dry clothes and go change in the bathroom."

"You both need to change too," Mila objected.

"We can't all do it at once," Daphne pointed out logically. "Now hurry."

When Mila walked into the kitchen a few minutes later, toweling her wet hair, Daphne was at the stove in her bathrobe, heating milk for hot chocolate. Quin was standing by the back door shivering.

"Lily and Ben are already asleep?" she asked in surprise.

Daphne nodded. "They were exhausted, poor babies. They didn't even make it through one book."

Quin put a hand on the doorknob. "I'd better go out to my camper to get dry clothes," he said through chattering teeth.

"If you open up the camper in this deluge, everything you have will get wet," Mila told him. "Then you won't be any better off than you are now."

He shrugged. "I can't just stand here and drip on your floor."

Daphne smiled. "Go into the bathroom and take off your shirt and pants. Mila will put your clothes in the dryer and hand you a quilt to wrap up in until they're done. This hot chocolate will be ready in a few minutes."

Quin didn't look thrilled with this plan, but he trudged down the hall. Mila followed at a discreet distance, then stood outside the bathroom door until it opened a few inches. He held out his sodden clothes, and she passed him the quilt before heading to the kitchen, where she put his clothes in the dryer. She was settled at the table sipping hot chocolate when he walked in, swathed in the quilt. He took the seat beside her—out of her direct line of vision. She knew he was uncomfortable to be wearing only a blanket, so she didn't turn her head toward him when she spoke.

"Do you want some marshmallows?"

"Yes, thanks." He took a handful from the package she held out to him and dropped them into his mug.

"Drink up!" Daphne commanded. "We've got plenty."

"It's delicious," Quin said politely and took another sip. "I feel warmer already."

Daphne smiled with approval as she took the seat across from Quin. "There's nothing like hot chocolate on a rainy day."

"What are they saying about the weather?" he asked.

"Now we've got a tornado watch and a flood warning," she said cheerfully.

"Maybe I should put my shoes on, just in case," he said, and Mila was pleased to find that even in these humiliating circumstances, he had retained his sense of humor.

"Only if they have rubber soles," she murmured as she blew on the steaming liquid in her cup.

A few minutes later, after a particularly loud crack of thunder, he said, "Do you think Cleo's under her bed yet?"

Mila laughed. "I think there's a very good chance."

And then the power went out.

"So much for my clothes getting dry," Quin muttered.

Daphne stood and started opening drawers. "I think I saw a flashlight over here somewhere." She found the flashlight and a small transistor radio and two weak batteries, so they had to alternate sitting in the dark and sitting in silence. Just as the radio weatherman announced that the tornado watch had expired, there was a knock on the door.

Daphne frowned. "I wonder who in the world would be calling on folks during a thunderstorm?"

"Only one way to find out," Mila said grimly. She pulled open the door and came face to face with a slightly waterlogged Belinda Wallace.

Mila stared speechless until the former Ryathon research assistant said, "Can I come in?"

CHAPTER 17

Belinda Wallace had lost weight, and her hair was cut in a modern, layered style similar to Mila's own. It also seemed lighter than it had in the snapshot the neighbor, Mrs. Creel, had given them. In spite of the terrible weather, she was wearing nice leather boots, designer jeans, and a denim jacket. Mila's practiced eye recognized an effort to change her appearance as much as possible.

Mila stepped aside to admit Ms. Wallace, then made brief introductions and invited their guest to sit on the couch. If the woman thought it was strange that Quin was wearing a blanket, she didn't comment on it.

"You know we've been looking for you?" Mila began, and the research assistant nodded.

"Oh, yes. That's why I've come here tonight. You've got the police and the FBI searching too, and eventually someone is going to find me. Then I'll be dead."

Even Mila, who had heard numerous shocking revelations during her years of police work, was surprised by this remark. "Who would kill you?"

"Ryathon, of course."

"Why?" Quin asked.

"To silence me, just like they did Larsen."

"And Theresa?" Mila guessed.

Belinda nodded. "Probably. I'm not sure about that."

Mila shifted into interrogation mode. "Were you romantically involved with Larsen Womack?"

Belinda laughed. "You must have been talking to Carol Harmon."

Mila and Quin exchanged a quick glance as Belinda continued. "She's so starved for male attention she probably fancied herself in love with him. All the romance rumors about me and Larsen were products of Carol's sick imagination."

"Did you ask him to give you rides to work?"

"I had an old car that was undependable," Belinda explained. "Larsen had to drive almost past my house to get to Ryathon, so I did ask him for rides sometimes."

"And you ate lunch together?"

"Is there a law against that?" Belinda demanded in exasperation. "I was friends with Theresa too. I went over to their house often for family events like birthdays and holidays."

"Why did you leave Roanoke?"

Belinda looked away, obviously reluctant to answer.

"If you don't tell us, we'll be forced to find out for ourselves," Mila reminded her.

Belinda sighed. "My husband had taken a construction job in Memphis, and he wanted me to join him. After all that happened with Larsen, I was seriously considering it. Then the threats started."

"What kind of threats?" Quin demanded. "Physical or legal?"

"Both—veiled at first," she said. "But gradually becoming more frightening. So I packed up and left."

"You're going to let your house be repossessed?" Mila asked.

She shrugged. "That didn't seem very important in comparison to my life."

Mila acknowledged this with a small nod. "Did the threats have something to do with an express mail envelope that Larsen was carrying around on the day of the fire?"

Belinda looked surprised. "How did you know about that?"

"We've kind of put two and two together. Larsen had been running unsanctioned tests in his little lab and came up with negative results. He was going to send the information to the FDA, but was . . ." Mila didn't want to say "killed" in front of Quin, so she changed it to, "stopped before he could."

"Yes," Belinda confirmed. "But they didn't recover the envelope, so they assumed I had it."

"But you didn't?" Quin asked.

"No. I don't know what happened to it," Belinda said. "Maybe it burned up in the fire."

Mila frowned. "But Ryathon wasn't taking any chances."

Belinda shook her head. "No, there was too much money involved."

"Why would they think you would have the envelope?" Quin asked.

"I guess because everyone thought Larsen and I were having an affair, thanks to Carol."

"We spoke to your neighbor, Mrs. Creel," Mila said. "She told us that Larsen came over to your house frequently in the evenings and sometimes stayed all night."

Belinda sighed. "Larsen was afraid that someone at the company was watching him, so he asked if he could use my spare bedroom as sort of a mini lab. I let him type up his notes on my computer. He may have stayed all night occasionally. I don't know because I was asleep in the other room."

"So Larsen determined that there was something wrong with the new blood thickener that Ryathon had developed and was about to submit the information to the FDA," Mila led Belinda, hoping for more information, but the research assistant just looked confused.

"Larsen never did any testing on the new drug. His obsessive research was related to a prenatal vitamin that has been on the market for almost a year."

Now Mila was confused. "Why would he be testing something that had already been approved?"

"It was sort of a compulsion of his, and sometimes he did find little mistakes. Mr. Ryan always praised him for it because if they could find problems and correct them, it saved them a lot of money. But this time when he showed Mr. Ryan his research, he was told to ignore it."

"But Larsen didn't," Mila guessed.

"No. Once he got onto something like that he couldn't let it go—even though he knew it was pointless." Belinda looked up at them. "I mean, it was just a vitamin, and it wasn't like they put poison in it or something."

"What was wrong with it then?" Mila asked.

"A few lots were deficient in folic acid. Most of the pills were fine, and if Larsen wasn't so obsessive about random sampling he never would have found the bad ones."

Daphne stepped in at this point. "Would you like some hot chocolate?" she asked Belinda. "Even though the power is out it's probably still warm."

Belinda smiled. "I appreciate the offer, but I'd better go. I took a terrible risk coming here at all."

Mila stood and walked the young woman to the door. "I'm glad you came, and I promise you that I'll do everything I can to bring whoever was involved in Larsen's death to justice."

Belinda studied her for a minute, then nodded. "Good luck."

Shortly after Belinda left, the power came back on. Daphne went into the kitchen to turn on the dryer and clean up. Once her mother was gone, Mila leaned close to Quin. "Well, that explains all of Larsen's erratic behavior except the smell of alcohol, and maybe that was another of Carol Harmon's lies."

"You sure were right about her," Quin said in admiration. "I wonder if Smiley DeFore is in on it too."

"I'd be willing to bet that he is," Mila replied grimly.

"Larsen was going to send his research on the vitamin to the FDA, and rather than let him do it, they killed him."

Mila shook her head. "If it had been over the new drug I could almost understand it."

Quin gave her a horrified look.

"I said *almost,*" she emphasized. "They had millions of dollars tied up in the new drug, but the prenatal vitamin probably wasn't all that expensive to make, and since it had been on the market for a year, it should have paid for itself by now. So what was the big deal?"

"A recall would have hurt them."

"But not much, especially if only a few lots were involved." Mila shook her head. "I don't understand."

"Maybe they don't know," Quin said softly as he pulled his blanket a little tighter around his chest. "Maybe they think Larsen *did* have information on the new drug."

Mila considered this. "Either way, I think Mr. Ryan needs to be questioned again."

He nodded. "I agree. Do you need to call Chief Monahan first?"

She shook her head. "If we ask him he might say no."

"So you're going with the old it's-easier-to-get-forgiveness-than-permission approach?" he asked with a smile.

"I'm not sure I could get either one from Chief Monahan, but solving this case is what's important, so I think we'd better talk to Mr. Ryan unofficially."

"If he's smart he won't tell us anything."

"We'll just have to hope he's not that smart."

Quin pulled Brandon Ryan's card from the file and held it out to her. "Maybe this time we should bypass Mr. DeFore."

"A sneaky idea, but a good one," she said with a smile. "I'm rubbing off on you."

He leaned forward and kissed her on the nose. "Is that what you're doing to me?"

She stepped back. "Sorry, but I don't kiss men wearing only a blanket."

* * *

Daphne brought Quin his dry clothes just as the children woke up from their naps. After changing into his clothes, he and Daphne gave the children hot chocolate. Mila called Dorcas and asked her to recommend a vitamin expert.

"Do I dare ask why you want this information?" Dorcas inquired.

"Ask me no questions, I'll tell you no lies," Mila replied.

There was a short pause, then Dorcas said, "I'll be back in touch."

Mila went into the kitchen and watched while Lily demonstrated that she could drink from a mug without spilling. Mila noticed that Daphne was taking no chances with Ben. His hot chocolate was in a sippy cup. Once the snack was over, Quin took the children into the living room and built them a tepee with the quilt he had been wearing. Daphne fashioned headdresses out of dishcloths and used some lipstick as war paint. Mila noticed that Quin also had a little towel tucked into the waistband of his blue jeans.

"What's that?" she asked.

"My loincloth, of course," he replied.

"Oh," she said with a nod. "I should have known you'd be a stickler for authenticity."

He laughed as she sat on the couch and listened to him explain Indian lore. Her phone rang. It was Dorcas with the name of a professor at Emory who would be able to answer her questions. She thanked Dorcas, then called the number. She got the professor's answering machine and had to leave a message. Putting her phone back in her pocket, she returned her attention to Quin and Lily and Ben.

"You're lucky that none of us know any real facts about Native Americans," she told him as he completed some story about using corn to make shampoo.

"It's all true!" he promised. "Or most of it, anyway." He flashed her a smile, and her heart skipped a beat. He was just so incredibly precious in his costume of assorted dishcloths.

They had just invited Mila into the tepee for a powwow when her phone rang again. "Don't start the powwow without me," she requested. "I'll be there in a few minutes." Then she walked into her bedroom before answering the call. It was the professor from Emory.

Pressing the small phone tightly to her ear, she explained to the professor what she needed to know. "Oh, folic acid is very important," the professor told her. "Especially to the developing fetus. A deficiency at crucial times during gestation could cause birth defects or something more subtle, like reduced intelligence."

Mila felt her hand start to tremble. "So not getting enough folic acid is very serious for a pregnant woman."

"Oh, yes," the professor agreed. "Very serious indeed."

Mila thanked the man and returned to the living room where the Indians were getting restless. She climbed into the makeshift tepee and sat cross-legged beside Quin. Between songs and stories, she told him what the professor had said, careful to avoid using Larsen's name.

"So his tests *weren't* pointless," Quin said. "Even if only a relatively small number of women took the defective pills, the results could be disastrous."

"But Ryathon didn't want anyone to know that," Mila mused. "Especially the women who took the bad pills."

"And they were willing to use extreme measures to keep it quiet." He looked down at her. "You still want to take on Mr. Ryan by ourselves?"

She nodded. "We don't have any proof yet. If I ask Chief Monahan to go with this, he'll laugh me out of his office."

He took her hand. "As soon as we get through with this powwow, we'll call Mr. Ryan. Somehow we'll get proof, and then no one will be laughing."

* * *

The children were having so much fun that in order to get away Quin finally had to tell them that a famous Navajo medicine woman was going to take over the powwow. Daphne dutifully donned a dish towel headdress and climbed into the makeshift tepee.

Mila led Quin into her room, and they sat on the edge of the bed. "Ready?" she asked, and he nodded.

"As much as I'll ever be."

She dialed the number for Brandon Ryan's private line and then held the phone out so that Quin could hear as it started ringing.

A few seconds later a man's voice answered. "This is Brandon."

"Mr. Ryan, this is Detective Edwards from the Albany Police Department."

"Hello, Detective," he said, his voice friendly. "Are you back in Roanoke?"

"No, I'm in Georgia, but I did think of a few more questions if you have time to talk."

"Certainly," he agreed.

"I had a conversation with Belinda Wallace recently." She waited to let this sink in, then continued. "She says that the information Larsen Womack was sending to the FDA related to a prenatal vitamin that has been on the market for almost a year. Apparently some of the lots didn't have the proper amount of folic acid."

She heard Mr. Ryan sigh. "I don't have my lawyer present, and I haven't given permission for this conversation to be taped, so I presume we're off the record."

Mila had to control a laugh. If he only knew just how far off the record they were. "This conversation is not official."

"Larsen came to me in early February, very upset. He had done some testing on the prenatal vitamin you mentioned and had determined that production mistakes caused a small percentage of the pills to be deficient in folic acid."

"Which could be very serious for the developing fetus," Mila said to make sure he knew she'd done her homework.

"*Could* is the operative word," Mr. Ryan said. "Many women don't even start taking prenatal vitamins early enough to enhance brain development. It was unquestionably a gray area."

"But the women who bought your vitamin trusted that it had everything their baby needed," Mila pointed out.

"Yes, that was the problem. Larsen felt very strongly that we should do a press release, but going public with something like that would have destroyed my company and there was absolutely no proof that the vitamins had harmed any of the women or their children," he said earnestly. "Ryathon pays a lot of taxes and provides a lot of jobs in the Roanoke area. The senseless destruction of my company would have been a tragedy not just for me, but for the whole community."

"Why would announcing the mistake ruin your company?"

"In a society as litigation happy as ours, the legitimate suits would break us and the frivolous ones would bury us."

"But surely you felt that you should do something," Mila replied.

"Of course!" Mr. Ryan agreed enthusiastically. "We set up a committee to identify and follow a cross section of the women who took the questionable vitamins. If we see a negative trend, we will approach them individually and offer compensation. But up to this point, there has been no such trend."

Mila glanced at Quin. "I assume that this plan didn't pacify Larsen?"

"No," Mr. Ryan confirmed. "He wouldn't be satisfied with anything except full disclosure."

"Larsen had too much integrity for compromise," Quin whispered, and Mila repeated the comment for Mr. Ryan.

"Yes, that's what I thought too," the CEO of Ryathon Pharmaceuticals said. "Until I got the blackmail demands."

Quin was visibly shocked by this accusation.

"Larsen blackmailed you?" Mila asked incredulously.

"Yes," Mr. Ryan claimed. "He said if I didn't give him what he asked for, he would give his research to the FDA. I made two payments of $100,000 each, but when the demand came for the next installment I refused. I decided that I'd rather lose my company all at once than slowly and painfully."

"How did Larsen react when you told him that you weren't going to pay him any more?"

"Violently. That's why he tore up the lab and set it on fire."

"Not because he was being terminated?"

"He was being terminated too. I wouldn't keep him as an employee after he blackmailed me," Mr. Ryan said with a trace of indignation.

"But the envelope never arrived at the FDA."

"Apparently not," Mr. Ryan confirmed. "I'm sure I would have heard from them if it had."

"There have been no more blackmail attempts?"

"No."

Mila took a deep breath. "In your opinion, is Larsen Womack dead?"

"I don't have an opinion on that matter," Mr. Ryan said. "I haven't heard from him since the day he tried to burn down my company."

"Is it possible that someone else besides Larsen was blackmailing you and just used his name?" Mila asked.

Mr. Ryan paused before answering, which seemed to indicate that he was giving her question some consideration. "I don't think so," he said finally. "The wording was very technical, and he included portions of the report he was preparing for the FDA. No one else would have had access to his research."

"What about his secretary and research assistants?" Mila knew she was grasping at straws, but felt she had to try. "Could any of them have accessed information on his computer?"

"We have very stringent security controls here for obvious reasons," the CEO told them. "Passwords are changed frequently and assigned at random. No one at Ryathon knows anyone else's password. It's company policy."

Mila frowned. "But it's possible that Larsen could have told someone. Or perhaps a coworker was standing behind him while he entered his password."

"I guess it's possible," Mr. Ryan's tone indicated that he found the idea highly improbable.

"What about security cameras?" Mila asked. "I presume you have them?"

"Of course," Mr. Ryan acknowledged.

"Could one have been manipulated into a position so that the password would be recorded?"

Mr. Ryan sounded aghast. "You're talking about conspiracy on a major scale if you think the security people are involved."

"We don't know who's involved," Mila told him. "We're just trying to consider all the possibilities."

"Based on the phraseology, the information, and even the nuances, I believe that those blackmail notes were written by Larsen Womack," Mr. Ryan reaffirmed. "You're making more of this than is really there."

"That may be true," Mila admitted. "But until I'm convinced that I've found all that *is* there, I'll have to keep looking. And I can't promise that in the course of our investigation word of your defective vitamin won't come out."

"I understand."

"Thank you for your time," Mila said, then disconnected the call.

"What now?" Quin asked, his arm pressed tightly against hers.

"Now I call Chief Monahan."

Mila placed the call and was surprised when she was put through to the chief quickly. She began by telling him about her trip to Roanoke the weekend before. The chief interrupted her at this point.

"You flew to Roanoke?" he clarified. "And I presume you were on a vacation of some kind since you had no permission to be there officially."

Mila licked her lips. "Yes, sir. It was just a pleasure trip." She rolled her eyes at Quin. "But while I was there enjoying the scenery, I had a little conversation with Brandon Ryan."

"And?" the chief prompted.

She told him what they had gleaned from both conversations with the CEO of Ryathon Pharmaceuticals and their interviews with the other employees and former employees.

"So all this information was gathered off the record?" the chief clarified.

"Yes, sir, but it wouldn't be hard to confirm it."

"You have no proof then?"

"Not really," she admitted. "But we should be able to get some if we subpoena the Ryathon company records."

"In Virginia?" the chief shouted. "You want me to try and arrange a subpoena in another state?" He didn't wait for her to respond, but continued. "You want me to accuse one of the largest pharmaceutical companies in the country of blatant negligence? And all of this without a shred of evidence."

"We have some circumstantial evidence—"

"No way," the chief cut her off. "But since you're finding the time to work on cases, you might as well come back to active duty. As of tomorrow, your leave is canceled."

Mila stared at the phone for a few seconds after the chief disconnected. Finally Quin reached up and turned it off. "What will you do?" he asked gently.

"I don't know," she replied.

"If Larsen's innocent, and I'm convinced he is, then someone else at Ryathon is guilty," Quin thought aloud. "Carol Harmon is the obvious suspect."

"Mr. DeFore also comes to mind."

"Mostly because he's smiley," Quin teased.

"And I don't think we can disregard Mr. Ryan," she said. "All we have is his word that he wasn't involved in Larsen's disappearance."

Quin nodded. "That's true."

"Since I'm making unofficial, useless phone calls, I think I might give Carol Harmon another try." She checked the file and dialed the main switchboard at Ryathon. When she was connected to Ms. Harmon's line she identified herself. "I wondered if I could ask you a few more questions."

"I won't answer any more questions without my lawyer present," Ms. Harmon said coldly, then hung up on Mila.

"Well, she's had a change of heart since last week," she said as she turned off her phone.

"So, what now?"

Mila leaned her head on his shoulder. "I'll probably get fired, but I can't give up now. We're close, I can feel it."

He put his arm around her and pulled her against him. "I feel it too." Then he pressed a kiss to her forehead. "And for what it's worth, I'm in it with you—all the way."

She allowed herself to relax against him. "Actually, that's worth quite a lot." As she listened to the beating of his heart, she considered the situation. Her career and possibly her life were in danger, but as long as Quin kept his arms around her, she didn't care.

CHAPTER 18

On Friday when Mila walked into the kitchen, she found Quin, Miss Eugenia, Lily, and Ben all settled around the table. Daphne was at the stove, cooking grits and eggs. It looked like her mother had made another batch of hot chocolate since everyone was drinking from mugs, except Ben who had his sippy cup.

"Good morning!" Miss Eugenia greeted. "Don't you look lovely?" She turned toward Quin, waiting for him to second her comment.

"Beautiful," he agreed, winking at her over his mug.

"What brings you here so early?" Mila asked Miss Eugenia, and Daphne gave her daughter a stern look from her position by the stove.

"Miss Eugenia has already visited the sick and is here enlisting volunteers to help set up the Faith Fair," Daphne said as she put a plate of fluffy eggs on the table. "Grits will be ready in a second. Mila, would you get the bacon out of the microwave?"

Once everyone had fixed their plates, Miss Eugenia said, "I asked Quin if he'd be able to help out with the Faith Fair this morning, and he said he'd have to check with you." She raised an eyebrow. "Which I thought was interesting."

Mila took a sip of orange juice, then replied, "We've had a couple of breaks in our case, so I'm sure he just wanted to see what my investigative plans are for today."

"Well," Miss Eugenia prompted. "Can the two of you help this morning?"

"What will we have to do?" Mila asked.

"Set up tables and chairs, fold programs, that sort of thing."

Mila looked over at Quin. "It's okay with me if you want to."

He smiled. "It's pretty much a civic duty to help with the first ever Haggerty Faith Fair."

Miss Eugenia studied him through narrowed eyes. "Young man, you have been spending way too much time with Mila."

Everyone laughed and then concentrated on eating.

"Cleo invited the children to come over and play, so while y'all are helping set up the fair I'll take them next door," Daphne suggested.

Lily put her hands into the air and cheered, then Ben did the same, ending any objections Mila might have had. She smiled at the children. "We'll walk you over, then keep them inside and the doors locked."

After her mother's nod of agreement, Mila took her plate to the sink and rinsed it. Quin came up close behind her and stacked his plate on top of hers.

"Hey, I'm not doing your dishes," she said.

"Mila Elizabeth Edwards!" Daphne cried from the table. "Quin is a guest in your house."

Mila smirked up at him, trying not to give any notice to the little pulse beating in his neck. "In that case I'll be *glad* to wash his dishes."

He laughed and slipped his hands around hers in the soapy water. "I'll wash the dishes. It's the least I can do to thank you for this wonderful breakfast."

Daphne got up and pushed both of them away from the sink. "I'll do the dishes. You two get ready to go help with the Faith Fair."

Mila dried her hands on a dish towel, then passed it over to Quin. "I've got to make a phone call first." Quin followed her out onto the front porch. They sat in Cleo's rattan loveseat and dialed Beau's cell number.

"Sounds like you've been a busy girl," he said by way of greeting when he answered.

"What makes you say that?" she replied cautiously.

"I just left the chief's office."

"Oh." She considered this for a second, then asked, "What did he say?"

"That you've been involved in an unofficial investigation of Larsen and Theresa Womack and that he'd better not find out that anyone in his office was helping you."

"Uh-oh."

"Don't worry." Beau certainly didn't sound concerned. "I don't think he even wants to know. He was just barking again."

"I hope so," Mila said, genuinely worried. She'd been careless with her own career, but she didn't want her decisions to affect anyone else.

"He also said you were back on active duty."

"Hmm," Mila murmured. "What did he say about the case?"

"He said you had some vague leads and that we could follow them in our spare time."

"Spare time?" Mila demanded. "In other words, he's going to give us a full workload in addition to the Womack case?"

"That's the way I see it," Beau agreed.

"I can't do that," she told him. "I'm close on this, I can feel it. I guess you'll have to tell the chief that I'm sick."

"Mila . . ." he began in a warning tone.

"Just help me out for a few more days. I've rattled some cages at Ryathon, and I think the monster will show his or her face soon."

"You'd better hope it's real soon. The chief may let you have until Monday, but after that I think you'll be on permanent leave, and I can't really blame him."

"Me either," Mila agreed. "But this is something I have to do."

After she hung up, Quin said, "Well, what's the next step?"

She frowned. "I don't have much time to force our mastermind into the open, so I'm going to have to do something drastic."

"Like what?"

"Like tell everyone involved that I've found the express mail envelope."

Quin put his arm around her shoulders. "Then what do you expect to happen?"

"Whoever killed Larsen will try to get it from me."

Now Quin looked truly alarmed. "Or kill you!"

Mila shrugged. "They may try."

"That's your plan?" he demanded. "To get yourself killed?"

"No, my plan is to smoke them out and then catch them red-handed." She smiled up at him. "Don't worry. I'll be careful."

Quin still looked doubtful as Miss Eugenia walked onto the porch. "So, are you two through cuddling and ready for some volunteer work?"

Mila patted Quin's shoulder briskly. "I guess we'll work for a while, but I reserve the right to revert to cuddling at some point in the future."

They escorted the children and Daphne over to the Ledbetters'. Mila went through her list of security instructions twice before Quin led her to the door. "Call 911 at the first sign of trouble!" she called as he propelled her firmly down the front steps.

"They'll be fine," he assured her. As they walked to the town square, Quin continued, "I want you to tell Beau what you're up to. Chief Jones and Bishop Iverson too. If you do attract a killer here, they have a right to be prepared."

She nodded. "You're right. I will."

"And I want you to promise not to go anywhere without me."

She smiled. "It's a deal."

When they arrived at the temporary fairgrounds they found Winston Jones and Mark Iverson talking together. "Here's your chance," Quin said, leading her over to them.

Both men listened carefully as she outlined what she and Quin had found out and what she was planning to do. "When are you going to make your calls?" Mark asked.

Mila checked her watch. "We've promised Miss Eugenia a couple of hours. I'll call them as soon as I get home."

Mark nodded. "If the person you're looking for is as ruthless as they sound, they'll act quickly." He turned to Winston. "Can you have a car in front of Mila's house for the next twenty-four hours?"

Chief Jones nodded. "Yeah, I should be able to handle that up until the fair starts. Then everyone will be involved here."

"That should do," Mark said.

"I'm going to send the children and my mother over to Cleo's so if I attract the kind of attention I'm looking for—they'll be out of danger."

"But I'm staying with her," Quin pointed at Mila.

Mark nodded again. "It sounds like you've got all the bases covered. I'll ask Miss Myrtle behind you if I can watch out her guest room window. That way I can keep an eye on the back of your house."

"So the FBI is officially involved?" Mila asked.

Mark shook his head. "No, I've taken the day off work. My surveillance will be done as your friend and your bishop—not in an official capacity for the FBI."

She nodded. "I appreciate the help in any capacity." Then she turned to Winston. "But can the policeman you send sit in an unmarked car? I don't want to scare off my prey."

"Sure," Winston agreed again.

"Then I think we're set."

"You're sure about this?" Mark asked her. "We'll do the best we can to protect you, but there are no guarantees."

"I know," she admitted. "But I don't think there's any other way to assure that the children will be safe. Besides, I don't like the idea that someone got away with blackmail, robbery, and possibly murder."

"Okay, then," Mark said. "I'll be in place shortly after noon."

"Thank you," Mila said, knowing the words were inadequate. "Both of you," she added with a quick glance at Winston Jones.

The police chief touched the rim of his hat. "Glad to help."

They reported for duty and received multiple assignments from Miss Eugenia and Cornelia Blackwood. It was noon before Mila and Quin could escape, and once they were headed home, Quin whispered, "I'll bet there were Egyptian taskmasters who were easier on their Hebrew slaves than those two were on us."

Mila took his hand and broke into a trot. "Let's pick up the pace. As long as they can still see us, there's the chance that they might call us back."

When they got to Aunt Cora Sue's empty house, Mila called the Ledbetters to make sure her mother and the children were safe. Then they made sandwiches for lunch. Finally, having put it off as long as she could, Mila sat on the couch with her Womack file in one hand and her cell phone in the other.

"Well, here goes nothing," she said, and Quin nodded gravely.

Mila started with Carol Harmon, and their conversation was predictably short.

"I told you not to call me again," the secretary said.

"I just thought you might want to know that I've found the express mail envelope Larsen Womack was carrying around on the day of the fire. The contents make for some very interesting reading."

"I couldn't care less," Carol Harmon claimed. "If you call me again, I'm going to file a harassment complaint." Then the line went dead.

"Well, I scared her to death," Mila said as her finger found the next name on her list. "Let's see how Mr. DeFore takes the news." She dialed the number and waited for him to answer. She got his secretary. Mila insisted that it was an emergency, and the woman put her on hold and promised to find the Ryathon executive.

A few minutes later a breathless voice spoke into the phone. "Detective Edwards!"

"Hello, Mr. DeFore. I'm sorry if I disturbed you," she lied.

"Oh, it's no bother. I was just out in the shed, and it's quite a hike back here. What can I do for you?"

"Well, actually this is just a courtesy call to let you know that I found the express mail envelope Larsen Womack was planning to send to the FDA on the day he disappeared."

"You did! Well, that's wonderful!" Mr. DeFore sounded both pleased and relieved. "If you will put it in the mail to us, we'll gladly reimburse you for the postage."

"I'm afraid I won't be able to send it to you, Mr. DeFore," Mila said, taking perverse satisfaction in her words.

"But it's Ryathon property," he replied, his confusion apparent.

"I felt it was my duty to look at the contents," Mila continued. "Based on what I saw, I'm trying to decide whether to give it to the police or the FDA. Once I decide, you can try to reclaim it from one of them."

"I don't understand, Detective. What was in the envelope?"

"I'm sorry, but I can't say more," Mila said firmly. "I just wanted to let you know. Good-bye."

As soon as she disconnected, she dialed Mr. Ryan's private line.

"I don't want to give Mr. DeFore a chance to get to him before I do," Mila explained, and Quin nodded. She returned her attention to the phone as Brandon Ryan answered. "Mr. Ryan, this is Mila Edwards from the Albany Police Department."

"Oh, hi, Mila," he said.

"I'm calling to let you know that I've found the express mail envelope that Larsen Womack was carrying around on the day of the fire.

Once I decide whether to give it to the police or the FDA, I'll let you know."

There was total silence on the other end of the line. Mr. Ryan didn't ask what was in the envelope or why she felt compelled to give it to a law enforcement agency. "Thank you for calling," he said finally, then broke the connection.

Mila leaned back against Quin and sighed. "Well, it's done."

"How long before people start shooting through the windows?" Quin asked.

"We probably have a few minutes," she replied, bringing her face up close to his.

"Then let's not waste them." His lips lowered until they were pressed firmly against hers.

A few moments later they were interrupted by a phone call from Dorcas James. "I ran a background check on all the people involved with Larsen Womack, and I found a few interesting results."

Mila looked longingly at Quin, then sat up straight and gave Dorcas her full attention. "That was very sensible of you," Mila praised the other woman. "Tell me what you found."

"None of it may be important," Dorcas warned.

"I understand," Mila assured her. "But you never know."

"Well, first of all, Carol Harmon has an impressive block of Ryathon stock."

Mila felt her stomach quiver with excitement. "Do you know how she got it or when?"

"I'm working on that," Dorcas promised. "Also, Mr. DeFore is Brandon Ryan's uncle. He actually ran the company between the time Brandon's father died and Brandon finished school."

"I wonder if he'd like the chance to run it again."

"I'm also looking for evidence of that," Dorcas assured her. "Pierce Maxwell was fired from his last job for theft. A coworker who hated him has promised to call me with details after she leaves work today."

Mila was impressed not only by Dorcas's resourcefulness but also by the multitude of sins she found in a small group of Ryathon employees.

"The only weird thing I found about Belinda Wallace is that her husband has an accounting degree. It made me wonder why he's been working construction."

Mila frowned as she considered this. "Maybe he didn't like being cooped up all day. It's probably not related, but check into it anyway. Does the chief know you're doing all this to help me?"

"What do you think?" Dorcas returned.

"Are you just a genuinely nice person or are you hoping I'll get fired so you can have my job?"

Dorcas laughed. "Maybe a little of both. I'll let you know when I find out anything else."

After she hung up, Quin asked, "What will we do now?"

"Just sit and watch a movie I guess."

"All we have are Disney movies and those educational things Cleo brought over to impress the child services guy."

She sat beside him on the couch. "We can find something on the classic movie channel." She cut her eyes over at him mischievously. "If you're lucky they'll be showing *Gidget* or one of those movies with Sandra Dee."

"Why would that be lucky for me?"

"They were about surfers," she explained.

"Oh. That *would* be lucky. Maybe I could copy their techniques."

Mila was still laughing when Beau called. "What are you doing?" he asked suspiciously.

"Sitting here waiting for the shooting to start," she replied. "How about you?"

"Trying to find the culprit that's been breaking into dry cleaners in downtown Albany."

"How did the chief take the news that I called in sick today?" she asked.

"You don't want to know," he assured her. "I thought I'd come by there when I get off and bring a pizza for dinner," Beau offered casually.

"Somebody told you my mother was over at Cleo's, and you think we'll starve!" she accused.

Beau laughed. "No, I just don't want you to have to resort to all those casseroles in your refrigerator. I'd like to hang around and get shot at myself, but . . ."

"Let me guess. You have a *hot* date," Mila teased.

"You know me well. See you around six o'clock."

When Mila hung up, Quin had settled on *Butch Cassidy and the Sundance Kid*. "Great," she said after the second shoot-out. "With so much gunfire on the television, we'll never know what hit us."

Quin reached for the remote control. "I'll change it."

She put her hand on his arm. "It's okay. I've got my gun." She patted her pocket. "And we've got a policeman outside. We'll be fine."

Miss Eugenia came by on her way home from the fairgrounds just as the movie ended. "Let's hope things turn out better for us," Mila remarked as she switched off the television. Quin laughed and let Miss Eugenia in.

"If I'd known you two were sitting around here wasting time I'd have had you helping us with Faith Fair preparations," Miss Eugenia grumbled as she came into the living room. "I ache all over." Her shoulders were drooping, and she rubbed her lower back.

"Sorry we couldn't help, but we've set a trap for the people who killed Larsen Womack, and we're sitting here waiting to spring it."

Miss Eugenia stood up straight, all semblance of pain disappearing. "What kind of a trap?"

Trying to hide her amusement, Mila explained.

"So, whoever the criminal is could arrive at any moment," Miss Eugenia said, eyeing the front window anxiously.

"At any moment," Mila agreed. "In fact, you could be the criminal," she teased.

"Me!" Miss Eugenia looked astounded.

"I'll vouch for Miss Eugenia," Quin said with a smile. "She may be a slave driver, but she's not a criminal."

Miss Eugenia nodded primly in his direction. "Thank you, Quin."

"How are things coming with the Faith Fair?" he asked.

"Oh, working with Cornelia is trying, but I think it's going to turn out nicely."

"From what I saw this morning I predict a big success," Quin was encouraging.

Miss Eugenia nodded and took a step toward the door. "That's another thing about working with Cornelia. She never accepts second best. If we have to work through the night, she'll have things the way she wants them tomorrow morning." She took another step and put her hand on the doorknob. "Well, I guess I'll be going. I see Arnold is watching the house."

"The policeman?" Mila clarified, looking over Miss Eugenia's shoulder to the car parked across the street. "Yes, he's our backup."

Miss Eugenia caught both of them in a serious gaze. "You two be careful. You hear?"

"Yes, ma'am," Mila promised.

After Miss Eugenia left, Mila called the Ledbetters again, and after a good report from Daphne, she took the remote control from Quin and announced that she would pick the next movie. She chose *Beaches* to torture him, but her plan backfired since she cried through the whole thing. Afterward she felt like she had the flu.

"Remind me never to watch that movie again," she begged as Quin stood and stretched. He reached to turn on a lamp, but she stopped him. "Sorry, but since it's getting dark outside, lights in here will just make us better targets if anyone is trying to shoot us."

He pulled his hand away from the lamp switch as if it had been burned. "That's a pleasant thought."

"It's kind of romantic," she said, moving close to him.

He kissed her gently. "I can't believe that *you* are looking on the bright side of anything."

She laughed. "I guess you're rubbing off on me too." After another kiss, she leaned back so she could see him better. "I've gotten used to having you around. I can't imagine not being able to talk to you in the evenings, then watching you laugh at my pain."

"I'll miss you too," he acknowledged.

"But I guess as soon as this is over you'll be going back to surfing."

Some of the humor left his face as he nodded. "My parents arrived in California yesterday. After handling some business, they'll be headed down here."

"To take over the foster care of Lily and Ben." Mila tried not to let the hurt show, but knew she failed when he reached out and stroked her cheek.

"I'm sorry."

"I know it's for the best," she assured him. "But I don't like to think about that. Where's your next tournament?"

"They're called competitions," he corrected her with a tolerant smile. "The next big one is in Australia, but I'm not planning to compete."

"Why not?"

"Well, I've been wanting to expand the retail side of my surfboard business. Once my parents get home, I won't have to house-sit anymore, so I should be able to concentrate on that. A friend of mine has a place in Hawaii that he's willing to rent out, and I've been thinking about taking him up on it."

"I guess surfboards are big business in Hawaii," she said.

"Oh, yes. And they have some good competitions too." He took her hand in his. "What about you? Are you going to stick it out here with Chief Monahan and the Albany Police Department?"

"I don't know," she admitted honestly. "I like Beau and am grudgingly fond of Dorcas, even though I know she wants my job. And who wouldn't love Haggerty?"

He smiled. "That's true."

"But after my mother and Lily and Ben and . . ." She wanted to add his name to the list, but pride wouldn't allow it. "And leave, it won't be the same here. I thought I might go back to school and do something like Wilma where I can put kids first and not feel guilty about it." She glanced around. "And maybe I'll buy a house that isn't falling apart."

"You've got to get all your fences back in place," he teased.

"Yes," she agreed, but she couldn't make herself smile. "I can't imagine life without fences."

He laughed, but it wasn't a particularly happy sound.

Mila pushed herself to her feet. "Well, I'd better walk through to make sure everything's still secure."

"Wouldn't we have heard if someone had tried to open a door or window?" he asked, following behind her.

"Probably, but I don't want to take any chances."

They finished their rounds, and Mila was wondering what they could do to further depress themselves when Beau arrived with the pizza.

"I got one with everything and one with only cheese," he informed them. "I figured that way I couldn't miss." He walked into the kitchen, then turned around and led them back to the living room. "Too many windows in there."

Mila got plates from the kitchen and cans of Sprite. While they ate, they filled Beau in on the recent developments in the case.

"When Miss Eugenia was here a little while ago we teased her about being the criminal, but since she left, that's been on my mind."

"You think Miss Eugenia killed Larsen?" Beau demanded as Quin choked on a bite of pizza.

Mila frowned at her partner. "No. But it made me think that the criminal might be someone I'd never suspect."

"Like me?" Beau looked even more offended now.

"No, I considered you briefly, but it makes no sense. You didn't arrange for me to come to Albany and had nothing to do with our being assigned as partners."

Beau put down his pizza. "You suspect Chief Monahan?"

"Well, he has been very resistant to this investigation. You've got to admit that."

"I'll admit that, but I won't consider him as a murder suspect." Beau picked up his pizza and took a sheet of paper out of his pocket with the other hand. "Which reminds me, Dorcas sent you this."

Mila reached for the paper, and Beau pulled it back. "Unless you suspect Dorcas too?"

She smirked at him and grabbed the sheet of paper from his fingers. "Pierce Maxwell. He was fired for stealing $235 out of the sympathy fund at his former employer," she read out loud. "That's interesting. And Carol Harmon's Ryathon stock was a recent acquisition, and there was no corresponding transaction to show that she used any of her own money to purchase it."

"They bribed her!" Quin guessed.

"It looks that way," Mila murmured as she continued to scan the page. Then she looked up. "Tell Dorcas I said thanks and if she has any more spare time, keep digging."

Beau raised an eyebrow. "You like to push your luck, don't you." He chewed his pizza in silence for a few minutes, then said, "You could be right about the killer being someone we're overlooking. Maybe I should take your Womack file home with me. Fresh eyes might spot something."

She picked up the file, put it in a large envelope, then extended it to him. "I don't mind you looking at it, just don't lose anything."

After they'd finished off most of the pizza, Mila put what was left in the refrigerator. Then Beau said he'd better go. "Don't want to keep my date waiting."

Mila rolled her eyes. "Actually Beau has to babysit his niece so his sister can go to night school. He just makes up all this stuff about dating."

Quin laughed, and Beau looked like he'd been shot. "I only babysit four nights a week, and I make up for lost dating time on the other three nights."

"Get out of here before one of us figures out that you're really a nice guy," Mila said, encouraging Beau's departure by putting a hand on his back.

"How do you think they'll attack?" Beau asked when they reached the front door. "Probably under the cover of darkness," Mila replied. "So we're in for a long night."

"But by this time tomorrow, it should all be over," Quin pointed out.

Beau frowned. "I hate to miss all the excitement, but I don't want my sister to miss class."

Mila opened the door for him. "Get out of here," she said. "We'll be fine."

Mila locked the door behind Beau and had just joined Quin on the couch when they heard the shot. "Get down," she ordered Quin, her hand pushing him to the floor. Then, gun drawn, she inched toward the window. She used her gun to push the blinds back slightly and saw that the young policeman was out of his car and kneeling beside a body on the sidewalk in front of Aunt Cora Sue's house.

"Use the list by the phone to call Chief Jones," she told Quin curtly. "But stay down."

"Where are you going?" he demanded.

"Outside," she replied, and she was out the door before he could stop her.

Moving her eyes from side to side, Mila approached the little gathering on the sidewalk. When she was close enough to see the victim, a groan ripped from her throat. "Oh, no!" she cried.

"He's still alive," Arnold said, looking around nervously. "And I've called for backup."

The sound of sirens rent the air as Mila fell to her knees beside Beau's prone form. "Beau Lambert, don't you dare die on me!" she ordered him, blinking to keep her eyes clear of tears. "Can you tell where the bullet hit him?" she asked the policeman.

"In the chest," Arnold replied, and Mila's heart pounded. Then she did an examination of her own and determined that the bullet hole was closer to the shoulder. She put her head against his chest. His heart was beating, but there was a distressing whistling sound.

"I think a lung is punctured," she said. "But I can't figure out why he's unconscious. He hasn't had time to lose that much blood."

"He hit his head pretty hard when he fell," Arnold told her.

"That's probably the reason," she said as Quin knelt beside her. She gave him a cross look. "I thought I told you to stay inside."

Before Quin could reply, Mark Iverson arrived on foot. "I heard the shot! What happened?" he asked, leaning down to examine Beau.

"He brought us pizza for dinner, and when he left, someone shot him," Quin said.

Mila directed a question toward Arnold. "Did you see who shot him?"

Arnold shook his head. "I saw him come out, then I looked away. When I heard the shot, I got out and saw someone running through those hedges at the back of your yard."

Mila glanced at the bushes in question and controlled a shudder.

"Man or woman?" Mark demanded.

Arnold shrugged. "I couldn't tell. They were dressed in black and wearing a mask."

Quin put an arm around Mila's shoulder as Winston Jones and another Haggerty policeman pulled up, lights flashing. Mark told them about the shooter, and they left to try to track him down. It seemed to take forever for the ambulance to get there.

"It has to come from Albany," Arnold said when Mila complained. "But it should be here soon."

It was actually another five minutes before the ambulance came to a halt near the curb. Mila and Quin stepped back while the attendants examined Beau.

"Collapsed lung," one of the paramedics said. "Bullet may have nicked the collar bone."

"Is he going to be all right?" Mila asked.

"I think so."

Mila sagged against Quin as they slid Beau onto a stretcher and lifted him into the ambulance. "We'll follow behind you," she said, and the attendant nodded vaguely.

Mila took a step toward the house. "I'll have to go inside and get my keys."

Quin grabbed her hand and pulled her to his Mustang. "I've got my keys. Get in."

As they ran for his car, Mila called to Arnold over her shoulder. "Could you go to the Ledbetters' house and wait with them until we get back?"

The young policeman nodded, and Mila ducked into the passenger seat of Quin's car.

During the drive to Albany, Mila called her mother at the Ledbetters and told them to expect Arnold. Daphne reported that Cleo was admitting the policeman as they spoke, then she asked several questions in rapid succession. Mila assured her mother that she and Quin were both fine, but told her that Beau had been shot.

"We're on our way to the hospital now. We'll let you know when we have more information."

After ending the call with her mother, Mila reluctantly called the switchboard at the Albany Police Department, but the operator told her that Chief Jones had already notified them. Knowing that she'd just reached an all-time low on Chief Monahan's popularity list, Mila sat back against the seat and watched the taillights of the ambulance in front of them.

They followed the stretcher into the emergency room, but were stopped at the huge double doors that led into the examination area. "You'll have to wait here," a no-nonsense nurse informed them. Then she handed Mila a clipboard with several forms attached. "When you have these completed, bring them back to me."

Mila knew Beau's name and cell number, but nothing else. She was staring at the woefully incomplete admission forms when Chief Monahan and Dorcas rushed in. He gave Mila a cursory glance, then demanded to speak to someone in authority. The chief was ushered into the back, and Mila sighed with relief. Dorcas walked over and sat down beside her.

"Are you two okay?"

"Yes," Mila said, unable to keep her voice from wavering.

"And the Womack children?"

"Fine." Mila pointed at the clipboard. "But I can't fill this out."

Dorcas took it from her. "I'll do it."

A few minutes later the chief returned, and Mila felt herself stiffen. "He's going to be all right," he said to no one in particular. Then he glared directly at her. "Can you explain why Beau was at your house tonight and how he happened to get shot?"

Mila licked her lips. "He brought pizza for dinner. When he was leaving someone shot him."

"Why was a Haggerty policeman sitting in an unmarked car in front of your house?"

Mila sighed. There was no way around it. She was going to have to tell him the truth. "I decided to smoke out whoever killed Larsen Womack. I called everyone I've interviewed so far and told them I found the express mail envelope Larsen was carrying around the day he disappeared."

"Where did you find it?"

"I didn't find it," Mila clarified. "I just said that so they'd make a move against me. I never meant for Beau to get hurt."

"Did he know about your little plan?"

"He might have overheard something," she said, determined not to get Beau into more trouble.

"Well, it looks like you were successful," the chief said. "You smoked out the killer, you just didn't catch him."

"He might try again," Mila began, but the chief cut her off.

"Am I supposed to consider that *good* news?" he demanded. "And who will get hurt this time? Or maybe you'll *really* be successful and someone will get killed."

Mila felt Quin tense and knew he was about to defend her, which would only make matters worse. So she spoke before he could. "I didn't start this, someone else did. I'm just trying to find out who."

"Without permission," the chief pointed out. "Without proper backup. Without following procedure. But then, that's what you do best."

"Most of the interviewing I did took place while I was on leave, so my actions were those of a concerned citizen," Mila said through clenched teeth.

Chief Monahan raised an eyebrow. "Did you use your rank and your association with the Albany Police Department to get people to cooperate with you?"

The mocking tone of his voice told her that he already knew she had. "Yes."

Now he looked disgusted. "Be in my office first thing on Monday morning." He turned to Dorcas. "We're going to have to find somewhere else to wait. I can't stay in here."

Dorcas gave Mila a sympathetic glance over her shoulder as she followed the chief to the nurses' station. After a brief conversation, a nurse led them through a set of doors, presumably to a private waiting room.

"Well, I guess that answers the question of whether I'll stick it out at the Albany Police Department," Mila said once they were gone.

Quin pulled her close. "You could always become my partner in the surfboard business and join me in Hawaii."

"I don't have a real good success rate with partners," she told him.

"You just haven't been working with the right partner," he whispered.

Mila snuggled close to him, grateful for his calming presence. She dozed for a few minutes and woke up when a young woman came over and introduced herself as Dr. Rankin. She unbuttoned her lab coat and said, "I've been working on Detective Lambert." Mila had to smile. The doctor was quite lovely, and she knew that the first thing Beau was going to do when he regained consciousness was ask Dr. Rankin out on a date.

"How is he?" Quin asked.

"He's going to be sore for a few days, but otherwise okay. We're keeping him overnight, then he'll be released tomorrow."

The chief and Dorcas walked into the waiting room, and Dr. Rankin repeated this information. Chief Monahan looked relieved, and Mila realized that he cared about Beau. After the doctor left, the chief turned to Quin, as if he couldn't bear the sight of Mila. "Take her home. There's nothing more to be done here tonight."

Mila allowed Quin to pull her toward the door. "Call if there's any change in his condition," she asked Dorcas, her eyes pleading, and the other woman nodded slightly.

Once they were settled in Quin's car, headed back to Haggerty, Mila let the tears fall. "I feel so responsible."

"You didn't ask Beau to bring pizza," Quin pointed out logically. "He knew it was a dangerous situation, and I'm surprised that he didn't take better precautions as a trained police detective. And he's going to be fine," he added. "Don't beat yourself up about it."

She had to admit that his arguments were sound, and they did make her feel a little better. Sniffling slightly, she called the Ledbetters again and gave them an update on Beau.

"Earl Sr. has his police scanner out, and we've been listening," Cleo told her. "Why don't you and Quin spend the night over here? Whoever shot Beau might still be hanging around your place."

Mila thanked her for the offer, but declined. "I hope I get a chance at the person who shot Beau," she told Cleo grimly.

When Quin parked in front of Aunt Cora Sue's house, Mila took a deep breath, then drew her gun and got out. A different car was parked across the street, and they could see another policeman sitting inside. Mila surveyed the area, then motioned for Quin to join her. She had a bad moment when they had to pass the place where Beau had been shot, but made it into the house without incident.

After locking the front door, Mila closed the living room blinds, then turned on one lamp so they could see. "We need to make sure there's no one inside," she told Quin, and he nodded. They walked slowly from room to room checking corners, closets, cabinets, and under beds. They found nothing out of the ordinary until they reached Mila's room. Propped up on one of her pillows was Beau's police badge, still splattered with his blood.

Mila staggered, and Quin put a hand under her elbow to steady her. Reluctantly she approached the bed and saw that in addition to the badge the shooter had left a little note. It said, *This is your final warning. Leave it alone or die.*

"He was in my room." She forced the words from between her stiff lips. "I'll never be able to sleep in here again."

"Well, not tonight, anyway," Quin agreed. "We'll both be sitting up in the living room—just in case he decides to pay us another visit."

After making a call to Mark Iverson to report the incident, they settled in the living room. After a few minutes Mila rubbed her hands up and down her arms. "I don't think I can."

"What?"

"Leave it alone."

"Of course you can't. It's like you said, the only way you or the children will ever be safe is to find out what happened to Larsen and Theresa." Mila gasped, and Quin sat up straight. "What?"

"I just realized that whoever shot Beau took my Womack file."

CHAPTER 19

Mila and Quin took turns dozing, but neither really slept, and both were tired when the sun rose on Saturday morning. Mila called the hospital and got a good report on Beau. Then she accompanied Quin out to his camper for him to get some fresh clothes. They took turns at guard duty with Mila's gun while the other showered, then Mila called Mark Iverson on his cell phone.

"Are you still watching our backyard?" she asked.

"I am," Mark confirmed.

"I think the danger is over, temporarily at least. I doubt that they'll try anything in broad daylight."

"If they're desperate enough, they might," he replied. "I'm going home for a while, but Winston is coming to take over for me. Just in case."

After Mila ended her conversation with Mark, she and Quin sat in dejected silence at the kitchen table until Daphne and the children walked in.

"You're home early," Mila said, hiding her gun in her lap.

"Cleo wasn't feeling very well, so we decided to get out of her way," Daphne replied.

"We got to sleep in a tent in the playroom!" Lily announced. "Even Ben!"

The baby smiled around the fingers in his mouth, and Mila felt her mood improve instantly. "Well, that sounds like lots of fun."

"It was!" Lily assured her. "Earl Jr. says that next time we spend the night, we'll stay outside so we can have a fire."

Mila's spirits plummeted at this comment, since she knew the chances of another sleepover at the Ledbetters' was unlikely to happen.

Quin and Mila helped the children unpack while Daphne started on breakfast. During the unpacking process it was discovered that Lily had left her pajamas at the Ledbetters. "What will I wear when I go to sleep tonight?" the little girl asked, concerned.

"Don't worry. I'll go over and get them after breakfast," Mila promised.

When they returned to the kitchen, Daphne had pancakes and sausage and fresh-squeezed orange juice arranged on the table. Lily asked to say the blessing, and permission was granted. She blessed everyone individually and each item of food by name. Once the prayer was concluded, Mila fixed Ben a plate and cut up his pancakes. Then Daphne questioned them carefully about the night before, using hand gestures and spelling out words to keep the children from comprehending.

"How is B-e-a-u?" she asked when the story was finished.

"I talked to the h-o-s-p-i-t-a-l this morning, and they said he's fine," Mila replied.

"No sign of the s-h-o-o-t-e-r?" Daphne inquired, and Lily looked up from her plate with a frown.

"Why does everyone keep doing that?" she asked. "You know I can't read yet."

Mila laughed, grateful for the comic relief. "I'm sorry, Lily. That was rude of us. Tell me some more about your campout."

Once breakfast was over, Lily and Ben begged Quin to help them make another tepee, so while they dragged him into the living room, Mila put her gun into her pocket and headed over to the Ledbetters. She walked up to the front door and rang the bell. She could hear the bell echo through the entryway on the other side of the door, but no one came to answer. She waited a minute or so, then rang again. A little chill ran down her spine. Daphne had said that Cleo wasn't feeling well, so it was unlikely that she had gone anywhere. All her instincts told her something was wrong. If she had brought danger to the Ledbetters she would never forgive herself.

Mila tried the doorknob, and it turned easily under her hand, which she considered a very bad sign. Pulling the gun from her pocket, she stepped into the entryway. The room was empty, and the big house was eerily silent. She decided not to announce her presence and crept stealthily toward the living room. It, too, was empty. Keeping her back to the wall, her eyes roving continuously, she moved through the dining room, into the breakfast nook, and finally into the kitchen. There she found Cleo lying on the floor. Earl Jr., dressed as usual in his police outfit, was sitting beside her. His walkie-talkie was clutched in his hand.

"I've called for backup," he said softly, and Mila could see unshed tears in his eyes. "But it always takes Daddy a while to get here."

Mila dropped beside Cleo, her eyes searching for a wound of some kind. "What happened?" she demanded.

"I fell," Cleo explained.

Mila frowned. "You fell?"

"It happens sometimes." She glanced at her son and gave him a reassuring smile. "But Earl Jr. knows just what to do. He called his daddy, and help is already on the way."

Now Mila was stupefied. "Help?"

"Earl Sr. will have to lift me up and take me to the hospital so I can get a shot," Cleo told her.

"Why?"

Mila could tell that Cleo was reluctant to answer, but finally she did. "I have multiple sclerosis, Mila."

Multiple sclerosis. The words echoed in her mind. Was that the disease Jerry Lewis used to have telethons for? And if so, how could Cleo have it. She was perfectly fine. "What are you talking about?" Mila demanded, getting irritated now.

"I have MS," Cleo repeated patiently. "It's a disease of the nervous system. It's incurable, so far, but they do have drugs to treat the symptoms. Usually I have some signs warning me when I'm about to have a flare-up, but this one caught me by surprise. Once I get my medicine, it will take a couple of days, and then I'll be good as new."

"You have an *incurable* disease?" Mila said, then cut her eyes quickly over to Earl Jr.

"It's not fatal," Cleo said matter-of-factly. "At least not directly. Sometimes complications develop that affect lifespan."

Mila was appalled, almost as much by Cleo's calm attitude as she was by the presence of the disease itself. Slipping her gun into her pocket, she demanded, "How long have you had it?"

"I was diagnosed when I was a teenager, so Earl Sr. knew what he was getting into when he married me. He's one fine man, I can tell you," Cleo continued. "We didn't think we'd be able to have children, and my doctors were not pleased when they found out that Earl Jr. was on the way. The doctors said the pregnancy might accelerate the progress of the disease, but I didn't care." She ruffled the little boy's hair. "He was worth it."

Now Mila understood why Cleo couldn't have more children and why child services took such an interest in her. Why they had an elevator and rarely used the beautiful spiral stairs. Why Earl Sr. came home and cooked lunch every day. "Is there anything I can do?" she asked, her voice thick with emotion.

"Just don't cry," Cleo begged. "Because if you do, there will be a chain reaction."

It was a struggle, but Mila held back the tears. Earl Sr. arrived a few minutes later, and she helped load Cleo into their SUV.

"Will they keep her at the hospital?" she asked Earl Sr. as she followed him around to the driver's side door.

He nodded. "She'll have to have an IV for a few days."

"Do you want Earl Jr. to stay with us?" Mila offered, desperate to do something useful.

He shook his head. "He likes to go. All the nurses know him by now, and they don't mind if he's there."

"Will you call and let me know how she's doing?" Mila pleaded.

"Sure," he agreed, swinging up into the driver's seat.

Mila stepped back and watched them drive away. Earl Jr. waved to her out the back window, and she wiped away the tears she could no longer contain. Then she turned and headed toward Aunt Cora Sue's house. She stopped and spoke to the young policeman, Arnold, who was sitting in the old truck across the street. He asked about Beau, and she told him that the Albany detective was doing well. There was a noise in the distance, and she looked up sharply.

"They're putting the finishing touches on the Faith Fair," Arnold explained shyly. "I'll be headed there myself in a little while."

Mila pursed her lips. "Do you think Miss Eugenia is there?"

Arnold nodded. "I know she is. I saw her walking that way an hour ago."

"Since you're here, I'm going to walk to the square and talk to her. Would you mind going inside and letting Quin and my mother know?"

"Sure," Arnold agreed and climbed from his truck. "I'll stay in the house until you get back."

Mila waited until Arnold was inside Aunt Cora Sue's house, then walked briskly down Hickory Lane and turned onto Maple Street, then up to Main, where the Faith Fair preparations were in full swing. She found Miss Eugenia helping to set up the watermelon-eating contest.

Miss Eugenia looked up just as Mila reached the booth. "Oh, Mila! I'm so glad to see you. I need an extra pair of hands."

Miss Eugenia gave Mila one end of a crepe-paper roll and started twisting it.

"I was sorry to hear about Beau Lambert getting shot, but Winston says he's going to be all right."

"It looks that way," Mila said as Miss Eugenia anchored a section of crepe paper with masking tape and continued her twisting. "I just came from Cleo Ledbetter's. Earl Sr. was taking her to the hospital."

Miss Eugenia looked up sharply. "Is she okay?"

"She fell," Mila replied. "But I don't think she hurt herself. She says once she gets her medicine she'll be fine."

Miss Eugenia nodded, tearing off a piece of masking tape with her teeth. "That's good."

"Why didn't you tell me?" Mila asked, trying to hide the hurt she felt.

"It wasn't my place to tell you."

"She's so young," Mila managed finally. "And she said it's incurable."

"That could change tomorrow," Miss Eugenia pointed out sensibly. "There's all kinds of scientists working on a cure."

"It's so sad."

"Disease is always a scary thing," Miss Eugenia acknowledged. "But look how well Cleo functions. You've spent a lot of time with her lately and had no idea she had anything wrong with her."

Mila shrugged, then said, "I'll bet if the people in this town knew she was sick they wouldn't treat her so bad!"

Miss Eugenia nodded. "That's the point exactly. Cleo's looking for friendship—not sympathy. So you'd better adjust your attitude before you see her again. She wants to be treated just like anyone else. And twenty-nine days out of thirty she *is* just like anyone else. But that thirtieth day is a doozy."

They finished the table decorations, and Mila told Miss Eugenia that she had to go check on Quin and the kids, but promised to come back soon. When she got home, she sent Arnold back out to his truck, then settled the children in front of the television before she told Quin and Daphne about Cleo.

"What a shame," Daphne said, dabbing at her eyes. "She's such a brave little thing."

"She's also very proud, so don't make a big deal over it the next time you see her," Mila insisted.

"I can't believe it," Quin said, sitting down at the kitchen table. "Cleo is one of the least helpless people I've ever met."

Mila smiled. "I'm sure she'll be glad to hear that you think so."

Quin didn't return her smile. "Earl Sr. took her to the hospital?"

"Yes. She has to get medicine intravenously for a few days, then she claims she'll be back to normal."

They sat quietly for a few minutes, all lost in their own thoughts. Then Mila stood and pulled out her cell phone. "I think I'll call the hospital and make sure that Cleo arrived, and maybe they'll let me talk to Beau."

She walked out onto the porch to make her calls. She was put on hold several times, but finally received confirmation that Cleo had been admitted to the hospital. Then she was transferred to the line for Beau's private room.

As soon as she identified herself, he said, "Let me guess. You got fired in Atlanta because your partner got shot after bringing you pizza."

She had to laugh. "No, but I promise full disclosure the next time I see you."

"Really?" he sounded pleased.

"It's the least I can do," she responded dryly. "Can you tell me anything about whoever shot you?"

"I didn't see a thing," he told her in obvious frustration. "I remember taking my keys out of my pocket, then nothing until I woke up in the hospital."

"I've got an idea, and I wanted to run it past you," Mila said, then gave him the details.

"Do you have a death wish?" he demanded when she was through.

"No, but until this is settled, I'll be looking for danger around every corner. And the Womack children will be at risk—"

"Okay," he interrupted with a weary sigh. "I'll call the chief."

"Make sure he understands that he can't stop me. His only choice is whether to help me or not."

"I'll spell it out for him."

When Mila turned off her phone, she saw that Quin was standing in the doorway, watching her closely. "I told you I couldn't let it go."

He nodded. "I knew you wouldn't. You really believe this is the only way?"

"I can't live my life watching for shadows and worrying about Lily and Ben. If my plan works, it should all be over with by tonight."

"So what's our next step?"

"We've got to tell Mark Iverson."

"Do you think he'll go along with your plan?"

She nodded. "I think so if I present it to him just right. I'll talk to him first, then I'll call someone at Ryathon."

"Who?"

She considered this for a few seconds, then said, "I think I'll call Mr. DeFore and count on him to spread the word."

Mila called Mark Iverson on his cell phone and explained what she wanted him to do. After a brief pause, he agreed. "I'll help you, but we have to make sure that innocent lives are protected."

"I've asked Chief Monahan from Albany to provide officers, some uniformed and some in street clothes," Mila told him. "We'll set the meeting place up away from the crowd, and I'll stay on the outskirts for the entire evening, just in case they try to relieve me of the package before the transfer."

"You seem to have thought of everything," Mark acknowledged. "Starting at seven o'clock, I'll call every fifteen minutes on your cell phone. If you don't answer, I'll know something is wrong. We also need to establish a code so that you can warn me of a problem if one arises and you are still able to answer your phone."

"What kind of code?"

"Something very simple," he replied. "Like if you answer, 'Hello,' I'll know that things are fine. If you answer, 'Edwards,' I'll know that you are in trouble."

"Okay."

She heard him sigh. "Unless you change your mind, I'll meet you by the library at seven o'clock."

"I won't change my mind," she assured him. After ending her call to Mark, Mila took a deep breath and called Mr. DeFore. "I've decided to give the information to the FBI," she told the Ryathon executive. "The resident agent in Albany is on vacation today, but he's going to come to Haggerty tonight. I'm meeting him in front of the Haggerty Library at seven o'clock if you want to have a representative present."

"I'll inform Mr. Ryan and see whether he wants to send someone to the meeting or just contact the FBI and request the return of our property." Then the ever-so-polite Mr. DeFore hung up without saying good-bye.

Mila looked up a Quin. "Well, that's that."

"He took the bait?"

She shrugged. "At least he knows. We'll have to see what happens from here." She chewed her lip for a few seconds, then said, "I have some errands to run, and I'd like to get a feeling for the area while it's still light. Would you like to walk into town with me?"

He nodded. "Sure."

They went inside and asked Daphne if she could watch the children while they went into town.

"You two go right on ahead," Daphne agreed. "The kids and I will be fine here."

"Don't leave the house," Mila instructed.

Daphne agreed with a roll of her eyes. "Don't worry."

"Maybe I'll have Arnold come inside again."

"He'll just make the children nervous," Daphne said as she herded them toward the door. "I'll call your cell phone if there's a problem."

Still uneasy, Mila walked outside with Quin. "Do you think they'll be okay?"

"Yes. You're attracting all the attention to yourself."

Some of the tension eased out of her shoulders. "That does make me feel a little better."

He took her hand in his. "Unfortunately, it doesn't help my feelings at all."

Once they reached the town square, they went to the post office and picked up an express mail envelope. Their next stop was the drugstore where Mila bought a package of loose-leaf paper, which she slipped inside the mailer. Then, after tucking the envelope under her arm, they proceeded to the fair site. They walked around the perimeter, taking note of the library in relation to the grandstand and booths set up in the square.

"The library was a good place to set up the meeting," Quin praised her. "It's at a far corner, well away from the grandstand where the festivities will be wrapping up."

"And there should already be Albany policemen in the adjacent buildings, watching for our prey."

They were feeling pleased with themselves and their plan when Miss Eugenia spotted them and drafted them into last-minute service. Unable to think of a reasonable excuse, they agreed. They worked all afternoon, and Mila was careful to keep the envelope in full view of anyone who might be watching.

At five o'clock they were dismissed to go home. When they arrived at Aunt Cora Sue's house, Mila walked over to the old truck to confer with Arnold.

"We'll be leaving for the fair in just a few minutes," she told him.

He nodded. "I'll wait and go with you."

Daphne had the children dressed and ready to go to the fair. They were excited and begged to leave at once.

Mila explained that she and Quin would have to clean up, but promised to hurry. She took a quick shower, then pulled her hair back into a ponytail so that she wouldn't risk it obscuring her vision. She dressed in a baggy pair of brown wool pants and an equally drab blouse.

When she returned to the living room, she found Quin waiting with the others. He had changed into dark-colored clothing and gave her a nervous smile. Mila took a deep breath and said, "Then let's go."

Arnold led the way, while Quin and Mila brought up the rear of their little procession. Under her left arm she carried the express mail envelope full of notebook paper. In her right hand she held her police revolver, hidden in the pocket of her loose-fitting slacks. When they reached the fairgrounds, she saw Frankie Cofield from the Albany PD and Winston Jones step up close. She walked casually over to the police chief.

"Is everyone in place?"

"The square is swarming with police, and we've got men in the buildings around the library. So I guess we're as ready as we'll ever be."

Mila glanced at her watch. "I'll start for the library a few minutes before seven o'clock. I'll pass by here on my way so you'll know I'm making my move."

He nodded. "I've got your cell number, and I'll call you if I see a problem."

She smiled. "Good luck on getting through. Mark Iverson's going to call every fifteen minutes."

Winston touched the brim of his hat, then they moved on. Quin and Mila walked through the booths and tables, careful to keep a safe distance from the children. They saw Miss George Ann, who accepted their compliments on the Faith Fair's success and confided that she was most likely going to be named president of the planning committee.

They found Miss Eugenia judging the pie contest with Polly Kirby, who had come to the fair in a wheelchair. "Talk about your dream job," Quin said as he watched the ladies sampling the pies. "Those pies look delicious."

Miss Eugenia laughed. "The only hard part is going to be choosing a loser!"

"Where are Kate and her children?" Mila asked, looking around.

"Mark asked them to stay home," Miss Eugenia said, and Mila realized that this was a safety precaution.

She grimaced. "If I survive the night, I'm going to owe Kate Iverson a trip to Disneyworld or someplace equally wonderful to make up for them missing the first annual Faith Fair."

Miss Eugenia laughed. "Kate understands. And it's not your fault that Mark is a worrywart."

"Mila knows all about that," Quin remarked, taking a bite of pie. "I vote for this one."

Mila pulled him away from the pie contest to the barbecue stand where they bought plate dinners. They sat on the grass across the street from the fair and watched the watermelon-eating contest.

"My money's on the big guy," Quin told her as he took a big bite of coleslaw.

Mila eyed the contestants. "I think the skinny man on the end will win."

A few minutes later her prediction proved correct, and Quin congratulated her.

"I had an unfair advantage," she told him modestly. "All that police training."

When they finished eating, they resumed their tour of the fair, stopping briefly at the LDS booth where they received a refrigerator magnet proclaiming *Love One Another.* Then they moved on to the Haggerty Baptist Church's booth where Cornelia Blackwood presented them with a Bible and an autographed copy of her cousin's book.

"He'll be our keynote speaker," she reminded them. "You'll have to sit down early if you want to have a seat!"

Quin stayed very close to Mila's side throughout the evening, often holding her hand or putting an arm around her waist. She appreciated the gestures of solidarity, but as seven o'clock approached, she had a serious talk with him.

"I'm a police detective," she began, and he smiled.

"I knew that."

"What I mean is that I'm trained for situations like the one tonight," she continued. "I can take care of myself, but if you get in the way, one of us might get hurt. When I meet Mark, I need you to stay back and let me do my job."

He didn't look happy, but finally he nodded. "Okay."

She took a deep breath. "Well, then, let's start toward the library. I'll tell you when to stop and let me go the rest of the way by myself."

He *really* looked unhappy about this, and she smiled.

"I won't actually be alone," she clarified. "Mark will be with me, and the police have the place surrounded."

"I know," he said. "But I still don't like it."

As they walked past the grandstand, the high school cheerleaders were just finishing a tumbling routine. Cornelia Blackwood stepped to the microphone and introduced her cousin. Mila nodded casually to Winston Jones, then proceeded toward the library.

Once they reached the sidewalk in front of the building, Mila pointed to a wooden bench. "Why don't you sit here?" *Out of the line of fire,* she thought. "That way if there's trouble you can go for help."

Instead of answering he pulled her into his arms and gave her a long, hard kiss. She could see the distress in his eyes, but he didn't argue. Instead he walked over and sat on the bench as she had asked. Mila took a deep breath, tucked the envelope more securely under her arm, and walked up the steps of the library and waited. Mark Iverson appeared a few minutes later, walking down the middle of Main Street, which had been closed off during the fair as a safety precaution.

He climbed the steps and came to a stop right in front of Mila. "Nothing yet?" he asked.

"Not so far." Her voice was full of tension.

"Dorcas James sent this to you," he said, handing her a sheet of paper.

Mila glanced at it with minimal interest. Itemized in neat print was the information about Carol Harmon's Ryathon stock. Apparently she had been offered early retirement effective at the end of the year and had accepted. The block of stock was part of the deal. Then there was a paragraph explaining that Belinda Wallace's husband had started working construction after a conviction for embezzlement. She had just lifted her eyes to make a comment to Mark when realization hit her like a ton of bricks.

Belinda asking Larsen for rides to and from work. Belinda allowing Larsen to use the computer in her spare bedroom to compile his report for the FDA. Belinda coming all the way to Haggerty to tell them about the vitamin with the folic acid deficiency. Belinda's husband having a degree in accounting and a conviction for embezzlement.

"What's the matter?" Mark asked, concerned.

"I just figured out who has been leading me around by the nose," she rasped, fighting nausea.

Before Mark could reply, they heard Daphne calling from the edge of the temporary fairgrounds. "Mila!" she cried, panic in her voice. "Ben is gone!"

Mila looked down and saw her mother holding Lily. The tears on Daphne's face convinced her that this was no joke. Mila ran to the bushes that edged the library and heaved her barbecue dinner into the shrubbery. Then, after wiping her mouth with the sleeve of her blouse, she hurried down the stairs where her mother and Lily stood surrounded by law enforcement personnel.

"What happened?" she demanded, forcing her emotions into submission.

"It was almost seven o'clock so we were headed home, just like you told us," Daphne explained through her tears. "Chief Jones was going to walk with us, but then Lily said she needed to go to the bathroom and couldn't wait." Daphne paused for a shuddering sob, then continued, "I took both the children with me into that portable bathroom trailer while Chief Jones waited outside." She looked at Mila with pleading in her eyes. "I had to put Ben down so I could help Lily in the stall."

Mila nodded. "And while you were helping Lily, someone took Ben?"

"But how is that possible?" Quin asked. "He would have screamed!"

"Not if the person who took him was someone he knew," Mila said grimly, thinking of Belinda's remarks about being invited to the Womacks' house for holidays and the children's birthday parties.

Dorcas pushed her way through the growing crowd and extended an envelope toward Mila. *Detective Edwards* was scrawled across the front. "We found this taped to the mirror in the bathroom."

Mila tore open the envelope with trembling fingers. It said, *Come to the abandoned gristmill out on Highway 27. Alone. If I see any sign of police or FBI, the baby gets a bullet in the head.*

She turned to Chief Jones. "Will you assign a policeman to take my mother and Lily home and stay with them until we get back?" Winston nodded, and she grabbed Quin's hand. "We've got to go, quickly."

"Where?" Mark demanded as they started down the sidewalk at a trot.

"To the marble quarry near Cartersville," Mila called over her shoulder. "Wait five minutes before following us and then stay back. I don't want to panic her into hurting the baby."

They sprinted down the street to Quin's car, then jumped inside. "Which way?" he asked breathlessly as he inserted his key in the ignition.

"Make a U-turn and head south," Mila instructed. "Keep your headlights off and drive as fast as you can. Once we get to the edge of town turn right on Highway 27."

Quin executed a beautiful, if illegal, turn, then sped down Hickory Lane, ignoring stop signs. "I thought Cartersville was to the north," he said without taking his eyes off the dark road.

"It is," Mila acknowledged. "I've sent the police to the wrong place. Belinda said she'd kill Ben otherwise."

Quin cut his eyes toward her for a split second, obviously shaken. "Belinda Wallace took Ben?"

"Yes. She orchestrated the whole thing," Mila replied, her teeth clenched with anger. "She and her husband blackmailed Mr. Ryan and probably killed Larsen. They kidnapped Theresa when she couldn't produce the express mail envelope, and they shot Beau."

She saw the muscles in Quin's jaw tighten. "There are some times I wish I could cuss," he muttered as they reached Highway 27. He turned right, his tires screeching. "How far?"

Mila leaned forward, peering out of the windshield. "About five miles. The entrance to the mill will be on your left, but it's overgrown, so we'll have to be careful not to miss it."

"Are you scared?" Quin asked quietly.

"I'm terrified," she admitted. "But I'll be darned if I'm going to let that woman get away with this."

Quin managed a nervous laugh. "Now I'm scared for Belinda Wallace."

Mila nodded without a trace of a smile. "As well you should be."

CHAPTER 20

When Mila and Quin pulled up in front of the old mill, the building was dark and appeared deserted. She said a silent prayer as he parked the Mustang. Then they walked slowly up to the entrance. The door was open. They went inside, and Mila called out. "I've brought Quin Drummond with me but not the police!"

There was no response, so they walked a little deeper into the building. The rotten boards under their feet yielded slightly under their weight. The floor was littered with debris.

Mila came to a stop in the middle of the room. "Please give me the baby, Belinda!"

"Give me the express mail envelope first," a voice said from the shadows.

Mila turned toward the sound and extended the envelope. "Here it is."

"Put it on the floor and step back."

Mila placed the envelope on the ground, but didn't step back. "What were you going to do with it? Mr. Ryan has refused to pay more blackmail money."

"Oh, I've got a wonderful new angle," Belinda said, and Mila could hear the amusement in her voice. "Which I have no intention of sharing with you. Now step back."

"What happened to Larsen?" Mila asked. The dim light and shadows cast by abandoned mill equipment distorted her depth perception, and she needed the sound of Belinda's voice to pinpoint the woman's location.

"He's dead," Belinda said calmly.

"You killed him?" Quin demanded.

"The idiot fell down my basement stairs and broke his stupid neck."

"What about Theresa?" Mila forced herself to ask.

"She's in a room upstairs."

Mila's heart skipped a beat. "She's still alive?"

In the dim light Mila could see the other woman raise a shoulder in a careless shrug. "I doubt it. We haven't checked on her for several days. Now, enough talking." Mila's eyes were adjusting to the darkness, and she could just make out Belinda's silhouette. She could also see the gun in her hand. "We've got to get this over with before the police find us," Belinda said with impatience.

"Where's the baby?" Mila asked.

"Steven," Belinda said, and a man stepped up beside her. He was holding Ben's limp form but didn't seem to be armed. The baby's head lolled to the side, and Mila heard Quin moan softly.

"You'll never get away with this." Mila slipped her hand into her pants pocket.

"Of course we will," Belinda said as Mila's fingers wrapped around the handle of her revolver. "Your bodies will be found with the empty express mail envelope. It will be obvious that someone at Ryathon silenced you. Just like they did Larsen. No one will ever suspect me."

Mila saw Belinda raising her gun and didn't wait to see whom she intended to shoot first. Mila jerked up her revolver and fired through the material of her pocket. The bullet caught Belinda in the right wrist, and the woman let out a bloodcurdling scream as her gun fell to the ground.

"You witch!" she shrieked, but Mila was unmoved by the insult. She covered the distance between herself and the injured woman in three quick strides. After kicking Belinda's gun toward Quin, she threw her full weight against Belinda, and they both fell to the floor.

"Quin!" she yelled as Steven Wallace started running away. "I'm sure there's a back exit. Stop him!"

Quin reached down and picked up Belinda's gun, then ran after the disappearing figure of Steven Wallace. Mila returned her attention to the woman underneath her. She twisted Belinda's arms viciously and whispered, "You came to their *birthday parties!* I ought to shoot you just for that." She took a deep breath and pressed Belinda's cheek roughly into the wooden planks of the floor, then said, "You have the right to remain silent . . ."

As she finished the Miranda statement there was a crashing sound at the back of the building, and Mila wished fervently for a pair of handcuffs so she could leave Belinda in order to help Quin. But under the circumstances she had to wait in anguished suspense.

"When did Larsen fall down your steps?" she asked, not really expecting a response.

"The day of the fire," Belinda replied. "He didn't start the fire, but he knew that Ryathon was going to blame it on him. If they could make him look like a nutcase and destroy all his evidence at the same time, he wouldn't have a chance with the FDA. So he was coming to my house to download his research off my computer. But by then Ryathon had e-mailed me a virus that destroyed everything on my hard drive."

"And he fell down your basement steps?" Mila prompted, her eyes searching the darkness for signs of Quin.

"We got into an argument when he arrived without the express mail envelope," Belinda said. "And he lost his footing on the stairs."

"You pushed him," Mila realized.

"You'll never prove it," Belinda returned.

Mila heard approaching footsteps and looked up as Mark Iverson pushed Steven Wallace into a circle of moonlight coming in through a hole in the roof.

"You found us in spite of my bad directions!" she said, very relieved to see the agent.

Mark frowned in her direction. "We'll talk about that later."

Then Quin emerged from the shadows, carrying Ben.

"He's breathing," Quin told her, cradling the baby against his chest. "He's got a bump on his head, so I guess he's unconscious. We've called an ambulance."

Mila pulled on Belinda's arms, stretching the woman's shoulder joints to their limits. "You hit Ben?" she demanded.

"No! I dropped him!" Belinda cried, her voice muffled by the dirty wood floor. "He fought me like a demon once he realized I wasn't taking him to you like I'd promised."

Mila felt tears blur her vision and prayed that it wouldn't take the ambulance as long to get there as it had to get to Aunt Cora Sue's house when Beau got shot.

At that moment uniformed police officers swarmed the old mill, weapons drawn and radios cackling and flashlights beaming. One of them took a pair of handcuffs from his belt and relieved Mila. Stepping away from the injured woman, Mila ran toward Quin. While drawing her hand across the baby's head she told Mark, "Theresa Womack is here somewhere."

Mark nodded and instructed a few of the officers to follow him as they began a search of the old building. Mila stroked the baby's head and whispered to him, "Lily's waiting for you at my house. When we get there we can read as many books as you want. And you're going to see your mother soon," she added, hoping that was true.

There was no response from Ben, but Quin gave Mila an encouraging smile. "He's going to be okay. I can feel it."

There was a commotion behind them as Mark returned with Theresa Womack in his arms. "She's still alive!" he told them. "She's in pretty bad shape, though. Dehydrated, and there are some bites on her legs. Probably rats."

Mila shuddered as they heard sirens approaching.

"We need to give them both blessings," Quin told Mark, reaching into his baggy shorts to pull out a key-ring oil vial. They performed the short prayers with the quiet competence of men who had done it often. Then they moved toward the entrance and ran directly into Chief Monahan and Dorcas James.

"They're both alive?" the chief indicated toward Theresa and Ben. All Mila could manage was a nod.

"Well, it looks like you did solve this case," he admitted grudgingly. "Someone called the television stations." The chief gave Dorcas a quick glance, but her face was expressionless. "So we're going to have to hold an impromptu press conference. Since you broke the case, you can stand beside me, but I'll do the talking."

The ambulances arrived, spraying gravel. Mark and Quin hurried toward them with Mila following close behind. "I'm not interested in the press conference," she told the chief over her shoulder. "I'll be at the hospital if you need me."

"In my office," the chief called after her. "First thing on Monday morning."

She nodded, then climbed into the ambulance with Theresa and Ben. One attendant crouched above the unconscious woman while the other slammed the door closed. Seconds later they lurched forward, headed to the hospital.

Mila watched as the attendant put an oxygen mask over Theresa's face and took her pulse. He was frowning as he started an IV and checked her pupils. Then he carefully removed the duct tape that circled his patient's wrists and ankles. Mila saw the bites on Theresa's legs, and fresh fury toward Belinda welled up inside her.

"Don't you quit, Theresa!" Mila said fiercely. "Lily and Ben need you!"

The attendant glanced over at her but didn't object, so she continued.

"They were alone for two days before I found them. Lily kept Ben happy by pretending to read books and singing songs. Then when the food ran out she made him peanut butter crackers . . ." Mila's voice broke, and she pressed a hand to her mouth to hold back the sobs.

"Blood pressure's coming up, and her color's improving," the attendant said. "Keep talking."

"That's a girl, Theresa," Mila encouraged. "Fight!"

The attendant nodded, so Mila described the past week, Lily teaching her to change diapers and test bathwater and play house. Then she told Theresa that Belinda and her husband were under arrest and would pay for their crimes. "I know that won't bring your husband back, but you've got the two greatest children in the world, and they've missed you so much."

Mila had to clutch the side of the swaying ambulance as the driver came to an abrupt halt at the emergency entrance of the hospital. The door opened, and Mila jumped out and moved quickly to the side so that she would be out of the way as Theresa and Ben were removed from the ambulance. She followed a few feet behind them into the emergency room and saw Quin waiting by the nurses' desk, holding another clipboard. Mark Iverson was beside him.

"Pretty soon everyone we know is going to be in this hospital," Quin said.

She gave him a weak smile. "Yeah, associating with me can be dangerous."

They did their best to fill out the admission forms while Mark made phone calls. They sat in anxious silence, waiting for word on the newest patients. They were still waiting an hour later when Winston Jones walked in, followed closely by Daphne, Lily, and Miss Eugenia.

Mila lifted Lily into her arms. "You found my mommy!" the little girl whispered.

"Quin helped," Mila replied generously with a smile in his direction.

"Okay," Daphne said as they settled in an assortment of plastic-covered chairs. "Tell us everything."

"I think I'll take Miss Lily here for a walk," Winston said with a meaningful glance at the group. "Maybe we can find a candy bar machine."

Once Lily was out of earshot, Mila and Quin explained everything that had happened. When they finished, Daphne beamed at her daughter. "I'll bet you get a medal for this! Or a commendation."

"At least a raise," Miss Eugenia added with practicality.

Mila couldn't help but be pleased by the look of pride shining in her mother's eyes. "Chief Monahan does want to see me in his office first thing on Monday morning."

Daphne nodded. "To thank you."

"And, I hope, to apologize for his less-than-gentlemanly behavior," Miss Eugenia inserted. "That Chief Monahan sounds like a rude sort of fellow."

Mila laughed, then asked Miss Eugenia to convey her apologies to Cornelia Blackwood. "I know that all this ruined the first annual Faith Fair."

Miss Eugenia hooted with laughter. "Are you kidding? You ensured her success."

Mila's forehead wrinkled with confusion. "How?"

"Because of you, every television station in Albany showed up at the fair just as the fireworks display started. Cornelia was interviewed, and a cameraman said the footage they got was so impressive that Channel Six said their national affiliate might run a clip on *Good Morning America* tomorrow!"

Mila smiled as Winston returned with Lily, who was clutching a candy bar in each hand.

Miss Eugenia pointed at the television mounted in the corner of the room. "Look!"

They looked, and there was Cornelia Blackwood, fireworks exploding as a backdrop, discussing the need for people all across America to attend the church of their choice. In spite of her anxiety about Theresa and Ben, Mila had to smile. Then another familiar face filled the television screen.

"Is that Brandon Ryan?" Quin asked.

Mila nodded. "The wordstrip on the bottom says this is national news."

They listened as the CEO of Ryathon Pharmaceuticals announced that there had been a problem with a prenatal vitamin, and women who had taken it were encouraged to contact the company immediately.

"Well, that was honest of him," Quin remarked.

Mila wasn't particularly impressed. "He probably figured it was all about to come out, and he'd save a little face by admitting it first."

"Always the optimist," he teased her.

"Always a *realist,*" she countered, but she smiled.

A few minutes later the press arrived at the hospital in force, and security had to be called to keep them out of the waiting room. During the confusion, Mila noticed a couple in their early fifties. They were allowed through the emergency entrance and, after surveying the waiting room, approached the little group waiting for word on Theresa and Ben. She touched Quin's arm, and he looked up, then stood.

He gathered the couple into a tight embrace.

"Quin's parents?" Miss Eugenia guessed.

Mila nodded. "They've come to take over the foster care of Lily and Ben."

"Those babies won't be needing foster care, thanks to Mila," Daphne said with another proud look in her daughter's direction.

"No, but Theresa is going to need help," Miss Eugenia pointed out. "So it's good that they've come."

After a quick, whispered conversation with his parents, Quin brought them over to the waiting group. Just as introductions were completed, the lovely Dr. Rankin walked in. She gave Quin and Mila a quizzical look and said, "You two are becoming frequent flyers here."

Mila acknowledged this with a brief nod, then asked, "How are they?"

"The baby is fine. He has a mild concussion, but he's awake. So far we haven't been able to get him to say much . . ."

"He doesn't talk," Mila said. "But the pediatrician doesn't think it's anything to worry about. Speech development in children occurs at different rates." Dr. Rankin smiled, and Mila blushed. "I guess you know that."

"I didn't know that he doesn't talk much yet, and I appreciate you letting me know. We'll adjust our expectations accordingly. And I think he'll be fine."

"How's Theresa?" Quin's mother asked.

"She's in guarded condition. She's seriously dehydrated, and there's some infection, but I expect her to recover completely." There was a collective sigh and the doctor smiled. "I'll allow each of them to have two visitors now for about a minute. Then we're going to admit them both and let them rest until tomorrow."

Mila and Quin exchanged a glance, then he said, "Mom and Dad, why don't you go see Theresa. We'll check on Ben."

"And I'll take Miss Lily for another walk," Winston volunteered.

"Thanks," Mila told him as she and Quin followed Dr. Rankin into the examination area. Mila caught just a glimpse of Theresa Womack in her cubicle, pale, but eyes open, before she was ushered into Ben's room.

The baby was strapped to the bed and started to struggle when he saw them. Mila and Quin stepped up to the bed and tried to soothe him. "It's okay, Ben," Mila said softly. "You're going to be just fine."

"You're such a brave boy," Quin added, stroking his chubby cheek. "And you helped us find your mommy."

"Mommy," Ben whispered, and Mila turned to the nurse.

"It will probably help them both if Ben and his mother could be put in the same room."

The nurse nodded. "I'll speak to Dr. Rankin about it."

Apparently the doctor hadn't been joking when she said she would allow a minute, because at this moment another nurse came and shooed them from the room.

They reassembled in the waiting area, then Quin filled his parents in on recent events. As the Drummonds talked, Mila took the opportunity to study them. Brother Drummond was taller than Quin and heavier, with white-gray hair and a genial expression. Sister Drummond was small, with dark hair and eyes very much like her son's. Mila noticed that she looked for excuses to touch Quin—straightening his collar and brushing lint from his sleeve. Quin gave Mila most of the credit for solving the case, and the Drummonds were complimentary when he finished his story.

"Quin's exaggerating," she assured them modestly.

Sister Drummond looked surprised. "That's most unlike him."

"I mean, I didn't solve the case single-handedly," Mila amended. "I had a lot of help, especially from Quin and Mark." She waved toward the agent.

Sister Drummond reached up and patted her son's shoulder. "He's always been brave."

"Quin says you were raised around here," Brother Drummond said, and Mila shrugged.

"My father was in the army," she told them, amazed by how easily the words came. "So I was raised all over the United States. But I did spend almost every summer about ten miles from here in the little town of Haggerty."

"Finest place on God's green earth," Miss Eugenia informed the Drummonds.

"We'll need to make funeral arrangements for Larsen," Sister Drummond said softly.

"Has the body been recovered?" Mila asked Mark, and he nodded. "That was quick."

"The husband gave the Roanoke police the location of the grave, and they collected the body immediately. An autopsy will be performed in Roanoke as soon as possible."

Mila considered this. "Any idea when they'll release the body?"

"I don't think it will be long, since the cause of death is obvious and the suspects are in custody." Mark turned to the Drummonds. "You could probably plan on services for next weekend and be safe."

Winston returned with Lily, who went happily into Sister Drummond's arms. When they started talked about taking Theresa and the children to Roanoke, Mila stepped back. She had never felt so unnecessary in her entire life. Daphne seemed to sense her distress and moved beside her daughter, offering silent support.

A nurse came by a few minutes later to report that Theresa and Ben had been admitted to the hospital and moved to a room on the fourth floor. She directed the group keeping vigil up to the appropriate waiting area. While Mila was pleased to hear that both patients were doing well, she couldn't shake the gloomy mood that had settled on her.

Finally Mark suggested that he take Miss Eugenia, Daphne, and Lily home.

"I don't think I can make myself go into Aunt Cora Sue's house after all this," Daphne said with a frown.

"You can spend the night at our house," Mark offered.

"Nonsense," Miss Eugenia said. "There's no point in waking up Kate and the babies this late. They'll stay at my house." Miss Eugenia turned to the Drummonds. "Have you checked into a hotel yet?" They nodded that they had. "Then you should go there now and get some rest. There's no point in all of you losing sleep, and I know that even a stick of dynamite won't get Mila out of here tonight."

Brother Drummond smiled. "You're probably right." He glanced at Quin. "You'll call us if there's a change?"

"Of course," he agreed.

The Drummonds looked grief-stricken as they said good-bye.

Once they were finally alone, Mila and Quin sat close together on one of the couches. "You were great tonight," Quin whispered.

"No, *you* were great. You trusted my experience and did just as I asked you to instead of trying something macho." She twisted to look into his eyes. "That's rare in a man."

He laughed. "I told you we'd be good partners."

She clutched him tightly as the adrenaline started to wear off and the reality of what they had been through set in. "Just hold me," she pleaded.

* * *

When Mila woke up, the first rays of sunlight were seeping through the miniblinds that covered the waiting room's only window.

Quin was already awake and smiled down at her.

"How are they?" she murmured, snuggling closer to him.

"Good. Dr. Rankin came by a few minutes ago and said Ben will be released this morning. Theresa's going to have to stay a couple of days, but she's doing much better." He stood and pulled her to her feet. "How about some breakfast?"

She waved a hand to encompass her less-than-impeccable appearance. "I doubt if they'll serve me in this condition."

He laughed. "This is a hospital cafeteria. They serve anyone."

"Thanks," she muttered.

He laughed again and pulled her toward the waiting room door. They left their cell numbers with a nurse, then walked down to the cafeteria. Mila was surprised to find that she had a voracious appetite. "I'm probably going to get fat," she said as she started on her second plate.

Quin found this very funny. "Yeah, I'd say you're right on the verge."

She gave him a smirk, then stuffed her mouth full of waffles.

After they were finished eating, they went to the information desk and asked for Beau's room number. They found the Albany detective sitting up in his hospital bed and scowling at a bowl of mush. "They call this food?" he demanded when they walked in. "I'll bet prisoners of war get better."

Mila smiled. "I just ate two huge plates of waffles with butter and maple syrup and sausage and bacon and . . ."

Beau held up a hand to stop her. "Enough!" He pushed the tray away from him in disgust. "You look like . . . well, not good," he finished lamely.

She fingered the bullet hole in the pocket of her pants. "We had quite a night."

"Tell me about it," Beau requested.

Mila and Quin sat down and took turns relating the events of the previous night. "What I don't know is how Belinda and her husband intended to make money off of the vitamin scandal," Mila said in conclusion.

"I know that," Beau told her. "And I'll tell you if you'll find a vending machine and buy me some candy bars."

Mila raised both eyebrows. "Aren't you on a special diet?"

"Heck no! I was asleep when they brought the menu by for me to choose my meals, so they gave me this slop!" He waved at the abandoned tray. "They don't care what I eat."

Mila looked suspicious, but Quin smiled and stood. "I'll go get your candy bars."

Once he was gone, Beau waved toward the empty doorway. "So, what's going on between you and surfer boy?"

Mila tried to look casual. "What do you mean?"

Beau laughed, then grabbed his shoulder. "Ow! You know exactly what I mean!"

She shrugged. "I'm not sure. We like each other. A lot," she finally admitted. "But I don't think there's any future in it."

"Just promise me one thing. If you decide to marry the guy, make him sign a prenuptial agreement swearing that he won't name your first son Quincy."

She laughed. "That name is kind of growing on me."

Beau shook his head. "Who could trust a guy named Quincy?"

The guy in question walked back a few seconds later, ending the conversation. Beau accepted his candy bars and ate hungrily.

"So, how do you know what Belinda's plan was?" Mila prompted.

"Dorcas came by a little while ago, but she wouldn't buy me any candy bars," he said around a mouthful of chocolate. "The husband is trying to cut a deal."

Mila frowned. "What a prince."

Beau laughed again, then glowered at her as he gently massaged the bandaged shoulder. "Since he's already got one conviction, if he gets another he'll get hard time. He claims Belinda is the one who kidnapped Theresa and shot me."

"How did Belinda plan to use the information in the express mail envelope?" Mila wanted to know.

"Apparently they were going to set up an advocacy group and file a class action suit for the women who took the deficient vitamins. The husband said they would have made millions just on legal fees, not to mention speaking engagements, book royalties, and interviews on *Oprah* and the *Today Show*."

"And they already had the $88,000 they stole from Ryathon and the money they blackmailed out of Brandon Ryan," Mila pointed out.

Beau nodded. "She tricked Larsen into signing a check for a lesser amount, then changed it. And since she had access to Larsen's research on her home computer, blackmailing Ryan was a cinch."

Mila considered this for a few seconds, then said, "I wonder when Theresa will be up to answering some questions."

Beau swallowed. "The chief and Dorcas talked to her this morning."

Mila leaned forward. "Did they ask her why she went into hiding?"

"She said Larsen called her after he left Ryathon the day of the fire."

"Why did Larsen set the fire?"

"He didn't. According to Theresa, Mr. DeFore had some security guards do it to destroy evidence. And he figured they'd try to blame it on him. He didn't dare go home, assuming that the police were already headed there. But he was afraid that if Ryathon was willing to set their facility on fire, they might not be opposed to kidnapping."

"He was afraid they would use Theresa and the kids to coerce him into giving them the information he'd prepared for the FDA," Mila guessed.

"Right. So he told Theresa to wait for the police to arrive and answer their questions honestly, since she really didn't know where he was. Then she was to pack up and leave Roanoke for an undisclosed location."

"Then how was he going to contact her?"

Beau smiled. "Once she was settled she was to contact the only person Larsen trusted at Ryathon." He paused for effect, then said, "Carol Harmon."

"The crabby secretary?" Mila was astounded that she could have misjudged the woman's character so completely.

"She was lying to us," Quin comforted her. "Just not about what we thought."

Mila gave him a grateful look, then asked Beau, "So the Ryathon stock really was just a part of her retirement package?"

"Well, according to Dorcas it was kind of a forced retirement."

This clarified things for Mila. "They were getting rid of her because she was loyal to Larsen."

"I guess," Beau agreed.

"Why did the secretary claim that Larsen came to work one day smelling of alcohol?" Quin asked.

"Apparently Belinda spilled it on him on purpose so she could convince Carol Harmon of the affair," Beau explained.

Mila grimaced. "Yes, Belinda used Carol very efficiently."

"Theresa said she checked in with the secretary regularly by e-mail," Beau continued, "waiting for word from Larsen that never came."

Mila frowned. "I wonder how Belinda got Theresa's address in Albany."

"The husband says Belinda was able to access the secretary's e-mail," Beau replied. "And once they had the address, they sent the postcard to Theresa."

"Who thought it was from Larsen," Quin guessed.

Beau nodded. "When she arrived at the meeting point, Belinda asked her about the envelope."

"But Theresa didn't have it," Mila said.

"No, but she did know about Larsen's findings, and Belinda couldn't risk the information leaking out before she had contacted all the possible victims. So she forced Theresa to come with her to the old mill."

"What ever happened to that envelope?" Quin asked.

Beau shrugged, then winced and rubbed his shoulder. "We may not ever know."

"What I can't figure out is how Belinda knew every move we made," Mila said.

"I hate to tell you this," Beau prefaced his remarks. "But she planted listening devices in some of the Womacks' stuff when they searched the apartment."

Mila pursed her lips with grudging respect. "So she heard everything we said—every plan we made."

"Not everything," Beau corrected. "Only conversations that were held close to one of the devices were picked up, but they heard enough."

"No wonder she was always a step ahead of us," Quin remarked. "It's too bad that Belinda Wallace didn't channel her intelligence into a useful direction."

"Well, the brilliant Ms. Wallace is now sitting smartly in jail while her own husband tries to put her away for the rest of her natural life." Beau polished off the last candy bar, then balled up the wrappers and tossed them skillfully into the wastebasket. "Now," he addressed Mila, "I think you have a little story to tell me. About your final days in Atlanta."

She took a deep breath, and related the events in an even, toneless voice. When she was finished, Beau whistled.

"Well, I can't say you were wrong," he said. "And I can't say you were right. It was a no-win situation."

"Even after all these weeks, I'm still not sure I made the right decision," she admitted. "But what I do know is that if I found myself in the exact same situation again, I'd do the exact same thing. I couldn't leave those kids. I just couldn't."

Before anyone could respond a nurse rushed in. "Time to change your bandage," she announced, then frowned at his breakfast tray. "If you don't eat, you'll slow the healing process."

"If you'll tell them to send me some actual food, I'll be glad to eat," Beau told her.

The nurse gave him a false smile and said, "Tell your friends good-bye."

Mila stood. "What will your sister do for a babysitter while you're stuck in here?"

"She doesn't have classes on the weekend, and by next week I should be fine."

Mila leaned forward and gave Beau a little hug. "I'm glad you're doing better."

"I won't be if you leave me with her!" Beau whispered, inclining his head toward the nurse. "She'll torture me!"

Mila laughed as she moved to the door. "Be a man."

After leaving Beau they stopped by to see Cleo, who looked fine and was anxious to get home. "It's the last day of the month," she pointed out. "That's when we do our itch treatment."

Mila's eyebrows shot up, and she had to resist the urge to scratch her scalp. "Itch?"

Earl Sr. chuckled from the corner of the hospital room. "Lice," he clarified, then chuckled again when he saw the look on Mila's face.

"We don't actually have them, but Cleo likes to treat our heads once a month as prevention."

"It seems like that would be bad for your hair," Mila murmured.

"Doesn't seem to hurt our hair, but I've heard if you use it too much for too long it can affect your brain," Cleo contributed.

"Now you *know* we use it regularly!" Earl Sr. said.

Cleo shot her husband a stern look, then demanded a recounting of the previous night's events. Once they were finished with what was becoming a well-polished presentation, Cleo looked at each of them in disbelief. "And I missed all of that?"

Mila nodded. "I'm afraid so."

"Isn't that just my luck," she griped.

Quin laughed at her dejection. "Only you would regret missing a kidnapping and shoot-out," he teased.

Earl Jr. walked into the room at that moment, dressed from head to toe in hospital paraphernalia. "Now he's into a doctor phase," Cleo explained unnecessarily.

Mila gave him an approving nod. "Very wise. Doctors make much more money, and they rarely get shot at."

Earl Jr. beamed at her, then insisted on taking her pulse and listening to her heartbeat. They finally escaped Earl Jr.'s ministrations and made it back up to the fourth floor waiting room. Mark Iverson and Daphne were waiting for them.

"Aren't you supposed to be at church?" Mila asked him.

"My counselors can handle things," he replied.

"We brought Lily in to visit with her mother," Daphne told them with tears in her eyes. "It was the most touching thing I've ever seen."

"They're ready to release Ben," Mark said, then looked at Quin. "Your parents are on their way to get him."

"Do you think they'd let me see them for a minute?" Mila asked. The Womacks were about to fade out of her life, and she didn't think she could bear it if she didn't get a chance to say good-bye.

Mark nodded. "They're in room 406 right down this hall. Just walk in and act like you have permission. I don't think anyone will stop you."

Mila looked at Quin. "Are you coming?"

He took her hand and let her lead the way.

Theresa was sitting up in her bed, Lily right beside her and Ben on her lap. "Quin," she said when she saw him.

He crossed the room and pressed a kiss on her forehead. "It's great to see you again, Theresa."

Mila hung back, feeling awkward. Then Theresa's gaze fell on her. "You must be Mila."

She nodded.

"How can I ever thank you?" Theresa whispered. "While I was in that . . ." she glanced at Lily, "horrible place I was so worried about the children. I prayed desperately and after a couple of days a feeling of peace came over me. I knew that the Lord had provided for them."

Mila felt her face color with embarrassment. "I'm glad the Lord chose me," she said. "You have wonderful children."

Theresa smiled. "I won't disagree with you there."

"I'm sorry about your husband."

Theresa nodded. "Me too, although it still doesn't seem real."

"I'm sure it will take you some time to adjust to all that has happened," Mila predicted.

"I hope you'll continue to be a part of our lives," Theresa offered kindly, and Mila began to feel a little optimistic. Then Quin's parents arrived.

There were more hugs and lots of tears, and Mila was pushed firmly into the background—an outsider. Finally she slipped out and walked to the waiting room. "I need to go home and change clothes," she told Daphne and Mark. "Can you give me a ride, Mother?"

"I rode with Mark," Daphne said.

"Since the Drummonds are here to take care of the children, I don't suppose any of us need to stay," the FBI agent said.

"You're sure you want to go, honey?" Daphne asked. When Mila nodded she gave the suitcase she had filled with Lily's and Ben's clothing and other personal items to the nurse at the desk. Then they got onto the elevator. As the doors closed in front of her, Mila felt more bereft than she had since the day she watched her father's casket descend into the ground, the sound of a twenty-one-gun salute echoing in her ears.

Quin called on Mila's cell phone during the trip back to Haggerty. He was surprised that she had left and sounded even more confused when she explained that she was trying to give him time alone with his family.

"Theresa wanted to talk to you some more, and my parents were planning to take us out to lunch."

"That's very nice of them," Mila replied, although she knew they were just being polite. "But I need to get the rest of Lily's and Ben's things packed."

"I'll be coming to Haggerty in a little while," he told her. "So I'll see you there."

"You'll be packing up your camper." It wasn't a question.

There was a brief pause, then he said, "I guess."

She took a deep breath. "I'll be watching for you."

After Mila turned off her cell phone, Mark invited her and Daphne to come to his house for Sunday dinner. "Kate would be honored to have you both as guests," he said. "And she'd love to have the opportunity to hear about your experience firsthand."

Mila smiled, thinking about how she and Quin had gotten into the routine of telling the story in tandem. Relating the events alone would be sad enough, but being around the Iverson children, who were very close in age to Lily and Ben, would be too painful. "Thanks, but I'd better go home and start packing up."

Mark dropped them off at Aunt Cora Sue's house, and Daphne made sandwiches while Mila took a much-needed shower. Then Mila sat at the empty table and pretended to eat.

"I called the bus station while you were in the shower," Daphne said. "I'm going home tomorrow morning."

"Please thank Terry for sharing you with me," Mila said around the lump in her throat. "I don't know what I would have done without you these past few days."

Daphne leaned down and gave her daughter a quick hug. "And I don't know how long I've been waiting to hear those words from you."

Mila went into the living room and started packing. Once Daphne had the kitchen cleaned up, she joined Mila. Miss Eugenia arrived a little later, still wearing her Sunday dress. She was uncharacteristically quiet and went straight to work without asking any questions.

"What about this stuff Cleo brought over?" Daphne asked, holding up one of the educational videos.

"Cleo said Earl Jr. had outgrown them," Miss Eugenia said. "Maybe Lily and Ben can get some use out of them."

Daphne nodded and added the series to the box of Disney videos. Having finished the living room, they were headed to the children's bedroom when Quin walked in. He looked fresh from a bath and boyishly appealing, but Mila steeled herself against him. He offered to help, but Mila told him they had things under control.

Daphne gave her daughter a confused look and insisted that Quin eat a sandwich or two. "I made a bunch, and goodness knows Mila won't eat them."

Quin accepted the offer, but Mila didn't join them in the kitchen. She kept packing.

Miss Eugenia worked efficiently beside her. Mila had to swat at tears when she put the bedtime books into the box, but Miss Eugenia pretended not to notice.

"You can still be a part of Lily's and Ben's life," Miss Eugenia said finally. "Especially if you marry Quin."

"Marry Quin!" Mila responded as if this were the most ridiculous suggestion. "Whatever makes you say that?"

"Well, because you're in love with each other for starters," Miss Eugenia replied calmly. "And he told me that he's asked you to come to Hawaii with him."

"He invited me to Hawaii as a partner in his surfboard business—not as his wife," Mila corrected.

"Maybe you misunderstood," Miss Eugenia suggested. "But even if you go as his partner, that's a start."

"A start that would require me to give up my career and move to Hawaii. And if we did decide to . . . marry," she forced the word out, "I'd have to live my life like a nomad, chasing surfing competitions until the business started making enough money to support us."

Miss Eugenia was staring at her now. "So? As long as you were together, what would it matter?"

Before she could answer, Quin stuck his head in the door. "You sure you don't need my help?" he asked.

She recognized the hopeful tone in his voice. But she knew a clean cut hurt less than a jagged tear, so she shook her head.

"No thanks. We've just about got it."

Miss Eugenia gave her a dark look. "If *you* don't need any help, I'll go help Daphne in the kitchen."

After the older woman left, Mila faced Quin, feeling shy and awkward. "I'm assuming that Theresa won't want this thrift-store furniture, so we're just packing the books and toys and . . . personal things. I'll leave the furniture in the house until it sells, so if she decides she does want something, she can let me know."

"You're putting the house back up for sale?" he asked, his voice soft.

She nodded. "Yes, I'll start looking for an apartment in Albany tomorrow."

His expression registered surprise and something else, maybe sadness or regret. "Oh. Then you've decided to stay with the Albany PD?"

She hadn't decided anything, but didn't want him to feel sorry for her, so she nodded. "Things should be okay between me and the chief now."

"Well," Quin said. "I wish you the best. You know that."

She nodded. "I do. And good luck with your surfboard business."

He looked over her shoulder at the window. "If you ever get tired of police work you can come see me in Hawaii."

She forced a smile and kept her voice brisk. "I might just take you up on that."

He pushed himself upright and took a step into the hallway. "Well, I should start packing up my camper."

"When do you leave?" She hated herself for asking, but couldn't help it.

"I guess I'll leave in the morning." Their eyes met for a few seconds, then she dragged hers away. "Well, I'll be in the Ledbetters' backyard if you need me."

After he was gone Miss Eugenia came back in, clicking her tongue. "I can't believe you're going to let him go."

"Were you eavesdropping?" Mila demanded, glad for somewhere to direct her frustration.

"No, I was standing in the living room and just happened to hear every word the two of you said. Now explain to me why you're going to let that wonderful young man slip through your fingers."

Mila sighed in exasperation. "We're just too different. Quin lives his life free of restrictions. He can wake up any given morning and drive away. I've lived my whole life within very specific boundaries." Miss Eugenia was staring at her blankly, so Mila tried another approach. "For me restrictions are like fences that define my life. For him they are just limits to his freedom. I can't imagine living without fences, and he can't imagine living with them." Mila was pleased with the analogy, feeling like it was borderline eloquent. Until Miss Eugenia laughed.

"I declare, if that's not the most ridiculous thing I've ever heard!" she exclaimed. "Instead of worrying about hypothetical fences, you'd better hold onto the man you love."

"I can't hold him if it will make him unhappy," Mila argued, now mildly annoyed.

"Humph!" Miss Eugenia said in derision. "Love is about compromises. Take your mother for instance."

"Yes, let's take her," Mila agreed, on safe ground now. "She lived a life she hated to please my father."

"She lived her life with the man she loved," Miss Eugenia countered. "There were aspects of that life that she didn't enjoy, but given the chance to do it all again I guarantee you she would. Because being with your father was worth the sacrifices."

Although Mila realized she'd lost another skirmish in this battle with Miss Eugenia, she had to admit this concept did make her feel a little better about her parents' marriage.

"When you marry someone you accept the limitation of your own dreams for theirs," Miss Eugenia continued. "And as long as they do the same for you—it works. Kind of like the *Gift of the Magi*."

"The gift of what?" Mila asked.

"Haven't you ever read O. Henry's short story?" Miss Eugenia was appalled. "And you consider yourself a well-educated young woman!" Shaking her head, Miss Eugenia proceeded to correct this scholastic oversight. "The *Gift of the Magi* is about a couple who are terribly poor at Christmastime. She has very long hair, and her husband wants to buy her some combs. He has a pocket watch his grandfather gave him, and she wants to buy him a chain for it. But neither have any money. So what do they do?"

Mila shrugged. "I have no idea."

"She cuts her hair and sells it to buy him the chain," Miss Eugenia said almost reverently. "And he sells the watch to buy her the combs."

"So they gave each other something useless?" Mila asked with a frown.

"No," Miss Eugenia corrected her. "They gave each other something *priceless*. By sacrificing the only thing of value they had for the other, they proved their love."

Mila shook her head in confusion. "So what are you saying?"

Miss Eugenia sighed. "Just something to think about. Now hand me that little lamp shaped like the sun."

They finally finished the packing up at eight o'clock that evening. Miss Eugenia was rubbing her back as Mila led her to the front door. "Think about what I said," the old woman instructed, then disappeared into the darkness.

"What does Miss Eugenia want you to think about?" Daphne asked.

"Fences and magis," Mila replied obtusely, then headed for the bedroom that she used to share with Ben and Lily.

She tossed and turned all night and woke up exhausted but determined to take Miss Eugenia's advice. She'd go into the Ledbetters' backyard and pour her heart out to Quin Drummond. She'd tell him that she loved him and that she was going to quit her job for him and follow him to Hawaii or wherever else his untraditional lifestyle took him. Terrified and ecstatic at the same time, she dressed quickly, then hurried outside.

With long, decisive strides she crossed the damp grass of Aunt Cora Sue's backyard and pushed through the hedges to the corner where Quin's campsite had been for over a week. But when she reached the spot, Quin and his camper were gone. Mila stood there in stunned silence, staring at the depressions in the grass where the wheels of Quin's Mustang had been recently. He had left without even saying good-bye.

"He left you a note," Cleo said from behind her.

Mila turned to see her friend sitting on the patio. "So, when did they let you out of the hospital?"

"Late last night. It was either that or add Earl Jr. to the medical staff," she said with a smile.

Mila walked over and sat beside her. "How do you feel?"

"Weak and a little depressed, but I'll be fine in a day or two."

"You said Quin left me a note?" she asked, trying to hide the emotion in her voice.

"He said he went over last night to say good-bye, but you were already in bed, and he didn't want to disturb you." Cleo extended a plain white envelope. It was the cheap security kind, and he had written his note on a sheet of plain typing paper. That was Quin, no frills.

It was short and unremarkable. He gave her his parents' address in California and said he would be there until the first of the next week. Then he'd be in Hawaii, and he provided that address as well. He wished her the best in the future and encouraged her to stay in touch. She felt worse after reading it than she had before.

"My mother's leaving today," Mila told Cleo.

"I know."

"And Quin's parents are taking Theresa and the kids back to Roanoke as soon as she's released from the hospital."

"He told me."

"So, I guess I'm right back where I started from. Alone."

Cleo laughed. "Poor Mila."

Mila was ashamed by her own selfishness. "I'm sorry, Cleo. You have so much more to deal with, and you never complain."

"I complain. Ask Earl Sr. sometime. He can tell you what I whiner I am."

"I think you're very brave."

Cleo smiled. "Coming from you, that's a big compliment."

"Mila!" Daphne's voice filtered through the hedges.

"I'm over here!" Mila called back.

"It's time to take me to the bus station, honey," Daphne said as she stepped into the Ledbetters' backyard. "Hey, Cleo. It's good to see you up and about."

"It's good to be up anyway," Cleo replied. "Have a safe trip home and come to visit me sometime."

"I might just do that," Daphne returned. "I've had a really nice stay here."

Mila was quiet on the way to the bus station, but Daphne kept up a steady stream of meaningless conversation. Finally, when it was time to part, Mila hugged her mother. "Thanks again. For everything."

Daphne smiled. "You'll come visit me, won't you? Terry would be so pleased."

Mila nodded. "I'll call you in a few weeks and arrange something."

Daphne gave her daughter a final squeeze, then hurried into the station.

Mila drove to the Albany Police Department, and for the first time, even riding in her beloved Mustang didn't cheer her up. When she walked in through the smoked-glass doors into the lobby, the receptionist smiled at her and put the call she was handling on hold.

"It's good to see you back, Detective," the woman said. "I'll let the chief know you're here."

Mila thanked her, then walked through the door beside her desk.

When the other occupants of the huge room saw her, all conversation stopped, much like it had on her first day there.

She acknowledged everyone with a nod, then started down the hall toward the chief's office. As she passed, one after another of the officers, secretaries, clerks, and even mailroom staff came to their feet. Those in uniform even went so far as to put their hats over their badges in a show of deep respect.

Mila faltered, staring around her in disbelief.

"We want you to know how proud we are of you," Frankie Cofield spoke for them.

"You're an example to us all," Dorcas James added.

"Thank you," Mila managed as tears flooded her eyes. She pushed on until she reached the chief's door. The last time she had been there the chief told her that the only way she'd be invited back is if she did something really good or really bad. Suddenly she wasn't sure which was the case. After taking a second to collect herself, she knocked.

"Come in!" he called.

After a deep breath she pushed inside.

The chief looked at her, then at his watch. "This is what you consider *first thing,* Detective?"

"I had to take my mother to the bus station, sir," she replied.

He pointed to a chair. "Have a seat."

She followed his instructions, then asked, "Do you know if Larsen Womack's body has been released by the medical examiner in Roanoke?"

He nodded. "They felt like the family had suffered long enough and needed the closure of a funeral, so they released the body early. The funeral is scheduled for Saturday. I guess you'll be going."

She shook her head. "No." The chief looked puzzled so she added, "I didn't really know Larsen, so my presence at the funeral would be awkward. I do think it's important that his name be cleared—publicly."

"I think so too." The chief surprised her by agreeing. "I've already talked to the police chief in Roanoke, and he's promised to make sure the local press gets enough information to guarantee front-page coverage of Larsen's murder and the Wallaces' arrest."

"Thank you." Mila was considerably relieved.

The chief cleared his throat, then said, "I want to commend you for your success with the Womack case." She knew this admission cost him and inclined her head in acceptance. "However, I must point out that once again you flagrantly disobeyed orders."

"That's true," she admitted.

He considered her for a few seconds. "You are intelligent and tenacious, but you're terrible at following police procedure. Personally, I think you'd be better off finding another line of work. However, if you're determined to be a detective, I'll arrange a job for you in another police department."

She assimilated this information, then smiled. "But not *your* police department."

He shook his head.

She laughed. "My mother and friends have been speculating about what you would say this morning. There were predictions of a raise, a promotion, and even a commendation, but nobody guessed that you were going to *fire* me."

His face darkened. "I know you think I don't like you," he said slowly. "Actually that's not true. You are a charming, likable person who is not cut out for police work. You follow your heart and ignore orders. In some professions that might work, but in law enforcement disregarding orders can get you killed, and others along with you."

"I know," she agreed. "And I can't tell you that I'll change. So maybe you're right. I've been thinking about going back to school, possibly getting a degree in social work."

He smiled. "If you do, heaven help the police chief in the jurisdiction where you get a job."

"They'll rue the day," she acknowledged.

"But the children you take under your wing will be the luckiest on the face of the earth," he added. "Because you'll fight for them tooth and nail."

She smiled at him. "Thank you for that."

He stood and reached his hand across the desk. "Good luck, Mila."

Taking his hand in hers, she shook it firmly. "Thank you, sir."

She made it to the door before he stopped her.

"I see in you the same courage your father had," he said softly. "And the same reckless disregard for your own safety. You're the kind of person I'd be glad to have on *my* side. I'm sure your father is very proud of you."

Afraid to trust her voice, Mila just nodded and stepped into the hall. Dorcas was waiting for her and led her out a side door, through a back hallway, and outside so that she wouldn't have to face the troops again after her dismissal.

"You knew what he was going to say?" Mila guessed as they reached the employee parking lot.

"Yes," the other woman said with calm competence. "And I also know that you don't want to be a police detective."

Mila had to smile. "You're right about that. I'm just not sure what I *do* want."

Dorcas paused and studied Mila for a few seconds. Then she said, "Well, my advice is to concentrate on that. Then once you have a decision, go for what you want with the same determination you showed in solving the Womack case."

"Thanks, Dorcas. You've been a friend, although I'm not sure why. Certainly not because I deserved it."

Dorcas smiled. "You don't have to earn everything, Mila. Keep in touch," she requested. Then she turned and walked back into the building through the side door.

EPILOGUE

One Month Later

Mila signed the legal papers under the direction of Nickel Phelps and the real estate attorney, and when she left the bank, Aunt Cora Sue's old house belonged to someone else—a young couple with two children for Earl Jr. to play with. And Mila had an extra fifty thousand dollars to finance her career change.

On the way back to Haggerty, Mila called Theresa.

"We're fine," she assured Mila. "Lily's started swimming lessons at the Y, and Ben's added two more words to his vocabulary."

Mila laughed. "Let me guess, *read* and *eat*?"

"Close," Theresa confirmed. "*Again* and *more*."

"Before you know it you won't be able to shut him up."

"I look forward to that day," Theresa admitted.

"Are you doing okay? Really?"

"I take it one day at a time, and I'm making it."

Mila was touched as much by Theresa's honesty as by her courage. "I'm leaving here soon," she said. "But you can always reach me by cell phone."

"I'll call you so often that you'll regret giving me your number," Theresa promised.

After ending her call with Theresa, Mila took a few minutes to regain her composure, then called her mother. "I'm finished at the bank," she said when Daphne answered. "Now I'm headed to Haggerty, and I've called for moral support."

"I have complete confidence that you can handle your new life as well as you did your old one."

Mila frowned at the road. "That's supposed to make me feel better?"

Daphne laughed. "You know what I mean."

Mila pulled to a stop in front of the Iversons' house. "I've got to go. I'll call you later." She ended the call, then walked up to the Iversons' front door and knocked. Kate answered a few seconds later.

"You're still here!" she greeted in surprise, pulling the door wide for Mila to enter. "I thought you were gone."

"My plane leaves this afternoon, so I'm saying my final good-byes."

"Well, I'm glad you stopped by." Kate closed the door and led the way down the hall, kicking toys aside as she went. "Mark's home for lunch."

Mila nodded. "I know. I called his office."

"He's out on the back porch watching the kids play on their new swing set. Would you like a sandwich?" Kate asked over her shoulder as they passed through the kitchen.

Mila shook her head. "No thanks."

Kate opened the back door and stepped onto the porch. "Mila's here," she told her husband.

Mark Iverson stood. "Is this an official visit?" he asked as he shook Mila's hand.

"Not really, but I did want to ask you a couple of questions."

"I'll answer anything I can," he offered as they sat down in patio chairs.

"And anything he *can't* tell you I probably can," Kate said with a smile as she sat beside Mark. "Thanks to all the gossip I've gleaned from Miss Eugenia and the other Haggerty ladies."

Mila managed a small smile, then asked, "Can you tell me the status of Belinda Wallace?"

Mark nodded. "She's been indicted on so many charges she'll have to hire an extra lawyer just to keep up with them."

"What about her husband?"

"He cut a deal with the district attorney, so he'll face lesser charges, but he'll spend a significant amount of time in jail."

"What about Mr. DeFore and Brandon Ryan?"

Mark sighed. "We're pretty sure that they tried to suppress evidence about their faulty vitamins by setting fire to the lab at Ryathon, but we haven't been able to prove that yet. Honestly, we're not trying all that hard since they've already been tried and convicted by the press. I have it on good authority that the company will file bankruptcy soon."

Mila couldn't help but be pleased. "I still can't believe that Larsen was willing to sacrifice everything—his family and his career—just to expose the vitamin deficiency. It seems like he should have at least waited until there was proof that any of the infants involved had problems."

Mark leaned forward. "This is just my personal opinion, not privileged information."

Mila nodded that she understood.

"I'm not sure that Larsen intended to sacrifice everything when he left Ryathon the day of the fire. He probably thought that he could use the evidence in the express envelope to force the company into being honest with the public. And he was too honest and naive to see Belinda for what she was."

"I think Lily's deformity made him more sensitive about birth defects," Kate contributed. "And less objective."

Mila nodded again. "I hadn't thought of that, but it does make sense."

They watched the children play for a few minutes, then Mila said, "I wonder if anyone will ever find the envelope."

Mark gave her a sheepish look. "We found it yesterday, with Kate's help."

Mila's eyes widened in astonishment, and Kate laughed. "Sometimes you criminal geniuses have to depend on simple people like me with good old common sense."

"We overlooked the obvious," Mark explained.

Mila frowned. "The obvious?"

Kate answered for him. "Miss Eugenia was over here, rehashing all the details of the case. When she got to the part about the missing envelope I told Mark I was surprised that Larsen didn't just mail it after he left Ryathon. That way he would know it was safe, and he wouldn't have to worry about losing it or having it taken from him."

"But we checked with the FDA," Mila pointed out. "They never received it."

"We didn't think it all the way through," Mark told her. "Mailing the envelope *was* the obvious thing to do, and that's exactly what

Larsen did. We figure that he put it in a drop box right outside the Ryathon complex."

"So why didn't the FDA ever receive it?"

"Because it didn't have postage on it," Mark replied.

"Then where did it go?"

"To the return address. Larsen basically mailed it back to himself."

"To his home?"

Mark nodded. "I'm sure he intended to claim it later. One of the instructions he gave Theresa on the phone was to have their mail held. She didn't mention it during questioning, because she thought it was just a household detail, like having her set up the automatic withdrawals for their house payments and transferring money from savings."

Mila was shaking her head in wonder. "So the envelope was in their unclaimed mail?"

Mark nodded. "I had the resident agent in Roanoke take Theresa over to get it. The envelope was in the box—returned to sender for insufficient postage."

Mila smiled at Kate. "Congratulations."

Mark turned his fond gaze toward his wife. "It's not the first time she's helped me solve a big mystery."

Kate waved a hand dismissively. "I'm glad to do what I can for the cause of justice."

Mila laughed as she stood. "I'd better get going. I still have to go over and speak to Miss Eugenia."

"You certainly do," Kate agreed. "She'll never forgive you if you don't."

Mila waved to the Iversons and crossed their lawn into Miss Eugenia's yard. She knocked on the screen door that led into the utility room and waited until the old woman appeared.

"Well," Miss Eugenia said when she saw Mila. "I wondered if you'd come to say good-bye."

"That's why I'm here," Mila acknowledged, stepping into the house. "To say good-bye and to tell you that I'm about to do the craziest thing I've ever done in my life, and if it backfires, I'm holding you personally responsible."

Miss Eugenia laughed as they settled around the kitchen table. "It's the smartest thing you've ever done," she countered. "Although from what I've seen of how you handle your life, that's not saying much."

Mila glanced at her watch. "As much as I enjoy being insulted, I'd better get on to the airport."

"You've got some time," Miss Eugenia said. "So, you've been accepted at the Mormon college in Hawaii?"

Mila nodded.

"And you've sold Cora Sue's house so you can invest in Quin Drummond's surfboard business."

"If he still wants me as a partner."

"Humph," was Miss Eugenia's response. "If you have any sense at all, you'll marry the boy the first chance you get."

Mila stood. "If Quin and I get married, you'll be the first to know. But right now, I've got to get to the airport or I'll miss my flight."

They walked out the back door and around the side of Miss Eugenia's house. When they passed the storage shed, the old woman said, "I guess I'm going to have to call Nickel Phelps."

Mila looked up, startled. "Surely you're not planning to sell your house?"

"No, but I do need to return all those For Sale signs I took out of your aunt Cora Sue's yard."

"That was you!" Mila cried in astonishment.

"I knew selling it then was the wrong thing to do. I didn't know why, but I knew you were going to need that house."

Mila had to laugh. "You may be the wisest woman I've ever met."

Miss Eugenia frowned. "What man do you know that's wiser than me?" she demanded.

Mila shook her head. "That you're smarter than all men goes without saying." They turned the corner of the house and stopped in the front yard beside a gorgeous climbing rosebush. "Please take care of Cleo for me," Mila requested. "She acts tough, but she's not."

"Wasn't I taking care of her long before you came along? Not that Cleo needs me," Miss Eugenia said with a dismissive gesture. "She's the darling of Haggerty now. Everybody's tripping over themselves trying to be her friend."

Mila smiled. "You look like you could use a hug," she teased and pulled the old woman into an embrace. "Tell Miss George Ann and Miss Polly and Cornelia good-bye for me. If things work out, maybe you could all come visit me in Hawaii."

"We might just do that." Miss Eugenia walked with Mila to the rental car parked at the curb. "Where's your Mustang?"

Mila shrugged. "I sold it so I could buy a watch chain that Quin doesn't even need."

Miss Eugenia was still cackling when Mila drove down Maple Street, headed toward Albany and the airport.

* * *

Mila returned her rental car, then checked her luggage and was standing in the security line when she saw him. He looked pretty much the same. His tan was a little darker, and the tips of his hair had been bleached by exposure to sunshine and salt water. Stepping out of the line, she waited until he crossed into the public area and called his name.

"Quin!"

He turned toward the sound of her voice, surprised. "Mila!" He reached for her, and she slipped naturally into her arms.

"I thought you were in Hawaii," she murmured against the warm skin of his neck.

"I was," he said. "But I found paradise was a little lonely. So I thought I'd give life behind fences a try."

Her breath caught in her throat. "What do you mean?"

"I mean that I can be happy anywhere as long as you're there too. If you want to stay here and be a police detective, I'll make Albany the home base for my surfboard business. If you decide to go back to school—I'll go wherever you're accepted and work from there." He paused, looking a little unsure for the first time. "That is if you want to marry me. I guess I should have asked that first."

She couldn't speak, so she held up her airline ticket.

He took it from her, read the destination, then looked back in wonder. "You were coming to me?"

She nodded as tears spilled down onto her cheeks. "I thought I might give life without fences a try."

He crushed her against his chest, his fingers tangled in her hair. Then he kissed her, mindless of the people passing on both sides. "My friend may have let someone else rent his house."

"We can pitch tents on the beach if we have to," Mila murmured.

He laughed. "I don't think they'll let us do that, but we'll find someplace. Our first order of business will be to get married. To keep it simple, maybe we could just elope to the Hawaii Temple."

"Can you elope to the temple?"

He kissed her nose. "I don't see why not."

She clung to him. "We're very different."

"Yes, our lives will be full of compromise," he agreed.

"But we'll be together," she whispered. "And that's what counts."

"In the end, that's *all* that counts," he assured her. Then his lips claimed hers again.

ABOUT THE AUTHOR

Betsy Brannon Green currently lives in Bessemer, Alabama, which is a suburb of Birmingham. She has been married to her husband, Butch, for twenty-four years. They have eight children, one son-in-law, and one granddaughter. Betsy is an assistant nursery leader in her ward.

Although born in Salt Lake City, Betsy has spent most of her life in the South. Her writing has been strongly influenced by the small town of Headland and the gracious, generous people who live there.

Her first book, *Hearts in Hiding,* was published in 2001, followed by *Never Look Back* (2002), *Until Proven Guilty* (2002), *Don't Close Your Eyes* (2003), *Above Suspicion* (2003), and *Foul Play* (2004).

If you would like to be updated on Betsy's newest releases or correspond with her, please send an e-mail to info@covenant-lds.com. You may also write to her in care of Covenant Communications, P.O. Box 416, American Fork, UT 84003-0416.